THE SLAVE

THE SLAVE

ISAAC BASHEVIS SINGER

Translated from the Yiddish by the author and Cecil Hemley

Goodreads Press

The author wishes to thank Miss Elizabeth Pollet for her assistance in the preparation of this book.

TABLE OF CONTENTS

Part One: Wanda.. 1
Chapter One.. 3
Chapter Two... 23
Chapter Three.. 44
Chapter Four... 59
Chapter Five... 75
Chapter Six... 89
Chapter Seven..113

Part Two: Sarah 125
Chapter Eight.. 127
Chapter Nine.. 155
Chapter Ten.. 184
Chapter Eleven...204
Chapter Twelve 231

Part Three: The Return 243
Chapter Thirteen..245

PART ONE

WANDA

ONE

I

A single bird call began the day. Each day the same bird, the same call. It was as if the bird signaled the approach of dawn to its brood. Jacob opened his eyes. The four cows lay on their mats of straw and dung. In the middle of the barn were a few blackened stones and charred branches, the fireplace over which Jacob cooked the rye and buckwheat cakes he ate with milk. Jacob's bed was made of straw and hay and at night he covered himself with a coarse linen sheet which he used during the day to gather grass and herbs for the cattle. It was summer, but the nights were cold in the mountains. Jacob would rise more than once in the middle of the night and warm his hands and feet on the animals' bodies.

It was still dark in the barn, but the red of dawn shone through a crack in the door. Jacob sat up and finished his final allotment of sleep. He had dreamed he was in the study house at Josefov, lecturing the young men on the Talmud. He stretched out his hand blindly, reaching for the pitcher of water. Three times he washed his hands, the left hand first and then the right, alternating, according to the law. He had murmured even before washing, "I thank Thee," a prayer not mentioning God's name and therefore utterable before cleaning oneself. A cow stood up and turned its horned head, looking over its shoulder as if curious to see how a man starts his day. The creature's large eyes, almost all pupil, reflected the purple of the dawn.

"Good morning, Kwiatula," Jacob said. "You had a good sleep, didn't you?"

He had become accustomed to speak to the cows, to himself even, so as not to forget Yiddish. He threw open the barn door and saw the mountain stretching into the distance. Some of the peaks, their slopes overgrown with forests, seemed close at hand, giants with green beards. Mist rising from the woods like tenuous curls made Jacob think of Samson. The ascending sun, a heavenly lamp, cast a fiery sheen over everything. Here and there, smoke drifted upward from a summit as if the mountains were burning within. A hawk, wings outstretched, glided tranquilly with a strange slowness beyond all earthly anxieties. It appeared to Jacob that the bird had been flying without interruption since creation.

The more distant mountains were bluish, and there were others, the most distant of all, that were scarcely visible – unsubstantial. It was always dusk in that most remote region. Caps of clouds sat on the heads of those unearthly titans, inhabitants at the world's end where no man walked and no cow grazed. Wanda, Jan Bzik's daughter, said that that was where Baba Yaga lived, a witch who flew about in a huge mortar, driving her vehicle with a pestle. Baba Yaga's broom was larger than the tallest fir tree, and it was she who swept away the light of the world.

Jacob stood gazing at the hills, a tall, straight man, blue-eyed, with long brown hair and a brown beard. He wore linen trousers which did not reach to his ankles and a torn, patched coat. On his head was a sheepskin cap, but his feet were bare. Though he was out of doors so much, he remained as pale as a city dweller. His skin did not tan and Wanda said that he resembled the men in the holy pictures that hung in the chapel in the valley. The other peasant women agreed with Wanda. The Gazdas, as the mountaineers were called, had wanted to marry him to one of their daughters, build him a hut, and make him a member of the village, but Jacob had refused to forsake the Jewish faith, and Jan Bzik, his owner, kept him all summer and until late fall in the barn high on the mountain where the cattle could not find food and one had to feed them with grass pulled from among the rocks. The village was at a high elevation and lacked sufficient pastures.

Before he milked the cows, Jacob said introductory prayer. Reaching the sentence, "Thou hast not made me a slave," he paused. Could these words be spoken by him? He was Jan Bzik's slave. True, according to Polish law, not even the gentry had the right to force a Jew into servitude. But who in this remote village obeyed the law of the land? And of what value was the code of the gentiles even prior to Chmielnicki's massacre? Jacob of Josefov took the privations Providence had sent him without rancor. In other regions the Cossacks had beheaded, hanged, garroted, and impaled many honest Jews. Chaste women had been raped and disemboweled. He, Jacob, had not been destined for martyrdom. He had fled from the murderers and Polish robbers had dragged him off to somewhere in the mountains and had sold him as a slave to Jan Bzik. He had lived here for four years now and did not know whether his wife and children were still alive. He was without prayer shawl and phylacteries, fringed garment or holy book. Circumcision was the only sign on his body that he was a Jew. But heaven be thanked, he knew his prayers by heart, a few chapters of the Mishnah, some pages of the Gemara, a host of Psalms, as well as passages from various parts of the Bible. He would wake in the middle of the night with lines from the Gemara that he himself had not been aware he knew running through his head. His memory played hide and seek with him.

If he had had pen and paper, he would have written down what came to him, but where were such things to be found here?

He turned his face to the east, looked straight ahead, and recited the holy words. The crags glowed in the sunlight, and close by a cowherd yodeled, his voice lingering on each note, resonant with yearning as if he too were being held in captivity and longed to thrust himself into freedom. It was hard to believe that such melodies came from men who ate dogs, cats, field mice, and indulged in every sort of abomination. The peasants here had not even risen to the level of the Christians. They still followed the customs of the ancient pagans.

There had been a time when Jacob had planned to run away, but nothing had come of his schemes. He did not know the mountains; the forests were filled with predatory animals. Snow fell even in summer. The peasants kept guard over him and did not permit him to go beyond the bridge in the village. There was an agreement among them that anyone who saw him on the other side of the stream should immediately kill him. Among the peasants there were those who wanted to kill him anyway. Jacob might be a wizard or a braider of elflocks. But Zagayek, the count's bailiff, had ordered that the stranger be permitted to live. Jacob not only gathered more grass than any other cowherd, but his cattle were very sleek, gave abundant milk, and bore healthy calves. As long as the village did not suffer from famine, epidemic, or fire, the Jew was to be left in peace.

It was time for the cows to be milked and so Jacob hurried through his prayers. Returning to the barn he mixed with the grass in the trough the chopped straw and turnips he had prepared the day before. On a shelf in the barn were the milking pail and some large earthen pots; the churn stood in a corner. Every day late in the afternoon Wanda came up, bringing Jacob his food and bearing two large pitchers in which to carry the milk back to the village.

Jacob milked the cows and hummed a tune from Josefov. The sun climbed beyond the mountains and the coils of fog dissolved. He had been here so long now and had become so acquainted with the plants that he could detect the odor of each flower and each variety of grass, and he breathed in deeply as the smells of vegetation were wafted into the barn through the open door. Every sunrise in the mountains was like a miracle; one clearly discerned God's hand among the flaming clouds. God had punished His people and had hidden His face from them, but He continued to superintend the world. As a sign of the covenant which He had made after the Flood, He had hung the rainbow in the sky to show that day and night, summer and winter, sowing and reaping would not cease.

II

All day Jacob climbed on the mountain. After gathering a sheetful of grass, he carried it to the barn, and then returned once more to the woods. The other cowherds, when he had first come, had attacked and beaten him, but now he had learned how to strike back, and these days carried an oaken stick. He scampered over the rocks with the agility of a monkey, mindful of which herbs and grasses were good for the cattle and which harmful. All those things which are required of a cowherd he could do: light a fire by rubbing wood against wood, milk the cows, deliver a calf. For himself, he picked mushrooms, wild strawberries, blueberries, whatever the earth produced, and each afternoon Wanda brought him a slice of coarse black bread from the village, and sometimes, also, a radish, carrot, or onion, or maybe an apple or pear from the orchard. In the beginning Jan Bzik had jokingly sought to force a piece of sausage into his mouth, but

Jacob had refused stubbornly to partake of forbidden food. He did not gather herbs on the Sabbath, but gave the animals feed he had prepared during the week. The mountaineers no longer molested him.

But this was not true of the girls who slept in the barn and tended the sheep. Night and day they bothered him. Attracted by his tall figure, they sought him out and talked and laughed and behaved little better than beasts. In his presence they relieved themselves, and they were perpetually pulling up their skirts to show him insect bites on their hips and thighs. "Lay me," a girl would shamelessly demand, but Jacob acted as if he were deaf and blind. It was not only because fornication was a mortal sin. These women were unclean, and had vermin in their clothes and elflocks in their hair; often their skins were covered with rashes and boils, they ate field rodents and the rotting carcasses of fowls. Some of them could scarcely speak Polish, grunted like animals, made signs with their hands, screamed and laughed madly. The village abounded in cripples, boys and girls with goiters, distended heads and disfiguring birthmarks; there were also mutes, epileptics, freaks who had been born with six fingers on their hands or six toes on their feet. In summer, the parents of these deformed children kept them on the mountains with the cattle, and they ran wild. There, men and women copulated in public; the women became pregnant, but, climbing as they did all day on the rocks, bearing heavy packs, they often miscarried. The district had no midwife and mothers in labor were forced to cut the umbilical cord themselves. If the child died, they buried it in a ditch without Christian rites or else threw it into the mountain stream. Often, the women bled to death. If someone descended to the valley to fetch Dziobak, the priest, to confess the dying and administer Extreme Unction, nothing came of it. Dziobak had a game leg and besides he was always drunk.

In comparison with these savages, Wanda, Jan Bzik's widowed daughter, seemed city-bred. She dressed in a skirt, blouse and apron, and wore a kerchief on her head; moreover, her speech could be understood. A bolt of lightning had killed her husband Stach and from then on she had been courted by all the bachelors and widowers of the village; she was constantly saying no. Wanda was twenty-five and taller than most of the other women. She had blond hair, blue eyes, a fair skin, and well-modeled features. She braided her hair and twisted it around her head like a wreath of wheat. When she smiled, her cheeks dimpled and her teeth were so strong she could crush the toughest of pits. Her nose was straight and she had a narrow chin. She was a skillful seamstress and could knit, cook, and tell stories which made one's hair stand on end. In the village she had been nicknamed "The Lady." As Jacob knew very well, according to the law he must avoid her, but if it had not been for Wanda he would have forgotten that he had a tongue in his head. Besides she assisted him in fulfilling his obligations as a Jew. Thus, when in winter, on the Sabbath, her father commanded him to light the oven, she got up before Jacob and lit the kindling herself and added the firewood. Unbeknown to her parents, she brought him barley kasha, honey, fruit from the orchard, cucumbers from the garden. Once when Jacob had sprained his ankle and his foot had swollen, Wanda had snapped the bone back into the socket and applied lotions. Another time, a snake had bitten him in the arm, and she had put the wound to her mouth and sucked out the venom. This had not been the only time Wanda had saved his life.

Yet Jacob knew that all this had been contrived by Satan; throughout the day he missed her and could not overcome his longing. The instant he awoke he would start to count the hours before she would come to him. Often he would walk to the sundial that he had made from a stone to see how much the shadow had moved. If a heavy downpour or cloudburst prevented her coming, he would walk about morosely. This did not stop him from praying to God to preserve him from sinful thoughts, but again and again the thoughts returned. How could he keep his heart pure when he had no phylacteries to put on and no fringed garment to wear? Lacking as he did a calendar, he could not even observe the holy days properly. Like the Ancients he reckoned the beginning of the month by the appearance of the new moon, and at the end of his fourth year, he rectified his computations by adding an extra month. But, despite all these efforts, he was aware that he had probably made some error in his calculations.

As he figured it, this long and warm day was the fourth of the month of Tammuz. He gathered great quantities of grass and leaves; he prayed, studied several chapters of the Mishnah, said those few pages of the Gemara which he repeated daily. Finally he recited one of the Psalms and chanted a prayer in Yiddish that he himself had composed. He begged the Almighty to redeem him from captivity and allow him to live the life of a Jew once more. This day, he ate a slice of bread left from the day before and cooked a pot of groats over the fireplace in the barn. Having said the benediction, he felt tired, and walked outside and lay down under a tree. He had found it necessary to keep a dog to protect the cattle from wild animals. At first he had disliked the black creature with its pointed muzzle and sharp teeth, repelled by its barking and obsequious licking which had reminded him of what the Talmud said on the subject and how the holy Isaac Luria, along with other cabalists, compared canines to the Satanic hosts. But at length Jacob had grown accustomed to his dog, and had even named him, calling him Balaam. No sooner had Jacob lain under the tree, than Balaam sat down near him, stretched out his paws, and kept watch.

Jacob's eyes closed, and the sun, red and summery, shone through his lids. Above him the tree was filled with birds, littering, singing, trilling. He was neither awake nor asleep, having retreated into the weariness of his body. So be it. This was the way God had willed it.

Ceaselessly he had prayed for death; he had even contemplated self-destruction. But now that mood had passed, and he had become inured to living among strangers, distant from his home, doing hard labor. As he drowsed, he heard pine cones falling and the coo of a cuckoo in the distance. He opened his eyes. The web of branches and pine needles strained the sunlight like a sieve, and the reflected light became a rainbow-colored mesh. A last drop of dew flamed, glistened, exploded into thin molten fibers. There was not a cloud to sully the perfect blue of the sky. It was difficult to believe in God's mercy when murderers buried children alive. But God's wisdom was evident everywhere.

Jacob fell asleep and Wanda walked into his dreams.

III

The sun had moved westward; the day was nearing its end. High overhead an eagle glided, large and slow, like a celestial sailboat. The sky was still clear but a milk-white fog was forming in the woods. Twisting itself into small ovals, the mist thrust out tongues, and sought to evolve into some coherent shape. Its inchoateness made Jacob think of that primeval substance which, according to the philosophers, gave birth to all things.

When he stood at the barn, Jacob could see for miles around. The mountains remained as deserted as in the days of the Creation. One above the other, the forests rose like steps, first the leaf-bearing trees, and then the pines and firs. Beyond the woods were the open ledges, and the pale snow, like gray linen unfolding, was slowly moving down from the summits ready to enshroud the world in winter. Jacob recited the prayer of Minchah and walked to the hill from which one could see the path to the village. Yes, Wanda was on her way up. He recognized her by her figure, her kerchief, her manner of walking. She looked no larger than a finger, like one of those imps or sprites about whom she told so many stories, fairies who lived in the crevasses of rocks, in the hollows of tree trunks, under the eaves of toadstools and who came out at dusk to play, dressed in small green coats and wearing blue caps and red boots. He could not remove his eyes from her, charmed by her walk, by the way she paused to rest, by her disappearance among the trees, then by the sight of her, emerging from the woods higher up the slope. Now and again, the metal pitcher in her hand gleamed like a diamond. He saw that she was carrying the basket in which she brought him food.

As she approached nearer and nearer, she grew larger and larger, and Jacob ran toward her, ostensibly to be of assistance, although the pitchers she was carrying were still empty. She caught sight of him and stopped. He was moving toward her like a bridegroom seeking his bride. When he reached her, shyness and affection, both equally intense, mingled within him. Jewish law, he knew, forbade him to look at her, yet he saw everything: her eyes which were sometimes blue, sometimes green, her full lips, her long, slim neck, her womanly bosom. Like any other peasant she worked in the fields, but her hands remained feminine. He felt awkward standing beside her. His hair was unkempt, his pants too short and as ragged as a beggar's. Being descended on his mother's side from Jews who had had constant dealings with the nobility and had rented their fields, he had been taught Polish as a child, and now in his captivity he had learned to speak the language like a gentile. At times, he even forgot the Yiddish name for some object.

"Good evening, Wanda."

"Good evening, Jacob."

"I watched you coming up the mountain."

"Did you?"

The blood rushed to her face.

"You looked no larger than a pea."

"Things look that way from a distance."

"They do," Jacob said. "The stars are as large as the whole world, but they are so far off, they appear to be little dots."

Wanda became silent. He often used strange words which she did not understand. He had told her his story, and she knew that he was descended from Jews who lived in a far-off place, that he had studied books, and that he had had a wife and children whom the Cossacks had slaughtered. But what were Jews? What was written in their books? Who were the Cossacks? All of these things were beyond her comprehension. Nor did she understand his statement that the stars were as large as the earth. If they were really that large, how could so many cluster above the village? But Wanda had long since decided that Jacob was a profound thinker. Who knew, perhaps he was a wizard as was whispered by the women in the valley? But whatever he was, she loved him. Evening for her was the festive part of the day.

He took the pitchers from her and they finished the ascent together. Another man would have taken her by the arm or placed a hand upon her shoulder, but Jacob walked beside her with the timidity of a boy, exuding a sunny warmth and trailing the odors of grass and barn. Yet Wanda had already proposed marriage, or, if he was unwilling to commit himself to that, cohabitation without the priest's blessing. He had pretended not to hear her suggestion and only later had he remarked that fornication was forbidden. God looked down from heaven and rewarded and punished each man according to his deeds.

As if she were unaware of that! But in the village love was a random matter. The priest had fathered a half dozen bastards. Such a proposal as she had made to Jacob would have been refused by no other man. Were not all the villagers pursuing her, including Stephan, the bailiff's son? Not a week passed without some boy's mother or sister approaching her to arrange a match. She was forever receiving and returning gifts. Wanda found Jacob's attitude perplexing and she walked with bowed head thinking about this puzzle which she was unable to solve. She had fallen in love with the slave at first sight, and though over the years they had been much together, he had stayed remote. Many times she had come to the conclusion that from this dough would come no bread, and that she was wasting her youth on him. But the strength of the attraction he exerted upon her did not abate, and she could scarcely endure waiting for evening. She had become the subject of gossip in the village. The women laughed at her and passed sly comments. It was said that the slave had bewitched her; whatever it was, she was unable to free herself.

Thoughtfully she bent down, plucked a flower, and tearing away its petals began, "He loves me; he loves me not." The last petal assured her that the answer was "yes." But if so, how long would he go on tormenting her?

Now the sun sank rapidly, dropped behind the mountains. Accompanied by the croaking and screaming of birds, the day ended. Smoke rose from the bushes and the cowherds yodeled. The women were already preparing the evening meal, perhaps roasting some animal which had fallen into a trap.

IV

In addition to bread and vegetables, Wanda, without the knowledge of her mother and sister, had brought Jacob a rare gift, an egg laid by the white hen, and while she milked the cows, he prepared supper. He placed a few dry branches on the stones, lit a fire, and boiled the egg. He had left the barn door open although it was already dark, and the flames from the pine branches mottled Wanda's face with fiery spots and were reflected in her eyes. He sat on a log remembering the meal eaten before the fast of the ninth day of the month of Ob. An egg was consumed then as a sign of mourning: a rolling egg symbolized the changeability of man's fate. He washed his hands, let them dry, said grace, and dipped his bread into the salt. There was no table in the barn and so he used a pail turned upside down. He gained his sustenance from vegetables and fruit; meat he never tasted. As he ate, he glanced at Wanda out of the corner of his eyes, Wanda who was as devoted to him as a wife, and who every day prepared him something special. "In the mercy of the nations is sin," he said to himself, quoting a commentary on a passage from the Bible and trying to strangle the love he felt for her. Had all this been done by her for the sake of God? No, it was desire for him that had prompted her. Her love depended upon outward show, and should he become a cripple, God forbid, or lose his manhood, her love would cease. And yet such was the power of the flesh that man looked only at the surface and did not probe into such matters too deeply. He heard the sound of the milk falling into the pail and he paused in his eating to listen. Grasshoppers were singing and there was a buzzing and humming of bees, gnats, flies, multitude upon multitude of creatures each with its own voice. The stars in the heavens had kindled their fires. A sickle of a moon was aloft in the sky.

"Is the egg all right?" Wanda asked.

"Good and fresh."

"Could anything be fresher? I saw the hen lay it. The moment it fell to the straw, I thought, this is for Jacob. The shell was still warm."

"You're a good woman, Wanda."

"I can be bad as well. It depends on whom I'm with. I was bad to Stach, peace be with him."

"Why was that?"

"I don't know. He demanded, he never asked. If he wanted me in the night, he woke me from the middle of sleep. In the daytime, he would push me down in an open field."

Her words aroused both passion and disgust in Jacob.

"That was not right."

"What does a peasant know of right or wrong? He just takes what he wants. I was sick once and my forehead was as hot as an oven but he came to me and I had to give myself."

"The Torah says that a man must not force his wife," Jacob said. "She must be wooed by him until she is willing."

"Where is the Torah? In Josefov?"

"The Torah is everywhere."

"How can it be everywhere?"

"The Torah tells how a man should conduct himself."

Wanda was silent.

"That's for the city. Here the men are wild bulls. Swear to me that you'll never reveal what I tell you."

"Whom would I tell?"

"My own brother threw himself on me. I was only eleven years old. He'd come back from the tavern. Mother was asleep but my screams woke her. She picked up the pail of slops and poured it over him."

Jacob paused a moment before speaking again.

"Things like that don't happen among the Jews."

"That's what you say. They killed our God."

"How can a man kill a God?"

"Don't ask me. I'm only telling you what the priest says. Really, are you a Jew?"

"Yes, a Jew."

"It's hard for me to believe. Become one of us and we'll get married. I'll be a good wife and we'll have our hut in the valley. Zagayek will give us our share of land. We'll work our time for the count, and what's left over we'll have for ourselves. There's nothing we won't have—cows, pigs, chickens, geese, ducks. You know how to read and write and when Zagayek dies you'll take his place."

It was some time before Jacob answered.

"No, I cannot. I am a Jew. For all I know, my wife is alive."

"You've said many times that everyone was killed. But even if she still lives, what's the difference? She's there and you're here."

"God is everywhere."

"And it will hurt God if you are a free man instead of a slave? You walk around barefoot, half naked. Summers you spend in the barn, winters you freeze in the granary. Sooner or later they'll kill you."

"Who will kill me?"

"Oh, they'll kill you all right."

"And so then I'll be with the other holy spirits."

"I pity you, Jacob. I pity you."

Both fell into a long silence and in the barn there was quiet except when a cow now and again stamped its hoof. The last embers in the fireplace died, and when Jacob had finished eating he walked out into the open air to say the benediction in a place unpolluted by dung. Evening had fallen but in the west the last shreds of the sunset lingered. Usually, the women who brought food to the cowherds did not loiter on the mountain since at night the way home was considered dangerous. But Wanda would often stay late despite her mother's scolding and the women's persistent gossip. She was as strong as a man and she knew the proper incantations to drive off the evil spirits. She had finished milking the cows and, in the darkness of the barn, she poured milk from the pail into the pitchers. She scrubbed the churn with straw and cleaned globs of mud off the hips of the cows. All this she did swiftly and with great skill. Her tasks accomplished, she went outside, and the dog ran from Jacob to her, wagged its tail and jumped on her with its front paws. She bent down and he licked her face.

"Balaam, enough," she ordered. "He's more affectionate than you," she said to Jacob.

"An animal has no obligations."

"But they too have souls."

She delayed going home, sat down near the barn, and Jacob sat also. They always spent some time together and always on exactly the same rocks. If the moon was not out, she saw him by the light of the stars, but it was as bright this evening as at the full moon. Gazing at her in silence, Jacob was seized by love and desire, and restrained himself with difficulty. The blood in his veins seethed like water about to boil, and hot and cold fire zigzagged down his spine. "Remember this world is only a corridor," he warned himself. "The true palace lies beyond. Don't let yourself be barred from it for the sake of a moment's pleasure."

V

"What's new with your family?" Jacob inquired.

Wanda awoke from her reverie.

"What could be new? Father works, chops down trees in the woods and drags them home. He's so weak the logs almost knock him down. He wants to rebuild our hut, or God knows what. At his age! He's so tired at evening he can't swallow his food, and drops on the bed as though his legs had been cut off. He won't live much longer."

Jacob's brow furrowed.

"That's no way to talk."

"It's the truth."

"No one knows the decrees of Heaven."

"Maybe not, but when your strength gives out, you die. I can tell who's going to go—not only the old and sick, but the young and healthy too. I take one look and it comes to me. Sometimes I'm afraid to say anything because I don't want to be thought a witch. But all the same, I know. There's no change with Mother, she spins a little, cooks a little, plays at being sick. We only see Antek on Sundays, and sometimes not even then. Marisha is pregnant, will be in labor soon. Basha is lazy. Mother calls her the lazy cat. But a dance or a party revives her. Wojciech gets crazier and crazier."

"What about the grain? Is the crop good?"

"When has it ever been good?" Wanda answered. "In the valley you get rich, black earth, but here it's all stony. You could drive a cart of oxen between the stalks. We still have some rye from last year, but most of the peasants eat their knuckles. What little good earth we have belongs to the count and anyway Zagayek steals everything."

"Doesn't the count ever come here?"

"Just about never. He lives in another country and doesn't even know he owns this village. About six years ago, a bunch of them descended upon us in the middle of summer—like now, before harvest. They got the idea they wanted to go hunting and tramped back and forth in the fields with their horses and dogs. Their servants snatched calves, chickens, goats, even a peasant's rabbit. Zagayek crawled after them kissing everyone's behind. Oh, he's high and mighty enough with the people around here, but as soon as he meets someone from the city he becomes a boot licker. When they went away, there was nothing but a wasteland left. The peasants starved that winter; the children turned yellow and died."

"Couldn't someone have spoken to them?"

"The nobles? They were always drunk. The peasants kissed their feet and all the thanks they got were a few strokes with a riding crop. The girls got raped; they arrived home with bloody shifts and an ache in their hearts. Nine months later they gave birth to bastards."

"We do not have such murderers among the Jews."

"No? What do the Jewish aristocrats do?"

"The Jews have no gentry."

"Who owns the land?"

"The Jews have no land. When they had a country of their own, they worked the earth themselves and possessed vineyards and olive groves. But here in Poland, they live by trade and handicraft."

"Why is that? We have it bad, but if you work hard and have a good wife, you at least own something. Stach was strong but lazy. He should have been Basha's husband, not mne. He kept putting off everything; he'd cut the hay and let it lie around until the rain soaked it. All he wanted to do was sit in the inn and talk. The truth was his time was up. On our wedding night I dreamed he was dead and his face black as a pot. I didn't tell anyone but I was sure he wouldn't last long. The day it happened, the weather wasn't bad. All of a sudden lightning struck and came straight through our window. It rolled along like a fiery apple, looking for Stach. He wasn't in the hut, but it went into the granary and found him. When I reached him his face was charred like soot."

"Don't you ever see anything good in your dreams?"

"Yes, I've told you. I foresaw that you would come to us. But I wasn't dreaming, I was wide awake. Mother was frying rye cakes and father had slaughtered a chicken that was starving because it had a growth in its beak. I poured some soup on the cakes and I looked into the bowl which was filled with great circles of fat. A mist rose and I saw you there as plain as I see you now."

"Where did you get such powers?" Jacob asked after a pause.

"I don't know, Jacob. But I've known all along that we were fated for each other. My heart knocked like a hammer when father brought you home from the fair. You weren't wearing a shirt and I gave you one of Stach's. Wacek and I were about to be betrothed, but when I saw you his image was erased from my heart. Marila has been laughing ever since. He fell into her hands like ripe fruit. I saw him at a wedding a short time ago and he was drunk. He started to cry and talk to me the way he used to. Marila was beside herself. But I don't want him, Jacob."

"Wanda, you must get such ideas out of your head."

"Why, Jacob, why?"

"I've already told you why."

"I never understand you, Jacob."

"Your faith is not my faith."

"Haven't I said that I'm willing to change my faith?"

"One can't belong to my faith unless one believes in God and his Torah. Just because one wants a man is not enough."

"I believe in what you believe."

"Where would we live? If a Christian becomes a Jew here, he's burned at the stake."

"There must be some place."

"Perhaps among the Turks."

"All right, let's escape."

"I don't know the mountains."

"I know them."

"The country of the Turks is very distant. We'd be arrested on the road."

The two once more fell into silence. Wanda's face was completely wreathed in shadows. From somewhere in the distance came a cowherd's yodel, muted and languorous as if the singer was expressing Wanda and Jacob's dilemma and bewailing the harshness of fate. A breeze had begun to blow and the rustle of branches mingled with the sound of the mountain stream as it coursed among the rocks.

"Come to me," Wanda said and her words were half command and half entreaty. "I must have you."

"No. I cannot. It is forbidden."

TWO

I

For Wanda the way down the mountain was more dIfficult than the way up. She was burdened now by the two pitchers filled with milk, and a heavy heart. But, terrified, she almost ran down the slopes. The path took her through towering grass, underbrush, forest; strange murmurs and rustles came from the thickets. Hostile imps and derisive spirits were abroad, she knew. They might play nasty pranks on her. A rock might be put in the path; the imps might swing from the pitchers and make them heavier; they might weave elflocks in her hair or dirty the milk with devil's dung. Demons abounded in the village and surrounding mountains. Each house had its familiar spirit dwelling behind the stove. Werewolves and trolls swarmed the roads, each monster with its own peculiar type of cunning. An owl hooted. Frogs croaked with human voices. Kobalt, the devil who spoke with his belly, was wandering somewhere in the neighborhood; Wanda heard his heavy breathing which sounded like a death rattle. And yet fear could not dull the pain of love. Her rejection by the Jewish slave intensified her desire. She was ready to leave the village, her parents, her family, and follow Jacob naked and empty-handed. She had told herself many times that she was a fool to be angry. Who was this man? If she wished she could get one of the village boys to kill him, and no tears would be shed.

But what was the use of murder when you loved the victim? The ache in her throat choked her. Her face stung as if it had been slapped. Men had always chased after her—her own brother, the urchin who tended the geese. Jacob's spirit was stronger.

"A sorcerer!" Wanda said to herself. "He's bewitched me."

But where was the charm hidden? Slipped into a knot in her dress? Tied to a fringe of her shawl? It might be hidden in a lock of her hair. She searched everywhere, found nothing. Ought she to consult old Maciocha, the village witch? But the woman was insane, babbled out all her secrets. No, Maciocha could not be trusted. Wanda became so occupied with her thoughts she didn't know how she managed the descent. But suddenly she was at the bottom of the mountain approaching her father's hut. It was little more than a hovel with crumbling beams overgrown with moss and birds' nests hanging from the thatch. The building had two windows, one covered with a cow's bladder and the other open to permit the smoke from the fire to escape. In summer Jan Bzik permitted no illumination but on winter evenings a wick burned in a shard or kindling was lit. Wanda entered, and though it was dark inside, she saw as clearly as if it had been day.

Her father lay on the bed. He was barefoot and in torn clothes. He seldom undressed. She couldn't tell whether he was asleep or just resting. Her mother and her sister Basha were busy braiding a rope of straw. The bed that Jan Bzik lay on was the only one in the hut; the whole family slept in it, Wanda included. Years before when her brother Antek had still been unmarried Jan Bzik would have intercourse with his wife before going to sleep and the children would have something to amuse them. But Antek no longer lived at home and the couple had become too old for such games. Everyone expected Jan Bzik to die shortly. Antek who was anxious to take over the house appeared every few days to ask shamelessly, "Well, is the old man still alive?"

"Yes, still alive," his mother would answer. She also wanted to be rid of this nuisance. He wasn't worth the bread he ate. He had become weak, morose, irritable. All day he belched. Like a beaver, he kept gathering wood, but the thin, crooked logs he brought home were only good for the fire.

They scarcely spoke to each other in that hut. The old woman had a grudge against Wanda for not remarrying. Basha's husband Wojciech had gone home to live with his own parents; he had become despondent after the marriage. Basha had already borne three children, one by her husband, and two bastards; all of them had died. Jan Bzik and his wife had also buried two sons, boys who had been as strong as oaks. The family had become embogged in bitterness and sadness; silent antagonism simmered and bubbled in that household like kasha on a stove.

Wanda didn't say a word to any of them. She poured the milk from the pitchers into some jars. Half of what the cows gave belonged to Zagayek the bailiff; he owned a dairy in the village where cheese was made. The Bziks would use their half the following day for cooking and drinking with bread. The family lived well compared to those around them. In a shed behind the house were two sacks, one of rye and one of barley, and also a handmill in which to grind the grain. Bzik's fields, unlike most, had been partially cleared of stones over the years and the rocks used to build a fence. But food isn't everything. Jan Bzik continued to mourn his dead sons. He couldn't tolerate Antek or his daughter-in-law Marisha. Basha he disliked because of her indiscretions. Wanda was the only one he loved and she had been a widow for years and had brought him no joy. Antek, Basha, and the old woman had become allies. They kept their secrets from Wanda as though she were a stranger. But Wanda managed the household. Her father even consulted her on how to sow and reap. She had a man's brain. If she said something, you could rely on it.

Stach's death had brought her humiliation. She had been forced to return to her parents and again sleep with them and Basha in one bed. Now she would often spend the night in the hayloft or granary, although these places were crawling with rats and mice. She decided to sleep in the granary that night. The hut stank. Her family conducted themselves like animals. It hadn't occurred to any of them that the stream that flowed before their house could be used for bathing. It was the same one that passed near Jacob's barn.

Wanda picked up her pillow; it was stuffed with straw and hay. She walked toward the door.

"Sleeping in the granary?" her mother asked.

"Yes, in the granary."

"You'll be back tomorrow with your nose bitten off."

"Better to have your nose bitten than your soul."

Often Wanda herself was amazed by the words that issued from her lips. At times they had the pithiness and wit of a bishop's talk. Basha and her mother gaped. Jan Bzik stirred and murmured something. He liked to boast that Wanda resembled him and had inherited his brain. But what was intelligence worth if you didn't have luck?

II

The peasants went to bed early. Why sit around in the dark? Anyway they had to get up again at four. But there were always a few who hung around the tavern until it was late. The tavern was presumably the property of the count; it was in fact owned by Zagayek. He supplied its liquor from his still. That evening Antek was among the customers. One of Zagayek's bastard daughters waited on tables. The peasants nibbled pork sausage and drank. All sorts of strange and curious occurrences were discussed.

The previous harvest a malevolent spirit named the Polonidca had appeared in the fields, carrying a sickle and dressed in white. The Polonidca had wandered around asking difficult riddles and demanding answers of all she met. For example: What four brothers chase but never catch each other? Answer: The four wheels of a wagon. What is dressed in white but black to the sight and wherever it goes speaks right? Answer: A letter. What eats like a horse, drinks like a horse, but sees with its tail as well as with its eyes? Answer: A blind horse. If the peasant didn't know the right answer the Polonidca tried to cut off his head with her sickle. She would pursue the man as far as the chapel. He would become ill and lie sick for many days.

The Dizwosina was another savage spirit. This terrifying succubus had stringy hair and came from Bohemia on the other side of the mountains. Recently she had entered the hut of old Maciek and had tickled his heels until he had died from laughter. She had taken three of the village boys as her lovers and had forced them to lie in the fields and do her will. One boy had become so emaciated he had died of the phthisis. It was also the custom of the Dizwosina to lie in wait for girls and win their confidence by braiding their hair, putting garlands around their necks, and dancing with them in a circle. But then after amusing herself with the maidens, she would spatter and cover them with filth.

Skrzots also had been seen this year in the granaries. This was a bird that dragged its wings and tail on the ground. As was well known, it came from an egg which had been hatched in a human armpit. But who in the village would do such mischief? It clearly couldn't be the men; only women would have the time and patience for things like that. In the winter the Skrzot got cold in the granary and would knock at the door of a hut and seek to be let in. Then the Skrzot brought good luck. But in all other respects it was harmful and consumed vast amounts of grain. If its excrement fell on the human eye, blindness followed. The opinion of those in the tavern was that a search party should be organized to find out what women were carrying eggs under their arms. But by far the strangest thing that had happened recently concerned a young virgin. The girl swore she had been attacked by a vampire. The monster had fastened its teeth to her breasts and had drunk until dawn. In the morning the girl had been found in a swoon, the teeth marks on her skin clearly visible.

And yet concerned though they were with vampires and succubuses, they spoke even more about Jacob who lived on the mountain and who tended Jan Bzik's cattle. It was a sin, they said, to maintain an infidel in a Christian village. Who knew where this man came from or what his intentions were? He said that he was a Jew, but if that was so he had murdered Jesus Christ. Why, then, should he be given asylum? Antek said that as soon as his father "croaked," he would take care of Jacob. But the listeners replied that they couldn't wait that long.

"You've seen how your sister crawls to him every day," one peasant remarked to Antek. "It'll end up with her giving birth to a monster."

Antek deliberated before he replied.

"She claims he doesn't touch her."

"Eh, woman's talk!"

"Her belly's flat."

"Flat today, swollen tomorrow," another peasant interjected. "Did you hear about the beggar that came to Lippica? This one was a fine talker and the women followed him around. Three months after he left, five monsters were born. They had nails, teeth, and spurs. Four were strangled but one woman out of pity tried secretly to nurse hers. It bit off her nipple."

"What did she do then?"

"She screamed and her brother picked up a flail and killed it."

"Bah, such things happen," an old peasant said, licking the pork fat off his mustache.

The tavern was half in ruins. Its roof was broken; mushrooms grew on its walls. Two tables and four benches were in the room which was lit by a wick burning in a shard; the single flame smoked and sputtered. The peasants cast heavy shadows on the wall. There was no floor. One of the men got up to relieve himself and stood at a heap of garbage in the corner. Zagayek's daughter laughed with her toothless gums.

"Too lazy to go outside, little father?"

Heavy steps could be heard, and a groaning and snorting. Dziobak, the priest, entered. He was a short, broad-shouldered man; he looked as if he had been sawed in half and glued and nailed together again. His eyes were green as gooseberries, his eyebrows dense as brushes. He had a thick nose with pimples and a receding chin.

Dziobak's robe was covered with stains. He was bent and hunched up, supported himself by two heavy canes. Priests are clean shaven, but coarse, stiff hairs like the bristles of a pig sprouted on his chin. For years the charge had been made that he neglected his duties. Rain leaked into the chapel. Half of the Virgin's head had been smashed. On Sundays when it was time to say Mass Dziobak often lay in a drunken stupor. But his one defender was Zagayek, who ignored all the denunciations. As for the majority of the peasants, they continued to worship the ancient idols that had been the gods of Poland before the truth had been revealed.

"Well, good householders, I see you're all busy with the bottle," Dziobak's hollow voice came from his chest as if from a barrel. "Yes, one needs a drink to burn out the devil."

"Well, it's a drink," Antek said, "but it doesn't burn."

"Does she mix it with water?" Dziobak asked, pointing at the barmaid. "Are you swindling the householders?"

"There's not a drop of water there, little Father. They run from water like the devil from incense."

"Well said."

"Why don't you sit down, Father?"

"Yes, my small feet do ache. It's a hard job for them to carry the weight of me."

Grandiose language was still available to him; he had studied in a seminary in Crakow, but everything else he had learned he had forgotten. He opened his froglike mouth, exposing his one long black tooth which resembled a cleat.

"Won't you have a drink, Father?" the barmaid asked.

"A drink," Dziobak repeated after her.

She brought him a wooden mug filled with vodka. Dziobak eyed it suspiciously and with visible distaste. He grimaced as if he had a pain in his stomach.

"Well, good people, to your health." He quickly gulped down the liquid. His face became more distorted; disappointment gleamed in his green eyes. It was as if he had been served vinegar.

"We're talking about the Jew Jan Bzik keeps on the mountain, Father."

Dziobak became incensed.

"What's there to talk about? Climb up and dispose of him in God's name. I warned you, did I not, little brothers? I said he would bring only misfortune."

"Zagayek has forbidden it."

"I count Zagayek as my friend and defender. We can be sure that he does not want the village to fall into the hands of Lucifer."

Dziobak peeked at the wooden mug out of the corner of his eyes.

"Just another drop."

III

Jacob awoke in the middle of the night. His body was hot and tense; his heart was pounding. He had been dreaming of Wanda. Passion overwhelmed him and an idea leaped into his brain. He must run down to the valley and find her. He knew she sometimes slept in the granary. "I'm damned already," he told himself. But even as he said it he was aware it was Satan speaking within him.

He must calm himself. He walked to the stream. The brook had its source in glacial snows and its waters were ice cold even in summer. But it was necessary for Jacob to perform his ablutions. What else remained for him but the doing of such acts? He took off his pants and waded into the stream. The moon had already set, but the night was thick with stars. Rumor had it that a water devil made its home in these waters and sang so beautifully in the evening that boys and girls were lured to their destruction. But Jacob knew that a Jew had no right to be afraid of witchcraft or astrology. And if he were dragged down into the current, he would be better off.

"Let it be His will that my death redeem all my sins," he murmured, choosing those words which in ancient times had been spoken by those put to death by the Sanhedrin. The stream was shallow and filled with rocks, but at one spot the water reached to his chest. Jacob walked carefully. He slipped, almost fell. He was afraid that Balaam would begin barking, but the dog continued to sleep in his kennel. He reached the spot that was deepest and immersed himself. How strange. The coldness did not extinguish his lust. A passage from the Song of Songs came to his mind: Many waters cannot quench love, neither can the floods drown it. "What a comparison," he admonished himself. The love referred to in Scriptures was the love of God for his Chosen People. Each word was filled with mystery upon mystery. Jacob continued to immerse himself until he became calmer.

He came out of the water. Before, desire had made him tremble but now he shivered from the cold. He walked to the barn and threw his sheet over him. He murmured a prayer: "Lord, of the universe, remove me from this world, before I stumble and arouse Thy wrath. I am sick of being a wanderer among idolaters and murderers. Return me to that source from whence I came."

He had now become a man at war with himself. One half of him prayed to God to save him from temptation, and the other sought some way to surrender to the flesh. Wanda was not married, she was a widow, the recalcitrant part of him argued. True, she did not undergo ablution after her periods, but the stream was here, available to her for this ritual. Were there any other interdictions? Only the one that forbade the marrying of a gentile. But this interdiction did not apply here. These were unusual circumstances. Had not Moses married a woman from Ethiopia? Did not King Solomon take as his wife Pharaoh's daughter? Of course, these women had become Jewesses. But so could Wanda. The Talmudic law stating that a man who cohabits with a gentile could be put to death by anyone in the community was only valid if there had first been a warning and the adultery was seen by witnesses.

In Jacob's case the normal order of things had been reversed. It was God who spoke in the simplest language wile evil overflowed with learned quotations. How long did one live in this world? How long was one young? Was it worth while to destroy this existence and the one that would follow for a few moments of pleasure? "It's all because I don't study the Torah," Jacob said to himself. He started to mumble verses from the Psalms, and then an idea came to him. Hereafter to occupy his time he would enumerate the two hundred and forty-eight commandments and the three hundred and sixty-five prohibitions to be found in the Torah. Although he didn't know them by heart, his years of exile had taught him what a miser the human memory is. It didn't like to give, but if one remained stubborn and did not cease asking, it would pay out even more than what was demanded. Never left in peace, it would at last return all that had been deposited within it.

To be fruitful and multiply was the first of all the commandments. ("Perhaps have a child by Wanda," the legalist within Jacob interjected.) What was the second commandment? Circumcision. And the third? Jacob could not think of another commandment in the entire book of Genesis. So he began to reflect upon Exodus. What was the first commandment in that book? Very likely the eating of the Passover offering and of the unleavened bread. Yes, but what was the use of remembering these things when tomorrow he might forget them? He must find a way to write everything down. Suddenly he realized that he could do what Moses had done. If Moses had been able to chisel the Ten Commandments into stone, why couldn't he? Chiseling wasn't even necessary; he could scratch with an awl or a nail pried from one of the rafters. He recollected having seen a bent hook somewhere in the barn. Now Jacob found it impossible to return to sleep. A man must be clever in battling the Evil One. He must anticipate all of the Devil's stratagems. Jacob sat waiting for the light of the morning star. The barn was quiet. The cows slept. He heard the sound of the stream. The entire earth seemed to be holding its breath awaiting the new day. Now he had forgotten his lust. Once more he remembered that while he was sitting here in Jan Bzik's barn God continued to direct the world. Rivers flowed; waves billowed on the ocean. Each of the stars continued on its prescribed way. The grain in the fields would ripen soon and the harvest would begin. But who had ripened the grain? How could a stalk of wheat rise from a kernel? How could tree, leaf, branch, fruit emerge from a pit? How could man appear from a drop of semen in a woman's womb? These were all miracles, wonders of wonders. Yes, there were many questions one might ask of God. But who was man to comprehend the acts of divinity?

Jacob was now too impatient to wait for sunrise. "I thank Thee," he said, rising, and then he washed his hands. As he did so a purple beam appeared in the crack beneath the door. He walked outside. The sun had just risen from behind the mountains. The bird which always announced the coming of day chirped shrilly. This was one creature that did not oversleep.

It had become light enough to reach for the hook. Its place was on the shelf where the milk pots were stored. But it had disappeared. Well, that was Satan's work, Jacob thought. He did not wish Jacob to engrave the six hundred and thirteen laws. Jacob took down the earthen pots, one by one, and put them back on the shelf. He rummaged on the ground, searching among the straw. He remained hopeful. The important thing was not to give up. Good things never came easily.

At last he found it. It had slipped into a crack on the shelf. He didn't understand how he could have missed it. Yes, everything, it seemed, was ordained. Years before someone had left the hook there so that Jacob could engrave God's edicts.

He left the barn to find a suitable stone. He did not have to search far. Behind the barn a large rock protruded from the earth. There it stood as ready as the ram which Father Abraham had sacrificed as a burnt offering instead of Isaac. The stone had been waiting ever since Creation.

What he wrote would be visible to no one; it would be hidden behind the barn. Balaam began to wag his tail and jump as if his canine soul comprehended what his master was preparing to do.

IV

Harvest time was approaching and Jan Bzik brought Jacob down from the mountain. How painful it was for the slave to leave his solitude! He had already scratched forty-three commandments and sixty-nine interdictions into the rock. What wonders issued from his mind. He tortured memory and things he had long forgotten appeared. His was a never ending struggle with Purah, the lord of oblivion. In this battle force and persuasion were both necessary; patience was also required, but concentration was most important of all. Jacob sat midway between the barn and rock, concealing himself with weeds and the branches of a midget pine. He mined within himself as men dig for treasure in the earth. It was slow work; he scratched sentences, fragments of sentences, single words into the stone. The Torah had not disappeared. It lay hidden in the nooks and crannies of his brain.

But now he was forced to interrupt his task.

It had been a dry summer, and though there was never much of a harvest in the village, this year's crop was particularly meager. The stalks of grain grew further apart than usual and their kernels were small and brittle. As always, the peasants prayed to both the image of the Virgin and the old lime trees which commanded the rain spirits.

These were not the only rites. Pine branches, lurers of rain, were set among the furrows. The village's wooden rooster, a relic of ancient times, was wrapped in green wheat stalks and decked with saplings. Dancing around the lime trees with the decorated image, the villagers doused it with water. In addition to such public ceremonies, each peasant had his own unique rituals which had been handed down from father to son. Relatives of men who had hanged themselves visited the suicides' graves and begged the unsanctified bones not to cause drought. But rain was not the only problem. As everyone knew, a wicked Baba hid in the stalks and an evil Dziad in the tips. As soon as one furrow was reaped the Baba and Dziad fled and concealed themselves in another. Even when the whole crop had been bound in sheaves, no one could be sure that the danger was over as tiny Babas and minuscule Dziads sought final refuge in the unhusked kernels, and had to be thrashed out with flails. Until the last small Baba had been crushed, the crop was not safe.

This year all the customs had been scrupulously followed, but somehow had been of no avail. There was a grumbling among the peasants when they learned that Jan Bzik had brought Jacob down from the mountain. The poorness of the harvest was perhaps his work. A complaint was made to the bailiff Zagayek, but his answer was, "Let him do his job first. It's never too late to kill him."

So from early morning until sunset Jacob stood in the fields, and Wanda did not leave him. It was she who taught him how to reap, showed him how the scythe should be sharpened, brought him the food he was permitted to eat: bread, onions, fruit. The law did not allow him to drink milk now since he had not been present at the milkings. But fortunately the chickens were laying well and Wanda secretly gave him an egg each day, which he drank raw. He could also take sour milk and butter since the law stated that the milk of unclean animals does not turn. His sin was heinous enough merely eating the bread of the gentile; his soul could not tolerate further sullying.

The work was difficult, and his fellow harvesters never stopped ridiculing him. Here was a man who wouldn't drink soup or milk and never touched pork. This fellow fasted while he worked.

"You'll wither away," he was warned. "The next thing you know you'll be stretched out flat."

"God gives me strength," Jacob answered.

"What God? Yours must live in the city."

"God is everywhere, in both city and country."

"You don't cut straight. You'll ruin the straw."

The women and girls giggled and whispered.

"Do you see, Wanda, how your man sweats?"

"He's the strongest in the village."

Hearing that remark, Jacob cautioned her.

"The man who can control his passions is the most powerful."

"What's that fool saying?"

The women winked at each other and laughed, exchanged lewd gestures. One girl ran over to Jacob and pulled up her skirts. This made the peasants whinny with laughter.

"That's a fine show for you, Jew."

As he reaped, Jacob kept up a constant recitation, repeating to himself Psalms and passages of the Mishnah and Gemara. He had been there when the oxen plowed the fields and the seed was sowed. Now he was harvesting the grain. Weeds grew among the stalks and corn flowers on the sides of the furrows. As the scythes moved, field mice ran from their blades, but other creatures remained in the harvested fields: grasshoppers, lady bugs, beetles, flyers and crawlers, every variety of insect, and each with its own particular structure. Surely some Hand had created all this. Some Eye was watching over it. From the mountain came grasshoppers and birds that spoke with human voices, and the peasants killed them with their shovels. Their efforts were to no avail, since the more they killed, the more gathered. Jacob was reminded of the plague of locusts that God had visited upon the Egyptians. He himself killed nothing. It was one thing to slaughter an animal according to the law and in such a way as to redeem its soul, another to step on and crush tiny creatures that sought no more than man did—merely to eat and multiply. At dusk when the fields were alive with toads, Jacob walked carefully, so as not to tread on their exposed bodies.

Now and again when the ribald songs of the harvesters resounded in the fields, Jacob would take up a chant of his own, the Sabbath service, or the liturgies of Rosh Hashana and Yom Kippur, or sing the Akdamoth, a Pentecost song. Wanda joined in, for she had picked up the tunes from Jacob, singing Jewish chants and recitatives with a voice that had been accustomed to ballads of a different kind. Jacob's soul throbbed with music. He kept up a constant debate with the Almighty. "How long will the unholy multitudes rule the world and the scandal and darkness of Egypt hold dominion? Reveal Thy Light, Father in Heaven. Let there be an end to pain and idolatry and the shedding of blood. Scourge us no longer with plagues and famines. Do not allow the weak to go down to defeat and the wicked to triumph. ... Yes, Free Will was necessary, and Your face had to be hidden, but there has been enough of concealment. We are already up to our necks in water." So absorbed did he become in his chant that he did not notice that all the others had become silent. His voice sang alone and everyone was listening. The peasants clapped hands, laughed, and mimicked him. Jacob stood with bent head, ashamed.

"Pray, Jew, pray. Not even your God can make this a good harvest."

"Do you think he's cursing us?"

"What language is that you're speaking, Jew?"

"The Holy Language."

"What Holy Language?"

"The language of the Bible."

"The Bible? What's the Bible?"

"God's Law."

"What's God's Law?"

"That one neither kill nor steal nor covet a man's wife."

"Dziobak says things like that in the chapel."

"It all comes from the Bible."

The peasants became silent. One of them handed Jacob a turnip.

"Eat, stranger. You won't get strong from fasting."

V

The crop had been poor, but nevertheless the peasants celebrated. Girls appeared in the fields with wreaths on their heads and the older women assembled also. The time had come for Zagayek to superintend the selection of the maiden who would reap the last Baba. The choice was made by drawing lots and the girl chosen cut the last sheaf of grain, thereby becoming a Baba herself. Once selected, she was wrapped in stalks tied round her body by flax, and paraded from hut to hut in a wooden-wheeled cart drawn by four boys. The whole village accompanied the procession, laughing and singing and clapping hands. It was said that in ancient times when the people had still been idol worshipers the Baba was thrown into the stream and drowned, but now the village was Christian.

The night following this ceremony, the peasants danced and drank. The Baba performed with the boy who was chosen to be rooster. The rooster crowed, chased chickens, did all kinds of antics. He had a pair of wings on his shoulders, a cockscomb on his head and on his heels wooden spurs. Last year's rooster was also there, and the two fought, pushing out their chests, charging each other, tearing each other's feathers. It was so funny the girls couldn't stop laughing. This year's rooster always won, and then danced with the Baba who was now disguised as a witch, her face smeared with soot, and with the broom in her hand on which she rode to the Black Mass. The Baba seated herself in a barrel hoop and lifted her skirts, preparing to make a journey. The peasants forgot their troubles. The children refused to go to bed, sipped vodka, laughed and giggled.

Since it was no longer permissible to drown the real Baba, the boys made an effigy from straw. So skillfully did they model face, breasts, hips and feet, that the scarecrow, with two coals in the head for eyes, seemed alive. Just as the sun rose, the Baba was led to the stream. The women scolded the scapegoat, demanding that she take with her the evil eye and all their misfortunes and illnesses. The men and children spat on her, and then she was thrown into the stream. Everyone watched the straw Baba move downstream, bobbing up and down in the current. As the peasants knew, the river flowed into the Vistula and the Vistula emptied into the sea where bad spirits were awaiting the Baba. Though she wasn't alive, the over-compassionate girls wept for her. Was there such a great difference between flesh and straw? The ceremony over, vodka was passed around, and Jacob was given a drink. Wanda whispered into his ear, "I wish I were the Baba. I would swim with you to the end of the world."

The next day, the threshing began. From sunrise to sunset there was the sound of flails rising and falling. Occasionally a muffled cry or sob rose from the stalks. One of the small Babas was dying. The evenings were still warm enough for the threshers to stay out of doors, and so after supper they gathered branches and lit a fire. Chestnuts were roasted, riddles asked, stories told of werewolves, hobgoblins, demons. The most spine-tingling tale concerned the black field where only black grain sprouted and where a black reaper reaped with a long black scythe. The girls screamed and clutched each other, huddled closer to the boys. The autumn days were brilliant, but the nights were dark. Stars fell; frogs croaked, spoke with human voices from the bogs. Bats appeared and the girls scurried, covering their heads and screaming. If one of these nocturnal creatures entangled itself in a girl's hair, it meant that she would not live out the year.

Someone asked Jacob to sing and he performed a lullaby he had learned from his mother. The song pleased the peasants. He was asked for a story. He told them several tales from the Gemara and Midrash. The one they liked best was about a man who had heard of a harlot living in a distant country whose fee was four hundred gulden. When the man went to the harlot, he found she had prepared six silver beds with silver ladders and one golden bed with a golden ladder. The harlot had sat before him naked, but the fringes of his ritual garment had suddenly risen and struck him angrily in the face. At the end of the story the man converted the harlot to the Jewish faith and the beds she had prepared for him were finally used on their wedding night. The story was not easy to translate into Polish, but Jacob managed to make the peasants understand. They became fascinated by the fringes. What kind of fringes were they? Jacob explained. The glow from the fire lit up Wanda's face. She pulled his arm to her lips, kissed and then bit it. He sought to free himself but she hung to him tenaciously. Her breasts rubbed against his shoulder and the heat she gave off was like an oven's.

The story had been told for her, he knew. In the form of a parable he had promised that if she did not force him to cohabit with her now, later he would take her as a wife. But could he make such a promise? His wife might be alive. How could Wanda become a Jew? In Poland a Christian who became a Jewish convert was put to death; moreover, Jewish law forbade the conversion of gentiles for reasons other than faith.

"Well, every day I sink deeper into the abyss," Jacob thought.

Then on the last day of the threshing, a circus arrived in town. It was the first time Jacob had seen anyone from another district. The troupe included two men beside the owner, and they had a monkey, and a parrot who not only talked but told fortunes by selecting cards with his beak. The village was in an uproar. The performance was given in an open field near Zagayek's house and all of the men showed up with their wives and children. Jacob was permitted to go also. The bear whirled around on his hind legs, the monkey smoked a pipe and did somersaults. One of the men was an acrobat and did stunts like walking on his hands and lying bare-backed on a board of nails. The other was a musician and played a fiddle, a trumpet, and a drum with bells. The peasants screamed with joy and Wanda jumped up and down like a little girl. But Jacob disapproved of such entertainment, which he considered only one step away from witchcraft. More than a desire for amusement had brought him there. Circus men wandered from town to town, and perhaps this troupe had stopped at Josefov. They might have news of Jacob's family. So when the performance was done and the monkey and bear had been chained to a tree, Jacob followed the performers into their tent. The proprietor looked at Jacob in astonishment when he heard his question: had the circus stopped at Josefov.

"What business is it of yours where I've been?"

"I come from Josefov. I am a Jew and a teacher. I am a survivor of the massacre."

"How do you happen to be here?"

Jacob told the proprietor and the man snapped his whip.

"If the Jews knew where you were would they ransom you?"

"Yes, to free a captive is considered a holy act."

"Would they pay me if I told them you were alive?"

"Yes, they would."

"Give me your name. And I must have a way to convince them that I am telling the truth."

Jacob confided to the circus owner the names of his wife and children as well as that of his father-in-law who had been one of the community elders. Although the man could not write, he made a knot in a piece of string and told Jacob that he had not as yet been to Josefov, but he might well stop there. If any Jews were left in the town he would tell them that Jacob was alive and where he could be found.

THREE

I

After the harvest, Jacob returned to the barn on the mountain. He knew that he would not be there long. Soon the cold weather would set in and the cattle would have no food. Already the days had become shorter and when he gathered grass in the morning, he found the fields covered with frost. Haze hung over the autumn hills and it was increasingly difficult to distinguish between fog rising from the earth and the smoke of camp fires. The birds screamed and croaked more shrilly these days, and the winds blowing down from the summits carried the taste of snow. Though Jacob gathered as much fodder as he could, it was never enough for the cows. The hungry beasts bellowed, stamped on the earth, even pounded with their hoofs while they were being milked. Once more Jacob proceeded with his task of engraving the six hundred and thirteen laws of the Torah onto a stone, but he had little spare time during the day and at night it was too dark to work.

On the seventh day of the month of Elul—according to Jacob's calculations—dusk came quickly. The sun fell behind a massive cloud which covered the entire west. But was it really that date? For all he knew his reckonings might be erroneous and when the ram's horn was blown all over the world and the Rosh Hashana litanies sung, he would be out as usual gathering fodder. He sat in the barn and thought about his life. For as long as he could remember he had been considered lucky. His father had been a wealthy contractor who bought up the gentry's timber, supervised the felling of the trees and floated the logs down the Bug River to the Vistula and from thence to Danzig. Whenever his father had gone off on such trips, he had returned bearing gifts for Jacob and his sisters. Elka Sisel, Jacob's mother, was a rabbi's daughter and came from Prussia where she had been brought up in comfortable circumstances. Susschen, as she was called, spoke German and wrote Hebrew and conducted herself differently from the other women. She had rugs on the floor of her house and brass latches on the door. Coffee, a rarity even among the rich, was served daily in her home. An expert cook, seamstress, knitter, she taught her daughters how to do needlepoint and instructed them in Bible reading. The girls married young. Jacob himself was only twelve when he became engaged to Zelda Leah, who was two years younger, and the daughter of the town's elder. He had always been a good student. At eight he had read a complete page of the Gemara unassisted; at his engagement party he delivered a speech. He wrote in a fine, bold hand, had a good singing voice, and was a gifted draughtsman and wood carver. On a canvas on the east wall of the synagogue he painted the twelve constellations in red, green, blue and purple circling Jehovah's name, and in the corners put four animals: a deer, a lion, a leopard, and an eagle. At Pentecost he decorated the windows of the town's most important citizens and for the feast of Succoth adorned the tabernacle with lanterns and streamers.

Tall and healthy, when he made a fist, six boys could not force it open. His father had taught him to swim side and breast stroke. Zelda Leah, on the other hand, was thin and small—prematurely old, his sisters maintained. But of what possible interest was this ten-year-old child to Jacob? He was more interested in his father-in-law's library of rare books. Jacob received four hundred gulden as dowry, room and board at his in-laws for life.

The wedding was noisy and boisterous. Josefov was only a small town but after his marriage Jacob immersed himself so deeply in study that he forgot the outside world. True, his wife, he discovered, had odd habits. If her mother scolded her, she petulantly kicked off her shoes and stockings and overturned the soup bowl. She was a married woman and had not as yet menstruated. When her period finally came, she bled like a slaughtered calf. Every time Jacob approached her, she howled in pain. She was a perpetual sufferer from heartburn, headaches, and back aches. She screwed up her face, wept, complained. But Jacob was given to understand that only daughters were always like that. Her mother was constantly tugging her from him, but Zelda Leah bore him three children, Jacob scarcely knew how. Her recriminations and sarcasms sounded like the babblings of fools or school children; she belonged to that class of spoiled daughters whose whims can never be satisfied. Her mother, she said, was envious of her good looks. Her father had forgotten her; Jacob didn't love her. It never seemed to occur to her that she should try being lovable. Her eyes grew prematurely old from too much crying and her nose turned red. She didn't even take care of the children. That too became her mother's responsibility.

When the rabbi died, Jacob's father-in-law wanted him to take over the office, but Zaddock, the late rabbi's son, had a considerable following. True, Jacob's backer was the town's elder, a rich and influential man, but the people of Josefov had decided that this one time they were not going to let him have his way. Despite himself, Jacob found that he was involved in a quarrel. He didn't want to become rabbi, was actually in favor of Zaddock, and because of this his father-in-law became his enemy. If he refused to become rabbi, let him at least lecture to the boys in the

study house. Jacob would have liked to stay in the library, studying the Gemara and its commentaries, meditating on philosophy and cabala, subjects he preferred even to the Talmud. From
childhood on he had been searching for the meaning of existence
and trying to comprehend the ways of God. He was acquainted
with the thought of Plato, Aristotle, and the Epicureans through
the quotations he had found in *A Guide for the Perplexed*, the
Chuzary, *The Beliefs and Ideas*, and similar works. He knew the
cabalistic systems of Rabbi Moshe of Cordova and the holy Isaac
Luria. He was well aware that Judaism was based upon faith and
not knowledge and yet he sought to understand wherever it was
possible. Why had God created the world? Why had He found it
necessary to have pain, sin, evil? Even though each of the great
sages had given his answer, the questions remained unsolved. An
all-powerful Creator did not need to be sustained by the agony of
small children and the sacrifice of His people to bands of assas-
sins. The atrocities of the Cossacks had been talked about for
years before the attack on Josefov. Hearts had long been frozen
with fear, then one day death had struck.

Jacob had just turned twenty-five when the Cossacks had
advanced on Josefov. He was now past twenty-nine, so he had
lived a seventh of his life in this remote mountain village,
deprived of family and community, separated from books, like
one of those souls who wander naked in Tophet. And here it was
the end of summer; the short days, the cold nights had come.
He could reach out his hand and actually touch the darkness
of Egypt, the void from which God's face was absent. Dejection
is only one small step from denial. Satan became arrogant and
spoke to Jacob insolently: "There is no God. There is no world
beyond this one." He bid Jacob become a pagan among the
pagans; he commanded him to marry Wanda or at the very least
to lie with her.

II

The cowherds also had their autumn celebration. They had sought by threats and promises to make Jacob join them ever since he had first appeared upon the mountain with Jan Bzik's herd. But, one way or another, he had always put them off. He was forbidden to eat their food or listen to their licentious songs and brutal jokes. For the most part, they were a crippled, half-mad crew with scabs and elflocks on their heads and rashes on their bodies. Shame was unknown to them, as if they had been conceived before the eating of the forbidden fruit. Jacob often reflected that as yet this rabble had not developed the capacity to choose freely. They seemed to him survivors of those worlds, which, according to the Midrash, God had created and destroyed before fashioning this one. Jacob, when he saw them approaching, had acquired the habit of turning his head, or looking through them as if they didn't exist. If they foraged for grass on the lower slopes, he moved up toward the summit. He avoided them like filth. They were crawling all about him on the mountain, yet he went days and weeks without meeting any. Nor was it only disgust that kept him apart from this vermin; they were dangerous and, like wolves, would attack for no reason. Sickness, suffering, the sight of blood amused them.

That year they had made up their minds to seize him by force, and one evening after Wanda had left they surrounded the barn, deploying themselves like soldiers stealthily preparing to storm a fortress. One moment there was a stillness in which only the song of the grasshoppers was heard, and the next, the silence had been broken by howling and shrieking as both men and girls charged from all sides. The attackers were equipped with sticks, stones, and ropes. Jacob thought they had come to kill him, and like his Biblical namesake prepared to fight, or, if possible, to ransom himself through entreaties and a "gift" (the shirt off his back). He picked up a heavy club and swung it, knowing that his adversaries were so debilitated by illness he might be able to drive them off. Soon an emissary stepped forward, a cowherd who was more fluent than the others, and who assured Jacob no harm was intended. They had merely come to invite him to drink and dance with them. The man dribbled, stammered, mispronounced words. His companions were already drunk and laughed and screamed wildly. They held their stomachs and rolled about on the ground. He would not be let off this time, Jacob knew.

"All right," he finally said, "I'll go with you, but I'll eat nothing."

"Jew, Jew. Come. Come. Seize him. Seize him."

A dozen hands grasped Jacob and started to tug him. He descended the hill on which the barn was located, half running, half sliding. An awful stench rose from that mob; the odors of sweat and urine mingled with the stink of something for which there is no name, as if these bodies were putrefying while still alive. Jacob was forced to hold his nose and the girls laughed until they wept. The men hee-hawed and whinnied, supported themselves on each other's shoulders, and barked like dogs. Some collapsed on the path, but their companions did not pause to assist them, but stepped over the recumbent bodies. Jacob was perplexed. How could the sons of Adam created in God's image fall to such depths? These men and women also had fathers and mothers and hearts and brains. They too possessed eyes that could see God's wonders.

Jacob was led to a clearing where the grass was already trampled and soiled with vomit. A keg of vodka three-quarters empty stood near an almost extinguished fire. Drunken musicians were performing on drums, pipes, on a ram's horn very like that blown on Rosh Hashana, on a lute strung with the guts of some animal. But those who were being entertained were too intoxicated to do more than wallow on the ground; grunting like pigs, licking the earth, babbling to rocks. Many lay stretched out like carcasses. There was a full moon in the sky, and one girl flung her arms around a tree trunk and cried bitterly. A cowherd walked over, threw branches on the fire, and nearly fell into the flames. Almost immediately a woolly looking shepherd attempted to put out the blaze by urinating on it. The girls howled, screamed, catcalled. Jacob felt himself choking. He had heard these cries many times before, but each time he was terrified by them.

"Well, now I have seen it," he said to himself. "These are those abominations which prompted God to demand the slaying of entire peoples."

As a boy, this had been one of his quarrels with the Lord. What sin had been committed by the small children of the nations Moses had been told to annihilate? But now that Jacob observed this rabble he understood that some forms of corruption can only be cleansed by fire. Thousands of years of idolatry survived in these savages. Baal, Astoreth, and Moloch stared from their bloodshot and dilated eyes.

He was offered a cup of vodka by one of the merrymakers but the liquid seared his lips and throat; his stomach burned as though he had been forced to drink molten lead like those culprits the Sanhedrin had condemned to death at the stake in ancient times. Jacob shuddered. Had he been poisoned? Was this the end?

His face became contorted and he doubled up.

The cowherd who had given him the drink let out a yell, "Bring him more. Make the Jew drink. Fill up his cup."

"Give him pork," someone else shouted.

A pock-marked fellow with a face like a turnip grater tried to push a piece of sausage into Jacob's mouth. Jacob gave the man a shove. The cowherd fell and lay as still as a log.

"Hey, he's killed him."

Jacob approached the fallen man with trembling knees. Had this also been destined? Thank God, the man was alive. He lay there, foam bubbling from his lips, the sausage still clutched between his fingers, screaming abuse. His comrades laughed, threatened, cursed.

"God murderer. Jew. Scabhead. Leper."

A few feet away a cowherd jumped on a girl but was too drunk to do anything. Yet the two wrestled and squirmed like a dog and a bitch. The surrounding company laughed, spat, dribbled from their noses, and goaded the lovers on. A monstrous square-headed girl with a goiter on her neck and tangled matted hair sat on a tree stump sobbing out a name over and over again. She was wringing her hands, which were as long as a monkey's and as broad as a man's, their nails rotted away. Her feet were covered with boils and as flat as a goose's. Some of the cowherds sought to comfort her and gave her a cup of vodka. Her crooked mouth opened, exposing a single tooth, but she only wailed louder.

"Father! Father! Father! "

So she also cried out, Jacob thought, to a father in heaven. Compassion for this creature who had fallen from the womb deformed and misshapen, a mooncalf, swept over Jacob. Who could tell what frightened her mother at the moment of conception, or what sinful soul had been incarcerated in the girl's body? Hers was not an ordinary cry but the wail of a spirit who has gazed into the abyss and seen a torment from which there is no escape. Through some miracle this animal comprehended its own bestiality and mourned its lot.

Jacob wanted to go and comfort her, but he saw in her half-shut eyes a fury undiminished by suffering. Such a woman might spring at him like a beast of prey. He sat down and chanted the third chapter of Psalms: "Lord, how are they increased that trouble me! Many are they that rise against me. Many there be which say of my soul, there is no help for him in God. Selah."

III

It stormed in the middle of the night. A flash of lightning lit up the interior of the barn, and the cows, dung heaps, earthen pots became visible for an instant. Thunder rumbled. After washing his hands, Jacob recited "The One Who Does the Work of Creation" and "His Power and Strength Fill the World." A gust of wind blew open the barn door. The downpour beat on the roof like hail. The rain lashed Jacob as he closed and latched the door. This was the beginning of bad weather, he feared, and not merely one of those torrential cloudbursts that occur in summer. So it was; for a few hours later, though the rain ceased, the sky remained overcast. An icy wind blew from the mountains. At dawn the storm started all over again. Though the sun had risen, the morning was as gray as twilight. There would be no foraging for grass and other vegetation on the slopes today. Jacob would have to feed his herd with the fodder he had prepared for the Sabbath. He built a small fire to make things more cheerful and sat by it praying; he rose, faced to the east, and recited the eighteen benedictions. A cow turned its head and gazed at him with a blank humility, yet the expression of the black muzzle, wet with saliva and bristling with a few sparse haks, made Jacob think that the creature nursed some grievance. It often seemed to him that the cattle complained, "You are a man and we are only cows. What justice is there to that?" He placated them by stroking their necks, slapping their sides, and feeding them tidbits. "Father," he often prayed, "Thou knowest why Thou hast created them. They are the work of Thy hand. At the end of days, they too must have salvation."

That morning his breakfast consisted of bread and milk and an apple brought the day before. If the rain continued, Wanda would not come. He would have to sustain himself on sour milk, a dish which he could no longer stomach. He chewed each bite of the apple slowly to savor the full flavor. In his father-in-law's house he had not known that one could have such an appetite and that bread with bran could be so delicious. As he swallowed each mouthful, he seemed to feel the marrow in his bones increase. The wind had died down, the door of the barn was now open, and from time to time he glanced up at the sky. Perhaps the weather would clear: wasn't it too early for the autumn rains? No longer was there a vista of distant places—nothing was visible but the flat crest of the hill surrounding the barn. Sky, mountains, valleys, forests, had dissolved and disappeared. Fog drifted across the ground. Mist rose from the pines as though the wet trees were burning. Here in his exile Jacob at last understood what was meant when the cabala spoke of God's hidden face and the shrinking of His light. Yesterday everything had been bright; now it was gray. Distances had shrunk; the skies had collapsed like the canvas of a tent; the tangible had lost substance. If so much could vanish for the physical eye, how much more could elude the spiritual. Every man comprehended according to his merit. Infinite worlds, angels, seraphim, mansions and sacred chariots surrounded man, but he did not see them because he was small and sinful and immersed in the vanities of the body.

As always when it rained, a variety of creatures sought shelter in the barn: butterflies, grasshoppers, gnats, beetles. One insect had two pairs of wings. A white butterfly with black markings resembling script alighted on a stone near the fire and appeared to be warming or drying itself. Jacob placed a crumb of bread near it, but it remained motionless. He touched it, but it didn't stir, and he realized it was dead. Sorrow overcame him. Here was one that would never flutter again. He would have liked to eulogize this handsome creature which had lived a day, or even less, and had never tasted sin. Its wings were smoother than silk and covered with an ethereal dust. It rested on the stone like a shrouded corpse.

Of necessity, Jacob had to war with flies and vermin which bit both him and the cows. He had no alternative but to kill. As he walked about, he could not avoid treading on worms and toads, and when he gathered grass he often encountered venomous snakes which would hiss and strike at him and which he crushed with a club or stone. But each time something like that happened he judged himself a murderer. He silently blamed the Creator for forcing one creature to annihilate another. Of all the questions he asked about the universe, he found this the most difficult.

There was nothing for him to do that day and so he stretched out on the straw and covered himself with his sheet. No, Wanda would not come. He was ashamed that he longed so much for this gentile woman, but the harder he tried to rid himself of desire, the stronger it became. His yearning stayed with him praying and studying, sleeping and waking. He knew the bitter truth: compared to his passion for Wanda, his mourning for his wife and children and his love for God were weak. If the desires of the flesh came from Satan, then he was in the Devil's net. "Well, I have lost both worlds," he muttered, and through half-shut eyes he maintained his watch. The petals of a flower stirred among the wet bushes. Field mice, weasels, moles, skunks, and hedgehogs were hiding in the thickets. All of these small creatures waited with impatience for the sun to shine. The birds, like clusters of fruit, weighed down the trees and the instant the rain let up, whistling, chirruping, croaking began. From somewhere far off came a muted yodel. A cowherd was singing in the foul dampness, and his distant voice pleaded and demanded, lamented the injustice visited on all living things: Jews, gentiles, animals, even the flies and gnats crawling on the hips of the cattle.

IV

Though the rain ceased before evening, it was clear that this was only a short respite. Thunderheads lay low in the west, red and sulphurous, charged with lightning, and the air was heavy with mist that might at any moment turn to rain. Crows dived and cawed. There was no hope that Wanda would come in such weather, and yet when Jacob ascended his lookout hill, he saw her climbing toward him, carrying her two pitchers and the food basket. Tears came to his eyes. Someone remembered him and cared. He prayed that the storm would hold off until she reached him, and apparently his plea was answered; a moment after she entered the barn the deluge came, pouring down from the heavens as if from barrels. Neither Jacob nor Wanda spoke much to each other that afternoon. She sat down and immediately began to milk the cows. She was strangely shy and embarrassed and so was Jacob. Now and again a flash of lightning illuminated the twilight of the barn and he saw her bathed in such a heavenly glow that it seemed to him the woman he had known before had only been a sign or a husk. Had she not been created in God's image? Did not her form reflect that emanation through which the Eternal reflected His beauty? Had not Esau come from the seed of Abrahrn and Isaac? Jacob knew only too well where these meditations were leading, but he could not push them from him. He ate, said the benediction, recited the evening prayer, but still they did not leave him. The weather did not clear; Wanda would be unable to return home. At this late hour, moreover, the road back had already become dangerous.

"I'll sleep here in the bam," Wanda said, "unless you drive me out."

"I drive you out? You are the mistress."

They sat conversing quietly with the ease that intimacy brings. Wanda spoke of Zagayek and his paralytic wife, of their son Stephan who continued to pursue Wanda, of Zagayek's daughter Zosia whom everyone knew consorted with her father. But the bailiff had a dozen mistresses besides his daughter and so many bastards he could not remember their names. He did not conduct himself like a retainer but like a lord or king. He exacted from the peasant brides "the right of the first night," a law that was no longer in force. The peasants he treated as slaves, although they had their own fields and were only required to work for the count two days a week. He whipped them with wet rods, illegally forced them to do his business, levied private taxes upon vodka, performed operations on the sick against their will, tearing out teeth with pliers, amputating fingers with a cleaver, opening up breasts with a kitchen knife. Often he acted as midwife and demanded a handsome payment for services.

"There's nothing he doesn't want," Wanda said. "He would swallow the village whole if he could."

Wanda's bed was not difficult to prepare. Jacob spread out some straw and she lay down on it, covering herself with her shawl. He slept in one corner of the barn and she in another. In the silence the cows could be heard chewing their cud. She went outside to relieve herself and returned drenched from the rain. "So modesty exists even among these people," Jacob reflected. They both lay there without saying a word. "I must be sure not to snore," Jacob warned himself. He feared that he would be unable to sleep, but weariness overcame him. His jaw sagged and darkness flooded his mind. Every night he dropped onto his bed like a log. Thank God there was something stronger than his lust.

V

He awoke trembling, opened his eyes, and discovered Wanda lying next to him on the straw. The air in the barn was cool but he felt the burning heat of her body. She caught hold of him, pressed herself against him, and touched his cheek with her lips. Though he was conscious, he submitted in silence, amazed not only at what was happening but at the fierceness of his own desire. When he sought to push her from him, she clung to him with uncanny strength. He attempted to speak to her, but she stopped his lips with her mouth. He remembered the story of Ruth and Boaz and knew that his lust was more powerful than he. "I am forfeiting the world to come," he said to himself. He heard Wanda's hoarse voice imploring him; she was panting like an animal.

He lay numb, unable now to deny either her or himself, as if he had lost his freedom of will. Suddenly a passage from the Gemara entered his mind: should a man be overcome by the Evil One, let him dress himself in dark clothing, and cover himself in black, and indulge his heart's desire. This precept appeared to have been lurking in his memory for the specific purpose of breaking down his last defense. His legs became heavy and taut, and he was dragged down by a weight he could not withstand. "Wanda," he said, and his voice was trembling, "you must first go and bathe in the stream."

"I have already washed and I have combed my hair."

"No, you must immerse yourself in the water."

"Now?"

"God's law requires it."

She lay there in silence, perplexed by this strange demand, and then finally said, "I will do this also."

She rose, and still holding tight to him, opened the barn door. The rain had stopped but the night was mired in darkness and wet. There was not a trace of the sky and the only evidence of the stream was the sound of water churning and bubbling as it rushed downward. Wanda clutched Jacob's hand as they groped blindly and with the abandon of those who no longer fear for their bodies. They stumbled over stones and shrubs, were splashed by the moisture dripping from trees. They were seeking the one spot in that shallow, rock-cluttered torrent where the stream was deep enough for a man to immerse himself. When they reached it, she refused to enter the water without him, and he, forgetting to slip out of his linen trousers, followed her in. The shock of the cold water touching him took away his breath; he almost lost his footing, so swollen was the stream because of the rains. They clung to each other as undergoing martyrdom. Thus, at the time of the massacres Jews had plunged into fire and water. At last, his feet on a firm bottom, Jacob said to Wanda, "Immerse yourself."

She let go his hand and submerged in the water. He reached about, unable to find her. She reappeared, and his eyes, now accustomed to the darkness, made out the dim contours of her face.

"Hurry," he said.

"I have done this for you."

He took her hand and together they ran back to the barn. The cold, he realized, had not extinguished the fire in his veins. Both of them burned with the heat of newly fit kindling. He dried Wanda's naked body with his sheet, breathing heavily, his teeth chattering. Wanda's eyes shone through the darkness. He heard her say to him again, "I have done this for you."

"No, not for me," he answered, "for God," and the blasphemy of his words frightened him.

Nothing could restrain him now. He lifted her in his arms and carried her to the straw.

FOUR

I

The sun rose and red could be seen through the chinks in the door. A purple beam of light fell across Wanda's face. They had been asleep, but awakened by lust they again sought each other. He had never known such passion as hers. She spoke words he had never heard before, called him in her peasant dialect her buck, her lion, her wolf, her bull, and even stranger epithets. He possessed her but it did not quench his desire. She blazed with an ecstasy—was it from heaven or hell? "More, more," she cried in a loud voice, "master, husband." He found himself possessed of powers that did not seem to be his—was it miracle or witchcraft? For the first time in his life he recognized the mysteries of the body. How was such desire possible? "For Love is as strong as Death," the Song of Songs said, and at last he understood. As the sun rose, he sought to tear himself from her. She clung to his neck and again thirstily kissed him. "My husband," she said, "I want to die for you."

"Why die? You are still young."

"Take me away from here to your Jews. I want to be your wife and bear you a son."

"You must believe in God to become a daughter of Israel."

"I believe in Him. I believe."

She was screaming so loudly that he covered her mouth with his hand so the cowherds outside would not hear. He was no longer ashamed before God, but he feared the ridicule of men. Even the cows turned their heads and stared. He pulled himself from her and was baffled to discover morning brought no repentance. The opposite rather! He was astonished now that he had endured his desire, The pitcher had overturned and he could not wash hands. He didn't even say "I thank Thee," fearing to utter holy words after what had happened. His clothes were damp, but he put them on anyway, and Wanda also tidied herself. He walked out into the cool, clear Elul morning, leaving her with the cows. Dew covered the grass and each droplet gleamed. Birds were singing, and in the distance a cow lowed, the sound echoing like the blast from a ram's horn. "Yes, I have forfeited the world beyond," Jacob muttered, and immediately Satan whispered into his ear, "Shouldn't you also give up being a Jew?" Jacob glanced at the rock on which he had already scratched a third of the commandments and interdictions and it seemed to him like a battered ruin, all that was left to him from a war that had been lost. "Well, but I am still a Jew," he said, quoting the Talmud in an attempt to rally his spirits. He washed his hands in the stream and said, "I thank Thee," and then he began the introductory prayer. When he came to the words, "Lead us not into temptation," he paused. Not even the sainted Joseph had been as tempted as he. The Midrash said that when Joseph had been about to sin, his father's image had been revealed to him. So Heaven had interceded in his behalf.

As he mumbled his prayers, he searched in himself for some extenuation of what he had done. According to the strict letter of the law, this woman was neither unclean nor married. Even the Ancients had had concubines. She could still be a pious Jewish matron. "Something done selfishly may end up as a godly act." But, nevertheless, as he prayed he contrasted, despite himself,

Wanda and Zelda, peace be with her. His wife had also been a woman, but frigid and cold, forever detracted. She had been a constant stream of complaints: headaches, toothaches, cramps in the stomach, and always fearful of breaking the law. How could he have known that such passion and love as Wanda's existed? He again heard Wanda's voice, the words she had whispered to him, her groans, the swift intake of her breath, and he again felt the touch of her tongue and the sharpness of her teeth. She had left marks on his body. She was willing to flee with him across the mountains in the middle of the night. She spoke to him exactly as Ruth had spoken: "Where thou goest, I go. Thy people are my people. Thy God is my God." Her body exuded the warmth of the sun, the breezes of summer, the fragrance of wood, field, flower, leaf, just as milk gave off the odor of the grass the cattle fed on. He yawned while he prayed. He recited the Shema and stretched his arms. He had scarcely closed his eyes the night before and lacked the strength to go hunting for grass. Bending his head low, Jacob was aware of his own weariness. During the few brief moments of sleep, he had dreamed, and although he did not remember his dream clearly, its aftertaste lingered. It seemed to him that he had been descending steps into a ritual bath or cave and had wandered across hills, ditches, and graves. He had met someone whose beard was composed of the roots of a plant. Who could it have been? His father? Had the man spoken to him? Wanda thrust her head out of the barn and gave him a wifely smile.

"Why are you standing there?"

He pointed to his lips to signify that she must not interrupt his prayer.

Her eyes shone with affection; she winked and nodded. Jacob closed his eyelids. Did he repent? He did not feel so much contrition as annoyance that he had been placed in a situation which made his sin possible. He stared into himself as though he were looking down the shaft of a deep well. What he saw there frightened him. Like a snake, passion lay curled at the bottom.

II

Rosh Hashana, Yom Kippur, and Succoth, according to Jacob's calendar, were past. The day which he thought to be Simchath Torah, Jan Bzik appeared on the mountain accompanied by Antek, Wanda, and Basha. The smell of snow was in the air; the time had come to drive the cattle down the valley. Both bringing them up and taking them down were difficult tasks. Cows are not mountain goats and do not climb slopes nimbly. The beasts had to be held by short, thick ropes, and restrained at every step. A cow might dig its hoofs into the ground and then one man would be forced to drag the creature while another whipped it. Others might stampede and break backs or legs bolting from the herd. But on this occasion all went well. An hour or so after the cattle had entered Jan Bzik's barn, snow fell. The mountains were no longer accessible, and were enveloped by columns of mist. The village, turned white, looked unfamiliar. Food was not plentiful in the homes of the peasants, but there was no lack of wood; smoke rose from the chimneys. The frames of the windows had been weather-proofed with lime and sealed with straw. The peasant girls had also made out of straw longnosed monsters with horns on their heads whose task was to tease and annoy Winter.

This year, as every year, Jacob was asked to move into the hut with the family, but he preferred to take up his old abode in the granary. He made himself a straw bed and Wanda sewed him a pillow stuffed with hay; he had a horse blanket for a cover. The granary had no windows but light seeped through the cracks in the wall. Now Jacob longed for the mountains. It was better up there than down here. How strange and remote his peak seemed to him, a giant with a white beard, coiffured in clouds and with curls of mist. Jacob's heart cried out. The Jews were celebrating Simchath Torah, were reciting "Unto Thee it was shown," and circling the lectern. The Bridegroom of the Torah, who would finish the reading of the Pentateuch, was being called up from the congregation, to be followed by the Bridegroom of Genesis who would start once more the Mosaic Books, beginning with the Creation. Even boys were being summoned to the lectern, while those too young to participate were parading with flags decorated with candles and apples. Girls also were coming to the study house to the holy scrolls and to wish for long life and happiness. There was dancing and drinking; people were going from house to house, partaking of wine and mead, strudel, tarts, cabbage with raisins and cream of tartar. This year, if Jacob was correct, Simchath Torah had fallen on a Friday, and the women were preparing the Sabbath pudding, dressed in their velvet capes and satin dresses.

But now all of this seemed dreamlike to him. He had been torn from his home not four but forty years ago! Indeed, were there Jews remaining in Josefov? Had Chmielnicki left a saving remnant? And if so, could the survivors rejoice in the Torah as they once had, now that all of them were mourners? Jacob stood in front of the granary and watched the snow falling, Some of the flakes dropped straight to earth and others swirled and eddied as if seeking to return to the heavenly storehouses. The rotting thatch of the roofs was covered with white, and the clutter of broken wheels, logs, poles, and piles of shavings was decorated with fleece and the dust of diamonds. The roosters were crowing with wintery voices.

Jacob reentered the granary and sat down. Some lines from the Simchath Torah liturgy which he had not thought of for four years came to his mind:

Gather you angels

And converse with each other.
Who was he? What was his name,
The man who ascended the heights
And brought down the strength of confidence?
Moses ascended the heights
And brought down the strength of confidence.

Jacob started to sing these words to the traditional Simchath Torah melody. Even the cantor had usually been a trifle tipsy by the time he reached this song. Every year it had been the same, the rabbi finding it necessary to admonish those of priestly descent not to bless the congregation while under the influence of wine. Jacob's father-in-law had himself brewed beer and vodka using grain raised in the fields he leased from the town's overlord. At this time of year, a keg with a straw in it had always stood near the water barrel of his house, and nearby had hung a side of smoked mutton. Whoever visited the house sipped vodka from the straw and took a nibble of the smoked meat.

Jacob sat there in the dark, alone with his thoughts. Slowly the door was pushed open, and Wanda entered, carrying two pieces of oak bark, and some rags and string.

"I've made you a pair of shoes," she said.

He was ashamed of how dirty his feet were, but she lifted them to her lap, and while taking their measure, caressed them with her warm fingers. She took a long time making certain the shoes fit. When she was satisfied, she insisted that Jacob get up and walk about to see if they were comfortable, just as Michael the shoemaker had him do in Josefov.

"They fit, don't they?"

"Yes, they do."

"Why are you so sad, then, Jacob? Now that you are near me, I can take care of you. I don't have to climb the mountain to see you."

"Yes."

"Doesn't that please you? I was looking forward so much to this day."

III

The day began as though it were already ending. The sun flickered like a candle about to go out. Zagayek and his men were in the woods hunting bear, and the bailiff's son Stephan strode about the village in high boots, dressed in a rawhide jacket embroidered with red, a marten cap with ear flaps on his head, and a riding whip in his right hand. Stephan wAS called Zagayek the Second by the peasants. His career with girlS had started early and by now he had his own crop of bastards. He was a short, broad-shouldered man, with a square head, a nose as flat as a bulldog's, and a chin which dimpled in the middle. He had the reputation of being a fine horseman and kept himself busy training his father's dogs and setting traps for birds and animals.

Stephan took over in the village whenever his father went hunting. On such days he went from hut to hut, throwing open doors and sticking in his head and sniffing. The peasants always had something which by law belonged to the landlord. That morning he entered the tavern and ordered vodka. His half-sister, one of Zagayek's bastards, waited on him, but their relationship did not prevent him from hiking her skirts. Then, after having his drink, Stephan proceeded to Jan Bzik's. Bzik had once been a man of importance in the village, one of those whom Zagayek had taken under his protection, but now the old man was worn out and sick. The day he had brought the cattle down from the mountain he had had a seizure and he now lay on top of the oven as his strength ebbed. He talked, spat, muttered to himself. Bzik was a small, lean man; his hair, long and matted, surrounded a single bald spot. He had deep sunken cheeks, a face as red as raw meat, and bulging, bloodshot eyes underlined by two puffy bags, a few scraggly hairs drooping from his chin. That winter he had been so sick they had measured him for a coffin. But then his condition had improved. He lay, his face turned toward the room, one eye glued shut, the other only half open. Ill though he was, this did not prevent him from running the household and overseeing each detail. "It's no good," he would grumble often. "Butter fingers!"

"If you don't like the way we're doing things, climb down from the oven and do them yourself," his wife would answer. She was a small, dark, half-bald woman, with a wart-covered face, and the slanty eyes of a Tartar. The couple did not live in peace; she kept insisting that her husband was finished and that it was time to cart him off to the graveyard.

Basha resembled her mother. Stocky and dark, she had inherited the high cheekbones and almond eyes of the older woman. She was known for her indolence. At the moment she sat at the edge of the bed studying her toes and every now and again searching for lice between her breasts. Wanda was at the oven, removing a loaf of bread with a shovel. As she bustled about the kitchen, she repeated to herself the lesson Jacob had taught her: The Almighty had created the world. Abraham had been the first to recognize God. Jacob was the father of the Jews. She had never before received any instruction and Jacob's words had fallen on her brain like a shower on a parched field. She had even memorized the names of the Twelve Tribes and knew how Joseph's brother had sold him into Egypt. When Stephan entered, he stood at the open door listening to her mutterings.

"What's that you're saying?" he asked. "Some sort of an incantation?"

"Close the door, Pan," she directed over her shoulder. "You're letting in the cold."

"You're hot enough to keep from freezing."

Stephan walked into the room.

"Where's the Jew?"

"In the granary."

"Won't he come into the house?"

"He doesn't want to."

"They say he lays you."

Basha opened her wide, gap-toothed mouth in laughter; she licked her lips with delight, hearing her proud sister insulted. The old woman left off spinning, and Bzik wriggled his feet.

"Dirty mouths will say anything."

"I understand you're carrying his bastard."

"Pan, that's a lie," the old woman interrupted. "She just got over her period."

"How do you know? Did you investigate?"

"There was blood on the snow in front of the house," the old woman testified.

Stephan struck his boot tops with his whip.

"The householders want to get rid of him," he said after a slight hesitation.

"Who does he hurt?"

"He's a sorcerer, and that's the least of it. How is it your cows give more milk than anyone else's?"

"Jacob feeds them better."

"All sorts of things are said about him. He'll be done away with. Father will haul him into court."

"For what reason?"

"Don't grasp at straws, Wanda. He'll be taken care of, and you'll give birth to a demon."

Wanda could no longer restrain herself. Not everything the wicked desire comes true, she told Stephan. There was a God in heaven who avenged those who suffered injustice. Stephan pursed his lips as if about to whistle.

"Where did you hear that? From the Jew?"

"Dziobak says so also."

"It was the Jew, the Jew, who told you," Stephan said. "If his God is such a great defender, how come he's a slave? Well, answer that!"

Wanda could think of nothing to say. There was a lump in her throat and her eyes were burning; she could scarcely keep back the tears. She wanted to run quickly to Jacob and ask him this difficult question. With fingers that had become inured to heat, she picked up a fresh loaf of bread and sprinkled it with water. Anger had made her face, flushed already from the warmth of the oven, even redder. Stephan stood surveying her legs and buttocks like a connoisseur. He winked at the old woman and Basha. The latter responded flirtatiously, smiled obsequiously at him with her gap teeth. At length he walked out whistling, slamming the door behind him. Wanda stood at the window and watched him stride off in the direction of the mountain. He was a man filled with iniquity like Esau or Pharaoh. Ever since she could remember he had spoken of little else but killing and torturing. It was Stephan who assisted his father in the slaughtering and scalding of the pigs. It was he who did the actual whipping when Zagayek ordered a peasant punished. Even the trail left by Stephan's boots in the snow seemed evil to Wanda. "Father in Heaven," she began to pray, "how long will You remain silent? Send down plagues as you did against Pharaoh. Drown him in the sea."

"He wants you, Wanda. He wants you," she heard her mother raying.

"Well, he'll just keep on wanting."

"Wanda, he's Zagayek's son. He may set fire to the hut. What would we do then? Sleep in the fields?"

"God will not permit it."

Basha started to guffaw.

"What are you laughing about, Basha?"

Basha didn't answer. Wanda knew that her mother and sister were on Stephan's side. They wanted to see her humiliated. There was a crooked wrinkle on the old woman's forehead and her toothless mouth was fixed in a smile which seemed to say, "Why quarrel over such nonsense? Stephan's powerful. There's no alternative."

The old man lying on the stove mumbled something.

"Did you say something, Father?"

"What did he want?"

The old woman laughed nastily.

"What does a tomcat usually want?"

"Father's forgotten about that kind of thing," Basha said scornfully.

"You did right, Wanda. Don't let him put a bastard into your belly." Bzik spoke haltingly and with the dirge-like tone of the mortally sick uttering a last testament. "The moment you're with child, that skunk will forget you. He has enough bastards already." The old man's singsong voice was mournful, other-worldly. Wanda remembered the Ten Commandments Jacob had taught her; one must honor one's father and mother.

"Do you want something, Father?"

Jan Bzik did not answer.

"Are you hungry or thirsty?"

He had to pass water, he said in a voice which was half cry, half yawn.

"Well, crawl outside," his wife ordered. "This isn't a stable."

"I'm cold."

"Here, Father." Wanda gave him a pan.

The old man sought to raise himself from the oven but the low ceiling interfered. He attempted to pass water and Basha giggled when he couldn't. His wife shook her head contemptuously. His member had shrunk to the size of a child's. A single drop of water fell into the pan.

"He's worthless," the old woman said.

"Mother, he's your husband and our father," Wanda replied sharply. "We must honor him."

Basha began to guffaw again. Wanda felt a cry rising in her throat. Jacob said that God was just, that He rewarded the good and punished the wicked, but Stephan, idler, whoremaster, assassin, flourished like the oak, while her father, whose whole life had been dedicated to work and who had done injustice to no one, crumbled into ruins. What sort of justice was this? She gazed toward the window. The answer could come only from Jacob in the granny.

IV

Jacob in the old days would have considered himself ridiculed if anyone had ever suggested to him that a time would come when he would discuss such matters as the freedom of the will, the meaning of existence, and the problem of evil with a peasant woman. But one never knows where events are leading. Wanda asked questions and Jacob answered them to the best of his ability. He lay close to her in the granary, the same blanket covering them both, a sinner who ignored the restrictions of the Talmud, seeking to explain in a strange tongue those things he had studied in the holy books. He told her that God is eternal, that His Powers and Nature have existed without beginning, but that, nevertheless, all that was possible for Him had not as yet been accomplished before Creation. For example, how could He have been Father until His children were born? How could He have shown pity until there was someone to pity? How could He have been redeemer and helper until there were creatures to redeem? God had the power to create not only this world but a host of others. However, Creation would have been impossible if He, Himself, had completely filled the void. So that the world might appear, it had been necessary for Him to dim his effulgence. Had He not done this, whatever He created would have been consumed and blinded by His brilliance. Darkness and the void had been required, and these were synonymous with pain and evil.

What was the purpose of Creation? Free Will! Man must choose for himself between good and evil. This was the reason God had sent forth man's soul from the Throne of Glory. A father may carry his child, but he wishes the infant to learn to walk by itself. God was our Father, we His children, and He loved us. He blessed us with His mercy, and if now and again He let us slip and fall, it was to accustom us to walking alone. He continued to watch over us, and when we were in peril of falling into ditches and pits, He raised us aloft in His holy arms.

Outside, frost glowed everywhere, but it wasn't too cold in the granary. Wanda snuggled close to Jacob, her body tight against his, her mouth leaning toward his. He spoke and she continued to question. At first it seemed to him that he was both a fool and a betrayer of Israel. How could a peasant's brain comprehend such profundities? But the more Wanda questioned, the more obvious it became to him that she grasped his meaning. She even posed problems he could not solve. If the animals did not possess Free Will, why was it necessary for them to suffer? And if the Jews alone were God's children, why were gentiles created? She clasped him so tightly he could hear her heart beating; her hands dug into his ribs. She lusted for knowledge almost as fiercely as she did for the flesh.

"Where is the soul?" she inquired. "In the eye?"

"Yes, in the eyes, but in the brain also. The soul gives life to the entire body."

"Where does the soul go when a man dies?"

"Back to heaven."

"Does a calf have a soul?"

"No, it has a spirit."

"What happens to the spirit when the calf is slaughtered?"

"It sometimes enters the body of the eater."

"Does a pig have a spirit too?"

"Yes. No. I guess so. It has to have something."

"Why can't a Jew eat pork?"

"God's Law forbids it. It is His Will."

"When I become a Jew, will I also be God's daughter?"

"Yes, if you let Him enter your heart."

"I will, Jacob."

"You must become one of us not because of love for me but because you believe in God."

"I believe, Jacob. Honestly I do. But you must teach me. Without you I am blind."

A plan was forming in Wanda's mind; they would run away together; she knew the mountains. True, a Christian could not become a Jew, but she would disguise herself as a Jewess. She would shave her head and not mix meat with milk; Jacob would teach her to speak Yiddish. She insisted that he begin immediately. She said a word in Polish and he repeated it in Yiddish. *Chleb* meant bread; *wol* was an ox; *stol*, a table, and *lawka*, a bench. Some words were the same in both languages. Wanda asked him if the two tongues were really identical.

"The Jews spoke the sacred tongue when they lived in the Land of Israel," Jacob replied. "The tongue they speak today is a mixture of many languages."

"Why aren't the Jews still in their own country?"

"Because they transgressed."

"What did they do?"

"They bowed down to idols and stole from the poor."

"Don't they do that any more?"

"They don't worship idols."

"What about the poor?"

Jacob considered this question carefully before answering it.

"The poor are not treated justly."

"Who is ever just to the poor? The peasants work hard all year round and yet go naked. Zagayek wouldn't think of soiling his hands, but he takes everything, the best gram, the finest cattle."

"Every man will have to make an accounting."

"When, Jacob? Where?"

"Not in this world."

"Jacob, I must go. It's almost sunrise."

She clung to his neck, pressed deeply into his mouth, kissing him one final time. Her face became hot once again, but finally she tore herself from him. As she threw open the granary door, she murmured something and smiled shyly. There was no moon but the reflection of the snow fell across her face. Jacob recalled the story of Lilith, she who seeks out men at night and corrupts them. He and Wanda had now lived together for weeks, and yet each time he thought of his transgression he shivered anew. How had it happened? He had resisted temptation for years, then suddenly had fallen. He had changed since he had cohabited with Wanda. At times he didn't recognize himself; it seemed to him his soul had deserted him and he was sustained like an animal by something else. He prayed but without concentration. He still recited Psalms and portions of the Mishnah but his heart did not hear what his lips uttered. Whatever was within him had frozen. He no longer hummed and sang the old melodies, and was ashamed to think about his wife and children and all the other martyrs whom the Cossacks had slaughtered. What connection did he have with such saints? They were holy and he, unclean. They had sacrificed themselves for the Sacred Name while he had made a covenant with Satan. Jacob could no longer control his thoughts. Every kind of absurdity and non sequitur crammed his brain. He imagined himself eating cake, roast chicken, marzipan; drinking wine, mead, beer; hunting among the rocks and finding diamonds, gold coins, becoming a rich man, and riding around in coaches. His lust for Wanda reached such intensity that the moment she left the granary he began to miss her.

As with the soul, so with the body! He grew lazy and wanted only to lie on the straw. He suffered more from the cold that year than any other. When he chopped wood, the ax stuck and he couldn't pull it free. When he shoveled the snow from the yard, he tired quickly and had to rest. How strange it was! Even the cows he had reared sensed his predicament and turned nasty. Several times they tried to kick and gore him when he was milking them. The dog barked at him as if he were a stranger.

His dreams changed also. His father and mother no longer appeared in them. The moment he fell asleep he was with Wanda. Together they roamed through forests, crawled through caves, fell into pits, ravines, abysses, sank into swamps filled with putrefaction and filth. Rats and beasts with shaggy tails, large udders, and pouches chased him; they shrieked with strange voices, dribbled, spat, and vomited upon him. He awoke from these nightmares in a cold sweat but still burning with passion. A voice within him called out constantly for Wanda. He even found it difficult to stay away from her on those days when the Mosaic law declared her unclean.

V

The moon shone in a cloudless sky. That night, it was nearly as bright as day. Jacob, standing at the door of the granary, looked up at mile upon mile of mountains. Crags rising from the forests resembled shrouded corpses, beasts standing erect on their hind legs, monsters from another world. The silence in the village was so intense Jacob's ears rang as though a multitude of grasshoppers were singing under the snow. Although it had stopped snowing, occasional flakes drifted slowly to earth. A crow started from sleep and cawed once. In the granary and surrounding sheds, field mice and weasels scratched in their winter burrows as if expecting the sudden advent of spring. Even Jacob awaited a miracle. Perhaps summer would come more quickly than usual this year. There was nothing beyond God's power. The Almighty, if he wished, could remove the sun's cover as he had in the time of Abraham. But for whom would the Lord perform such a miracle? For Jacob the profligate, Jacob the sinner? He looked about him at the trees in the yard, snow hanging from their branches like white pears, petals of ice dropping from the twigs. He listened intently. Why didn't she come? The hut was dark, it seemed like a mushroom protruding from the drifts. Yet Jacob thought that he heard footsteps and voices. The door of the hut opened and Wanda appeared, but not as usual barefooted and enveloped in a shawl. She had on shoes and a sheepskin coat and she carried a cane. "Father is dead," she said, walking over to Jacob.

His mind froze.

"When? How?"

"He went to sleep like always, groaned, and that was the end of it. He died as silently as a chicken."

"Where are you going?"

"To fetch Antek."

They stood there in silence, and then Wanda said, "Hard times have begun for us. Antek's no friend of yours. He wants to kill you."

"What can I do?"

"Be careful."

She turned away from him; Jacob stood and watched her move into the distance, diminishing in size until she appeared no larger than an icicle. There had been no tears, but he knew she was grieving. She had loved her father— at times she had even used that word "father" addressing Jacob—now she had lost him. Whatever soul a peasant possessed had deserted the old man's body. But where was it now? Still in the hut? Or had it already begun its ascent? Had its departure been like smoke through the chimney? The custom of the village required Jacob to visit the family and say a few words of comfort. But he was doubtful whether he ought to go. Without Wanda the hut was a nest of snakes. He was not even certain Jewish law permitted him to make this condolence call, but at length he decided to. He opened the door of the hut. The old woman and Basha stood in the middle of the room; a wick was burning in a shard. On the bed lay the body, its appearance altered by death, the face yellow as clay, the ears chalk white, only a hole where once the mouth had been. How difficult to imagine that only a few minutes before, this corpse had been alive. Yet in the wrinkled eyelids and sockets a hint of the live Jan Bzik remained, a smile, the look of a man who has encountered something both come and propitious. The old woman sobbed hoarsely.

"He's gone, finished."

"May God comfort you."

"There wasn't a thing wrong with him at dinner. He ate a whole bowl of barley dumplings." Her remarks were only half directed at Jacob.

He stood there while the neighbors gathered. The women arrived in shawls and battered shoes, the men in sheepskins and boots made of rags. One woman wrung her hands, forced tears from her eyes, crossed herself. The widow kept repeating the identical sentence. "He had barley dumpling for supper and ate every morsel." With these words she was accusing death and giving evidence of what an exemplary wife she had been. All the faces were immersed in shadow, filled with the mystery of the night. Soon the air became fetid. Someone went to fetch Dziobak; the coffin maker arrived to take Jan Bzik's measure. Jacob slipped out of the hut. He was an alien among these people, but not as much a stranger now since Jan Bzik could almost be regarded as his father-in-law. The thought of this frightened him. "Well, aren't we all descended from Terah and Laban?" he said to himself. He was cold and his teeth were chattering. Jan Bzik had been good and just, had never ridiculed him, nor called him by a nickname. Jacob had become accustomed to him. There had been a secret understanding between the two men as if Bzik had somehow sensed that some day his cherished Wanda would belong to Jacob. "Well, it's a mystery," Jacob said to himself, "the profoundest mystery. All men are made in God's image. Perhaps Jan Bzik will sit with the other God-fearing gentiles in paradise."

Again he yearned for Wanda. What was keeping her? Well, from now on there would be an end of peace. The dog barked; more and more peasants were entering the hut. Zagayek arrived, a small rotund man dressed in a coat of fox pelts, felt boots, and a fur cap similar to those Jews wore on the Sabbath. Zagayek's mustaches flared underneath his thick nose like the whiskers of a tomcat. Dawn broke and the stars faded. The sky paled and turned rose. The sun blossomed behind the mountains and reddish specks of light glistened on the snow. The shrill voices of winter birds were heard, chattering. Jacob entered the barn and found that Kwiatula, the youngest of the cows who only a short time before had been a heifer, was about to give birth. She stood with bloated stomach, saliva dripping from her black muzzle. Her moist eyes looked straight at Jacob as though imploring his help.

He started to prepare the feed. It was also necessary to milk the animals. He mixed chopped straw, bran, and turnips together. "Well, we are all slaves," Jacob murmured to the cattle, "God's slaves." Suddenly the door opened and Wanda came in. Her cheeks were moist and red. Wanda, taking hold of Jacob, cried out as had his mother, peace be with her, before she rolled the large candle preparing for Yom Kippur Eve. "Now I have no one but you," she said.

FIVE

I

The scarcity of food in the village was rarely discussed, and Christmas was celebrated with great pomp despite the dearth. Though many of the peasants had already slaughtered their hogs and suckling pigs, there was sufficient meat for the holiday meal, nor was there a lack of vodka. Children went from hut to hut singing carols. The older boys collected gifts, leading around one of their company dressed as a wolf. Since the roof of the chapel leaked, the creche showing the birth in the manger had been set up in Zagayek's granary; there, too, was put on the pageant showing the arrival of the kings and wise men come to adore God's newborn son. Staffs, flaxen beards, the gilded star, everything required for the play was on hand, having been used year after year. But the sheep were real and the sound of their bleating cheered up the dejected spirits of the peasants.

The winter had been a hard one. Sickness and pestilence! The number of small and large graves had increased in the cemetery, and gales had toppled most of the new wooden crosses. But now the time to be merry was here, Zagayek distributed toys to the children and he gave white flour to the women so that the wafers could be baked. Wanda now knew from Jacob that the Jews believed in a God who had neither son nor division into persons. Yet she had to participate in the holiday and go with the others

Christmas Eve to Midnight Mass. She even took part in the pageant, stood near Stephan with a halo around her head looking like one of the saints. Stephan wore a mask, a white beard, and a miter. His breath stank of liquor, and he surreptitiously pinched Wanda and whispered obscene words into her ears.

Time after time Wanda had begged Jacob to enter the hut and take part with the others in the feasting. Even Jacob's enemy Antek sought to make peace during the holidays. Inside the hut stood a Christmas tree hung with ribbons and wreaths. The old woman had made pretzels, baked pork, stuffed cabbage, and a variety of other dishes. An extra man was needed to even out the number of guests, but Jacob remained stubborn. None of the food was kosher; all of this was idolatry, and it was well known that it was better to die than participate in such ceremonies. He stayed in the granary and ate dry bread as usual. It hurt Wanda to see him separate himself from the others and hide. The girls ridiculed him and her as well since he was her lover. Her mother openly spoke of the need to rid themselves of that accursed Jew who had brought bad luck and disgrace to the family. Now Wanda was more careful about seeking him out at night, knowing that the boys were planning to play all sorts of tricks on him. They considered dragging him out of the barn and forcing him to eat pork. Someone suggested that he be thrown into the stream as a sacrifice to the river spirit or be castrated. Wanda had brought him a knife so he might defend himself. She began to drink vodka to dispel the bitterness in her heart.

On the third day after Christmas, the village celebrated the sacred day of Turon that honored the ancient god of horses and courage, wind and power. Dziobak demanded the abolition of this pagan holiday, pointing out that with Jesus' birth all the idols had been deprived of their power, and in addition that no one in the large cities ever remembered such days. But the village paid no attention to him and there was dancing at Zagayek's house and in the huts. The musicians fiddled, banged cymbals, beat drums, played "The Little Shoemaker," "The Shepherd," "The Dove," "Good Night," and the "Dirge of a Dying Man," the last of which brought tears to the eyes of the women. The boys and girls danced a mazurka, a polka, a cracowiak, a goralsky. Everyone forgot his troubles. Sleighs crowded with young people raced across the snow, the bells on the reins and harnesses of the horses jingling. Here and there a sled yoked to a dog passed. Wanda had promised Jacob not to participate in these pagan revels, but with each passing hour she grew more restive. She had to dance and drink with the peasants. As long as she stayed in the village, it was impossible not to be one of them. The very fact that she planned to run away with him and accept his faith made the avoidance of suspicion more necessary. She hurried into the granary, her face flushed, and her eyes shining. Hurriedly she threw Jacob a few kisses, put her face on his chest, and started to sob. "Don't be angry with me," she said. "I've already become a stranger in my own home."

II

This was the first of the month of Nissan according to Jacob's calendar, two weeks before Passover. Not once in his captivity had he eaten bread during that holiday, subsisting those eight days on milk, cheese, and vegetables. The cold had set in again and a heavy snow had fallen. Antek had gone to buy another cow in a nearby village, and had taken Wanda along to get her opinion. She had been forced to agree to the trip, fearing to quarrel with her brother as long as Jacob was there. Jacob spent the morning milking the cows and chopping wood for the fire, which was the work he liked best. His ax rose and fell and the chips flew. The heavier pieces he split by hammering wedges into them. Little by little the pile grew until there was a sizable quantity. He went into the granary to rest, lay down, closed his eyes and dreamed of Wanda, but this dream did not have the village as its setting. Suddenly he felt himself being poked and he opened his eyes. The granary door was ajar and Basha stood near him. "Get up," she said. "You're wanted at Zagayek's."

"How do you know?"

"He's sent one of his men."

Jacob rose, realizing only too well what had happened. Zagayek had learned of his plan to escape and this was the end. Only recently Stephan had prophesied to Wanda that the Jew would be disposed of. "Well, my time has come," Jacob thought. All through the years he had been expecting this outcome. His knees trembled, and crossing the threshold, he bent over, picked up a handful of snow, and rubbed the palms of his hands with it so that he might pray. "Let it be Thy Will that my death redeem all my sins," he mumbled. For one instant he thought of making a break for it, but then saw how useless it would be. He was barefoot and without a sheepskin. "No, I won't run," he decided. "I have sinned and earned my punishment." Zagayek's man was waiting outside; he was unarmed.

"Let's go," he said to Jacob. "The gentlemen are waiting."

"What gentlemen?"

"How the devil do I know?"

"So they are going to try me," Jacob said to himself. The barking of the dog brought the old woman out of the hut; she stood there, broad and squat, yellow-faced, neither joy nor pity in her slanty eyes. Basha stood next to her mother, another one of those who, cow-like, accept docilely. The dog became silent and his tail drooped. Jacob was relieved that Wanda was not there; by the time she returned it might be all over. He thought of reciting, "Hear, O Israel," but decided he should do that when the noose was fixed about his neck. His stomach felt heavy; he was cold. He hiccupped, belched, started to recite the third chapter of Psalms, but paused when he came to the verse, "For Thou, O Lord, art a shield to me, my glory, and the lifter of my head." It was too late for such hopes. When he nodded at the old woman and Basha, they remained as unresponsive as stuffed images. The one thing that astonished Jacob was that not only was his attendant unarmed but he made no attempt to manacle him. "Well, there is an end to everything," Jacob thought, walking with bowed head and measured steps. For years he had been curious about what lay on the other side of flesh and blood. He was only anxious to get the death agony over with, and was prepared to sanctify God's name if he were asked to deny or blaspheme Him.

Women came from their hovels to stare blankly. Barking dogs ran after him; others peacefully wagged their tails. A duck waddled across his path. "Well, you'll outlive me," Jacob comforted the creature. He bid the world and the village goodbye. "Do not let anxiety make her ill," he prayed, thinking of Wanda. She had not been destined to reach the truth and he sorrowed for her. He raised his eyes and saw that the sky was once more blue and vernal. The only cloud resembled a single horned beast with a long neck. The mountains looked down on him from the distance, those hills to which he had planned to flee from slavery. "It has been ordained that I be with them," he said, thinking of his father and mother and his wife and children.

The man led him to Zagayek's house and there in front of the building stood a covered wagon hitched to a team of horses. Jacob didn't think that either the wagon or the team were from the neighborhood. The horses were covered with blankets and their harnesses were decorated with brass; a lantern hung from the rear axle of the vehicle. Jacob walked up a meticulously scrubbed staircase to the second floor. He had almost forgotten staircases existed, but here, it seemed, was a piece of the city in the center of this hamlet. As he walked down the hall, he smelled cabbage cooking; the midday meal was being prepared. He passed doors which had the kind of brass latches his parents' house had had. Straw mats lay before them. A door was thrown open and what he saw was strange and dream-like. Three men sat at a table, Jews with beards, sidelocks, and skull caps. The coat of one was unbuttoned and a fringed garment peeped through. Jacob recognized another but in his confusion forgot where he had met him. Jacob stood with his mouth open, and the Jews gaped back. At last one of them addressed him in Yiddish, "Are you Jacob from Zamosc?"

Everything went dark before Jacob's eyes.

"Yes, I am," he answered, speaking with a Polish accent.

"Reb Abraham of Josefov's son-in-law?"

"Yes."

"Don't you recognize me?"

Jacob stared. The face was familiar but he couldn't place it. "So this is not the day of my death," he thought.

He was unable to grasp what was happening, but he was ashamed that he was barefoot and dressed in peasant clothes. Inside of him all was still and frozen and he became as tongue-tied and shy as a boy. "Perhaps I am already on the other side," he thought. He wanted to say something, but couldn't utter a word. For the moment Yiddish eluded him. Another door opened and in walked Zagayek, short and stocky, red-nosed, his pointed mustaches resembling two mouse tails. He had on a braided green coat and low boots. The riding crop he carried had a rabbit's foot for a handle. Though it was early in the day, he had already drunk enough to make him walk unsteadily. His eyes were bloodshot and watery. "Well, is this your Jew?" he shouted.

The man who had just addressed Jacob spoke hesitantly. "Yes, this is he."

"All right, then, take him and go. Where's your money?"

One of the Jews, a small, pampered-looking man with a broad fanlike beard and dark eyes set widely apart, silently pulled a purse from his coat and commenced to count out gold pieces. Zagayek tested each of the coins by placing them between his thumb and index finger and trying to bend them. Only now did Jacob realize what had happened. These Jews had come for him; he was being ransomed. The man with the familiar face was from Josefov, one of the town elders. Suddenly Jacob felt terribly awkward as though the nearly five years he had lived in the mountains had taken effect this very instant and changed him into an uncouth peasant. He didn't know where to hide his calloused hands and dirty feet. He was ashamed of his torn jacket, and his unruly hair, resting upon his shoulders. A desire to bow peasant-like to the Jews and grasp their hands and kiss them seized him. The man who had counted out the gold pieces lifted his eyes.

"Blessed be Thou who revivest the dead."

III

The speed with which things now happened to Jacob was eerie. Zagayek extended his hand and wished him a pleasant trip. A moment later, the Jews escorted him outside and told him to get into the covered wagon. A number of peasants had gathered at Zagayek's house, but none of Jan Bzik's family was in the group. Before Jacob could say anything, the gentile driver—Jacob had not noticed him before – snapped his whip and the wagon careened downhill. Jacob thought of Wanda, but he didn't mention her. What was there to say? Could he ask that his peasant mistress be taken along? She was not in the village and so he couldn't even say goodbye to her. With the same suddenness that he had been enslaved he had now been ransomed. In the wagon the men spoke to him all at once and confused him so he scarcely knew what they were saying. Their speech sounded almost like a foreign tongue. A quilt was thrown over his shoulders and a skull cap placed on his head. He sat among them feeling naked. Slowly he grew accustomed to their words, gesticulations, odor, and asked how they had known his whereabouts. "A circus proprietor informed us," they said.

He became silent again.

"What happened to my family?" he asked.

"Your sister Miriam is alive."

"No one else?"

They didn't reply.

"Should I rend my clothes?" he inquired, intending the question not merely for them but for himself also. "I have forgotten the law."

"Yes, for your father and mother. But not for your children. More than thirty days have passed."

"Yes, that is now a distant event," Jacob said, employing the technical term.

Although he had known all along that his loved ones were dead, he sat there grieving. Miriam was the only one of the family who had survived. He feared to ask for details, kept looking straight ahead; the men spoke, for the most part, to each other. They discussed the clothes he must have: a shirt, a fringed garment, trousers, shoes. One of them remarked that his hair must be cut, and another untied a leather sack and rummaged in it. The third offered him cake, vodka, jam. Jacob refused to eat: he must remain in mourning for at least one day. Now he recollected the name of the man from Josefov: Reb Moishe Zakolkower, one of the town's seven most prominent citizens. The last time Jacob had seen him, he had been a young man sprouting his first growth of beard.

"It's exactly like Joseph and his brethren," one of the men remarked.

"Now we have lived to see this, we must say a benediction," another interjected, and he started to intone, "Oh, Thou who hast sustained me and made me live to reach this time."

"And I must say 'Thou hast done mercy,' " Jacob mumbled as if to prove that he too was a Jew and that no error had been made in ransoming him. But even as he said this, he was conscious of having erred. The correct thing was to praise God without further ado, but his voice sounded so coarse to him, he was embarrassed to speak before such fine people. His companions were small in stature but his head touched the roof of the wagon. He felt penned in, and so unfamiliar was the smell of the vehicle, it was difficult for him to keep from sneezing. These men should be thanked, but he didn't know the correct words for the occasion. Each time he tried to say something, Yiddish and Polish mingled in his head. Like an ignoramus about to talk to learned men he knew in advance that he would make a fool of himself. But he did ask finally, "Who is left in Josefov?"

The men appeared to have been waiting for this question and all started talking at once. The Cossacks had nearly leveled the town, had killed, slaughtered, burned, hanged, but there had been some survivors, widows and old men mostly, and a few children who had hidden in attics and cellars or taken refuge in peasant hamlets. The men mentioned some names Jacob knew, but others, since Josefov had acquired new inhabitants, that he had never heard before. The wagon continued to roll downhill, sunlight seeping through the covering, and the conversation remained elegiac. Every sentence ended with the word "killed." Now and then Jacob heard "died in the plague." Yes, the Angel of Death had been busy. The massacres and burnings had been followed by sickness, and people had died like flies. Jacob found it difficult to comprehend so much calamity. But as always, there was a saving remnant. The speakers appeared weighed down by an enormous burden and Jacob bowed his head. It was as if he had slept seventy years, like the legendary Choney, and awakened in another age. Josefov was no longer Josefov. Everything was gone: the synagogue, the study house, the ritual bath, the poor house. The murderers had even torn up the tombstones. Not a single chapter of the Holy Scroll, not a page from the books in the study house remained intact. The town was inhabited by fools, cripples, and madmen. "Why did this happen to us?" one of the men asked. "Josefov was a home of Torah."

"It was God's will," a second answered.

"But why? What sins did the small children commit? They were buried alive."

"The hill behind the synagogue shook for three days. They tore out Hanan Berish's tongue, cut off Beila Itche's breasts."

"What harm did we do them?"

No one answered these questions and they raised their eyes and stared at Jacob as if expecting him to reply. But he sat in silence. The explanation he had given Wanda that free will could not exist without evil nor mercy without sorrow now sounded too pat, indeed almost blasphemous. Did the Creator require the assistance of Cossacks to reveal His nature? Was this a sufficient cause to bury infants alive? He remembered his own children, little Isaac, Breina, the baby; he imagined them thrown into a ditch of lime and buried alive. He heard their stifled screams. Even if these souls rose to the most splendid mansion and were given the finest rewards, would that cancel out the agony and horror? Jacob wondered how it had been possible for him to forget them for an instant. Through forgetfulness, he had also been guilty of murder.

"Yes, I am a murderer," he said to himself. "I am no better than they."

SIX

Passover was at an end. Pentecost came and went. At first each
day was so crammed with incident it seemed like a year to Jacob.
Not an hour passed, scarcely a minute, without his coming
upon something new or something he had half forgotten. Was
it so trivial a matter to return to Jewish books, clothes, holidays,
after years of slavery among the pagans? Alone in the mountain
barn or in the Bziks' granary, he had felt that no trace of this
world remained. Chmielnicki and his Cossacks had wiped out
everything. At other times he had been half convinced that there
never had been a Josefov and that all his memories were illu-
sions. Suddenly he found himself dressed again as a Jew, praying
in synagogues, putting on phylacteries, wearing a fringed garment, and eating strictly kosher food. His trip down the road
from Cracow to Josefov had been one long continual holiday.
Rabbis and elders had greeted and feasted him in every town.
Women had brought their children to be blessed and had asked
him to touch coins and speak incantations over pieces of amber.
The martyrs were beyond help, and so everyone's goodness was
lavished on this man who had been ransomed from captivity.

His sister Miriam and her daughter Binele awaited him in
Josefov. Besides these two only a few distant relations were left
to him. Josefov was so changed it was unrecognizable: grass

was growing where houses had once been, buildings now stood where goats had pastured. There were graves in the middle of the synagogue yard. The rabbi, his assistant, and most of the elders came from other towns. Jacob was given a room and the authorities scratched together a yeshiva class so that he could support himself teaching. His sister Miriam had once been well-to-do, but now she was toothless and in rags. Meeting Jacob, she ran to him with a wail and never stopped sobbing and crying until she returned to Zamosc. He feared she was out of her mind. She screamed, pressed against him, bobbed up and down, all the time wringing her hands, pinching her cheeks, and enumerating all the tortures the family had undergone. She made Jacob think of those mourners and hand clappers who in the old days, according to the Talmud, had been hired for funerals. Her voice became so shrill at times that Jacob covered his ears.

"Alas, poor Dinah, they ripped open her stomach and put a dog in. You could hear it barking."

"They impaled Moishe Bunim, and he didn't stop groaning all night."

"Twenty Cossacks raped your sister Leah and then they cut her to pieces."

Jacob was not under the misapprehension that one had a right to forget how the dead had been tortured. What was said in the Bible of Amalek was true of all Israel's enemies. Yet, he did beg Miriam not to heap so many horrors on him at once. There was a limit to what the human mind could accept. It was beyond the power of any man to contemplate all these atrocities and mourn them adequately. A new Tischab'ov and a new seventeenth day of Tammuz had to be proclaimed. The year was not long enough to pray for and lament each of these saints singly. Jacob would have liked to run off and hide in some ruined building where he could remain in silence. But there was no such place in Josefov, which was all hustle and bustle. Houses were being built, buildings roofed; on every side men were mixing lime and carrying bricks. There were new stores in the market place and once again the peasants flocked to town on market day to deal with the Jews. Jacob, returning, was immediately involved in religious activities. It was the time when the matzoth were baked and he helped prepare them for the town's most pious citizens, drawing the water and assisting in the rolling. On the first night of Passover he entertained some widows at his seder, and it seemed strange to him now to speak of the miracles that had transpired in Egypt when in his day a new Pharaoh had brought to pass what the old Pharaoh had been unable to accomplish. There was not a prayer, law, passage in the Talmud that did not seem altered to him. The questions that he asked about Providence became increasingly sharp and searching and he found he had lost the power to stop asking them.

But, as he realized with astonishment, what was so new for him was stale for everyone else. The yeshiva boys laughed and played practical jokes on each other. Alert young men wove chains of casuistry. Merchants were busy making money, and the women gossiped in the same old way. As for the Almighty, He maintained his usual silence. Jacob saw that he must follow God's example, seal his lips, and forget the fool within, with his fruitless questions.

So the days flew by: Passover, Pentecost! Jacob's body had returned home but his spirit remained restless. No, if anything, his condition was worse, for now he had nothing to hope for. To prevent himself from thinking, he kept busy all day: teaching, studying, praying, reciting Psalms. Other towns had contributed a number of worn out, dog-eared books to Josefov and Jacob mended the pages and filled in the missing letters and words. The new study house needed a beadle, and he took that job also.

His day began at dawn and did not end until he was ready to collapse from exhaustion. If his thought could dwell only on complaints against Heaven or on memories of lechery in a barn on a mountain, then it was unclean. Let those whose minds were pure indulge in meditation.

Those pious women who took care of Jacob sought to repay him for his years of exile, but an undeclared war developed between them and their charge. They prepared him a bed of down and he stretched out on the hard floor and lay there all night. They cooked him soups and broths, and he wanted dry bread and water from the well. When visitors came to speak to him about his years of absence, he answered curtly. How else could he behave? The windows of the study house overlooked the hill where his wife and children lay buried. He could see cows grazing there in the newly grown pasture. His parents, relations, friends, had been tortured. As a boy he had pitied the watchman in the cemetery at Zamosc whose life had been passed near the cleansing house, but now the whole of Poland had become one vast cemetery. The people around him accommodated themselves to this, but he found it impossible to come to terms with. The best he could do was to stop thinking and desiring. He was determined to question no longer. How could one conceivably justify the torments of another?

One day seated alone in the study house, Jacob said to God, "I have no doubt that you are the Almighty and that whatever you do is for the best, but it is impossible for me to obey the commandment, Thou Shalt Love Thy God. No, I cannot, Father, not in this life."

II

How revolting to lust for some peasant woman and not adore the Creator. Out of contrition, one should bury oneself alive. But what then could be done with the gross body and its desires? How silence the criminal within? Jacob lay on the floor moving neither hand nor foot. The window was open and the night billowed in. He traced the path of the constellation in the ascendant and saw the stars drift from roof to roof, noting how these lights, whiter than the sun, twinkled and shimmered. The same God, who had given the Cossacks strength to chop off heads and rip open stomachs, directed this heavenly multitude. The midnight moon floated in mother-of-pearl and its face, said by the children to be Joshua's, stared straight at Jacob.

Josefov by day was a confusion of sounds: chopping, sawing; carts arriving from the villages with grain, vegetables, fire wood, lumber; horses neighing, cows bellowing; children chanting the alphabet, the Pentateuch, the commentaries of Rashi, the Gemara. The same peasants who had helped Chmielnicki's butchers strip the Jewish homes now turned logs into lumber, split shingles, laid floors, built ovens, painted buildings. A Jew had opened a tavern where the peasants came to swill beer and vodka. The gentry, having blotted out the memory of the massacres, again leased their fields, woods, and mills to Jewish contractors. One had to do business with murderers and shake their hands in order to close a deal. It was rumored that Jews, too, had fattened on the catastrophe, dealing in stolen goods and digging up caches hidden by refugees. Deserted wives were another subject of gossip. These women wandered through town searching for their husbands or for witnesses to testify they were dead. Many Jews had not been strong enough to resist conversion and the Polish government had decreed that those unwillingly baptized might reassume their own faith.

But the greatest sensation of all was caused by the Cossack wives, Jewish women forced into marriage, who now fled the steppes and returned. One of them, Tirza Temma, who had arrived in Josefov shortly before Jacob, had forgotten how to speak Yiddish. Her first husband was still alive, having escaped to the forest where he had lived on roots at the time of the massacre. He had not recognized Tirza Temma and had denied it was she. She had exhibited her evidence in the bath house, a honey-colored speck on one of her breasts and a second birthmark on her back. But her petition that her husband be forced to divorce his second wife had been denied. Tirza Temma, informed by the court that it was she who would be divorced, had berated the community in Cossack, and still persistently sought to break into her old home and take over the household. Another woman had been possessed by a dybbuk. One girl barked like a dog. A bride whose groom had been murdered on their wedding day suffered from melancholia and spent her nights in the cemetery dressed in her bridal gown and veil. Only now, years after the calamity, did Jacob realize how deep were the wounds. Moreover, new wars and insurrections were feared. The Cossacks on the steppes were again preparing an invasion of Poland, and Muscovites, Prussians, and Swedes stood poised with sharpened swords. The Polish nobility did nothing but drink, fornicate, whip peasants, and quarrel among themselves over the distribution of honors, privileges, and titles.

Only at night was there silence—the song of grasshoppers and the croak of frogs. Warm breezes wafted the smell of flowers, weeds, ripening grain from the fields, and Jacob recognized each faint aroma. He heard birds and animals stirring among the thickets. Lately he had taken a solemn oath, to root Wanda from his heart and never think of her again. She was a daughter of Esau who had lured him into adultery, a woman whose desire to accept his faith came from impure motives. In addition she was there, he here. What good was this brooding? Nothing but sins and imps born of evil thoughts arose from it. He marshaled the images of the cripples he had seen on the road and here in Josefov, men without noses, ears, tongues— each time he lusted for her, he thought of them. He should be more concerned with the misery of these unfortunates than with dreams of luxury in the lap of their torturer's sister. He determined to punish himself: every time he thought of Wanda he would fast until sunset. He drew up lists of torments: pebbles in his shoes, a stone beneath his pillow, bolting his food without chewing it, going without sleep. The debt he owed for allowing Satan to ensnare him had to be paid off once and for all. But Belial was as persistent as a rat. Who was the rat? Jacob, himself? Some force beyond him? But there was, as he well knew, a Spirit of Good and a Spirit of Evil. In his case the latter was more firmly seated in his brain and had much more to say. The instant Jacob dozed off, Evil took over, sketched lascivious pictures, brought Wanda's voice to the sleeper's ears, revealed her naked body to him, defiled and polluted Jacob. Sometimes he heard her voice even when he was awake. "Jacob, Jacob," she called. The sound came from without, not within him: he saw her working in the fields, grinding the grain, bearing food to the cowherd who this year slept in the barn with the cattle. She had taken up residence within him and he could not drive her forth. She nestled close to him beneath the prayer shawl when he prayed. She studied with him as he sat poring over the Torah. "Why did you show me how to be a Jew if you meant to leave me among the idolater?" she complained. "Why did you pull me to you only to thrust me away?" He looked into her eyes, heard her sob, walked with her among the cattle in the fields. Once more they bathed together in the mountain stream and he bore her in his arms to the straw. Balaam barked; the mountain birds sang. He heard her panting, "More, more." She whispered, bit his ear, and kissed it.

The matchmakers were busy trying to marry off Jacob, and one of the men who had ransomed him was among those who had found a prospect. Jacob at first said "no" to all these suggestions. He had no intention of remarrying, would remain celibate. But the contention was that he should not travel so dangerous a road. Why endure temptation daily? Moreover, he should obey the precept: "Be fruitful and multiply." A widow from Hrubyeshoyv was among the possibilities and she was to come to Josefov shortly to meet him. She had a drygoods store in the Hrubyeshoyv market and a house that the Cossacks had neglected to burn. The widow was a few years older than he and had a grown daughter, but this was no great handicap. The Jew does not tempt Evil by denying the body but harnesses it in the service of God. Jacob knew that he could never love this woman from Hrubyeshoyv, but possibly he might be able to find forgetfulness with her.

He was exhausted by the struggle within him, sleepless at night, weary during the day. He found he lacked the patience to teach and had lost his taste for Torah and prayer. He sat in the study house longing for the open air, dreaming of gathering grass again, scaling crags, chopping wood. The Jews had ransomed him but he remained a slave. Passion held him like a dog on a leash. The hounds of Egypt bayed but he could not drive them off.

One day when he was seated in the study house explaining the procedures involving the horns of rams sacrificed as burnt offerings, a small boy entered and said, "My father would like to see you, Reb Jacob." Jacob shivered as he always did now when he saw a child.

"Who is your father?"

"Moishe Zakolkower."

"Do you know what he wants with me?"

"The widow from Hrubyeshoyv is here."

The class burst out laughing and Jacob, becoming confused, blushed. "Recite the Gemara while I am gone," he directed. But even before he left the building, he heard his pupils pounding on the table and arguing querulously. Active boys, accustomed to playing wolf and goat, hide and go seek, tag, they were forever joking among themselves and laughing boisterously. One of the principal objects of their humor was gloomy Jacob seated before them lost in somber thoughts, and, now that he was being led away to meet a woman, they had something more to ridicule. Jacob walked beside the boy, having decided not to go home to change to his Saturday gabardines. The child, who had not even been alive at the time of the massacres, prattled about a bird that had flown through his bedroom window. They came to Moishe Zakolkower's newly erected house, even more comfortable than the one the Cossacks had burned, and Jacob, entering, found himself in a hall, smelled food, cutlets, and onions frying. The door of the kitchen was open and he could see Moishe's second wife (his first had been killed) standing near the oven. Another woman was kneading dough and a girl was grinding pepper in a mortar. For a moment he caught a whiff of the past and then Moishe, the man who had counted out the gold pieces for Zagayek, opened the living room door and bade Jacob enter. In the room, Jacob noted the newness of everything, walls, floors, tables, chairs, newly bound books from Lublin in the bookcases. The evil ones destroyed, the Jews created. Once more Jewish books were being printed and authors were traveling here and there to sign up subscribers. Jacob felt a stab in his heart every time he saw the past visibly resurrected. No doubt the living must go on living, but this very affixation betrayed the dead. A song he had heard a wedding jester sing came to his mind: "What is life but a dance across graves?" Yes, his coming to meet a prospective bride was a scandal. Only a few feet from here his wife and children lay buried. Yet better a wife than this perpetual brooding about a gentile woman.

Moishe and he were deep in a discussion of yeshiva and community matters when the woman of the household entered, bringing cookies and a dish of cherries—the hospitality of the wealthy. Blushing, she apologized for not being properly dressed, and nodded as if to say, "I know what you think, but you can't do a thing about it. This isn't a man's world." Finally the widow from Hrubyeshoyv arrived, a small dumpy woman, decked out in a silk dress and satin cape, wearing a matron's bonnet decorated with colored ribbons and pearls. Her round face had so many wrinkles that it looked as if it had been pieced together, and her eyes were black and soft, resembling those pulps found in cherry brandy. From her neck hung a gold chain with a dangling pendant, her fingers gleamed with rings. The odor of honey and cinnamon trailed into the room with her, and she looked Jacob over shrewdly.

"My, what a giant of a man! May the evil eye not fall on you."

"We are as God created us."

"True, but better big than a midget."

She spoke with a lilt and a sob, and kept wiping her nose with a batiste handkerchief. The wagon that had brought her to Josefov had lost a wheel, she said, and they had had to stop for repairs at a blacksmith's. Then she sighed and began to fan herself, meanwhile talking about her drygoods store and how hard it was to get the goods that the customers wanted. She refused the refreshments that Moishe's wife offered her, and then broke down and drained a glass of blueberry wine while she swallowed three cookies. Some crumbs fell on the folds of her cape and she picked them up and ate them. True, her business was large, thank God, but the girls she had working for her, on the other hand, couldn't be trusted. "A stranger's hand is useful only for poking a fire," she said, quoting the proverb and looking at Jacob slyly from the corners of her eyes. "One needs a man in the house, otherwise everything goes."

She liked him, Jacob saw, and was ready to sit down and write the preliminary agreement. But he hesitated. This woman was too old and syrupy, too cunning. He didn't want to spend his life overseeing clerks and bargaining with customers. Such a person needed a husband who was wrapped up, body and soul, in money. She was going to add a new wing to the house, she said, and also enlarge the store. The more she spoke, the more disconsolate Jacob became. I have ceased being a part of this world, he said to himself, the match would be good for neither of us. "I am not a business man by nature," he said aloud.

"Who's born a business man?" she asked, picking up a cluster of cherries with her flabby fingers.

She began to examine Jacob on his years of captivity— a subject usually avoided since the Jews regarded time spent among the pagans as wasted and better not discussed —but such a wealthy woman did not have to conform to convention. Jacob told her of Jan Bzik, of the barn on the mountain in which he had spent his summers, of the granary where he had slept in the winter. "How did you get food when you were on the mountain?" she asked. "It was brought from the valley."

"Who brought it? The peasant?"

"No, his daughter."

"Unmarried?"

"A widow."

"Did you collect grass on the Sabbath?"

"I never broke the Sabbath. Nor did I eat unkosher food." He was ashamed to hear himself boasting of his piety.

The woman thought over what he had said carefully, and then remarked as she reached out her hand to take another cookie, "What choice did you have? Oh, what those murderers did to us!"

III

It was noon; the boys went for their midday meals, some to their families and others to the houses where they boarded. Alone in the study house, Jacob prepared a lecture. He was pleased to be once more deep in the study of books, yet he found earning his living by teaching distasteful. Most of his students were bored and the clever ones spent their time in hair-splitting or in complicating the obvious. His years away from Torah had changed his views. Now conscious of much he had not realized, he saw that one law in the Torah generated a dozen in the Mishnah, and five dozen in the Gemara; in the later commentaries laws were as numerous as the sands of the desert. Each generation added its own strictures, and during his years of exile the Shulcran Oruch had been further interpreted and additional forbiddances added. A wry thought occurred to him: if this continued, nothing would be kosher. What would the Jews live on then? Hot coals? And why had these interdictions and commandments not preserved the Jews from Cossack atrocities? What more did God require of his martyred people?

Moreover, as Jacob looked about him, he saw that the community observed the laws and customs involving the Almighty, but broke the code regulating man's treatment of man with impunity. His return before Passover had brought him to town when a quarrel was in progress. Flour for matzoths was scarce and the rabbi, finding no proscription in the Mosaic Law, in the Talmud, or even in Maimonides, had authorized the eating of peas and beans during the holidays. This ruling had incensed certain members of the congregation, some because they wanted to show how pious they were, others because they were angry at the rabbi; and they had broken the windows in the rabbi's house and driven nails into his bench at the east wall. One of the zealots had approached Jacob and sounded him out about becoming rabbi.

Yes, men and women who would rather have died than break the smallest of these ritualistic laws, slandered and gossiped openly, and treated the poor with contempt. Scholars lorded it over the ignorant; the elders divided privileges and preferments among themselves and their relatives and exploited the people generally. Money lenders gouged their clients—using loopholes in the law against usury; merchandise was kept off the market until it became scarce. Some went so far as to give false weight and measure. But when Jacob entered the study house he met them all: the angry, the haughty, the obsequious, the crooked. They prayed and schemed, erected tall towers of legalisms while they broke God's commandments. The catastrophe had impoverished the community, but the town still had more than its share of hatred and envy. Moishe Zakolkower told Jacob that there were those who were anxious to prevent his match with the widow of Hrubyeshoyv. An anonymous letter had been received denouncing Jacob.

Yet Jacob's thoughts worried him, since he knew his concern with such things was of evil origin. Satan tried to prove that corruption being general, sin could be taken lightly. The Spirit of Good replied: "Why concern yourself with what others do? Look to yourself." But Jacob had no peace. Everywhere he heard people asserting things that their eyes denied. Piety was the cloak for envy and avarice. The Jews had learned nothing from their ordeal; rather suffering had pushed them lower.

Chanting as he studied, he found it difficult now to keep the lilt of the cowherds' songs out of his voice. Moments came when he longed for the barn. His love for the Jews had been wholehearted when he was distant from them. He had forgotten the shifty eyes and barbed tongues of the petty—their tricks, stratagems and quarrels. True, he had suffered from the primitiveness and savagery of the cowherds, but what could be expected from such a rabble?

The marriage contract was almost completed, the date of the wedding set for the Friday after Tischab'ov. The widow, though well along in her thirties, could still bear children and was anxious to have a son. Already flatterers considered Jacob a rich man and showered him with compliments. Yet he lay awake worrying, still uncertain about this marriage. The widow needed a business man, a good mixer; he was withdrawn, a recluse. The years of slavery had estranged him from life; he looked healthy, but was shattered within. He kept rummaging in the cabala and leafing through books of philosophy. Sometimes he was overwhelmed by the desire to flee, but he didn't know where. He doubted everything, with, as the saying goes, the kind of doubt which "the heart does not share with the lips." He had not tasted meat in all the years of slavery and the idea of feeding on God's creatures now repelled him. Meat and fish were both eaten customarily on the Sabbath, but the food stuck in his throat. Jews treated animals as Cossacks treated Jews. The words "head," "neck," "liver," "gizzards," made him shudder. Meat in his mouth gave him the fantasy he was devouring his own children. On several occasions he had gone outside and vomited after the Sabbath dinner.

He was alone in the study house, not studying, but merely leafing through volume after volume. Possibly Maimonides had the answer. Or the *Chuzary*. Might it be contained in *The Duty of the Heart* or *The Vineyard*? He read a few words, turned the page, opened another book in the middle, turned pages again. Putting his hands to his face, he closed his eyes. He longed for both Wanda and the grave. The instant his desire for her left him, he wished to die. "Father in Heaven," his lips said as if possessed of a will of their own, "take me."

Footsteps approached; a charity worker entered, bringing him a bowl of soup. Jacob studied her. Lame though she was, with a wart on her nose and hair on her chin, this woman was a saint. Kindness, gentleness, candor dwelt in her eyes. She had lost her husband and children but exhibited no bitterness, envied no one, nursed no grievances, uttered no slander. She washed Jacob's linen, cooked for him, waited on him like a maid, and would not allow him even to thank her. Her answer to praise was, "for what other reason were we created?"

She placed the bowl on the table and brought bread, salt, a knife, as well as a pitcher of water for him to wash his hands; and then stood humbly at the door waiting for him to finish. What was the source of her kindness? Jacob wondered. Only the wise behaved as she. Even if she were the sole representative of virtue in Josefov, she would still be a witness to God's mercy, and this was the woman he should marry. Would she consider marriage, he asked, if a proper husband were found for her? Her eyes clouded. "God willing, in the next world with my Baruch David."

IV

Wanda came to Jacob one night as he lay sleeping. He saw her in the flesh, her body surrounded by light, her cheeks tear-stained, and knew she was pregnant. The smell of fields and haystacks entered with her. "Why did you leave me?" she asked wanly. "What will happen to your child? It will be brought up among pagans." Startled, Jacob awoke; the image lingered an instant at the boundary of sleep and waking. When it at last dissolved, the darkness retained an afterglow as if a lamp had just been extinguished. Hearing Wanda's voice re-echo in his ears, Jacob trembled. He could almost feel the warmth of her body. Straining his ears, he waited for her to reveal herself again. He dozed off. She reappeared, wearing a calico apron, carrying a kerchief with a fringed border, and approaching him, threw her arms about him and kissed him. Because of the child she bore, he had to bend to her and he tasted her lips and the salt of her tears. "It's yours," she said, "your flesh and blood."

Once more he awoke, and did not close his eyes again that night. He had seen her, she was carrying his child. Jacob began to recite Psalms. The eastern sky became scarlet; he rose and washed his hands. All was clear to him now. The law obliged him to rescue Wanda and his child from the idolaters. He had money, for as sole heir of his father-in-law he had received fifty gulden for the property in the market place where the old house had stood. He threw his belongings into a burlap sack and walked to the study house. Reb Moishe, always one of the first ten to enter God's house, had his Gemara already open, and was busily studying. His dark eyes grew large seeing Jacob approach with a sack slung over his shoulder.

"What are you up to?"

"I'm off to Lublin."

"But the date of the wedding's been set."

"I can't go through with it."

"What'll happen to your class?"

"You'll find another teacher."

"Why? And so suddenly?"

Wanting neither to lie nor tell the truth, Jacob said nothing. He counted out twenty gulden from a small bag. "Here's part of the money the town spent ransoming me." Astonished, Reb Moishe tugged at his beard. "Repaying the community," he mumbled. "We can expect the Messiah any day."

"It should be of some assistance."

"What do I tell the widow of Hrubyeshoyv?"

"Say we weren't meant for each other."

"Are you coming back?"

"I don't know."

"What's your plan—to become a recluse?"

Without waiting for the arrival of a quorum, Jacob turned his head and began the morning prayer. He had learned the day before that a wagon would leave for Lublin in the morning, and quickly finishing his devotions, he set out to find Leibush the carter. If he passed someone carrying a filled container, he had decided that would be an omen that there would be room on the wagon, and that Heaven approved of the trip. Lo and behold, there was Caiman the water carrier lugging two pails of water. "Well, we can always squeeze in one more," Leibush said.

The morning was warm; the village quiet. It was late in the month of Sivan. Shutters opened. Sleepy-eyed women poked out their bonneted heads. Men converged on the study house carrying bags containing their prayer shawls and phylacteries. Cows were being led to pasture. A great golden sun was aloft in the east, but dew continued to fall on the grass and the young trees planted after the destruction. Birds sang and pecked at the oats fallen from the horses' feedbags. On such a morning it was difficult to believe this a world in which children were slain and buried alive, and that the earth still drank of blood as in the days of Cain. "You sit with me on the box," Leibush said to Jacob. The other passengers were mostly women off to buy goods in the Lublin stores.

One woman had forgotten something. Another had to run home to nurse her baby. A man arrived with a package to be delivered to the Lublin inn. So the wagon did not start immediately as scheduled. Two men, storekeepers, who were seated among the women whiled away the time swapping spicy stories and innuendoes with the giggling matrons. Jacob heard his name mentioned and then the name of the widow of Hrubyeshoyv. Unintentionally, he had humiliated her. No matter what one does one stumbles into sin, he thought. He had been reading books of ethics, filled with the best advice on how to avoid the pitfalls of evil, but Satan always outwitted one. He participated in all business transactions and marriages; no human enterprise proceeded without him: touch something and you hurt someone. Have a little success, and, no matter how decent you were, you provoked envy. But why was he on his way to Lublin? He told himself he didn't know. He wanted advice from the city's wisest rabbis and would do as they recommended. Yet all the time he was aware he was traveling to Wanda, like one of the Israelite rabble that had wanted to turn and march back to Egypt and slavery for a kettle of meat. But did he dare let his child grow up among the pagans? He had not thought that the gentile woman would become pregnant. Generally he had withdrawn and spilled his seed like Onan.

Well, it makes no difference whether I go or stay, Jacob remarked to himself. I'm lost either way. The wagon had begun to move without his noticing it, and was now passing fields where the peasants were weeding and transplanting. How beautiful the countryside was and how contrary to his despair. Doubt, dissension, discord dwelt within him, but the fields exuded harmony, tranquillity, fruitfulness. The sky was blue, the weather warm with the mercy of summer, the air fragrant as honey, each flower exhaling its own perfume. A hidden hand had shaped and modeled each stalk, blade of grass, leaf, worm, fly. Each hovering butterfly's wings exhibited a unique design; every bird sang with its own call. Breathing deeply, Jacob realized how much he had missed the country. Grainfields, trees, every single growing thing refreshed his eyes. If only I could live in perpetual summer and do harm to no one, he murmured, as the wagon entered a pine wood which seemed less a forest than some heavenly mansion. The trees were as tall and straight as pillars and the sky leaned on their green tops. Brooches, rings, gold coins were embossed on the bark of their trunks. The earth, carpeted with moss and other vegetation, gave off an intoxicating odor. A shallow stream coursed through the woodland, and perched on rocks in the water were birds Jacob had never seen in the mountains. All of these creatures knew what was expected of them. None sought to rebel against its Creator. Man alone acted viciously. Jacob heard the women behind him slandering the whole of Josefov. Raising his eyes, he gazed through the screen of branches and needles where jewels glittered. The light which filtered through shone with all the colors of the rainbow. Cuckoos sang, woodpeckers drummed. Gnats circled quickly, dark, eddying specks. Jacob closed his eyes as though begrudging himself the sight of so much splendor. A roseate light seeped through his lids. Gold mingled with blue, green with purple, and, out of this whirlpool of color, Wanda's image formed.

V

Great crowds filled the community house in Lublin. The Council of the Four Countries was not in session, but the Council of Poland was. Deserted wives petitioning for the right to remarry, "Cossack brides" returned from the steppes and Russian Orthodoxy, widows whose brothers-in-law had refused to perform the Levirate ceremony or had insisted on being payed exorbitantly to do so, moved through the rooms. Mingled with them were husbands whose wives had run off or gone mad and who needed the consent of a hundred rabbis to remarry, fathers looking for prospective sons-in-law, authors asking religious authorities for endorsements, contractors seeking partners to invest in the lumber business, and individuals who merely wanted witnesses for wills. Both social and commercial activity went on in the Lublin community house. Merchants passed around samples; jewelers and goldsmiths displayed their wares; authors hawked their books and met with printers and paper jobbers;

usurers discussed loans with builders and contractors; managers of estates brought objects their gentile patrons wanted to pawn or sell—a carved ivory hand ornamented with rubies, a lady's gold comb and hairpins, a silver pistol with a mother-of-pearl handle studded with diamonds.

Despite the upheaval, Poland's commerce remained in the hands of the Jews. They even dealt in church decorations, although this trade was forbidden them by law. Jewish traders traveled to Prussia, Bohemia, Austria, and Italy, importing into the country silk, velvet, wine, coffee, spices, jewelry, weapons, and exporting salt, oil, flax, butter, eggs, rye, wheat, barley, honey, hides. Neither the aristocracy nor the peasantry had any real knowledge of business. The Polish guilds continued to protect themselves through every form of privilege, but nevertheless their products were more expensive than those of the Jews and often inferior in workmanship. Nearly every manor harbored Jewish craftsmen, and, although the king had forbidden Jews to be apothecaries, the people had confidence in no others. Jewish doctors were sent for, sometimes from abroad. The priests, particularly the Jesuits, harangued against infidel medicine from their pulpits, published pamphlets on the subject, petitioned the Sejm and the governors to disqualify Jews from medical practice, but no sooner did one of the clergy fall ill, than he called in a Jew to attend him.

Jacob had come to Lublin to get advice from the local rabbi or from the members of the Council, but he loitered in the city doing nothing. The Sabbath came and went. The more he reflected on the question perplexing him, the clearer it became that no one could advise him. He was familiar with the law. Would he find a man anywhere who could determine the authenticity of a vision or who could weigh in the scales which was the greater transgression, the abandonment of one's issue to the idolaters or the conversion of a woman lacking a true vocation? Once more Jacob remembered the saying, "Something done selfishly may end up as a godly act," and argued accordingly. Cakes, candies, and almonds were given a child starting cheder to encourage him to love the Torah. Didn't one speak of a convert as new-born? Who could know all the motives of those who had become Jews in the past? No saint was entirely selfless. Jacob decided to take the sin upon himself and instruct Wanda in the tenets of his faith. Now that the Polish government permitted converted Jews to return to their religion, Wanda could pass as one of them. No one would bother to investigate. She would shave her head, put on a matron's bonnet, and he would teach her every single law.

In Lublin, Jacob was known as that man from Josefov who spent so many years a slave. Speaking thus, they set him apart. The scholars addressed him as if he were a simpleton who had forgotten all he learned. When they mentioned a Hebrew word or quoted the Talmud, they translated it into Yiddish for his benefit. In his presence they whispered among themselves and smiled patronizingly as city people do when they converse with bumpkins. The elders were interested in how he had conducted himself in slavery: had he kept the Sabbath and the dietary laws? How odd that he had not attempted to escape but had waited to be ransomed. Jacob became convinced they knew something dreadful they dared not say to his face. Could they have been told about Wanda? Zagayek might have passed a comment to the group who had come to ransom him. If so, his secret was traveling from mouth to mouth.

From the first he had noted the difference between himself and the others, and the longer he stayed in Lublin, the sharper the contrast seemed. He was tall, blond, blue-eyed; they, for the most part, were short, dark-eyed, black-bearded. They liked esoteric scholarly jokes, used snuff, smoked tobacco, knew the names of all the rich contractors, were acquainted with who had married whom, and what Jew was the favorite of which nobleman. All this was foreign to Jacob. I have turned into a peasant, he said, rebuking himself. But he recalled that it had not been so different before the calamity. The rabbis, elders, and rich men in the old days had also been of one party and he of another. They had eyed him suspiciously as if they suspected he had gentile blood. But how could this have been? Descended from an eminent family, his grandfathers, and their fathers also, had all been Polish rabbis.

Stranger than this, however, was the attitude of the Jews who, having just survived their greatest calamity, behaved as if they no longer remembered. They groaned and sighed, but without feeling. The rabbis and elders were again quarreling over money and power. The problem of the deserted wives and "the Cossack brides" was for them an opportunity to display their casuistic brilliance in long, time-consuming discussions little connected with the spirit of the law. The unhappy petitioners waited weeks and months for verdicts that could have been handed down in a few days. The Council of the Four Countries had taken upon itself the task of collecting the Crown taxes in addition to those which went for its own support, and everywhere complaints were heard that the burden of the tax was inequitably distributed and the rate excessive. Occasionally an accuser pointed a finger at these eminent men, threatening to complain to the administration, to stand up in the synagogue and denounce them before the reading of the Torah, or to wait for them outside and give them a good beating. The man was immediately made a member of the elite, offered a few crumbs, and sent out to sing the praises of the very individuals he had been defaming. Jacob even heard of emissaries who misappropriated money they collected or took too high a percentage for themselves. The catastrophes over, the stomachs of many of the rabbis and elders had increased in size; their necks wrinkled with fat. All this flesh was dressed in velvet, silk, and sables. They were so heavy they wheezed; their eyes shone greedily. They spoke an only half comprehensible language of innuendoes, winks, and whispered asides. Outside the community house, angry men proclaimed these rulers robbers and thieves and warned prophetically of the plagues and afflictions their sins would produce.

Yes, it was clear to Jacob that these, the grabbers, were worthless, but there were also the givers, and more of these than the others. Thank God, not all Jews were community elders. Men still prayed, studied, and recited Psalms in God's house. Many of them still bore the wounds they had received from the Cossacks. Jacob saw cripple after cripple, men deprived of ears, fingers, noses, teeth, eyes, and all sang: "We will sanctify"; "Bless ye." They listened to the sermons, sat down to pore over the Mishnah. Anniversary candles were lit and men continued to mourn.

Wandering through the narrow alleys, Jacob saw how great the poverty was. Many lived in what were only dark burrows; tradesmen worked in shops that looked like kennels. A stench rose from the gutters; ragged women, often on the point of giving birth, foraged for wood shavings and dung to be used for heat. Half naked children with scabby heads and rashes walked around barefoot. Many of the urchins had rickety legs, sores on their eyes, puffed bellies, distended heads. There was some kind of epidemic in progress and hearses with corpses in them passed constantly, each followed by lamenting women. A beadle rattled his alms box and cried out, "Charity will preserve you from death." The insane were everywhere, wild in the streets, another remembrance of the Cossacks.

It shamed Jacob that he thought so much of Wanda. People were starving before his eyes. A groschen here could save a life. He was continually changing silver to smaller coins and distributing his money. But what he gave was little when confronted with this vast need. Bands of beggars pursued him, clutched at his coat, blessing and cursing him. They hissed, spat at him, threw lice in his direction, and he was barely able to escape. Where was God? How could he look down on such want and keep silent? Unless, Heaven forbid, there was no God.

SEVEN

I

Jacob traveled from Lublin to Cracow by wagon. Changing to peasant dress, he proceeded on foot from Cracow to the mountains. The sack slung over his shoulder contained bread, cheese, a prayer book and shawl, phylacteries, a volume of the Mishnah, and presents for Wanda: a matron's bonnet, a dress, a pair of shoes. He had made his plans in advance; he would avoid the high road and take meadow and forest trails. The sun had gone down before he left Cracow, and all night he walked, aware of the dangers around him. Wild beasts and robbers lived in the hills; he remembered Wanda's stories of vampire owls disguised as cats and of witches' mares galloping through darkness on their evil errands.

The roads were dangerous at night, as Jacob knew. The King's Daughter, filthiest of witches, confused travelers and shoved them into bogs. The demonic Lillies made their homes in caves and the hollows of tree trunks. Ygereth, Machlath, and Shibta enticed men off the highways until they defiled themselves with nocturnal emissions. Shabriry and Briry polluted the waters of springs and rivers. Zachulphi, Jejknufi, Michiaru, survivors of the generation that had built the Tower of Babel, confounded men's speech and drove them mad or into the mountains of darkness. But Jacob's longing for Wanda made him willing to take any risk. Even though the journey must result in sin, he sang Psalms and begged God to keep him safe. His investigations of the cabala since his return had uncovered the doctrine that all lust was of divine origin, even Zimri's lust for Kozbi, the daughter of Zur. Coupling was the universal act underlying everything; Torah, prayer, the Commandments, God's holy names themselves were mysterious unions of the male and female principles. Jacob thrashed this way and that, constantly seeking exoneration: a soul would be saved from idolatry; his seed would not be mingled with that of Esau. Such virtuous acts must tip the scales in his favor.

The summer night passed, but Jacob could not have told how. The sun rose and he discovered himself in a forest with a stream close by. Washing his hands, he recited the Shema, and said the morning prayer in his shawl and phylacteries. He breakfasted on bread, dried cheese, and water, and then, having said grace, rested his head on the sack and fell asleep. The analogy between him and his Biblical namesake had already occurred to him. Jacob had left Beersheba and journeyed to Haran for love of Rachel and had toiled seven years to win her. Had she not been the daughter of a pagan? Awaking with such thoughts in his mind, he resumed his own journey, heading upstream past mushrooms and blackberry brambles in bud, noting which plants were edible. Uncertain of the road, he kept his eye out for the blazes the Gazdas notched into trees. Cows bellowed close at hand; he could see camp fires. As long as the path climbed, it was taking him to Wanda.

Late in the afternoon, when the sun was moving westward, a strange figure appeared as if risen from the earth. White-haired, bearded, the man wore a brown robe and felt boots. A rosary and crucifix hung from his neck. He stopped before Jacob, leaning on a crooked staff. "Where are you bound for, my son?" he asked.

Jacob told him the name of the village.

"There is the way," the old man said, and he showed him the path.

Before leaving, he blessed Jacob. If it had not been for the cross he wore, the old man might have been mistaken for the prophet Elijah. But, perhaps, Jacob thought, he was an emissary of Esau, sent by those powers who wished Jews and gentiles to mate. Jacob was now nearing the village, and he lengthened his stride. He felt anxious: Wanda might have remarried or fallen ill. God forbid, she might be dead. She might be in love with someone else. The sun went down; though it was midsummer, it became cold. Columns of mist rose from the mountains. In the distance, a huge bird, an eagle perhaps, hung suspended in mid air, wings motionless as though kept aloft by cabala. The moon rose and one by one, like candles being lit, stars appeared. Suddenly there was a noise, a kind of roaring. An animal or the wind? Jacob wondered. Though he was prepared to fight, he recognized that Providence would be justified in allowing some predatory creature to destroy him. How had he deserved better?

Stopping, he looked about him. He was as solitary here as the original Adam, with no sign anywhere of man and his works. The birds silent, only the song of the grasshoppers and the bubbling of a stream were heard. Glacial breezes blew from the mountains. Jacob breathed in deeply, savoring the familiar odors. Strange how he had missed not only Wanda but this. The stale air of Josefov had been unbearable, windows tightly shut, nothing but books all day. Tired though he was from his exertion, the journey had invigorated him. The body required use as well as the soul. It was good for men to haul, drag, chop, run, perspire, to hunger and thirst and become weary. Raising his eyes, he saw more stars appearing, large and brilliant here in the mountains. The workings of the heavens were visible to him, each orbiting light going its prescribed way and fulfilling its function. Notions he had had as a boy returned to him. Suppose he had wings and flew in one direction forever, would he come to the end of space? But how could space end? What extended beyond? Or was the material world infinite? But if it was, infinity stretched both to the east and west, and how could there be twice infinity? And what of time? How could even God have had no beginning? How could anything be eternal? Where had everything come from? These questions were impertinent, he knew, impermissible, pushing the inquirer toward heresy and madness.

He continued to walk. How strange and feeble was man. Surrounded on every side by eternity, in the midst of powers, angels, seraphim, cherubim, arcane worlds, and divine mysteries, all he could lust for was flesh and blood. Yet man's smallness was no less a wonder than God's greatness.

Pausing, he took some dry cheese from his sack and refreshed himself. Would he find Wanda today or have to wait until tomorrow? He feared the peasants and their dogs. He began to mumble prayers—a slave returning to bondage, a Jew again putting on Egypt's yoke.

II

Jacob entered the village at midnight, stealing through fields and pastures at the back of the huts. The moon had set, but it was light enough for him to recognize each house and granary. The mountain where he had spent five summers was visible also and he constantly lifted his eyes to it. Those years seemed dreamlike now, a vanished miracle, an interlude achieved by sorcery. Thank God, the dogs slept. His feet no longer felt heavy and his steps were faunlike; his body was buoyant from lack of food. He broke into a run, down the hill leading to Jan Bzik's hut, his single desire to find Wanda. Was she in the house? In the granary? Could she have gone to Antek's? He thought of his life and was amazed at what had happened to him. He had been taken captive; his family had been wiped out. Now, disguised as a peasant, he was hurrying to find his beloved. This was the sort of ballad his sisters had told or sung when his father was absent, not daring to when the pious man was at home, knowing that he regarded the female voice as lascivious.

Jacob stopped and held his breath. There it was, Jan Bzik's hut. He was trembling. He could make out every detail: the thatched roof, the windows, the granary, even the stump on which he had chopped wood. The kennel in the center of the yard appeared to be empty. Tiptoeing toward the granary, he smelled an odor he only now remembered. Was Wanda there? Could he be sure she would not cry out and wake everyone? He recollected the code she had used during those months when he had feared an attack by Antek or Stephan – three knocks, two loud and one soft. He rapped out the signal. There was no answer. Now for the first time he realized how dangerous this undertaking was. If he were discovered, he might be killed as a thief. And what if he did find Wanda, where could they go? This adventure was putting him in constant jeopardy. The Christians burned gentiles who became Jews. Nor would the Jews accept the convert. It was still not too late to turn back, he knew. He tingled with anxiety. Where had passion led him? Quietly he pushed open the granary door, meanwhile defending himself—I am no longer responsible for my acts. He heard breathing. Wanda was there. Hands ready to stifle her scream, he approached. Now he saw her in the darkness: she lay on the straw, her breasts exposed, half-naked. The story of Ruth and Boaz floated through his brain. He was awake, yet dreaming. He put down his sack.

"Wanda."

Her breathing stopped.

"Wanda, don't scream. It's me, Jacob." He broke off, unable to say more.

She sighed. "Who is it?"

"Jacob. Don't scream."

Thank God she did not, but sat up like someone delirious from fever.

"Who are you?" she said uncomprehendingly.

"Jacob. I've come for you. Don't scream."

At that very instant she did. Her scream made Jacob shudder and he was certain those in the hut must have heard. He fell to the straw, and, struggling with her in the darkness, he clamped his hand over her mouth. She freed herself, got to her feet, and he clutched her again, glancing at the open door, expecting to see peasants running toward the granary.

"Be still," he said, his breath coming in gasps. "They'll kill me. I've come for you, Wanda. I couldn't get you out of my mind."

Scarcely knowing what he was doing, he pulled her closer. They dared not stay there, the granary was a trap. He was breathing hard and sweating; his heart was pounding. "We must leave here while it's still dark," he whispered.

No longer struggling, trembling now, she pressed herself to him, her teeth chattering as though it were winter. "Is it really you?" he heard her say.

"Yes, I. Hurry, we must go."

"Jacob. Jacob."

The scream must have gone unnoticed as no one was coming. But perhaps the peasants lay in wait outside. Now, for the first time, it occurred to him that this was not the Wanda of his vision. There was no indication that she bore his child. A dream had deceived him. Her arms about his neck, she whimpered like a sick animal, "Jacob, Jacob." He could not doubt that she had been longing for him. But every minute counted now. Over and over again he cautioned her that she must dress quickly and come with him. He grasped her by the wrists, shook her, begged her not to delay—they were in great peril. She pulled him to her again, pressing her face against his. In his anxiety he couldn't make out what she was saying. "We must leave," he warned her.

"One minute."

Turning, she ran from the granary. He saw her enter the hut and wondered if she would tell the old woman. He lifted his sack and walked out into the open air, prepared to run for the fields if there was trouble. It was difficult for him to believe that the woman he had awakened was Wanda. She looked smaller and thinner than she had been, more like a girl than a woman. Outside it was dark and still—that moment before dawn when night borders on day. Sky, earth, and mountains waited in an expectant hush. Though he remained terrified and shocked at what he had done, there was also a silence in Jacob. His mind seemed frozen. He no longer cared what the outcome of this adventure would be. His fate was decided. He had passed beyond freedom, was both himself and another. The still point within him watched as though his actions were those of a stranger.

He waited, but Wanda did not come. Had she decided not to leave with him? The sun must have risen already on the other side of the mountains. He stood enveloped in the chill darkness of dawn. Suddenly Wanda ran from the hut, now wearing shoes and with a kerchief on her head. A sack was slung over her shoulder. "Did you wake them?" he asked.

"No, they sleep like the dead."

III

Wanda chose another route to leave the village than the one he had had in mind. Like an elusive shadow she ran before him scarcely visible in the darkness. His legs shook from too much walking and too little sleep. He stumbled over rocks, slid into ditches. He wanted to call to her not to get too far ahead, but dared not raise his voice. How could she run so quickly bearing a sack? He felt drowsy; he kept dreaming. Something rose from the darkness. He drew back startled and instantly the image dissolved. An alien voice spoke inside him. Things were happening, but he didn't know what. Wanda had dressed and packed without waking her mother and sister – how? An absurd idea, patently false, came to him: could she have strangled them?

That instant a fragment of day fell on the mountains and made them shine. The east reddened and the sun lifted itself behind the peaks. Jacob caught up with Wanda and saw that they were in a meadow at the edge of the forest. He noticed that she had on the fringed kerchief and the calico apron she had worn in his dream. Yes, she had altered, was shrunken and emaciated. Though her face was tinted purple by the sun, nevertheless her complexion was as pale as that of a consumptive. Her eyes had grown large and protruded from their sockets. It was even more difficult now to understand how she could have run so swiftly.

"Let's stop for a moment," he said.

"Not here—in the forest," she answered in a whisper.

But they did not stop immediately upon entering the woods. Among the trees Wanda's figure became more elusive than ever, and Jacob feared he would lose sight of her. The grade became steeper. He slipped on the pine needles. Wanda climbed like a bear, or a doe. He had returned to a changed woman. How could she have altered so quickly?

The forest grew lighter as if a lamp had been lit. Golden light fell over everything. Birds whistled and sang. Dew fell. Wanda stopped at the narrow opening of a cave. She threw her sack into the aperture and crept in head first, her feet kicking outside for a second. Jacob pushed his sack in and followed her through the opening. He recalled the commentary in the Talmud on the passage in the Bible, "And the pit was empty, there was no water in it." The Talmud added, "There was no water in it, but there were snakes and lizards." Well, whatever happens, happens, Jacob said to himself. It was as if he had entered the mouth of an abyss. He slipped and Wanda gripped him by the shoulders. The dampness choked him. He stumbled into her, and they fell over the sacks. Finally the cave became larger and he was able to sit up. When he spoke, his muffled voice sounded far off and unfamiliar to him.

"How did you know about this cave?" he asked.

"I knew. I knew."

"What's wrong with you? Are you sick?"

Wanda did not speak immediately.

"If you'd waited a little longer, you would have found me dead."

"What's wrong?"

Wanda paused again.

"Why did you go away? Where did they take you? I was told you'd never come back."

"You knew that the Jews had ransomed me?"

"All they said was that some devils had seized you."

"What do you mean? They paid Zagayek fifty gulden. They arrived in a wagon."

"When I was out of the village. But I knew I wouldn't find you when I got back. I didn't need the women to tell me."

"How did you know?"

"I know everything, everything. I was walking with Antek and the sun became black as night. The horse Wojciech was riding began to laugh at me."

"The horse?"

"Yes, and then I knew that my enemies would revenge themselves on me."

Jacob considered what she had told him.

"I was lying in the granary, when your sister came to call me."

"That! I know. As soon as I came into the village, they all laughed at my bad luck. How did the Jews know where you were?"

"I spoke to that circus proprietor and he carried the message."

"Where to? Palestine?"

"No, to Josefov."

"You didn't even say goodbye to me. It was as if the earth had swallowed you up, as if there had never been a Jacob. Stephan came to me but I spat in his face. He got back at me by killing the dog. Mother and Basha said I was either possessed or crazy. The peasants wanted to tie me to a tree trunk but I ran away to the mountains and I stayed there until they brought up the herd. For four weeks I didn't taste a thing but snow and cold water from the stream."

"It wasn't my fault, Wanda. The Jews came and took me. What could I have told them? The wagon was waiting. When Zagayek sent for me I thought I was going to be hanged."

"You should have waited. You shouldn't have left me like that. If I'd had a child by you I would have had some comfort. But all I was left with was the stone behind the barn and what you had scratched on it. I beat my head against it."

"But I did come."

"I knew you would. You called to me but I didn't have the strength to wait. I went to the coffin maker and had myself measured. I had the priest confess me and I chose a grave next to father's."

"But you told me you no longer believed in Dziobak."

"What? He sent for me and I came. I fell on my knees and kissed his feet. All I wanted was to lie near Father."

"You'll live, but as a daughter of Israel."

"Where will you take me? I'm sick. I can't be a wife to you now. The witch told me what to do—it was she who brought you here and no one else."

"Wanda, what are you telling me? One cannot use witchcraft."

"You didn't come of your own free will, Jacob. I made a clay image of you and I wrapped it in my hair. I bought an egg laid by a black hen and buried it at the crossroads with a piece of glass from a broken mirror. I looked into it and I saw your eyes..."

"When?"

"After midnight."

"One mustn't do such things. That's sorcery. It's not allowed."

"You wouldn't have come by yourself."

Suddenly clutching him, she let out a wail that made Jacob shudder. Crying, she kissed his face, licked his hand. A howl tore itself from her throat.

"Jacob, don't leave me again, Jacob."

PART TWO

SARAH

EIGHT

I

Once more the Cossacks attacked Poland, once more they slaughtered Jews in Lublin and the surrounding areas. Polish soldiers dispatched many of the survivors. Then the Muscovites invaded from the east and the Swedes from the north. It was a time of upheaval and yet the Jews had to conduct business, supervise the tilling of leased fields, borrow money, pay taxes, even marry off daughters. A house built today would be burned tomorrow. Today a girl was engaged, a few days later raped. One day a man was rich, the next poor. Banquets were held one day, the next funerals for martyrs. The Jews were constantly on the march, from Lemberg and back to Lemberg, from Lublin and back to Lublin. A city that was secure one day was under siege the next. A wealthy man would wake to find he must carry a beggar's sack. Entire communities of Jews turned Christian and though some later reassumed their own faith, others remained in darkness. Poland teemed with deserted wives, raped women, brides run away from their gentile husbands, men who had been ransomed or who had escaped from prison. God's wrath poured down on his people. But the moment the Jews caught their breath, they returned to Judaism. What else could they do? Accept the religion of the murderer?

A handful of Jews, survivors of burned-out and pillaged towns, gathered in Pilitz, a village on the other side of the Vistula, having gained the consent of the overlord to settle there. The Swedish war had ruined Adam Pilitzky, but not even the Swedes could steal earth, sky, and water. Again the peasants plowed and sowed. Again the earth, soaked with the blood of the innocent and the guilty, brought forth wheat and rye, buckwheat and barley, fruit and vegetables. The retreating Swedish army had set fire to Pilitzky's castle, but a rain storm had extinguished the blaze. A revolt of the peasantry had followed the withdrawal of the Swedes and one of Pilitzky's marshals had been stabbed. Arming his retainers, Pilitzky attacked the rebels, hanging some, and flogging others to death. He ordered the heads of the executed to be placed on poles and publicly exhibited as a warning to the serfs. Birds pecked at the flesh until only naked skulls remained.

Pilitzky had no time for his manor and was a poor manager; his Polish bailiffs were drunkards, drones, and thieves. True, the Jews also swindled if they got the chance, but the owner could brandish a whip over them. A Jew could be flogged like a peasant, imprisoned in a sty, even beheaded. Moreover the Jew was thrifty, saved money, and put it out for usury. One could always go bankrupt and make a settlement with him.

Though Adam Pilitzky was already fifty-four, he looked much younger. He was tall, dark, had brown hair untouched by gray, black eyes and a small goatee. He had spent his youth in France and Italy and had returned with what he termed new ideas. For a time he flirted with Protestantism, but that mood passed and he soon became a zealous Catholic and an enemy of the Reformation. The neighboring landowners found him strange, spoke of him as an "odd bird." He continually predicted the collapse of Poland. All of the prominent leaders were rascals, thieves, scum. He himself had taken no part in the Cossack and Swedish wars but accused his countrymen of cowardice. He swore by all that was holy that everyone in Poland could be bought, from the smallest clerk in a town hall to the king. Phrases from the diatribes of the priest Skarga were perpetually on his lips, though he drank heavily and was considered a libertine. The *jus primae noctis* (obsolete elsewhere) was in force in his estates. It was said that his daughter had drowned herself after having been possessed by him. His son had gone mad and had died of jaundice. The rumor was that his wife Theresa was his procuress and had taken the coachman as her lover. Another report was that she copulated with a stallion. Both wife and husband had recently become religious enthusiasts. When the monastery at Czestochow was besieged and Kordecki put up his heroic resistance, they had worked themselves into a religious frenzy.

Pilitzky's castle was crowded with his and his wife's relatives, who, though they belonged to the aristocracy, did the work of maids and lackeys. Once when Lady Pilitzky found a hole in the tablecloth she emptied a glass of wine over a female cousin. She required that the tablecloths, towels, shirts, underwear, silver, and porcelain be counted weekly. When Adam Pilitzky became angry, he took a rod and beat the old maids. The great fortune he and his wife had inherited between them had been dissipated. The neighborhood joke was that all that remained of Theresa Pilitzky's jewelry was a single gold hairpin. At every opportunity Adam Pilitzky warned that Poland would have no peace until all Protestants, Cossacks, and Jews were killed—particularly the Jews who had secretly bribed the traitor Radziszewski and conspired with the Swedes. Pilitzky had given his word to the priests that when Poland was rid of its enemies, no Jew would lay foot on his property. But, as usual, he did the opposite of what he said. First he permitted a Jewish contractor to settle. This Jew began to complain that he needed a quorum. Soon the Jews were granted the right to build a synagogue. Someone died and a cemetery was necessary. Finally the Jews of Pilitz imported a rabbi and a ritual slaughterer. So now Pilitz had become a community. Adam Pilitzky cursed and spat, but the Jews had done much to get him back on his feet. It was they who saw to it that the peasants plowed, harvested, mowed hay. They paid cash to Pilitzky for grain and cattle, repaired the pond in which he stocked fish, built a dairy. They even brought beehives for honey into the estate. Pilitzky no longer had to go looking for a tailor, a shoemaker, a furrier, a bell maker. Jewish craftsmen repaired his castle, patched the roof, rebuilt the overa. Jews could do anything; rebind books, mend parquet floors, put glass in windows, frame pictures. When someone was ill, a Jewish doctor bled him or applied leeches and had a stock of medicines ready. A Jewish goldsmith made a bracelet for Lady Pilitzky and took a note instead of cash. Even the Jesuits, despite their slander and pamphlets, dealt with the Jews and used their handicraft.

At first Pilitzky had kept count of the number of Jews who settled on his property. But before long, he lost track. He didn't know their language and could scarcely tell one Jew from another. He warned constantly, "Unless the Poles change radically, there'll be another Chmielnicki. Anyway, everything's collapsing."

II

One day a man and woman trudged into Pilitz, sacks on their shoulders, bundles in their hands. The Jews emerged from stores and workshops to welcome the newcomers. The man, tall, broad-shouldered, blue-eyed, had a brown beard. Wearing a kerchief, seemingly younger than her husband, the woman looked almost gentile. The man was called Jacob. Asked where he was from, he mentioned the name of a distant city. The women soon learned that the young wife was a mute, and at first were amazed that so handsome a man should have made such a marriage. But, then, was it so astonishing? Marriages were made in heaven. Jacob gave his wife's name as Sarah, and she was immediately nicknamed, "Dumb Sarah."

The Jews inquired if Jacob was a scholar because they were looking for a teacher. "I know a chapter or two of the Pentateuch," Jacob said hesitantly.

"That's all that's needed."

It was springtime, the period between Passover and Pentecost. So now Pilitz had a school. Jacob and his mute wife were given a room and promised a house of their own if Jacob proved a good teacher. Pilitzsky owned many forests and lumber was cheap in the town. The new teacher was supplied with a table, a dunce's stool, and a cat-o'-nine-tails; he whittled a pointer and printed the letters of the alphabet on paper. Most of the children were in the early grades and the class assembled under a tree. Jacob sat with his charges in the shade, teaching them the alphabet, how to read syllables and words, instructing each child according to his age and knowledge. Because of the great amount of construction in progress, logs and lumber were piled all around, and the children built swings out of the boards and made little houses from chips and shavings. The town had no woman teacher and some of the parents sent daughters as well as sons to the cheder to learn their prayers and master a little writing. The girls made mud pies and sang and danced in a circle. The smaller boys and girls played house. The husband went to the synagogue to pray, his wife fixed supper for him and served it on a broken plate. The bread was a sliver of bark, the soup sand, the meat a pine cone. Jacob misplaced his cat-o'-nine-tails. He never whipped the children or scolded them, but lovingly pinched their cheeks and kissed their foreheads. These children had been born after the catastrophe.

The community liked Jacob immediately and pitied him for having a mute wife. True, Dumb Sarah behaved as a Jewess should, went to the ritual bath, soaked the meat and salted it, on Friday prepared the Sabbath pudding, burned a piece of chalah dough, blessed the candles; on the Sabbath, she stood in the woman's section of the synagogue and moved her lips as though praying. But sometimes she behaved in a way unbecoming a teacher's wife, took off her shoes and walked barefooted, laughed unrestrainedly, exhibiting a mouthful of unblemished peasant-like teeth. Dumb Sarah labored with the skill of a country woman, chopped wood, tended a vegetable garden she had planted behind the house, washed clothes in the river. When her own washing was done, she helped other women who had small children. She was remarkably strong and worked for everyone— and for nothing. Once she undressed in front of the women and swam in the river naked. Certain that she would drown at the spot where the waters swirled dangerously, the matrons, none of whom knew how to swim, broke into screams. But Dumb Sarah fearlessly crossed the whirlpool. Her audience was astounded. Dumb all right! Just like an animal.

This incident was soon followed by another which gave the people of Pilitz more to gossip about. The construction of Jacob's house was begun; and not only did Jacob assist in the work but Sarah also, although she was already pregnant and had stopped going to the ritual bath. Jacob went to the forest and felled trees, trimmed them with his ax and dragged them to the village. Sarah hauled logs and lumber as though she were a man. The house didn't cost the community a groschen. Nor was Jacob as unlearned as everyone had believed. One Saturday the reader lost his voice and Jacob read from the scroll; several times he was observed opening a Gemara in the study house. When he prayed he stood in a corner, swaying piously, and occasionally sighing.

He said little about his past and the community concluded that he must have lost his family in the massacres. If they sought to engage him in conversation, he walked away, saying, "What happened happened. One must start over again."

The men respected him and the women liked him. When the matrons sat on their benches in front of their houses Sabbath afternoons, they agreed among themselves that Dumb Sarah had more luck than brains. No one denied that she was young, good-looking, and healthy, but what did a man want with a dumbbell? A husband liked to talk to his wife and hear her opinions. What a calamity, God forbid, the child should take after its mother. Such things happened. One woman known as a wit remarked: "Well, some men would regard a silent wife as a blessing. No tongue, no torment."

"Oh, that's just talk."

"Well, it's better than having a blind one."

"Have you noticed," a young woman asked, "that as soon as it's dark she closes the shutters?"

"What does that prove?"

"That she loves him."

"Who wouldn't?"

On the Sabbath, Dumb Sarah discarded her kerchief, put on a bonnet, pointed shoes, an embroidered apron, and a dress with flowers that she had brought from far off. Going to synagogue, she held a prayer book in one hand and a handkerchief in the other. [This was allowed since the town of Pilitz had been enclosed in a wire which removed the Sabbath ban against carrying things.] When the women tried to communicate with her by hand signs, she smiled and shook her head, apparently unable to understand. The women poked fun at her, yet agreed she had a kind heart. She visited the sick and massaged their bodies with turpentine and alcohol. She prepared stewed apples and prunes as a treat for her husband's pupils on the Sabbath afternoon. Her stomach swelled, became pointed, and the women calculated she would give birth around Succoth or early in the month of Cheshvan.

Since the mute are also deaf, the women did not watch their words in her presence. Once, while Sarah sat with her prayer book open, a woman remarked, "She reads as well as the sacrificial rooster."

"Perhaps she's been taught."

"How can you teach the dumb?"

"Maybe she became dumb with fright."

"She doesn't look frightened."

"Perhaps the murderers cut out her tongue."

The women asked to see her tongue. At first, Sarah didn't seem to understand, then she began to laugh and her cheeks dimpled. She stuck out a pink tongue, as pointed as a dog's.

III

Wanda, not Jacob, had thought of playing the mute, realizing Yiddish would take her too long to learn; the few words she knew she spoke like a gentile. Her idea of passing herself off as a "Cossack bride" who could now only speak the language of the steppes was discarded because she didn't know that tongue either. She was not an adroit liar and would have been unmasked immediately. Jacob and she underwent many hardships and dangers before she decided on the role of a mute. They went to distant Pilitz because Jacob was too famous in Lublin and the surrounding areas as the slave who had returned. At night when Sarah, as all Jewish converts were called, closed the shutters, Jacob spoke with her and instructed her in their religion. He had already taught her the prayers and how to write Yiddish and now they studied the Pentateuch, the Books of Samuel and Kings, the Code of the Jewish Law; he told her stories from the

Gemara and Midrash. Her diligence was amazing, her memory good; many of the questions she asked were the same the commentators had raised. Teaching her, he dared not lift his voice. Not only did he dread the gentiles and their laws, but also the Jews who would expel him from the village if they learned his wife was a convert. Sarah's presence in Pilitz imperiled the town. If the Polish authorities learned that a Christian girl had been seduced into Judaism, there would be reprisals. God knows what accusations would be made. The priests only wanted a pretext. And if the Jews got wind of it, the elders would immediately investigate the circumstances of the conversion and would guess correctly that Sarah had left her own religion because of Jacob—women being little interested in speculative matters; and Jacob would be excommunicated.

There was so much concern with the lineage and matrimonial connections of scholars that Jacob had not divulged that he was learned. The few scholarly books he had brought he kept hidden. He built his house with thick walls and constructed an alcove, windowless and hidden from the world by a clump of trees, where he and his beloved wife could study in secret. True, they had lived together illicitly, but since then they had fulfilled the law of Moses and Israel by standing under the canopy. Sarah now fervently believed in God and the Torah and obeyed all the laws. Now and then she erred, doing things upside down according to her peasant understanding, or speaking in a manner that was inappropriate. But Jacob corrected her kindly and made her understand the reason for each law and custom. Teaching others, Jacob realized, one also instructed oneself; correcting Sarah's behavior, answering her questions, eradicating her errors, many problems about which he would not have otherwise thought were clarified for him. Often her questions demanded answers which were not to be found in this world. She asked:

"If murder is a crime, why did God permit the Israelites to wage war and even kill old people and small children?" If the nations distant from the Jews, such as her own people, were ignorant of the Torah, how could they be blamed for being idol worshipers? If Father Abraham was a saint, why did he drive Hagar and her son Ishmael into the desert with a gourd of water? The question that recurred more often than any other was why did the good suffer and the evil prosper. Jacob told her repeatedly he couldn't solve all the world's riddles, but Sarah kept on insisting, "You know everything."

He had warned her many times about the unclean days, reminding her that when she was menstruating she could not sit on the same bench with him, take any object from his hand, nor even eat at the same table unless there was a screen between her plate and his. He was not allowed to sit on her bed, nor she on his; not even the headboards of their beds ought to touch at this time. But these were some of the things that Sarah either forgot or ignored, for she kept on insisting she must be near him. She was capable of running over and kissing him in the middle of her period. Jacob rebuked her and told her such acts were forbidden by the Torah, but she took these restrictions lightly, and this caused Jacob sorrow. She was very scrupulous about less important things. She immersed all the dishes in the ritual bath, and kept on inquiring about milk and meat. At times she forgot she was a mute and broke into song. Jacob trembled. Not only was there the danger of her being heard, but a pious daughter of Israel should not provoke lust with the lascivious sound of her voice. Nor had she let the bath attendant shave her head like the other women's, though Jacob had asked her to. Sarah cut her own hair with shears; occasionally ringlets pushed out from under her kerchief.

Though Jacob had built them a house, Sarah complained nightly that she wished to leave Pilitz. She could not remain silent forever, and she feared what would happen to her child. The young must be taught to speak, and given love. She kept asking whether her Yiddish had improved; Jacob assured her she was doing well but it wasn't so. She mispronounced the words, twisted the constructions, and whatever she uttered came out upside down. Often her mistakes made Jacob laugh. Even a few words dropping from her tongue and there was no mistaking she had been born a gentile. Now that she was pregnant Jacob was more frightened than ever. A woman in labor cannot control her screams. Unless she could endure the birth pangs in silence, Sarah would give herself away.

Yes, the day Jacob had left Josefov for the village where he had been a slave for five years, he had picked up a burden which became heavier with the passage of time. His years of enforced slavery had been succeeded by a slavery that would last as long as he lived. "Well, Gehenna is for people and not for dogs," he had once heard a water carrier say. Yet he had saved a soul from idolatry, even though he had stumbled into transgression. At night when Sarah and he lay in their beds which were arranged so as to form a right angle (the room wasn't long enough to have one at the foot of the other), the couple whispered to each other for hours without tiring. Jacob informed Sarah about the moral life, spicing his text with little parables. She spoke of how much she loved him. They often recalled the summers he had lived in the barn when she had brought food to him. Now those days were far off and as shadowy as a dream. Sarah found it difficult to believe that the village still existed and that Basha and Antek and possibly her mother still lived there. According to the law, Jacob said, she no longer was a member of her family. A convert was like a newborn child and had a fresh soul. Sarah was like Mother Eve who had been formed from Adam's rib; her husband her only relative. "But," Sarah argued, "my father is still my father," and she began to cry about Jan Bzik who had had so hard a life and now lay buried among idolaters. "You will have to bring him into Paradise," she told Jacob. "I won't go without him."

IV

The peasants, now busy in the fields preparing for harvest, rarely brought produce to town. Jewish peddlers traveled to the country with packs on their backs to buy chickens, millet and corn. Sarah, needing supplies, picked up a sack and set out, though Jacob had insisted this was no errand for a pregnant woman, much less the wife of a teacher. But Sarah longed for the fields and pastures. The moment Pilitz was behind her, she kicked off her shoes and slung them over her shoulder. The townswomen smirked, seeing her go, asked each other, "Now how will the dumbbell bargain?"

Sarah's presumed deafness left the women free to slander and ridicule her in her presence. She was referred to as a dumb animal, a golem, a simpleton, a cabbage head. Jacob was pitied for having brought home such a goose. The guess was she had a rich father who had given a substantial dowry to marry her off. Still, Jacob was a fool to have led such a nanny goat under the canopy. Sarah had to keep smiling though she could scarcely retain her tears. The peasants were openly scornful. Running their fingers across their throats, they would point toward the road, pretending the Cossacks were coming. Pan Pilitzky, they said, was infesting Poland with Jewish lice, and they prophesied wars, plagues, and famines, Heaven's revenge for permitting the God murderers to settle there. Sarah found it difficult to remain silent.

When she was alone with Jacob at night she cried and repeated what the Jews said. "You must not repeat such things," Jacob scolded her. "That's calumny. It's as great a sin as eating pork."

"So they're allowed to abuse us but I can say nothing?"

"No, they're not behaving properly either."

"Well, they all do it, even Breina, and she's the wife of an elder."

"Those who do such things will be punished in Heaven. The sacred books warn that all those who gossip, ridicule, or speak evil of others, will burn in the fires of Gehenna."

"All of them?"

"There's no lack of room in Gehenna."

"The rabbi's wife laughed too."

"There are no favorites in Heaven. When Moses sinned, he was punished."

Sarah became thoughtful.

"No, speaking evil can't be one thousandth the sin of eating pork, or no one would do it."

"Come, I'll show you what it says in the Torah."

Jacob, opening the Pentateuch, translated the text and told her how each of the sins had been interpreted by the Gemara. Several times he walked to the door to assure himself no one was listening or looking through the keyhole. "Why do the Jews obey some laws and break others?" Sarah whispered.

Jacob shook his head.

"That's the way it's always been. The prophets denounced it. The temple was destroyed for that reason. It's easier not to eat pig than to curb your tongue. Come and I will read you a chapter from Isaiah."

Jacob turned to Isaiah and translated the first chapter. Sarah listened in amazement. The prophet said the same things as Jacob: God had had enough of the blood of bullocks and the fat of lambs; people were not to come into his presence with bloody hands. The elders of Israel were compared by the prophet to the lords of Sodom God had destroyed. Late though it was, the wick in the shard continued to burn and moths cycled the flame. The shadow of Jacob's head wavered on the ceiling. A cricket chirped from behind the oven. Love and fear mingled in Sarah. She dreaded the angry God who dwelled in Heaven and overheard every word and thought; she feared the peasants desirous of murdering Jews again and burying children alive; she was anxious about the Jews who were provoking the Almighty by obeying only one part of the Torah. Sarah promised not to repeat the evil gossip she heard, though as it was she had not told him everything. It was said in town that one of the storekeepers gave false measure. There was a rumor that a man had stolen from his partner at the time of the massacres. Sarah had been told that the Jews were the chosen people and she wanted to ask how they could be so favored when they committed such crimes. But that Jacob was righteous was evident to her. If God loved him as much as she did, he would live forever.

In her prayers she told God that she had no one but Jacob. She could never love another. She had joined a community but felt like a stranger. Though she had fled the peasants, she had not become one of the Jews of Pilitz. Jacob was husband, father, and brother to her. The moment the candle was extinguished she called him to her bed. "You, gentile," Jacob said jokingly: "Don't you know that a daughter of Israel musn't be immodest or she'll be divorced without a settlement?"

"What can a daughter of Israel do?"

"Bear children and serve God."

"I intend to bear you a dozen."

He would not lie with her immediately, but first told her stories of upright men and women. She asked what went on in Paradise and what would occur when the Messiah came. Would Jacob still be her husband? Would they speak Hebrew? Would he take her with him to the rebuilt temple? When the Messiah came, Jacob said, each day would be as long as a year, the sun would be seven times as bright, and the Saints would feed on leviathan and the wild ox and drink the wine prepared for the days of redemption.

"How many wives will each man have?" Sarah asked.

"I'll have only you."

"I'll be old by then."

"We'll be young forever."

"What kind of a dress will I wear?"

Lying with Jacob was for her a foretaste of Paradise. She often wished that the night would last forever and she could continue to listen to his words and receive his caresses. That hour in the darkness was her reward for what she had endured during the day. When she fell asleep, her dreams took her to her native village; she entered the hut where she had lived; she stood on the mountain. Strange events involving Antek, Basha, and her mother occurred. Her father, once more alive, spoke wisely to her, and though she forgot his words as soon as she awoke, their resonance rang in her ears. Sometimes she dreamed Jacob had left her, and cried in her sleep. Jacob always awakened her.

"Oh, Jacob, you're still here. Thank God." His face would become hot and wet from her tears.

V

A coach drawn by a team of four horses, with two coachmen in front and two footmen in the rear, rode into the market place at noon. One of the coachmen blew his horn. The Jews of Pilitz became alarmed. Pilitzky rarely came to town in such pomp, and never in summer before the harvest. He was carrying a sword; he looked drunk. Leaping from the coach, he drew his sword from its scabbard and screamed, "Where is Gershon? I'm going to cut off his head. I'm going to tear him to pieces and pour acid into his wounds—him and his family as well. I'm going to throw the whole batch of them to the dogs."

Some of the Jews scurried off. Others rushed to Pilitzky and threw themselves at his feet. The women began to wail. The children in Jacob's class heard the tumult and came running to have a look at the lord, at the coach, at the horses with their heads held high in their fine harnesses. One of Gershon's sycophants hastened to him and warned him that Pilitzky was drunk and looking for him. Gershon was the most powerful man in Pilitz, since he leased the fields of the manor and managed them as if they were his own. He was known in town as a shady dealer. He'd built himself a large house and had acquired three sons-in-law, all from wealthy families, who had become respectively the town's rabbi, ritual slaughterer and public contractor. The last supplied the flour at Passover and had built the synagogue. Gershon had retained the wardenship of the burial society and charged exorbitant prices for graves, although Pilitzky had donated the land for the cemetery. Gershon also collected the taxes, usurping the function of the town's seven elders as set forth by the Council of the Four Countries. Taxation in Pilitz worked on the principle that the friends and flatterers of Gershon paid little or nothing; all others tottered under the weight of his levies. Gershon was ignorant but had granted himself the title "Our Teacher" and did not allow the cantor to intone the eighteen benedictions until he, Gershon, had said them over to himself. When he got the whim to take a steam bath in the middle of the week, the bath attendant was forced to heat the water at the community's expense.

Those whom Gershon had trampled threatened to denounce him to Pilitzky and to the Council in Lublin, but Gershon feared no man. He had friends who sat on the Council and he held Pilitzky's note for a thousand gulden. He was an intimate of other landowners, Pilitzky's enemies. Gershon, it seemed, had forgotten that the Jews were in exile. Yes, Pilitzky was looking for him and Gershon was advised to take cover in an attic or cellar until the wrath of the lord of Pilitz subsided. But Gershon was not one to have himself thought a coward, and he put on his silk overcoat, his sable hat, wrapped a sash around his waist, and walked out to meet Adam Pilitzky. Though Gershon dressed like a rabbi, he had the florid complexion of a butcher. His nose was flat, his lips thick; his belly stuck out as though he were pregnant. One of his eyes higher and set in a larger socket than the other. He had heavy, bushy eyebrows. Not only was he aggressive but stubborn. When he rose to make a speech, every third word was a barbarism; he babbled until everyone fell asleep, and the opposition never had a chance to voice its opinion.

Now, walking slowly, Gershon approached his overlord. He did not come alone but accompanied by his entourage: the butchers, the horse dealers, and the men of the burial society whom he banqueted twice a year and who got all the sinecures in town. Before Gershon could open his mouth, Pilitzky screamed: "Where's the red bull?"

Gershon considered the question for a moment and then replied. "I sold him to the butcher, my lord."

"You dirty Jew. You sold my bull."

"Sir, while I lease the manor land, I'm in control."

"So you're in control. Seize him, boys. We'll hang him here." All the Jews shouted in terror – even Gershon's enemies joined in. Gershon tried to speak and retreated a few steps, but the coachmen and footmen caught hold of him. Pilitzky cried out, "Get the rope."

Some of the Jews fell to their knees, prostrated themselves, bowed—as on Yom Kippur when the cantor repeats the ritual service of the ancient temple in Jerusalem. Women screamed.

Gershon struggled with his captors. The sash was torn from his waist. Pilitzky shouted, "A pole. Bring me a pole."

"We can hang him from the lamp post, my lord."

Jacob, hearing the clamor which was not unlike that when the Cossacks had attacked Josefov, came running. Gershon's wife was clasping one of Pilitzky's knees, refusing to let go. Pilitzky was trying to shake himself free of her and had his sword raised as if about to sever her head. The women were pushing and milling and wailing insanely. One dug her nails into her cheeks, another clutched her breasts, a third scratched at her husband to do something. Gershon was a crass man. The Jews of Pilittz disliked him but they could not stand by and see him hanged summarily. Gershon's daughters-in-law fell into each other's arms. The rabbi also prostrated himself at Pilitzky's feet; his skull cap having come off, his long side locks dragged in the dirt. It was almost as if the massacres had again begun. Gershon's followers, instead of disarming Pilitzky's servants which they might have done easily, just stood gaping with legs spread wide, amazed it seemed at their own impotence. But when had a Jew ever defied a Polish noble? Then out of the study house walked the beadle bearing the holy scroll as if it would quiet Pilitzky's wrath. There were shouts bidding the old man advance closer; others among the crowd motioned him back, protesting the sacrilege. He stood swaying indecisively on his rickety legs as though about to fall. Seeing him totter, a great cry of lamentation rose from the people. Jacob stood transfixed, knowing he must say nothing, yet equally certain he could not remain silent. Stepping forward, he ran quickly to Pilitzky and took off his hat.

"Mighty lord, a man is not killed for selling a bull."

The market place became quiet. Everyone knew that Gershon had declared war on Jacob because Jacob had taken the place of

the reader. Gershon didn't like scholars, would never have tolerated Jacob's appointment if he had known that this was a man
who could understand both text and footnotes. Now Jacob came
to his assistance. Astonished, Pilitzky stared at the Jew in front
of him.

"Who are you?"

"I am the teacher."

"What's your name?"

"Jacob."

"Oh! Are you that Jacob who cheated Esau out of his birth-
right?" An inhuman laugh burst from Pilitzky's throat.

Hearing the lord of Pilitz laugh, everyone joined in— the
Jews, Pilitzky's men; Pilitzky doubled up with mirth. Was it
merely a joke, a nobleman's prank such as the Polish landowners
often played on their Jewish tenants? These games always terrified the Jews since such fun sometimes turned serious. But the
men still held onto Gershon—who was the only one not laughing. His yellow eyes had lost none of their arrogance; his thick,
mustached lip was drawn back into a snarl, revealing sparse, yellow teeth. Gershon looked like an animal at bay about to die in a
struggle with a stronger adversary. Pilitzky howled with laughter,
clapped his hands, clutched at his knees, and gasped. Those who
had prostrated themselves rose and, relieved, bellowed with a
mad exuberance. Even the rabbi laughed. The women collapsed
into each other's arms, their knees buckling, their laughter turning to tears.

"Mommalas, Poppalas, tsitselas," Pilitzky mimicked and
started braying again. The whole community joined in, every
face with its own particular expression and grimace. The sight
of one old matron, who had lost her bonnet and whose unevenly
clipped scalp resembled a newly sheared ewe, started the women
off once more, but this time their laughter was genuine.

Then all laughter ceased. Pilitzky gave a final burst and scowled again.

"Who are you? What are you doing here?" he asked Jacob. "Answer me, Jew."

"I am the teacher, my lord."

"What do you teach? How to steal the host? How to poison wells? How to use Christian blood to make matzoth?"

"God forbid, my lord. Such acts are prohibited by Jewish law."

"Prohibited, are they? We know. We know. Your cursed Talmud teaches you how to fool the Christian mob. You've been driven from every country, but King Casimir opened our gates wide to you. And how do you repay us? You've established a new Palestine here. You ridicule and curse us in Hebrew. You spit on our relics. You blaspheme our God ten times a day. Chmielnicki taught you a lesson, but you need a stronger one. You love all Poland's enemies—Swedes, Muscovites, Prussians. Who gave you permission to come here?" Pilitzky screamed at Jacob, shaking his fist. "This is my earth, not yours. My ancestors shed blood for it. I don't need you to teach Jewish vermin how to defile my country. We have enough parasites already. We're more dead than alive."

Pilitzky ceased his invective and foamed at the mouth. Once more, eyeing each other in dread, the Jews bent, ready to fall to the ground and beg for mercy. The elders signaled among themselves. Picking up his skull cap, the rabbi placed it, still dirty, on his head. The woman whose bonnet had fallen off clapped it back on, askew, its beaded front to the side. Pilitzky's men tugged at Gershon again, as though trying to shake him out of his clothes. The beadle still swayed back and forth with the scroll. Evidently the story was not to end happily. Men and women began to detach themselves from the crowd and to slip away, some going to close their shops, others running into their houses and locking the doors. "Don't run away, Jews," Pilitzky shouted. "There's no escape. I'll strangle you wherever you are. When I finish with you, you'll mourn the day your wretched mothers squeezed you from their leprous wombs."

"Magnanimous lord, we are not running away. Mighty benefactor, we await your pleasure."

"I have asked you something," Pilitzky shouted, turning to Jacob. "Answer me."

Jacob didn't remember the question. Pilitzky reached out as if to grab the teacher by his collar. But Jacob was too tall for him.

"Forgive me, my lord," Jacob bowed his head. "I have forgotten the question."

Pilitzky, having forgotten himself, looked confused. He had noticed that this Jew, unlike the others, spoke good Polish. His anger left him and he felt something akin to shame at having made such a display before these paupers, the survivors of Chmielnicki's blood bath. He had always considered himself a compassionate man. Tears came to his eyes. Prayers to Jesus and the apostles passed through his head. From boyhood on, he had expected to die young; a fortune teller had predicted an early end. Now he looked for some excuse to terminate this saturnalia. His turbulent spirit stood midway between contrition and anger. Should he ask forgiveness of the Jews, that wilful people God had chosen? There was a bitter taste in his mouth and his nose tickled. I wouldn't behave this way if my life weren't chaos. That cursed woman has ruined me. Suddenly he had an impulse to toss coins to the crowd. That would show them that he was no Haman. But when he reached into his pocket he remembered he didn't have a groschen, and he was overwhelmed with self-pity. That's what these Jews have done to me, he thought, bled me dry. Seeing the old beadle, swaying unsteadily with the holy scroll on his shoulder, he yelled, "Why did you bring out the scroll? How can that help you? It would be better if you followed what is written there instead of using it to mask your crimes. Carry it back to the synagogue, you old rascal."

From every side shouts came, "Carry back the scroll. Carry back the scroll." The lord of Pilitz had relented, the Jews sensed. The beadle gave a final sway and bore the scroll into the study house. But the men still held Gershon pinioned. Pilitzky's mood might change again. He surveyed the crowd, a bitter look in his eyes as if searching for another victim. Dumb Sarah walked into the square carrying an apronful of herbs. Having gone into the fields, she had not heard the noise of Pilitzky's arrival and knew nothing of what had happened. She saw the coach and horses, Pilitzky's men, Pilitzky himself, and Jacob, hat in hand, standing humbly before the lord of Pilitz. Sarah raised her arms, wailed, and the herbs fell from her apron. What she had dreaded had come to pass. Her nightmares had been true omens. Breaking through the crowd, she pushed her way to Jacob, and screaming wildly threw herself at Pilitzky's feet. Pilitzky turned pale and retreated. She followed him, crawling like a worm and clutching at his legs. "Have pity, Pan," she lamented in Polish. "Mercy, gentle lord. He's all I've got. I carry his child in my womb. Kill me instead. My head for his. Let him go free, Pan. Let him go free."

"Who is this woman? Get up."

"Forgive him, my lord. Forgive him. He's committed no crime. He's honest, my lord. A holy man."

Jacob bent to raise her and then paused, terrified. Only then did he realize that Sarah had given herself away: she had spoken. In the confusion, no one appeared to have understood what had happened. Then men spread their hands and raised their eyebrows; women clutched their heads; Pilitzky's servants momentarily let go of Gershon. Even the horses, until then standing silently, lost in equine meditations remote from the struggles of men, turned their heads. Gershon looked baffled and outraged. Like many overbearing men, he resented having things happen he could neither control nor comprehend. A woman slapped both of her cheeks screaming, "Oh, I've seen everything."

"What is this? Who is she?" Pliitzky asked.

"My lord, she's a mute."

"What? A mute?"

"Gracious lord, she's as dumb as a fish. Deaf and dumb."

"Yes, gracious lord, dumb, dumb, a mute." Cries came from all directions.

"Hey, rabbi, is that a fact? Is this woman a mute?" Pilitzky said, turning to the rabbi.

"Yes, my lord, she's the wife of the teacher. She's deaf and dumb. This is a miracle."

"Children, I'm going to faint"—and a woman fell to the ground.

"Help. Water! Water!"

"Oh, my God"—and another woman fainted.

Jacob, bending, pulled Sarah to her feet. Her limp body lay against his shoulder, supported by his arm; she trembled, gasping, sobbing. Pilitzky rested his hand on the hilt of his sword. "What is this, Jew? Some kind of farce?"

"No farce, my lord. She's deaf and dumb. Deaf as the wall and dumb as a fish."

"My lord, we all know she's mute," witnesses from the crowd attested.

"Are you prepared to swear to that?"

"My lord, we've invented nothing."

"Hey, you, Jew, is your wife really dumb?"

"Yes, my lord."

"Always been that way?"

"As long as we've been married."

Jacob did not consider this a lie since Sarah had assumed her role before stepping under the canopy. All around him the townswomen were screaming that it was indeed so, swearing by their husbands and their children that this was Dumb Sarah who everyone knew was unable to talk. Pilitzky's men stood gaping while their master considered strange occurrence.

"I don't believe you, Jews, not a word of it. This is just another one of your tricks. You want to fool me and make me look ridiculous. Remember Jews, if this is a lie, you'll be flayed alive, I'll herd you into your synagogue and set it on fire. We'll roast you slowly, as sure as my name is Adam Pilitzky."

"Gracious lord, we are telling the truth."

VI

Pilitzky realized the Jews were telling the truth. Their open mouths and bewildered looks told him this was a miracle. Adam Pilitzky had been waiting for a miracle ever since the start of the wars and invasions. One was needed to save Poland. Prior Chodecki's resistance at Czestochow and Stephan Czanecki's campaign against the Swedes, which had rallied the Polish armies and revived the cause of Catholicism, had seemed to be that miracle. Now from every side came reports of new wonders. An image of the Virgin had wept real tears which the people gathered in a silver chalice. On church steeples stone crosses flamed in the dark of night. Dead armies, dressed in the uniforms of a hundred years ago, marched against the enemies of Poland and drove them from fortified positions. Ghost riders were seen galloping on phantom horses. Legendary heroes, dressed in helmets and breastplates, brandished swords and spears as they led charges. Monks and nuns, long since residents of Paradise, put on bodies again and roamed the countryside comforting the people and urging them to pray.

Here a church bell rang by itself, and there an ancient coach was seen driving down a road into a wall and disappearing as if swallowed up. Birds spoke with human voices and a dog led a battalion out of ambush. In one village it had rained blood, in another fishes and toads. In one instance wine had been lacking for the mass and God's mother had opened her lips and wine had flowed out. An almost blind crone had watched a flaming ship flying the Polish ensign sail across the sky. These signs and portents had invigorated the nation's spirit and renewed its belief in heaven.

Nevertheless, Adam Pilitzky had seen no miracles himself and resented this. The devil subverted and denied the wonders of God in a thousand ways; hidden in every heart was some doubt. Often when Pilitzky lay awake thinking of what was going on in the country, Lucifer came and whispered in his ear: "Don't they all speak of miracles? The Greek Orthodox, the Protestants, even the infidel Turks? How does it come about that God sometimes rides with the Protestants bringing them victories? Why doesn't he visit them with the plagues of Pharaoh or rain down stones as he will on Gog and Magog?" Pilitzky listened to Lucifer; at heart, he may have believed man merely an animal who returns to dust, and hence condoned his wife's licentiousness.

The revolt of his serfs and the cruelties with which he had suppressed the rebellion had further mortified Pilitzky's spirit. He knew that widows and orphans sorrowed because of him. At night he had visions of bodies hanging from the gibbets, their feet blue, their eyes glassy, their tongues extended. He suffered from cramps and headaches; his skin itched. There were days when he prayed for death or planned suicide. Not even wine and vodka could calm him now. Nor were the pleasures of the body as intense as they had been. He was always on the lookout for new sensations to stave off impotence. Because of the perverseness of that witch Theresa, now only her infidelities aroused his lust. He made her describe her affairs in detail. When she had exhausted the catalog of her debauchery, he forced her to invent adventures. Husband and wife had driven each other into an insane labyrinth of vice. He procured for her and she procured for him. She watched him corrupt peasant girls and he eavesdropped on her and her lovers. He had warned her many times that he would stab her, she teased about poisoning his food. But both were pious, lit candles, went to confession, and contributed money for the building of churches and religious monuments. Often Adam Pilitzky opened the door of their private chapel and found Theresa, her cheeks wet with tears, a crucifix pressed to her bosom, kneeling before the altar deep in contemplation. Theresa spoke of entering a nunnery; Pilitzky toyed with the idea of becoming a monk.

Pilitzky could never have described the torment he had endured during the last few years. Only God, aware of all the temptations and pitfalls besetting man, and compassionately viewing His creatures' follies and weaknesses, knew how much Pilitzky had suffered through shame and guilt. What the lord of Pilitz wanted was a sign that some supernal eye looked down and took notice, some proof that more than blind chance governed the world. Now heaven, it seemed, had decided to put an end to his doubts.

Pilitzky looked at Sarah and Jacob, the wife clinging to the husband. No, this was no fraud. He could see the Jews glancing at each other and staring at the couple incredulously. There was a lump in Pilitzky's throat; he found it difficult to keep from crying. Then, remembering that the mute had spoken of Jacob as a holy man, he said in a firm voice, "Forgive me, Jacob. I did not mean to insult you. If you are truly a holy man as the mute has attested, I respect you even though you are a Jew."

"Gracious lord, there is nothing holy about me. I am an ordinary individual, a Jew like all the others; perhaps even less than they."

"What? Saints are all modest. Hey, there, men, let that crook Gershon go. I'll settle with him some other time. You are no longer my tenant, Gershon," Pilitzky said. "Don't step on my land again or let me see your face. If I find you trespassing, I'll unleash the dogs."

"Your excellency owes me money," Gershon said. His voice did not waver; his manner showed he did not fear the bluster of overlord. "I have leased the manor lands. I have a contract and your note."

"Huh? Jew, you have nothing. You can wipe yourself with those papers."

"My lord, this is not just. A man's word is sacred. There is a court in Poland."

"Drag me into court, will you, Jew? You're crazy, Jew. You'd be already swinging and the birds would be eating the flesh of your head, as the Bible says, if what just happened had not. You thief, you swindler. I've heard that you filch from the Jews, even. I intend to investigate and see you're punished. As for the court: I fear no one. I am the court and the law. I rule supreme on my manor. Poland is not France where the king tyrannizes over the nobles. Here we have more power than the king. We make and break our kings. Keep that in mind and you'll also keep your head on your shoulders."

"I have paid for the contract."

"What you paid, you got back a long time ago. I'll have no further dealings with you. Move – before I break every bone in your body."

There was a murmuring among the Jews. Gershon's friends and family whispered to him to leave the market place immediately. His wife and daughter tugged at his sleeves, begging him to come home. But Gershon shook his head; his nose wrinkled and his heavy under lip sagged. Powerless though a Jew was against a nobleman, Gershon did not intend to stand by and see himself ruined. He had friends who were richer and more eminent than Pilitzky. He knew that the lord of Pilitz had broken every law of church and state. Moreover, he was involved in law suits that threatened to ruin him. The nobility still preserved their code and demanded that notes and contracts be honored, even those made with the contemptible Jews. Gershon took a step forward.

"I am still the tenant until the expiration of my lease."

"All you are is a dead dog."

Adam Pilitzky turned violently, drew his sword, and ran at Gershon. The Jews wailed and screamed.

NINE

Jacob saw that he had lost control of himself. Satan fiddled and he danced. "Transgression draws transgression in its train," the Book of Aboth said, and this was surely true in his case. His lust for a forbidden woman had involved him in deception. An entire Jewish community—no, not merely one, a host of them—had been deluded into believing his wife was a mute. Now, grieving women sought out Sarah who was already in her eighth month and begged her to lay her hands on them and bless them. Nor would the elders of Pilitz hear of Jacob not accepting Pilitzky's offer. Gershon had lost the contract; Pilitzky warned that if Jacob refused to become his administrator, he would import one from another town. He even threatened to expel the Jews from Pilitz. A deputation of the elders, led by the rabbi, came to plead with Jacob. Gershon let it be tacitly understood that he was not opposed to this arrangement; Jacob should administer the estate for the time being. Gershon's appraisal was that the teacher, unable to distinguish rye from wheat, would mismanage Pilitzky's interests and this would lead the nobleman to conclude that Gershon was indispensable.

As is usual in the affairs of men, the relationships were complex, and all were based on deception. Woe to the house founded on falsehood. But what could Jacob do? If he told the truth, Sarah and he would be burned at the stake. Sacred though the truth was, the law did not permit one to sacrifice oneself for it.

Lying awake at night, Jacob addressed God: "I know that I have forfeited the world to come, but nevertheless you are still God and I remain your creation. Castigate me, Father, I will submit to your punishment willingly."

The punishment might arrive any day. Sarah would shortly go into labor, and might scream and talk. The truth would sooner or later make itself known. Jacob waited for the rod to strike and worked; there was more than enough for him to do. God had blessed the fields with plenty; the Polish and Swedish armies had not trampled the newly sown crops that year. Jacob woke early and retired late; the lord of Pilitz expected a profit. Gershon also anticipated getting a covert share. However, Jacob, unlike Gershon, received no contract and was only Pilitzky's manager, supervising the peasants and dealing with the grain merchants. He took as wages merely what he needed to subsist.

It was strange to be in the fields surrounded by vegetation again. Sarah and Jacob lived in the house Gershon had built for himself near the castle. Jacob's own house as well as the school he had begun to build remained unfinished. The town was looking for a new teacher – meanwhile someone tutored the children a few hours a day— and the current joke was that since Jacob was managing Pilitz, Gershon should take over the cheder.

Jacob had always been aware that everything in this world is transitory. What was man? Today alive, tomorrow in his grave. The Talmud spoke of the world as a wedding; the poet in the liturgy compared man to a drifting cloud, to a wilting flower, to a fading dream. Yes, everything passed. But never before had Jacob felt the transience of things so keenly. One week a field of grain stood ripening; the next the field was bare. The days were now bright and clear, but rain and snow would soon follow. Jacob had become important in Pilitz; the lord of the manor was now accessible to him. When he passed peasants, they tipped their caps and addressed him as "Pan." The Jews considered him the husband of a holy woman. Jacob knew the end of all this would be disgrace and a walk to the gallows. But meanwhile he saw to it that the grain was harvested, threshed, and stored. He superintended the autumn plowing and the sowing of the winter crop. What he had learned in those years of slavery had become useful. Now when Sarah and he retired at night, they discussed not only the Torah but also the affairs of the manor. Even though Jacob did not keep the account books, little by little he uncovered evidence of Gershon's bad practices. True, Pilitzky in turn stole from the peasantry and he who robs a thief is guilty of no crime; nevertheless Gershon had broken the Eighth Commandment, made enemies for Israel, and committed sacrilege. Well, but everyone has his temptations.

Jacob had risen in the world, but he knew his ascent was of that kind of which it is written, "Pride goeth before a fall." The peasants did not seek to trick him, as they had Gershon, but followed his instructions and even offered him advice. The inhabitants of the castle, Pilitzky's dependents as well as his servants, respected Jacob. The dogs, whose ferocity had made Gershon tremble, for some mysterious reason took to Jacob immediately, wagging their tails when he approached the gate. Everyone in the castle was kind to him, and Lady Pilitzky sent a maid to help the pregnant and mute Sarah. Pilitzky, himself, went out of his way to talk to Jacob and admired the manager's fluent Polish. Gershon had been another sort, an ignoramus unable to answer any of his patron's questions about Jews and their religion. Jacob replied quoting the holy books. Accustomed to discussing difficult questions lucidly, he invented parables the gentile mind could accept. Pilitzky brought up the same problems that had disturbed Wanda.

One day when Pilitzky sat with Jacob in the library showing him a Bible concordance in Latin which had Hebrew marginalia, Lady Pilitzky entered. Jacob rose from his chair and bowed deeply. Theresa Pilitzky was a small, plump woman with a round face, short neck, and a high bosom. Her blond hair, twisted in a coronet, reminded Jacob of a Rosh Hashana chalah. She had on a pleated, black silk dress, decorated with ribbons, and around her neck lay a gold cross set with jewels. She had a small nose, full lips, bright dark eyes and a smooth forehead. Jacob had been told that she behaved like a whore, but she walked with sprightly steps and seemed almost girlish, despite her stoutness. She smiled upon seeing the men and her cheeks dimpled. Pilitzky winked at her, "This is Jacob."

"Of course, I've seen you many times from my window."

Lady Pilitzky offered her hand to Jacob who hesitated an instant and then, bowing again, carried her fingers to his lips. One more sin, Jacob thought, kissing her hand, and blushing to the roots of his hair. Pilitzky laughed.

"Well, now that that's done let's have a glass of wine together."

"Forgive me, my lord, but my religion forbids it."

Pilitzky's body tensed.

"Oh, so you're forbidden. It's all right to fleece the Christians, but you mustn't drink wine with them. And who forbids it? The Talmud, naturally, which teaches you how to cheat the Christians."

"The Talmud makes no mention of Christians, only idolators."

"The Talmud considers Christians idolators. Your people gave the world the Bible, but then you denied God's only begotten son, thereby turning from the Father. Today Chmielnicki punishes you; tomorrow another *hetman* will continue your castigation. The Jews will never have peace until they recognize the truth and…"

Lady Pilitzky frowned. "Adam, these discussions have no value."

"No, I will not keep back the truth. That Jew Gershon was a crook and a jackass besides. He didn't know a thing, not even his own Bible. Jacob appears to be not only honest but well-educated. That's why I want to ask him a few questions."

"Not now, Adam. He's busy seeing to the fields."

"Where are the fields running? Sit down, Jew. I'm not going to hurt you. Sit here. Very good! Neither Lady Pilitzky nor I believe in forcing our Faith on anyone. We don't have an inquisition here as they do in Spain. Poland is a free country, too free for its own good. That's why it's collapsing. But that's not your fault. Let me ask you this. You've been waiting for the Messiah for a thousand years— what am I talking about?—for more than fifteen hundred, and he doesn't appear. The reason is clear. He has come already and revealed God's truth. But you are a stubborn people. You keep yourself apart. You regard our meat as unclean, our wine as an abomination. You are not permitted to marry our daughter. You believe you are God's chosen people. Well, what has he chosen you for? To live in dark ghettos and wear yellow patches. I've been out of the country and seen how Jews live abroad. They're all rich and all they think about is profit. Everywhere they're treated like spiders. Why don't you take a good look at yourself and throw away the Talmud? Perhaps the Christians are right after all. Have any of you visited heaven?"

"Really these religious argument are stupid," Theresa Pilitzky protested.

"What's so stupid about them? People have to discuss things. I'm not speaking to him in anger, but as an equal. If he can convince me that the Jews are right, I'll become a Jew." Pilitzky laughed.

"I can convince no one, my lord," Jacob began to stammer. "I inherited my faith from my parents and I follow it to the best of my ability."

"The idolators had fathers and mothers too. And they were taught that a stone is God. But you Jews demanded the destruction of their temples and the annihilation of their children. The Old Testament says so. Doesn't that prove that one doesn't necessarily follow the parents' faith?"

"The Christians also regard the Bible as sacred."

"Naturally. But one must be logical. Everyone but your people and the infidel Turks have accepted Christianity. You Jews consider yourself cleverer than anyone in Europe or the world. All right, God loves you. What kind of love?—your wives are raped and your children buried alive."

Jacob swallowed hard. "Those were the acts of the Christians."

"What? The Cossacks are no more Christians than I am Zoroastrian. Only the Catholics are Christian. The Russian Orthodox are as idolatrous as their allies the Turks. Protestants are even worse. But this is all irrelevant, Jew."

"None of us knows the ways of Providence, my lord. The Catholics also suffer. They wage war against each other ..." Jacob broke off in the middle of his sentence. For a moment Adam Pilitzky meditated in stance on Jacob's words.

"Of course we suffer. As the Bible says, man was born to suffer. But we suffer for a reason. Our souls are purified through what we endure and rise to heaven. But the real torment begins for the unbeliever after death."

Theresa Pilitzky shook her head. "Really, Adam, where's this getting you? The truth cannot be proved. It can only be found here." Theresa Pilitzky pointed to her heart.

"Yes, that is true, my lady," Jacob said softly.

"Well, I suppose it is. But of what use is this stiff-necked clinging to your faith? In your misguided way, you are attentive to God, and your synagogues are always filled. Once when I was in Lublin, I walked past your prayer houses. Such ecstatic singing! A song rose as if from a thousand voices. But a few years later ten thousand Jews were slaughtered. I talked to someone who saw the Cossacks enter Lublin. The Jews crushed each other in their panic. More died from being trampled on than were killed by the invaders. While this went on, was the sky any less blue? Did the sun stop shining? Where was the God you praise and beseech, whose dear children you claim to be? How do you deal with these facts, Jew? How can you sleep at night remembering?"

"When you're tired enough, your eyes close by themselves."

"I see you avoid answering me ..."

"He's right, Adam, he's right. What's there to say? Can we explain our misfortunes any better than he can his? Even searching for an answer is blasphemous. You know that very well."

Pilitzky drew his eyeballs downward and stared cross-eyed at Lady Pilitzky. "I know nothing, Theresa. Sometimes I think that the Epicureans and Cynics were right. Have you ever heard of Democritus, Jew?"

"No, my lord."

"Democritus was a philosopher who said that chance ruled everything. The Church has proscribed his writings, but I read him. He believed in neither idols nor God. The world, he said, was the result of blind powers."

"Don't repeat those heresies," Theresa Pilitzky said, interrupting.

"Perhaps he was right."

"Really, Adam."

"Very well, I'll go and lie down. Your eyes close by themselves," he said, echoing Jacob. "Isn't there something you have to say to Jacob, Theresa?"

"Yes, there is."

"Goodbye, then, and don't be afraid of us. Is your wife really a mute?"

"Yes, my lord."

"That means that miracles also happen among the Jews, doesn't it?"

"Yes, my lord."

"Well, I'll go and take a nap."

II

As he left the room, Pilitzky glanced back over his shoulder. Jacob bowed. Lady Pilitzky slowly moved her fan of peacock feathers.

"Sit down. So! Where do such discussions ever lead? One has to trust that God knows how to manage the world. When the Swedes took the manor, they flogged me in my own castle. I thought it was the end. But the Almighty wanted me to continue living."

Jacob paled. "They flogged you, my lady?"

Lady Pilitzky smiled.

"My dear Jacob, the rod is not particular about rank. Dukes, ladies, your royal highnesses even, are all the same to it. It strikes. The officers found it more amusing just because I was an aristocrat."

"Why did they do this, my lady?"

"Because I said no to the general. My husband was in hiding and I had no one to protect me. If my suitor had been young and handsome, or at least healthy" (Lady Pilitzky's tone changed) "I might have been tempted. 'All's fair in love and war,' as they say. But not with that ugly ape. One look and I said, 'Sir, death is preferable.'"

"I had thought such behavior was limited to Muscovites and Cossacks."

Lady Pilitzky smiled. "Ah, the Swedes are angels? No, Jacob, all men are alike. Frankly, I don't blame them. Women have only one use for them. A child must nurse and doesn't care if the breast belongs to a peasant or a princess. Men are like children."

Demureness and coquetry met in Lady Pilitzky's smile. She looked Jacob straight in the eye and fluttered her lids slightly. Jacob's neck became hot.

"A man has his wife."

"What? To begin with, in wartime, wives don't count. Secondly, one gets tired of a woman. My tailor makes me an expensive dress; so after I wear it three times I'm bored with it and give it to one of my husband's cousins. Men feel the same way. A woman's no longer attractive to a man when he can have her as much as he pleases—and he's off after another. But why should I tell you this? You're a man – tall and with blue eyes…"

The blood rushed to Jacob's face. "The Jews do not behave so."

Lady Pilitzky petulantly shook her fan. "Jew or Tartar, a man is a man. Why, your men were allowed a host of wives. The great kings and prophets had harems."

"Now that's forbidden."

"Who forbade it?"

"Rabbi Gershom, the Light of the Diaspora. He issued the edict."

"The Christians forbid it too. But what does human nature care about edicts? I don't condemn a man for wanting. If he gets a woman to say 'yes' I don't condemn her either. My view is that everything comes from God – including lust. And not everyone's a saint, and not every saint was always saintly. Anyway, how does it hurt God? Some take the position that a secret sin where there is no sacrilege injures no one. My husband spent a few years in Italy. There the ladies have both a husband and lover. The lover is called an 'amico.' When a lady goes to the theater, she is escorted by both her gentlemen. Don't forget this happens in the shadow of the Vatican. The amico is often a cardinal or some other Church dignitary. The Pope knows of it, and, if it were such a crime would he tolerate it?"

There was a pause in the conversation. Finally, Jacob said, "Nothing like that occurs among the Jews. A man may not even glance at another woman."

"Just the same they do glance. I know a man's a hypocrite if he claims to be only interested in his wife. Let me ask you something."

"Yes, my lady."

"Where are you from? How does it happen you settled here? Don't think it odd that I pry; I have my reasons. It seems strange that you married a mute. Most Jews aren't as good-looking as you, or as well-bred, and you speak good Polish. You could have had the prettiest girl." Jacob shook his head. "This is my second marriage."

"What happened to your first wife?"

"The Cossacks killed her and our children."

"In what town?"

"I am from Zamosc."

"Well, that is sad. What do they have against the women and children? And where does your present wife come from?"

"From near Zamosc."

"Why did you marry her? There must have been other women."

"Only a few. Most of the women were killed."

"You must have liked her. It can't be denied that she's good-looking."

"Yes, I did."

Lady Pilitzky rested her fan on her bosom.

"I'll be frank with you, Jacob. Your enemies among the Jews—don't think you don't have any—are spreading the story that your wife is not as mute as she pretends. When my husband first heard this, he was out of his mind with rage, and he wanted to put your Sarah to the test. But I dissuaded him. His idea was to shoot off a pistol behind her and see what happened. I told him you don't play such tricks on a pregnant woman. Adam Pilitzky listens to me. He does whatever I tell him to. In this one respect he's an unusually good husband. You understand yourself that the Jews of Pilitz will suffer if there was no miracle. The clergy in this part of the country, particularly the Jesuits, have their own interests to look out for. All that I want you to know is that you have a close friend in me. Don't be shy and secretive. We are all only flesh and blood underneath our clothes. I want to protect you, Jacob, and I am afraid that you may need protection."

Jacob raised his head slowly.

"Who is spreading these rumors?"

"People have mouths. Gershon is sly and even conspires against my husband. He will come to a bad end, but before that happens he will make trouble."

III

Fear such as he had felt when Zagayek sent for him, arose in Jacob. But now Sarah's life was in danger, also. The Jesuits had interests to protect. Pistols were to be fired near Sarah! I am in a trap, thought Jacob. I must flee. But the child must be born first. With winter approaching, where could he run? What course should he follow—tell Lady Pilitzky the truth? Deny the rumor? He sat silent and helpless, ashamed of his cowardice. Lady Pilitzky surveyed him expertly out of the corner of her eyes, a polished smile on her lips.

"Don't be afraid, Jacob. You remember the saying, 'A great wind but a small rain.' Nothing bad will happen."

"I trust not. Thank you, my lady. I can't thank you enough."

"You can thank me later. Have you seen the castle?"

"No, only this room."

"Come, I will show it to you. The invaders did a great deal of damage, but they left something. At times I agree with my husband—everything's collapsing. The peasants report having seen a huge comet in the sky with a tail stretching from one horizon to the other. It's as it was at the end of the first millennium, or during the Black Plague."

"When did they see the comet? I've seen nothing."

"Nor have I. But my husband has. It's a sign that we can expect some cataclysm: war, pestilence or flood. The Turks are sharpening their scimitars. Suddenly the Muscovites are a power. The Prussians, of course, are always ready for pillage. 'Eat, drink, and be merry. For tomorrow we die.' "

"A life lived in constant fear loses its flavor."

"What? Some have the opposite attitude. I've been through one war after another. But I know how to keep calm when others shiver. I laugh when most people cry. 'Draw the curtains,' I order my maid, and say to myself, 'Theresa, you have only one more hour to live.' Do you ever drink in bed?"

"Only when I'm sick…"

"No, when you're well. My husband's room is across the hall from mine and so I can isolate myself completely. I prop myself up with a pillow and order the maid to bring me wine. I like mead especially, although it's supposed to be a peasant's drink. They call it 'the nectar of the Slavs' in other countries. But I'm happy when I'm just this side of being drunk. When my mind's a trifle foggy, I don't worry; I lose all sense of obligation. I only do those things that please me."

"Yes, my lady."

"Follow me."

As Lady Pilitzky led Jacob through the halls and chambers, he did not know what to admire first: the furniture, the rugs, the tapestries or the paintings. Everywhere were trophies of the hunt: stags' and boars' heads staring down from the walls; stuffed pheasants, peacocks, partridges, grouse, looking as if they were alive. In the armory were displayed swords, spears, helmets, and breastplates. Lady Pilitzky pointed out the portraits of the lords of Pilitz and their families. Pictures of the kings of Poland were also on the walls: the Casimirs, the Wladislaws, the Jagelos, King Stephan Batory, along with famous statesmen from the ancient families of Czartoryski, and Zamoyski. Whichever way he turned, Jacob's eyes fell on crosses, swords, nude statuary, paintings of battles, tournaments, and the chase. The very air of the castle smelled of violence, idolatry, and concupiscence. Lady Pilitzky threw open the door of a room in the center of which was a large canopied bed. Jacob caught sight of himself in a mirror, but his image, standing as it were in deep water, was barely recognizable. He saw himself hatless, blushing, his hair and beard disheveled, resembling, it seemed, one of the savages portrayed in the other room. "It isn't the best taste to show the bedrooms," Lady Pilitzky said, "but you Jews don't go in too much for courtly forms. My father had a manor Jew whom we were all fond of. He was very vivacious and would dress up like a bear when we had a ball. You know, he could dance exactly like a bear! But he wouldn't drink and though he took part in the fun, he stayed sober. My father always said only a Jew could do that."

"He had to do it."

"Do you know, not only could he speak in rhymes but in a mixture of Polish, Yiddish, and the patois of the peasants? The Jews considered him a scholar. He married his daughter to the son of a rabbi and the fellow lived at his expense and just sat swaying over prayer books."

"What happened?"

"You mean to the old fellow? He was killed by brigands."

Strange, but Jacob had known she was going to say that. His skin prickled. When Lady Pilitzky spoke, he had the impression she understood that what she told him had made him sad.

"Well, he had had a full life. But what difference does it make how long one lives? One thing is certain; we all die. Sometimes I find it impossible to believe that the world will go on after I'm gone, that the sun will shine, the trees blossom—but I won't be there. No, it's unimaginable. But then, one often hears old people speak of things that happened before one was born. Well, while one's here one longs for happiness, particularly at night. I lie by myself with the darkness surrounding me. Jacob, have you ever seen a werewolf?"

"No, my lady."

"Nor have I. But there are such creatures, There are nights when I want to crawl out into the dark on my hands and knees and howl."

"Why, my lady?"

"Oh, for no reason. I may decide to visit you one of these nights, Jacob, and then be on your guard because I'm dangerous."

Suddenly Lady Pilitzky took hold of Jacob's wrists and said, "I am not so old yet. Kiss me."

"My lady, I am not allowed to. My religion forbids it. I must humbly beg your pardon, your excellency."

"Don't apologize. I'm a fool and you're a Jew. You have borscht, not blood in your veins."

"My lady, I fear God."

"Well, go to him."

IV

It was a warm, summerlike evening in the month of Elul. The crops had been harvested and the fields lay bare. A tepid mist rose from the empty furrows. Jacob as he walked heard the croak of frogs; he kept his eyes fixed on the heavens where a half moon shone, attended by a brilliant blue-green star twinkling with a strange light. Jacob could almost see this small point as the vast orb it really was. Here on earth he was as good as destroyed by the dangers hemming him in on every side. But it was a comfort to realize that God and his angels and seraphim dwelt in their heavenly mansions. Jacob, not wanting to lay himself open to investigation and persecution, had to be careful about opening a book in Pilitz; he did not want to be known as a scholar and certainly not as a cabalist. But here on the manor, he could study whatever he wanted in his free moments. He had brought with him the Book of Creation, Angel Raziel, and the Zohar to use as charms against devils and to put under Sarah's pillow when she was in labor. These were the books he kept returning to now. A man like himself could not expect to understand what was written in such volumes, but the very words had a sacred look about them. Merely gazing at a page edified him. Even if you were a sinner, it was a privilege to exist surrounded by so many spheres, chariots, powers, and potentates. Jacob remembered from his readings in *The Tree of Life* that evil, synonymous with absolute emptiness, only arose because God had contracted and hidden his face. Repentance could change sins to pieties, justice to mercy. A transgression might at times even lead to good. So, he, Jacob, had sinned when he had lusted for Wanda, but now Wanda had become Sarah, the daughter of Abraham, and in giving birth to a child was about to summon a Jewish soul from the Throne of Glory. It had been right for him to rebuff Lady Pilitzky but would his virtue help him avoid the traps lying all around him?

He was walking on an embankment between fields and insects and other small creatures scurried from beneath his advancing tread. They had received their share of wisdom, but the Creator had left their bodies unprotected. Whoever had feet trod on them; they killed and fed on each other. Yet Jacob found no sadness anywhere but within himself. The summer night throbbed with joy; from all sides came music. Warm winds bore the smells of grain, fruit, and pine trees to him. Itself a cabalistic book, the night was crowded with sacred names and symbols – mystery upon mystery. In the distance where sky and earth merged, lightning flashed, but no thunder followed. The stars looked like letters of the alphabet, vowel points, notes of music. Sparks flickered above the bare furrows. The world was a parchment scrawled with words and song. Every now and then Jacob heard a murmur in his ear as if some unseen being was whispering to him. He was surrounded by powers, some good, some evil, some cruel, some merciful, but each with its own nature and its own task to perform. At times he heard laughter, at other times sighs. He tripped but his foot was guided to the ground. The struggle was going on without as well as within him. He trembled thinking of Lady Pilitzky's wrath but thanked God continually that he had not involved himself with her. He longed for Sarah who might already be in labor, and wished he were home. The maid was in the house, and in an emergency the servants' midwife could be sent for, but Jacob wanted a daughter of Israel to bring the baby into the world. He would not stay on in the manor during the High Holidays. The moment he had finished his most important work he would move back to Pilitz. That is if he were still alive.

"Don't be frightened," Jacob said to himself to keep up his courage, and suddenly a few lines of commentary entered his mind. They concerned the Biblical passage in which the patriarch Jacob blesses his son Jehudah, saying, "Jehudah thee shall thy brethren praise." His teacher at cheder had given the following gloss: Jehudah had been hiding in a corner from his father afraid that he would be reminded of his transgression with Tamar. But Jacob had said reassuringly, "Don't be afraid and don't tremble. Thy brethren will praise you because King David will descend from your loins."

So many years had passed since he had been a school boy, but his teacher's voice still rang in his ears. The old man had died a martyr; Jacob could see his wrinkled face and his gesticulating hands. He remembered the cheder boys also, each with his particular facial expression and mannerism. Where were Moishe'le, Kople, Chaim Berl? Probably dead; and inhabitants now of higher worlds, where thousands upon thousands of mysteries had already been revealed to them. As Jacob walked, his shadow paced with him, a double shadow, composed of a light shell and a dark kernel. He had come to a swamp and, fearful of sinking into the slime, retraced his steps and made a long detour. Nets of moonlight fell in front of him; he heard the hissing and rapid retreat of frightened snakes. Sorcery lay all around him. The castle appeared and disappeared, one moment in front of him, the next to the rear, and he realized that he was lost. He noticed a light in one of the castle windows and thought he caught a glimpse of Lady Pilitzky.

When, at length, he reached home, he found Sarah preparing supper on a tripod, and looking almost girlish despite her pregnancy. Thank God she was all right. The pine branches over which she was cooking blazed and smoked and Jacob smelled the odors of resin and fresh milk. Before he had a chance to speak,

Sarah pointed to the rear. On a log outside the house sat three women and a man who had heard of Sarah's miracle and come to be blessed.

Jacob covered his face with his hands. His lies had made him a party to this abominable fraud. These people had left home, wasted their money, exhausted themselves to seek out Sarah. He walked outside and saw a broad-shouldered man with a ragged beard, heavy eyebrows, and a pimply nose. The man's tattered coat was unbuttoned revealing his hairy chest and long fringed garment. A beggar's sack stood close by on the ground. The man rose upon seeing Jacob. The three women were all small and wore kerchiefs and aprons. One of them had a bundle in her lap, the second a basket; the third nibbled on a piece of turnip. They also rose when Jacob appeared.

"Good evening, visitors. Bless you."

"Good evening, rabbi," the man answered in a deep, gruff voice.

"I am not a rabbi," Jacob said, "only a humble Jew."

"God has granted you a saint for a wife," one of the women answered, "so you must be a saint also."

V

The guests were invited to remain for the night and Sarah prepared supper for them. When the meal was over she blessed the travelers, placing her hands on the womens' heads and mouthing a silent prayer over the man. Then, knowing that this was a wasted evening, she wearily retired to her bed in the alcove. There would be no studying of the Torah that night; the guests had to be hospitably treated. Though the women had had beds made up for them in the adjoining bedroom, and the man his in the shed, none of the travelers felt like retiring and they walked out into the warm evening. Jacob followed, anticipating that this would be one of those nights when he would not close his eyes. The incident with Lady Pilitzky had made his position untenable. He expected to be arrested at any moment.

As always the talk turned to the catastrophe. In a rasping voice, the man, Zeinvel Bear, told how he had fled Chmielnicki's Cossacks.

"Yes, I ran. No, my body ran. I was scared. I meant to stay with my family, but my feet said 'no.' Look, I'm a wanderer now. Well, in the old days I just stayed put. All I did was pound cleats into shoes. So how did I, a shoemaker, know where to go? I'd heard of two hamlets, Lipcy and Maidan. In Lipcy there was this fellow who would walk through fire for me. Only a peasant, but a builder and wood carver too. The count humored him, let him dress like one of the gentry. I made his boots. Such boots aren't made any more. The king's aren't as good. But Maidan had a bad reputation. The peasants there were sorcerers and brigands, and secret allies of the murderers. So, there I stood at the crossroads, wanting to get to Lipcy, but not knowing whether it was right or left. Suddenly I saw a dog. Where had it come from? Out of the earth. It wagged its tail, and pointed its nose straight at me. It couldn't talk, but it was saying, 'Follow me.' It started off down one of the roads and kept turning its head. It was making sure that I was following. Where did it lead me? Right into Lipcy. When I saw the town I went to pat the dog and give it a piece of bread. But it vanished before my eyes. I knew then that it wasn't a dog at all but a messenger sent from heaven."

"Did the gentile really hide you?"

"I lived in the granary for weeks and he brought me everything I needed."

"What became of your family?"

"None of them are left."

The woman with the basket nodded her head.

"Heaven wanted you to be saved, so you were. But why was I kept alive? My husband and my little swallows were killed in front of me. Woe to a mother who must endure that. I begged them to do away with me first but they wanted to torture me. Two Cossacks held me while the others did their dirty work. They discussed the plans that they had for me. One of them had a rabbit and they were going to sew it into my stomach. Suddenly there was a scream and they ran like crazy. I still don't know who screamed. It was such an awful yell I get cold shivers even now when I think of it."

"They must have thought it was some soldiers."

"What soldiers?"

The woman, still holding on to her turnip, took a bite and spat it out. "Trine, tell them about the Cossacks," she said to the woman with the bundle.

Trine didn't answer.

"What's wrong? Are you angry?"

"What's there to tell?"

"She was the wife of a Cossack for three years."

"Be quiet. Why talk? It was worse than when the temple was destroyed. I look old, but I'm not as old as all that. I'll be thirty-six on the fast day, the seventeenth of Tammuz. My husband was a scholar and known all over Poland. When the rabbis were stumped by a question, they came to him. He would pick up a book and open it: there was the answer. They wanted to make him assistant rabbi, but he would have no part of it. 'When the town buys you bread, soon you wish you were dead.' He sat and studied and I took care of our drygoods store. When a fair opened, I went there with our stock, and God did not forsake me. My only grief was that I had no children. Ten years after our marriage, my mother-in-law (may it not be held against her) said that my husband should divorce me because I was barren. We married young. I was eleven and he twelve. He was bar-mitzvahed in my father's house. My mother-in-law had the law on her side, but my husband answered, 'Trine is mine.' He liked to talk in rhyme. He would have been a good wedding jester. Well, the murderers came. We all ran to hide, but he put on his prayer shawl and walked out to meet them. They made him dig his own grave. As he dug, he prayed. I sat in the cellar for days and I didn't have the strength to rise. I fainted from hunger. The others went out at night to hunt for food. I was already in the other world and I saw my mother. There was music and I didn't walk but floated like a bird. My mother flew beside me. We came to two mountains with a pass between. The pass was as red as sunset and smelled of the spices of Paradise. My mother skimmed through, but when I tried to follow someone drove me back."

"An angel?" the shoemaker asked.

"I don't know."

"What happened then?"

"I cried, 'Mother, why are you leaving me?' I couldn't make out her answer. It was just a faint echo in my ear. I opened my eyes and someone was dragging me. It was dark out. I was being pulled from the cellar by a Cossack. I begged him to kill me, but those who want to die live. He tied me to his horse. His name was Vassil."

"Is that the one you married?"

"Married-shmarried."

"Where did he take you?"

"Who knows? Some place on the steppes. We rode day and night. Maybe a week, maybe a month. I didn't even know when it was Sabbath."

"So?"

"Please let me alone."

"He kept her for three years," the woman with the basket said.

"I'll bet you had children by him, huh?" Zeinvel Bear asked.

His question remained unanswered.

No one spoke for a while, and everyone looked up at the moon. Then Zeinvel Bear asked, "What about the steppes? Is it like here?"

"It's beautiful, beautiful. They have strange birds there that talk like people. The grass is very tall and you have to watch out for snakes. The horses are small but faster than our big ones. The Cossacks ride bareback and laugh at anyone who uses a saddle. The women ride too. All the men wear a single earring, and they carry riding crops. When they get angry, they hit with their whips, first from the right, then from the left. They'll beat their own mothers. When a boy comes of age, he and his father wrestle in front of the village. They call it *stanitza*. If the son throws the father, they're jubilant, even the mother. We milk cows but they milk mares. I saw a lot of Tartars where I was. The Tartars shave off their hair and leave only a pigtail. They gamble with hard-boiled eggs on holidays. We do everything inside the house, but they wash and cook outside. They make a fire in a hole, and if they don't have wood, they burn cow dung. They don't have a king. If they have to decide something, all the men get together and talk it over. Every Cossack has his own sword and saber. If a man suspects his wife's unfaithful, he just kills her and no one says anything. Everyone sings there, even the women. At dusk they sit around in a circle and an old man starts the chant and the others join in. They also know how to dance and play musical instruments.

"When I got there, I was more dead than alive. My Cossack had ridden with me all day and half of the night. We didn't eat much, mostly only mushrooms and berries and whatever else he could find in the forest. When he went to look for food, he'd tie his horse to a tree and me to the horse. One time it started to rain and thunder and I tried to get free. But when they tie you up, you stay tied. The horse got frightened too and started to stamp his hoofs and neigh. He came back carrying a wild boar. I refused to put the meat in my mouth. He'd roasted it but it was still half raw. They all eat meat that's hard as a rock and filled with blood. I started to vomit, but he pushed the filthy stuff into my mouth. When a Cossack stops beating his wife, it means he doesn't love her any more. He doesn't beat her in private, but outside in front of everyone, and while he's doing it, he talks to the neighbors. All the men have beards just like the Jews.

"Where was I? Oh, yes, he takes me to the *stanitza* and I can't speak a word of their language. I already had hair on my head, but not as much as the Cossack women. Everyone came to watch him untie me from the horse. An old woman, dressed in pants and as ugly as a witch, began to mumble and spit. It was his mother. She ran at him and began to hit him with her fists and he drove her away with his whip. Then a young woman—it was his wife—came rushing up, screaming and cursing. I stood there like a clay image, ragged, half-naked, barefoot, as emaciated as the dead. I didn't know what to do but they all kept pointing at me as if asking, 'What do you need such a carcass for?' They looked me over as if I were a freak. He had already defiled me but I started to make my confession. What does a woman remember? 'Hear, O Israel.' 'I put my spirit into thy hands.' And a few benedictions. I spoke to God in Yiddish, knowing He understands all languages. 'Father in heaven, take me to you. Death is better than such a life.' But when one wants to go, one doesn't. They brought me into the house and put me to tending geese. They tried the Cossack for bringing home a foreign woman. The young men wanted to behead him, but the old men sided with him.

"What? No, I have no children. That's all I would have needed. He had children by the other one, and they loved me more than their own mother. She'd fly into rages when he wasn't around and beat me until I bled. But then she'd get sorry and bring me a bowl of soup. At first I wouldn't eat unkosher food but finally I had to. I threw up more than I swallowed. They know nothing about Jews. They live like savages. Do you know how they take a bath? They go outside and the husband pours a bucket over his wife and then she pours one over him. All the while the neighbors chat. When they kill a pig, it's a great event. Instead of cutting off its head, they all stab it with spears—men, women, and children. The old crones run up with a pot and catch the blood.

"They got to like me. Even the old bitch. I learned some Cossack, and they picked up some Yiddish. The old woman was always fighting with her daughter-in-law and she began to make up to me. I understood about one word in ten, but she kept on raving and chattering until I had water on the ear. You know they hardly fed her. She slept on a pile of straw and was half eaten by vermin. She didn't have a tooth in her head. Her son didn't know she existed. I gave her whatever I could. When she was dying, she left me her bracelets. I hid them carefully. The daughter-in-law would have devoured me if she had known.

"I thought about only one thing, running away. But where can you run to on the steppes? There are wild animals every-where. It's so hot in summer that the earth burns your feet. In the winter the snow is piled as high as your head. I didn't have clothes or money. But even if you have money there's not much to do with it. One thing I did not forget: I was a daughter of Israel. When I opened my eyes in the morning, I said, 'I thank Thee.' He'd ask me, 'What's that you're mumbling?' and I'd answer, 'None of your business.' If I'd known their language I could have converted them. They said to me openly, 'We want to become Jews.' If I'd been a man something would have come of that. But what use is a woman? I myself can't tell up from down. They know a little about the Christian holidays, but it's all topsy-turvy. Their priest has a wife. If his wife dies, he has to take another right away. Until he does, they won't listen to him bleating. During Lent they don't eat milk, butter, cheese, or eggs. Only cabbage and vodka. They have everything there but salt and wine which are as expensive as gold. The country's fine except for the flies and locusts which descend like the plagues of Egypt. And they give you elflocks ... ."

"How did you manage to get away?"

"What's the difference? I'm here. My mother came to me in a dream and told me to leave. When a Tartar passed through, I gave him the old woman's bracelets. He sold me what he had on him—a *bashmet* and a pair of their shoes— they're called *tshuviakis*. I started off trusting in God and good angels to lead me. A small flame ran before me and showed me the road. If I'm lying, may I not see another Yom Kippur. Animals chased me. A huge bird swooped down and tried to carry me off. I screamed and it flew away. But, dear friends, if I told you everything, we would be here for three days and nights. I got help. Yes, help was sent to me. But to whom or what was I running? I didn't even find a grave. I am all by myself in God's world, shamed and despised. When I remember all I went through, I spit on myself."

"So why have you come to be blessed?" Zeinvel Bear asked.

"I keep wandering. So as not to stay in one place. Perhaps there is some comfort for me somewhere in the world. When that blessed woman put her hands on me, a stone dropped from my heart."

Zeinvel Bear pointed with his finger, "See, a falling star!"

VI

The door of Lady Pilitzky's bedroom opened. The moon shone through the curtains. Lady Pilitzky opened her eyes. "Is that you, Adam?" she asked in a soft, mtimate voice.

"Yes, Theresa. Did I wake you?"

"No, I was just napping."

"I can't sleep. What should I do about that Jew? About all the Jews? I let in a few and suddenly there's a city. Savitzky is boiling. He's already consigned me to hell. Our dear neighbors are also conspiring. Each of them has his own little Jew, but when it comes to me, they're all pious Christians. This business with that mute is a farce. Even the Jews are laughing at me. It's just another of those damned Jewish tricks."

"Why are you standing? Sit down or come into bed."

"All right, I'll sit. I'm hot. Why has it turned so warm in the middle of the night? Maybe the world's coming to an end or something of the sort. I don't want those Jews around any longer. Gershon's a crook, and that Jacob's a trickster. Why should a woman pretend to be dumb? I just don't understand it."

"Perhaps she's not pretending. She may really be a mute."

"You said yourself that he admitted she wasn't."

"I said nothing of the kind. All I said was that he remained silent and didn't protest. Who knows what goes on among these people? They're a special tribe. It's best to ignore them."

"How can I ignore them? They have a finger in everything."

"Your Catholic administrators aren't any better."

"What is any good? The whole of Poland's collapsing. Mark my word, we'll be completely eradicated. What the Jewish lice don't eat, the Prussians or Muscovites will. You won't find our nobility crying. No, they consider every Polish defeat their personal victory. Things like this only happen in Poland. Every other country's anxious to prosper; we strangle ourselves."

"I don't know, Adam. I don't know anything anymore!"

"Why did you start with that Jew? It was like spitting in my face."

Theresa hesitated.

"But that's what you enjoy."

"Not when it's a Jew. You shouldn't have done it. I used to sleep at night. Now I don't. I wake every few minutes. I'm beginning to think I'm possessed. Theresa, I want to bring the matter to an end."

"What matter? What kind of an end?"

"I'll take some men and we'll march down to Pilitz and cut off a few Jewish heads. The rest of them will just pack up and run."

"Adam, you're mad. Whose heads? We have enemies all around us. Do something like that and you'll find yourself standing trial."

"Because of some Jews?"

"You know your enemies are just looking for something. All right, they hate the Jews, but if they find it useful, they'll take their side."

"I must do something."

"Do nothing, Adam. Go to sleep. Lie perfectly still with your eyes closed, and sleep will come. We must bide our time. Adam, dear, we must wait. What else is there to life? You wait and the days pass, and death comes and everything is over."

"I can't just lie waiting for death. Those spinster cousins are too much for me. They walk around glaring at me as if I were their worst enemy; and they're always whispering. This castle is filled with whisperers. You'd think I was keeping them imprisoned. If they're so unhappy, let them go elsewhere. I can't support all my distant relatives. It's not my fault that my uncles and aunts produced only spinsters."

"I've been saying just that for years."

"Yes, it was you who poisoned me against them. That's the tragedy. But now that your venom's worked, suddenly you're their protector and good angel."

"I knew it. Sooner or later everything ends up being my fault."

"Well, it's so. You're the cause of all my troubles. I've quarreled with everyone on account of you. You've isolated me. But I want to be finished with all this." Pilitzky's voice rose to a scream.

"Why must you shout? You'll wake everyone. You know that they eavesdrop."

"Here no one needs to eavesdrop. They all know everything. I can see it in their faces and hear it in their laughs. Theresa, this time you've gone too far."

"I? No, it was you who pushed me, Adam. If I were at the point of death, I would say it over again. You did it. When I testify before God, I will not change my story. No one but you was responsible. I came to you as an innocent girl and you—"

"I know, I know. That story's already grown a beard. You were pure as snow, as innocent as a white rose, and so on. What do you want me to do? Return your hymen?"

"No, all I want from you is a little peace."

"I can't go on living like this. What makes you think Jacob won't talk? I don't want those dirty Jews pointing their fingers at me."

"He won't say anything. He'll keep still. He has his own troubles. His wife's a puzzle—I don't know the answer, but there is one. He's as frightened as he is large and awkward. Maybe he ran away from jail. God knows what. Sooner or later the truth will out."

"Yes, and my shame also."

"You wanted it that way, Adam. For years you urged me to indulge you in your fantasies. God alone knows how I struggled against you and what I endured."

"Don't mention God."

"Who else? I have no one but Him. You drove our children to their deaths. It was as if you killed them with your own hands. Me you made—I dare not say the word; it would disgrace the souls of our parents in heaven. What you have done can not be undone."

Both husband and wife lapsed into silence and then Pilitzky said, "I ordered Antonia to kill the hog tomorrow afternoon."

"No, Adam, I am no longer interested. I don't want it to happen. Let the beast live."

"I have already told Antonia."

"I was not serious when I said it. I don't want to watch. It doesn't help anyway. Holy Mother, what has become of me? God in heaven strike me dead this instant. I want no tomorrow."

Theresa moaned, half in pain and half in disgust. Her body contorted on the bed as if she had been seized by a spasm.

"Take me, death."

TEN

The Jews of Pilitz were preparing for the High Holidays. The beadle blew his horn daily to scare off Satan, the Seducer, who led men into sin and then testified against them in heaven. Sarah, having moved back to Pilitz from the manor, in addition to holiday preparations, made ready for childbirth. Jacob had placed The Book of Creation and a knife under her pillow to discourage those she-devils who hover around women in labor and injure the newborn – Lilith, for example, or Shibta who broke the necks of children being delivered. Jacob had also acquired a talisman from a scribe which had the power to keep off Ygereth, the queen of the demons, Machlath, her attendant, as well as the Lillies who resembled humans but had bat wings, ate fire, and lived in shadows of the moon and tree trunks. As for Sarah, she secretly practiced the magic native to her village. Though now a daughter of Israel, who had learned the prayers said on the High Holidays, still she wore on her throat a piece of a meteorite; and she took the shell of a newly hatched chick, mixed it with dry horse manure and frogs' ashes and drank the concoction in milk. Another charm required her to sit naked on a pot in which mustard seed was burning, allowing the smoke to enter her. The prediction of the women of Pilitz was that she would give birth to a boy since her stomach was not round but pointed upward. Jacob had already bought a gold embroidered skull cap from a traveling pedlar as well as a bracelet that protected from the evil eye.

On Rosh Hashana it was Jacob who arose to begin the prayer, an honor which Gershon had bitterly opposed. On the previous Sabbath he had delayed the reading of the Torah while he railed against the community for allowing a stranger to stand at the lectern as its representative, but the elders had outvoted him. Jacob stood in his prayer shawl and robe singing "the King" and Sarah could not keep back her tears. She could remember him when he had been a barefooted slave who slept in her father's barn. Now he looked like a venerable sage. She, too, had changed, wore a gold colored dress, earrings which Jacob had ordered from a goldsmith and on which money was still owed, and a string of imitation pearls. She held a prayer book in her hands and its brass covers reflected her image— the image of a lady. Her lips moved in silent prayer. Jacob had been so scrupulous in his teaching that she knew more than most of the women around her. How strange it all was: her love for Jacob at first sight, his leaving her and returning to get her, their years of wandering together. Those had been years of constant danger and her life had almost been forfeited many times. God alone knew how many miracles had been required to rescue Jacob and her.

Next to her in the women's gallery stood Beile Pesche, Gershon's wife, dressed in silk and velvet and with a string of real pearls around her neck. But Sarah didn't envy her her finery, felt herself to be superior. Beile Pesche was old, couldn't read, had to listen to a woman reader, and was married to an ignoramus who was not allowed to represent the community at prayer. But Sarah was young, could read and understand a little Hebrew, and was married to a scholar. If the town only knew what a scholar Jacob really was! More than that, Jacob was Pilitzky's administrator, and was received at the castle. Those years that separated

Sarah from her peasant past stretched behind her like an eternity. What had occurred before must have happened to someone else. It was as if she had read about it in a story. She had once been Wanda, the wife of Stach, a drunken peasant. Whenever that thought came to her, she shivered, but often she went days without remembering it. She had become a Jewess. What Jacob had said was true: she had been born with a Jewish soul and he had merely brought her back to her point of origin.

Jacob's voice rang loud and clear as he sang and intoned. Her eyes misted. What had she done to deserve these blessings? She bore his child in her womb. Why had she been chosen from all the other Polish women? Her only special merit had been the suffering which had set her apart from childhood; sorrow and longing had always been part of her. She had had strange thoughts even before she could talk. Often she had cried for no reason. Asleep or awake she had odd dreams whose meanings she had not understood until now. She had always been afraid to talk to Jacob about them, fearing he would think her mad. When her grandfather had died—her father's father—she had seen the dead man standing among the mourners, and he had walked with the peasants as his body was carried for burial. She had wanted to scream out to him, but he had raised a finger and put it to his nose as a sign for her to be silent. Only when the cortege had reached the graveyard had the image dissolved slowly like a pocket of mist when the sun starts shining.

The next night her grandfather had come and left flowers on her bed.

She had had other visions as well, had foreseen Jacob's arrival and for this reason had refused other men. The truth was that since childhood she had been expecting and longing for him.

Around her now, the women motioned and made signs to her, assuming that she heard neither her husband intoning the prayers nor the ram's horn being blown. When they spoke to each other, they did so disregarding her presence. Only Beile Pesche loudly warned that she was no mute at all but a fraud. So great was this woman's hatred that when Sarah nodded a silent Good New Year to her after the prayers, Beile Pesche turned her back. At home the holiday dinner Sarah had prepared was waiting, the head of a fish, carrots, all the customary dishes that are eaten on Rosh Hashana. Jacob said the benediction over the wine and passed the goblet to her so that she might drink, and cut her a slice of chalah with honey. As she ate, she imagined she saw God in the pale, blue sky, seated on a fiery throne with the book of life and death open before Him, while angels trembled and fluttered their wings and the hand of each man inscribed his fate for the year. A secret fear gnawed at her. Perhaps her death had already been decreed. If so, at least Jacob and the baby must be allowed to live.

When the meal was over, Jacob went to the study house to recite Psalms. Sarah lay down on the bed. She could feel the child moving in her womb. It would soon be Yom Kippur when those who have lost their parents say the memorial prayer. But whom should she pray for? Jan Bzik, her father? She had asked Jacob, who had concluded after some hesitation that she should omit that part of the prayer where the names of the dead are mentioned. For she, Sarah, had not been orphaned through the death of Jan Bzik. Her real father was the patriarch Abraham.

II

In the middle of the night Jacob felt himself being shaken. He opened his eyes. Sarah stood by his bed.

"Jacob, it's begun."

"What, the spasm?"

"Yes."

Though he was still exhausted and longed for sleep, he rose quickly, yawning. Then he remembered and was afraid. In the half light Sarah's bloated body seemed a barrel taut with suffering.

"I'll go for the midwife."

"Wait. Perhaps there's still time."

She spoke in a whisper. No matter what happened, she continued to insist, she would not utter a word, not even in labor. But who could be certain how flesh and blood would behave at such a time? Jacob was surrounded by danger. He went and opened the shutters. The half moon that shines during the ten days of repentance had set, but stars glittered. Should he bring her something to eat, he wondered. That summer she had made gooseberry, currant, and blackberry jam, and some cherry wine. He glanced at the water barrel, saw it was half empty, and decided to go to the well for more water. He would not have left a woman about to go into labor alone if there had not been charms and inscriptions on the wall to protect her. But even so he kept the door open and he directed her to recite the incantation a scribe had written out for her:

The mountain is high; the sky is my skin.

The earth is my shoe; the sky is my dress.

Save me, Lord God.

Let no sword cut me,

No horn gore me,

No tooth bite me,

No waters flow over me.

Under the black sea lies a white stone.

In the throat of the hawk a hard bone is stuck.

YUHAH will guard me!

SHADDAI will save me!

TAFTIFIAH will be a wall for me.

During the period between Rosh Hashana and Yom Kippur the townspeople attended night prayers at the study house.

Jacob had not gone this year because Sarah was approaching labor. But he had seen Gershon walking with the others. Only a few days before this wilful man who dictated to everyone had been threatening violence if Jacob was allowed to become reader; he had even implied he would denounce Jacob to the nobles. Everyone knew how Gershon had acquired his wealth; during the massacres monies and other valuables had been entrusted to him for safekeeping by someone he knew. The man had perished and when his heirs had asked for their father's fortune, Gershon had denied ever receiving it, perjuring himself. Yet now he went with his wife, his daughters, and his sons-in-law to night prayers. Did he believe he could fool the Almighty? Despite the thirty-odd years he had lived in the world, Jacob was continually astonished at how many Jews obeyed only one half of the Torah. The very same people, who strictly observed the minor rituals and customs which were not even rooted in the Talmud, broke without thinking twice the most sacred laws, even the Ten Commandments. They wanted to be kind to God and not to man; but what did God need of man and his favors? What does a father want from his children but that they should not do injustice to each other? Jacob, leaning over the well, sighed. This was the cry of the prophets. Perhaps it was the reason the Messiah did not come. He pulled up a pail of water and hurried back to Sarah. She stood at the threshold bent double with pain.

"Get the midwife."

Leaving the pail of water standing, Jacob ran for the midwife, but when he knocked at her shutters, nobody answered. Jacob hurried to the study house and entered the woman's section, although it was not the correct thing to do. But childbirth is dangerous. He looked around and saw she wasn't there.

"My wife's in labor," he said aloud. "Where's the midwife?"

Several of the women scowled and slapped their prayer books, angry at the interruption. Others whispered words of advice and informed him that the midwife was delivering another child. One woman, however, closed her prayer book and rose.

"Life is more important than anything," she said. "I'll go to your wife."

Still in search of the midwife, Jacob found himself traveling down a street filled with bumps and holes and small hillocks. The house of the woman in labor had been described to him and he knew it was one of those he was passing but couldn't decide which, not hearing any screams. The only sound disturbing the silence was the chant rising from the study house. "Adonai! Adonai! Gracious and Merciful God." How strange the prayer sounded echoing in the dark with that peculiar intonation characteristic of night prayers. Despite all their catastrophes, the Jews still spoke of God as merciful and gracious. Jacob stared vacantly about him, uncertain whether to continue his search or hurry home. Sweat ran from his face, wetting his shirt. "Father in Heaven, preserve her," he said aloud, looking up at the sky crowded with stars. When his first wife, peace be with her, had given birth, he had been scarcely more than a boy. What went on among women had been a mystery to him, protected as he had been by his mother, sisters, aunts, and cousins. He had been reading when the women had come in to tell him that he was a father and wish him mazeltov. It had been that way with the second and third child also. But now all of this was so distant it seemed to have taken place in another life. Raising his voice, he called out the name of the midwife, and his cry echoed as though he were in a forest. Then, turning, he ran back home to find a fire already burning in the oven and a pot of water boiling. The woman who had come from the study house had also laid out linen and towels and had lit a wick in a shard of oil. Her sleeves were rolled up and her face wore the expression of one who is an expert in female matters. If she hadn't been there, Jacob would have asked Sarah how she felt. Sarah lay silent on the bed, her face contorted.

"Did you get the midwife?" the woman asked.

"No, I couldn't find her."

"Well, don't get upset. Nothing's happening yet. It doesn't go that easily." And she thrust another piece of wood into the oven.

Behind the anguish in Sarah's eyes was the trace of a smile which seemed to say, "Don't worry so." Jacob looked at her with both love and astonishment. This was Wanda, Jan Bzik's daughter, who every afternoon had brought food to him on the mountain. On her head was the kerchief worn by daughters of Israel, and around her throat a talisman. The walls of the room were hung with charms and verses from the Psalms, and under the pillow lay *The Book of Creation*. He had wrenched this woman from generations of gentiles, robbed her of mother, sister, sister-in-law, all her family. He had even deprived her of her speech. And what had he given in return? Only himself. He had wed her to dangers from which only a miracle could rescue her. For the first time he realized the ordeal to which she had been subjected, and came close to her and stroked her head. Responding like a peasant, she caught his hands in hers and kissed them. If the other woman had seen, the people of Pilitz would have had more to gossip about and ridicule.

III

Can a mute cry? Can she scream in pain? Sarah wept and screamed but said nothing. From the first, signs had indicated a difficult labor. The afternoon following the night of her first spasms she still had not given birth. Her body was wet with perspiration and her eyes protruded. The midwife hurried in and out; there was an assistant, an old crone who delivered the peasants' babies and who had left her turnip patch to run to the bedside; she also bustled about, her unwashed hands black with loam. Neighbors entered, having heard it was a difficult labor, and offered contradictory advice and suggestions. Some of the women stayed outside talking to Jacob, others approached the bed to signal to the mute. Various magical attempts were made to ease the delivery. A young nursing mother squeezed milk from her nipples and gave it to Sarah to drink. A piece of matzoth left over from Passover was placed between the suffering woman's teeth and she was directed to hold it there. A pious matron, noted for her acts of charity, placed her hand on Sarah's stomach and recited a spell. The man who had read the Torah on Rosh Hashana was sent for and he intoned the following passage, resting one hand on the mezuzah: "The captive exile hasteneth that he may be loosed and that he should not die in the pit." He also repeated the verse beginning, "And the Lord visited Sarah," three times, continuing to the words, "at the set time of which God had spoken to him." It was known that Beile Pesche had a bowl inscribed with sacred letters which if placed on the navel of a woman in labor pulled the child out—sometimes the woman's intestines as well if it were left on the body too long. But when Beile Pesche was asked to lend it, she said it had been broken.

When darkness fell and Sarah continued to scream, the women started to bicker. Should she be given the milk of a bitch mixed with honey? Or pigeon droppings in wine? A tip of the lemon used at Succoth was offered and a coin blessed by the pious Rabbi Michael of Zlotchev. Nothing worked. There was only one hope left—the most powerful of all remedies. A long string was brought and attached to Sarah's wrist, its other end carried to the study house and tied to the door of the Ark. Sarah tugged with her wrist as commanded, but instead of the door opening as it should have, the string snapped. This was a bad omen. The midwife said: "I'm afraid there'll be no bread from this oven."

"We must at least try to save the child."

The women spoke loudly, believing there was no need to watch their words.

"What would the widower do with a newborn baby?"

"Oh, he'll find a woman to help."

"Imagine, God already decreed this misfortune on Rosh Hashana," the pious woman remarked.

"No, you're wrong, the fates don't become final until Yom Kippur."

The words Sarah had been trying to hold back tore themselves from her throat:

"Don't bury me yet, I'm not dead." She spoke in Yiddish.

The women drew back.

"Oh, my God, she's speaking."

"It's a second miracle."

"Miracle nothing. She's not a mute."

"Gershon was right."

One of the women called out that her head was spinning and fainted.

Jacob, who had run to the beadle's to fetch more Passover matzoth since the piece in use had fallen from Sarah's and was spattered with blood, was not present. Everyone in the room began to yell at once and there was such a tumult it was heard on the street. From all sides people came running to Jacob's, among them the burial society women who supposed Sarah had died and were ready to lay the corpse on the floor and light the candles. Soon there was such a crush in the room that the bed on which Sarah lay was almost broken. Terrified, she started to shout in her native Polish:

"What do you want from me? Get out of here. You play at being good, but you're all rotten. You want to bury me and marry off Jacob to one of your own, but I'm still living. I'm alive and my baby's alive too. You're rejoicing too quickly, neighbors. If God had wanted me to die, He wouldn't have made me go through what I have."

Sarah's Polish was not that of a Jewess but that of a gentile and the women turned pale.

"That's a dybbuk speaking."

"There's a dybbuk in Sarah," a voice called out into the night.

Many strange events had occurred recently, but the Jews of Pilitz had never heard of a dybbuk entering a woman in labor, and of all things during the days of repentance. Now everyone came, screaming and running. Mothers warned their daughters not to go see the dybbuk unless they wore two aprons, one in the front and one in the rear. Even school children tried to shove into the room where Sarah lay uncovered, but the women turned them back at the door. The stool on which the wick stood was jostled and the light went out; the oil was spilled when someone attempted to light it from the oven. Those on the inside sought to get out and those on the outside tried to squeeze in. People blocked the door and quarrels started. Madness, it seemed, had become universal in Pilitz. Bonnets and kerchiefs fell to the floor, dresses were torn; a string of beads was ripped from a woman's neck. Rising above all this came Sarah's periodic screams. The darkness in the room frightened her and she spoke in a mixture of Polish and Yiddish.

"Why is the room so dark? I'm still living. I'm not in the grave. Where's Jacob? Jacob. Has he run off? Has he forgotten his Wanda?"

"Who's Wanda?" someone asked.

"Let me have light. I'm dying," the woman in labor moaned.

A piece of kindling was found and lit and fiery shadows danced on the walls. In the semi-darkness all the faces seemed distorted. The midwife who had been out of the room pushed her way through the crowd.

"What's come over you? Who's Wanda? Push down hard. Push, daughter."

"He's too big, too big. He takes after Jacob," Sarah cried in Polish. "He's tearing out my insides."

"Who are you? How did you enter Sarah?" a woman inquired of the dybbuk.

Realizing what she had done, Sarah did not reply. The spasms subsided momentarily and she lay exhausted, her hair damp, her body bathed in sweat, her lips and nose swollen. Her legs felt as heavy as logs, her fingers as if they had been stretched. She knew what a dybbuk was, having heard the women speak about them frequently.

"Who are you? How did you enter Sarah?" the women demanded again.

"I entered and here I am," Sarah said. "What do you care? Get out of here. All of you. I don't need you. You're my enemies."

She was speaking in Polish.

"Who is Wanda?"

"She is who she is. Get out of here. Out of here. Let me die in peace. Grant me this. Have pity on me."

The spasms returned and she let out a terrifying wail.

IV

Jacob had been told that a dybbuk had entered Sarah and his arrival started the crowd milling again. Somehow he managed to squeeze his way through.

"What's going on here?" he asked, annoyed and fearful.

"There's a dybbuk inside of her," a woman answered. "It talks Polish. It calls itself Wanda."

Jacob shrugged. "Where's the midwife?"

Sarah's mouth twisted into an expression of mockery.

"No midwife can help me," she said in Polish. "Your son is too large for my hips. Both of us are on our way there," and she pointed toward the cemetery.

Jacob stood, knowing all was lost, speechless with sorrow and shame.

"Save her," he begged those around him. "Please save her."

"No one can save me, Jacob," Sarah said. "The witch predicted I wouldn't live long. Now I see she was right. Forgive me, Jacob."

"Who are you? Where do you come from?" a woman asked.

"Bring the rabbi," another woman cried. "Let him exorcise the dybbuk."

"It's too late for that," Sarah said. "What's he going to drive out? When you bury me, I won't be here anymore and you won't have to trouble yourself gossiping about me. Don't think I didn't hear your nasty talk." Sarah's tone changed. "I heard every word. But I had to play the fool. Now I'm dying, I want you to know the truth. You call yourself Jews but you don't obey the Torah. You pray and bow your heads but you speak evil of everyone and begrudge each other a crust of bread. Gershon, the man who rules you, is a swindler. He robbed a Jew whom the Cossacks killed and because of that his son-in-law's a rabbi and—"

Jacob turned white. "What are you talking about, Sarah?"

"Be quiet, Jacob. My sorrow speaks, not I. I can no longer be silent. I kept still for two years, but now that I'm dying, I must talk. I'll burst if I don't. Thank you, Jacob, for everything. You are the cause of my death but I don't hold it against you. How is it your fault? You're a man. You'll find another woman. They're already talking of matches. The town won't let you remain single long. Pray for me, Jacob, because I have forsaken the God of my parents. And I don't know if your God will allow me into heaven. If you ever meet my sister Basha or my brother Antek, tell them how their sister died."

"What is she saying? What is she saying?" voices asked from all sides.

"It's a dybbuk, a dybbuk."

"Yes, a dybbuk. What are you going to do about it? I'll be in my grave along with my child before you can harm me."

Sarah suddenly started to howl. The spasms had begun again. Jacob was pushed from the room and rebuked for being there. He found himself among the men, women, and girls who had not been able to get in. Questions came at him from all sides but he did not answer.

"Why don't they bring the rabbi?"

"They went to get him."

"First they must remove the child and then the dybbuk," one man said.

"Why didn't Gershon's wife lend her bowl?"

"Because she's so noble."

"What's the sex of this dybbuk, male or female?"

"Female."

"I never heard of one female entering another."

There was silence and everyone listened to Sarah's groans. Men bowed their heads; women covered their faces as if ashamed of Eve's curse. The midwife stuck her head out the door.

"Run and bring the bowl. She's sinking fast."

Jacob lunged. "Let me in."

"No, not now."

The rabbi had entered the street, accompanied by his father-in-law, Gershon, and his brother-in-law, the ritual slaughterer.

The latter was carrying a utensil, which was at first thought to be Beile Pesche's bowl, but turned out to be a pan filled with burning coals. A ram's horn was stuck in the rabbi's pocket. At Gershon's command the crowd parted and the dignitaries walked through. Trailing behind, carrying a white robe and a prayer shawl, was Joel, the beadle and town grave digger. Gershon, as befitted his position, began to talk loudly.

"Women, make way for the rabbi. We are going to exorcise the dybbuk."

"No men can come in now," a woman called from inside.

"We can't just stand here and wait."

"It's not a dybbuk," Jacob said. "There's no dybbuk."

"What is it, then?" Gershon asked, even though Jacob and he were not on speaking terms.

"Leave her in peace."

"Men, in that room is a demon residing in the body of a woman. Dare we permit her to defile this whole community?" Gershon said, haranguing the crowd. Then, pointing at Jacob, he continued, "He came to us a mere teacher but now he's become a big man. He has a wife with a devil inside her. Because of such people plagues are sent down."

"First the child must be removed," a woman said sagely.

"Perhaps there isn't any child in her womb," another woman suggested. "It may be the dybbuk."

"I have seen the child's head."

"Demons have heads too."

"Demons have hair."

"No."

"If she dies with the child in her womb, the whole community will be imperiled," the rabbi warned.

"Shouldn't we blow the ram's horn out here?" the beadle asked.

"No, first we must implore the dybbuk to leave her," the rabbi announced.

Again there was silence. Roosters began to crow, answering each other. These fowl would be sacrificed on the day before Yom Kippur; there was something both solemn and awesome in their recitative as if they already knew what lay in store for them. The dogs, hanging around the butcher shops, started barking. A warm breeze blew from the fields and swamps; the night had turned hot and humid. Jacob covered his face with his hands.

"Father in heaven, save her."

V

I will say nothing, Jacob decided. Now that she is speaking I must be still. He stood, lips tightly sealed, determined to endure his tribulations to the end, knowing that now he could not escape unharmed. Sarah mortally ill, probably delirious, had divulged their closely guarded secret. Prayer alone was left to him but his lips refused to open even to prayer. Sarah's fate had been decided by heaven which had determined also that he and probably the child too must die with her. I must recite my confession, he thought, and he murmured inwardly: We have trespassed, we have been faithless, we have robbed, we have spoken basely ... He heard people talking to him but the words made no sense. Sarah wept continually, and then finally became silent. But she could not have died, because again they were speaking about driving out the dybbuk. The men were arguing unsuccessfully with the women who were now in charge, about entering the room. A compromise was reached: the men would stand in the doorway. Admonishing the dybbuk, the rabbi pleaded with it to desert the woman's body, but no voice issued from Sarah. At the rabbi's command, the beadle blew the ram's horn; first a long blast, then three staccato ones, then nine swift grace notes in succession.

A few minutes later, Pilitzky's carriages drove up to the house accompanied by retainers bearing torches. The entourage resembled an invading army or demons parading in Gehenna. Pilitzky dismounted, inquiring:

"What's going on here, Jews? Has the devil taken over?"

"My lord," someone answered, "a dybbuk has entered Jacob's wife. It's been screaming from her throat."

"I don't hear any screams. Where is she?"

"She's in labor. It was screaming before. Here's Jacob." Pilitzky glanced at Jacob.

"What's going on with your wife? Is she talking again?"

"I know nothing, my lord. I have ceased knowing anything."

"Well, it's clear enough to me. She's as dumb as I'm blind. I want to speak to her."

"My lord, no men are allowed," the women called from inside.

"Nevertheless, I'm going in."

"Cover her. Cover her."

Pilitzky entered and addressed Sarah, but she did not answer. The women listened in silence. The younger matrons had already gone home to nurse their babies, and many of the older women had hastened off to the study house. The rabbi had left too. Gershon lounged against a tree outside, appearing asleep on his feet. He had removed his hat on Pilitzky's arrival and had been about to run and kiss his master's hand, but the lord of Pilitz had turned his back on him. This was Jacob's second sleepless night, and he stood numb from fatigue but with his eyes still open. He had wrestled with God as had the Patriarch Jacob, but his defeat had brought more than a dislocated thigh. He, Jacob, the son of Eliezer, had been utterly destroyed by heaven. No longer did he fear anything, not even Gehenna. He deserved no better, having cohabited with the daughter of Jan Bzik and then illicitly converted her. What did he expect? In these days justice ruled untempered by mercy. Jacob heard Sarah groaning.

"Gracious lord, let me die in peace."

"So you are not dumb. You never have been. This was a little comedy that you and your husband played."

"It's the dybbuk, my lord, the dybbuk," someone interrupted.

"Silence. You don't have to tell me. I know what a dybbuk is," Pilitzky said, raising his voice. "When the devil enters a woman, he speaks with his own voice. She uses her own. That's the same voice I heard when she thought I meant to harm her husband. Isn't that true? What's your name? Sarah?"

"Let me die, worthy lord, let me die."

"You'll die, you'll die. And when your soul leaves your body, I won't stop it. But for the moment you're living. Tell me, why did you pretend to be mute?"

"I can tell you nothing."

"If you won't, your husband will. We'll pour hot oil on his head, then he'll talk."

"My lord, what do you wish from me? Have you no pity for the dying?"

"Tell the truth before you die. Don't go to the grave still lying."

"The truth is that I loved him and still love him. I regret nothing, my lord. No, nothing."

"Who are you? You speak like a mountaineer, not like a Jewess."

"I am a daughter of Israel, my lord. Jacob's God is my God. Where is the rabbi? I want to make my confession. Where is Jacob? Jacob, where are you?"

Jacob pushed his way through the crowd.

"Here is my husband. Why don't you eat something? Women, give him something to eat. Don't be so pale, Jacob, and frightened. I'll sit with the angels and look down on you. I'll see that no harm befalls you. I'll sing with the choiring angels and pray to God for you."

Sarah intoned all this in Polish and the women stood open-mouthed. Neither Sarah's way of speaking nor her manner was that of a daughter of Israel. Suddenly they remembered she didn't look Jewish, that she had a snub nose, high cheekbones, teeth which were strangely white, strong, and sharp, unlike those found among the Jews. Pilitzky asked:

"Where are you from? The mountains?"

"I have nobody, my lord, neither father, nor mother, nor sister, nor brother. I have erased them from my mind. My father was a good man, and I'll meet him if he's in heaven. Remember, all of you, don't hurt Jacob. You can find him a wife when I'm dead, but don't torture him with your talk. I'll defend him. I'll kneel before God's throne and pray for his safety."

"You were born a Christian, weren't you?"

"I was born when Jacob found me."

"Well, everything's clear."

"What's clear, my lord? It's clear that I'm dying and will take my child with me to the grave. And I had hoped that God would grant me a son, and that I would still have a few good years with my husband..."

Suddenly Sarah started to sing in a half yodel, half sob. The song was one Jacob had often heard on the mountain, the ballad of an orphaned girl who fell into the hands of a forest spirit and was carried to a Smok's cave. The Smok made her his concubine and, forced to endure his demonic love, she longed for the mountains, the Gazdas, and her lover at home. Now it seemed as if Sarah no longer knew where she was. She lay, her cheeks swollen, her eyes half shut, her head uncovered, and chanted in a hoarse voice. Pilitzky crossed himself. The women wrung their hands.

Suddenly Sarah was silent, her thoughts turned inward. Then, again, she started chanting; Jacob's eyes clouded and he viewed everything as if through water. He remembered a passage from the Book of Aboth: "Whosoever profanes the Name of Heaven in secret will suffer the penalty of it in public." He wanted to go and comfort Sarah, wipe the sweat from her brow, but his feet were like wood. Pilitzky took him by the arm and led him outside.

"Look, you'd better leave town," he said conspiratorially. "The priests will burn you. And they'll be right to do it."

"How can I run away at such a time?"

"She'll be dead shortly. I pity you, Jew. That's why I'm warning you."

Pilitzky stepped into his carriage and drove off.

ELEVEN

I

The baby, a boy, born the next day, arrived crying too loudly for a newborn child. Sarah remained in a stupor and the women took care of the infant; a young mother with an abundance of milk nursed him. It was the day before Yom Kippur and the townspeople were busy with the sacrificial fowl and preparations for the holiday. Yet Gershon demanded a meeting of the community elders. What was said in this secret conclave was never told; but the rabbi forbade the cheder boys to read the Shema at Sarah's bedside, and prohibited attendance at the ceremony requesting peace for the male child customarily held on the Sabbath after the birth. The rabbi went further and instructed his brother-in-law, the ritual slaughterer who also performed the circumcisions, that for the time being the child should not be circumcised. Pilitz was in an uproar. The uninstructed misunderstood the rabbi's decision and maintained that it was Gershon who had instigated his son-in-law to humiliate Jacob. But those who knew the Talmud explained the verdict. According to the law, the child is born into its mother's faith. It was clear Sarah was a gentile— even the name substantiated that she was a convert. But what rabbinical court would have upheld the conversion of a gentile when the punishment for such an act was death? How could the community accept her when acceptance meant a criminal indictment? God forbid. Misfortunes and evils could only attend such an act. In the study house, Gershon demanded that Jacob be excommunicated, publicly exhibited in an ox cart and driven out of Pilitz. What a heinous crime, Gershon shouted. Jacob from mere lust had passed off a gentile as a daughter of Israel. Now even those who had sided with Jacob agreed with Gershon. And since Gershon remained out of favor with Pilitzky another envoy was sent to explain the position taken by the Jews.

The next day Sarah still lay helpless. The women refused to visit her knowing that according to Polish law she too had committed a capital crime. Only one old woman came a few times to inquire after her and leave some chicken broth which Sarah couldn't swallow. Yom Kippur would begin at sundown and although eating before the fast day was considered an act of piety, Jacob had no food in the house nor could he have tolerated eating. He sat at the bedside and recited Psalms. The woman who was acting as wet nurse had taken the child to her own home and Jacob could not go to visit his son since he had no one to leave with Sarah. Nor was it certain that the family would have permitted him to enter their house, for though he had not as yet been officially excommunicated he soon would be. The townspeople, he noticed, no longer passed by his house. His acts, in a perverse way, were an offense to the government, the community and to God. He was ashamed to say the verses of the Psalms. How could his lips utter such holy words? How could his prayer be acceptable? Now he was receiving his retribution in all its harshness. Any day he might be burned at the stake.

As he sat with the sick woman, holding the Book of Psalms in his hands, he made a spiritual accounting. His family had been killed; for five years he had been Jan Bzik's slave, sleeping with the cattle in the barn or with the mice in the granary. True, he had lusted for Jan Bzik's daughter and had wanted her as his wife. But had not the author of the Psalms, King David, lusted for Bathsheba? And if the Bible was to be accepted as the literal truth, then David had committed a far worse sin than he had. God had forgiven David. Why not Jacob, who had never sent a man out to be killed in battle?

But Jacob knew that these thoughts themselves were forbidden. The Talmud explained that King David had not been a sinner, that Uriah the Hittite had left a divorce for Bathsheba before he marched out to battle. The Gemara and the Midrash also defended the people of the Bible. But, just the same, those great ancient figures had lusted carnally, and had married outside of their nation. Moses had taken an Ethiopian as a wife, and Miriam had become leprous when she slandered him. Jehudah who had given his name to the Jews had had intercourse with a woman he thought was a harlot. King Solomon, himself, the greatest sage, had married the daughter of Pharaoh, and yet the Song of Songs and the Proverbs were holy. And what of the Jews now? Did they all strictly obey the commands of the Torah? His years of wandering with Sarah had made him aware of many wrongs he had ignored before. Legalisms and rituals proliferated without diminishing the narrow-mindedness of the people; the leaders ruled tyrannically; hatred, envy, and competition never ceased. Before Yom Kippur the Jews made peace with one another, but the night after quarrels broke out all over again. Perhaps that was why God sent men like Chmielnicki, why the exile lasted so long and the Messiah did not come.

Jacob dipped a finger in water to moisten Sarah's lips, bent over her, touched her forehead, and whispered to her. She lay as if already in the beyond, sunk in contemplation, receiving, it seemed to Jacob, the answers to those unanswerable questions that the living ask. Her chin trembled; the veins of her temples throbbed. It was as if she were arguing with the higher powers. Is that how it is? the smile that occasionally came to her lips seemed to say. How could I, Jan Bzik's daughter, ever have known that? I wouldn't have guessed it in a million years.

She is good, he thought, really a saint, a thousand times better than any of the others. Have they been to heaven and learned what God likes? Worry and fear, the isolation in which he found himself, had made him rebellious. He was even ready to struggle with God himself. Of course, God was the only God, awesome and all powerful, but it was only fair that his justice be universal. He should not be a tyrant like Gershon, fawning on the strong and spitting at the weak. Was it Sarah's fault who her parents were? Had she had the freedom to choose her mother's womb? If such as she must burn in Gehenna, then there was even inequity in heaven.

Dusk was beginning to fall, and the Jews were going in slippers or in their stockinged feet to pray. They wore white robes, prayer shawls, and on their heads gold-embroidered miters. The women were adorned with capes, fancy headgear, dresses with trains. Candles burned in the windows. A wailing rose from the houses. Everyone in Pilitz had lost someone in the massacres, and now Jacob's anger turned to pity. A tortured people. A people whom God had chosen for affliction, raining down on them all the tortures in the Book of Punishment.

The door opened and the old woman entered bearing half a chicken, a chalah, and a piece of fish for Jacob to eat before the fast started. No one else would come near him but at her age she had nothing to lose. Her face was yellow as wax, dry as a fig, and the wrinkles on her forehead were like the script on an ancient parchment. For a few moments she stood at the sick woman's beside, her eyes still young, looking up at Jacob with a motherly understanding. Her hairy chin shook as she made an effort to speak. Finally she said:

"Let your prayer for a good year be answered. Everything can still be all right. God is good."

The old woman raised her voice in a wail.

II

Late that night, Sarah opened her eyes. Her lips moved and Jacob heard her half-choked voice coming to him as if from a distance. He had the feeling that her voice and body were no longer connected. He bent over her, and she muttered in Polish.

"Jacob, is it Yom Kippur yet?"

"Yes, Sarah, Yom Kippur eve."

"Why aren't you in the synagogue?"

"I'll go there again as soon as you are well."

Sarah closed her eyes and meditated on this. Jacob thought she had fallen asleep. When she opened her eyes again, she said:

"I will be dead soon."

"No, you will get better and live many more years."

"Jacob, my feet are dead already."

He tried to feed her some broth, but her teeth locked, and the soup dribbled out. He remained leaning over her, clasping her hands. He had prayed so much in the last days and weeks, but now he had given up and even the wish for prayer had evaporated. Heaven had not listened to his supplications. The gates of mercy had been closed to him. He looked at Sarah, realizing that he was her murderer. If he had not touched her, if she had remained in her village, she would still be healthy and vital. Every sin, no matter how small, ends in murder, Jacob said to himself. He felt a love such as he had never known before, but equally a helplessness. There was a midnight silence in the room. Two candles standing in a box of sand flickered and cast shadows. The kerchief had fallen from Sarah's head and her scalp, covered with short hair like a boy's, was the color of straw and fire. He didn't know what to do. Should he go and get someone? Disturb people on the holiday? No one could help anyway. He sat on a stool by the bed, unable even to think now. Within him there was a great emptiness. Crush me, Father in heaven, crush me! In the Psalmist's words, "And my sorrow is continually before me." Now his only desire was to die with her. He had forgotten the child. He wanted to descend into Sheol from which none return.

Suddenly Sarah opened her eyes and spoke, her voice firm and clear as if she were again well.

"Jacob—see Father."

Jacob looked around.

"What did you say?"

"Don't you see him? There he is." Sarah stared at the door.

"Good evening, Father," she said. "You've come for your Wanda. You haven't forgotten. I'll come with you soon, Father. But wait, wait another few minutes. How well you look, Father, all in light."

Jacob turned to the door and saw nothing. Sarah was silent. Her eyes began to shrink in their sockets, the pupils contracting into opaqueness. Jacob spoke to her but she did not answer, nor give any sign that she heard. Then she said:

"See Grandmother too. How beautiful you look. I was your favorite granddaughter. You've come for me too. Oh, how I loved you. You and Father. Now we'll always be together."

"Sarah," Jacob cried. "You'll get better. You are the mother of a child. You have a son."

"Yes."

"You must live—for him and for me."

"No, Jacob."

He continued to call to her but she did not answer. Her eyes stayed shut. She lay absorbed in meditations that could not be interrupted. Something was happening within her. Jacob could see that the journey to where she was going was not easy. She seemed to be engaged in a dispute with some power external to her, arguing with it, struggling. Whatever power was forcing her from life also would not accept her in death. An accusation was being made and her glazed eyes seemed to be imploring: No more. No more. I'm tired. Leave me in peace. Jacob sought to have her make her confession, wanted her to die with the words, Hear O Israel, on her lips, but it was too late for that. How strange that these gentile spirits had found their way here on of all nights Yom Kippur eve. But who knew the secrets of heaven and earth? Again and again, Jacob turned to look at the door. Perhaps he too would see the ghost of Jan Bzik.

His head slumped forward and he fell into the sweet forgetfulness of sleep. He awoke, glanced at Sarah, and knew that she was dead. Her jaw had sagged, one of her eyes was open, one closed. The face was no longer recognizable. Now the struggle had ended, her chapped lips seemed to say, I've passed through everything. All is well now. The face was peaceful and acquiescent; this was no longer the sick, the tormented, the martyred Sarah who had estranged herself from both Jews and gentiles, and lost her home and her language. The corpse, at last beyond the reach of finite good and evil, forgave. Sarah's body was here, but her spirit had already climbed to heights unreachable for flesh. Jacob's sight became as if visionary, and he saw her entering a heavenly mansion. He did not cry but his cheeks became damp. His love for her had begun with lust; now nine years later he watched over the body of a saint. But the burial society, Jacob knew, would refuse to inter her in a Jewish cemetery. Moreover, the gentiles threatened him direly. Nothing that was related to this earth was of any importance to him now. In the presence of this peace, all anxiety left him. He bent down and kissed her forehead.

"Holy soul."

The door opened and a few men and women from the burial society entered. A tall man in a fur hat and white robe cried out:

"What are you doing? That's forbidden."

"He's out of his head," another said.

A woman put a feather to Sarah's nostrils. The feather did not move.

III

Gershon breached custom once more and called a meeting of the elders and the burial society immediately Yom Kippur ended. After the debate had gone on for an hour, Jacob was sent for. He was sitting watch over the corpse, but the beadle now took his place. Offered cake and wine by the rabbi's wife, Jacob refused.

"A second Yom Kippur has begun for me," he said.

"You should eat. One fast day is sufficient," the rabbi answered.

At the insistence of those present, Jacob took a spoonful of rice and a cup of water. The meeting wanted information from Jacob, nothing less than the complete truth.

"What you have done bears on the welfare of the whole community," the rabbi pointed out. "We imperil the town if we break the law. You know well enough what we have suffered. So tell us the truth. If you have sinned, don't be ashamed. This is the night after Yom Kippur and all Jews have been purified."

The speech was unnecessary since Jacob had already decided to tell the truth. As soon as he started to talk everyone became quiet. He told them who he was, who his father and grandfather had been, how Polish robbers had captured him and sold him to Jan Bzik, and how he had lain illicitly with Bzik's daughter, how the Jews of Josefov had ransomed him, how, longing for Wanda, he had later returned to the village, and how, since she could not speak Yiddish correctly, she had pretended to be mute. So quiet was it in the study house that the buzzing of a fly could have been heard. Every once in a while a listener sighed. This was not the first strange story those assembled had listened to. Ever since the massacres all sorts of peculiar things had been heard of: Jews turned Christian or Mohammedan; daughters of Israel married to Cossacks, sold into harems; women who remarried only to find their husbands returning. Stories to tell for generations to come! Yet, that a young scholar from a fine family should fall in love with a peasant girl, convert her in defiance of both the Jewish and gentile law—this was something new. Gershon's yellow eyes bulged, his mustache quivered like a tomcat's, and he clenched his fist on the table. The others glanced at one another and shook their heads. The moment Jacob stopped talking, Gershon said:

"You have betrayed Israel. You're a monster!"

"Men, this is no time to preach morality," a white-bearded elder interrupted.

"You know the law," the rabbi said hesitantly to Jacob. "Your son is not a Jew. The mother was not converted with the consent of the community."

"She went to the ritual bath. She observed the laws."

"That is immaterial. She was not accepted. Moreover, the laws of this country apply to us, too."

"These are unusual times. Is it the child's fault?"

"He was born and conceived in sin."

"Must he remain uncircumcised?"

"Take your bastard and go elsewhere," Gershon shouted. "We're not going to pay with our heads for your lechery."

"What about the body?" the white-bearded elder asked. "Interment in the cemetery is out of the question." They were still arguing when Jacob rose and left. He walked slowly through the streets with bowed head. Now he knew what he was: a branch torn from its trunk. Excommunication was certain. He wanted to see the child but decided it was more important to watch over the corpse. While he had been sitting night and day at the sick bed, he had been meditating. What happened was no accident. Everything was preordained. True, the will was free, but heaven also made its ordinances. He had been driven, he knew, by powers stronger than himself. How else could he have found his way back from Josefov to the mountain village? It had been his feet that had led him. And Sarah had hinted, even before she became pregnant, that she would die giving birth. The night before, her words had returned to him, and he knew she must have been granted some prophetic power. But whom could he tell such things? Who would believe him?

But now he at least understood his religion: its essence was the relation between man and his fellows. Man's obligations toward God were easy to perform. Didn't Gershon have two kitchens, one for milk, and one for meat? Men like Gershon cheated, but they ate matzoth prepared according to the strictest requirements. They slandered their fellow men, but demanded meat doubly kosher. They envied, fought, hated their fellow Jews, yet still put on a second pair of phylacteries. Rather than troubling himself to induce a Jew to eat pork or kindle a fire on the Sabbath, Satan did easier and more important work, advocating those sins deeply rooted in human nature.

But what could he, Jacob, do? Become a prophet and castigate the people? He who had himself broken the Torah?

He arrived home and relieved the beadle, sat down to watch over the body. The corpse lay on the floor now, covered by his overcoat, the feet towards the door. Behind the head, the stumps of yesterday's candles still burned. The previous night, it had seemed to him several times that the corpse had moved, and he had uncovered Sarah's face, and tried to wake her, suspecting catalepsy. But hour by hour, she had grown stiffer. The body was altering, and one could see that she was moving further and further from this earth. Jacob raised the eyelids, but the pupils were blank. Even the expression of acquiescence had vanished. Clearly, she was no longer there. Unable to gaze at her longer, Jacob covered her again. He took out the Psalter from his bookcase and began to recite the Psalm: "Deliver me out of the mire, and let me not sink ... Reproach hath broken my heart; and I am full of heaviness ... Make haste, O God, to deliver me; make haste to help me, O Lord."

IV

The clatter of horses' hoofs sounded in the night. Jacob knew what that meant. The door slammed open and a dragoon with a plumed helmet and twisted mustache thrust his head in. He saw the corpse lying on the floor and was silent for a moment. Then he spoke:

"If you're Jacob, come with me."

"Who will watch over the body?"

"Let's go. I have my orders."

Jacob bent and for the last time uncovered Sarah's face, which seemed to be smiling. He had closed the mouth but the jaws opened again; the teeth no longer seemed to fit the gums; the tongue was lumpy and blackish. He wanted to say goodbye but he didn't know how. I should take some clothes or a shirt, he thought, but he didn't move. Again he covered the body and said:

"All right, I'm ready."

The moment he was in the street he thought of his prayer shawl and phylacteries and asked the soldier to let him return for them. But the soldier blocked his way. The moon, not yet full, had crossed the sky to the horizon. Everywhere, shutters were closed. Even the grasshoppers and frogs were silent. A

mounted dragoon held the first one's horse by the reins. Jacob
had the feeling that he had lived through this before or seen
it in a dream. He thought of calling out to the people not to
leave Sarah's body unattended, but was held back by a youthful
embarrassment. He was trembling, not from fear but from the
cold. He recalled that the night before a mouse had approached
the body and he had had to chase it away. But what difference
did it make whether the corpse was eaten by mice or worms?
The first dragoon dragged out a long chain, tied one end to
Jacob's wrist, and attached the other to his saddle. The second dragoon dismounted to help, the two handling the prisoner like butchers trussing an ox to be led to slaughter. They
spoke, but only to each other. Only now did Jacob remember
the child. Well, the boy would have neither father nor mother.
He had been born under a dark star. Jacob wanted to ask the
soldier to take him to the house where the baby was but realized that his request would be refused. He fixed his eyes on
the chinks in the shutter where could be seen the glimmer of
the candles burning at the head of the corpse. Does she know
what's happening to me? he asked himself. Or is her soul so
distant it is no longer connected with this world? The dragoons
rode slowly, Jacob following. He realized they were taking him
to another town. Pilitz was left behind, and they moved past
fields that had already been harvested. He was marching to
his death, yet Jacob breathed in deeply, filling his lungs with
the cool night air. For days now he had done nothing but sit
with the sick woman and then with her corpse. Inactivity and
stale air had enervated him. He was no longer accustomed
to not using his body. His feet wanted movement, his hands
demanded work. Now he walked between the horses, fearful
they might step on his feet or crush his ribs, although surely
such a death was more honorable than being hanged. He

wanted to recite chapters from the Psalms, but the chatter of the soldiers distracted him. The taller of the dragoons, the one who had arrested Jacob, said:

"All right, Czeslaw, how many men do you think Kasia's had already ?"

"More than you have hairs on your head."

"She only has one bastard."

"You can have her for half a grivnik."

"Still, she has a way with her."

"It's all false. She smiles at you with one eye and at your wont enemy with the other. She'll kiss you all over, but the moment you go she curses you and your mother. Then she's off to the priest to confess how she accidentally stepped on a cross of straw."

"That's a fact. Now all she talks about is getting married."

"Why not? Once she's your wife, she'll tell you to go whistle. You'll rot in camp and she'll do what she wants. You'll come home and she'll have a belly ache. With strangers she'll dance; with you she'll groan. Every year she'll present you with another bastard."

"Well, I've got to marry someone."

"Why?"

"Should I take my horse for a wife?"

"Your horse would be more faithful than Kasia."

Jacob wondered how a man who had just looked on death could speak so. Didn't these men ever contemplate their own fate? They lead me to the gallows and never bother to ask why. As if guessing his thoughts the soldiers became silent. The horses' pace slackened. Jacob, cooled by a breeze, felt a calm such as he had never known before, and raised his eyes to the sky. So, the heavens were still there, created by the same God who had formed both the rider and the horse. He had made the chain strong. Suddenly it occurred to Jacob that sometimes chains could be broken. Nowhere was it written that a man must consent to his own destruction. Instantly his mood changed. He was angry. Powers slumbering within him awoke. He now knew what to do. He wanted to laugh. The moon had set, he noticed. Edging over toward Czeslaw, the smaller of the two dragoons, he struck his horse with an elbow. The animal broke into a gallop, veered off into the underbrush. The tall dragoon shouted, reached for his sword. Jacob yanked the chain and the tall dragoon's saddle came apart. The horse stumbled and nearly fell. Regaining its balance, this mare also bolted. Jacob ran into the fields with a speed and lightness that astounded him. There was no place to hide, but the dragoons would not risk injuring the legs of their mounts pursuing him across the stubble. Soon all was silent and he was surrounded by darkness.

I must reach a forest before sunrise, he warned himself, amazed at what had happened. But which way should he run? He had outwitted the powerful, broken the chain of slavery, but despite his escape, he felt no elation. He kept on going blindly and for how long he did not know. Time had become dreamlike. The chain dragged; he felt its weight on his hand. Bending down, he groped on the ground, not realizing at first what he was looking for. He found a stone and used it to pry the chain from his wrist. Where would he hide it? There was no ditch or stream around; like a dog with a bone, he dug a hole with his fingers and buried the chain. Only half awake, he knew he was in the fields, but at the same time he seemed to be in Josefov. He was surprised to discover that Gershon and the widow of Hrubyeshoyv were married. How could this be? Gershon's wife hadn't died. Had the edict of Rabbi Gershom the Light of the Diaspora come to an end? Shaking his head to clear it, Jacob got up and stumbled on across the stubble. Sky and earth fused in the darkness. He heard someone sighing, and knew that it was neither man nor beast but one of those who hover in the night; something wet and warn, like spittle, fell on Jacob's forehead. Under his feet, the earth seemed to sway. He walked dragging his legs as if they were no longer a part of his body. He saw a red pool shining like blood on the ground before him. Billowing smoke mingled with sparks rose in front of him as if from a burning village. He fell face down on the ground, overcome by sleep.

He awoke and it was day. Coils of mist hovered over the naked fields. A crow flew low and croaked. At the edge of the horizon to his left a forest stretched like a sash of blue, and emerging from it like the head of a newborn child, small and bloody red, came the sun.

V

Jacob lay in the forest and slept. But even in his sleep he clutched a heavy stick. The day was warm and the sunlight filtered through the pines. His was the deep sleep of those who have ceased to hope. Each time he woke, he wondered, Where am I running? Why did I escape?—and then exhaustion overwhelmed him again. He dreamed he was in the barn on the mountain and Wanda brought him food. He stood on the rock and watched her climbing from the valley dressed like a queen in jewels and purple robes, a crown on her head, golden milk pails in her hands. When, he asked himself, did Wanda become a Polish queen? Where was her retinue? Why did she need gold milk pails? It must be a dream. He awoke. The forest echoed with the songs of birds. His stomach ached with hunger. He dozed again. Today is her funeral, he said to himself, waking. They will give her a donkey's burial, outside the fence. His grief was too great to permit him to stay awake. Sleep like an opiate drugged him.

He was with her again, but now she was both Wanda and Sarah; Sarah-Wanda, he called her, amazed at the coupling of these names. How strange: Josefov and the mountain hamlet had also merged. Wanda was his wife, and he sat in his father-in-law's library and she brought him the Sabbath fruit. The massacres and the years of slavery had become the dream. But as he told Sarah-Wanda this, her eyes filled with tears and her face paled.

"No, Jacob, it happened."

He heard her speak and knew she was dead.

"What must I do now?"

"Fear not, Jacob my slave."

"Where shall I go?"

"Go with the child."

"Where?'

"To the other side of the Vistula."

"I want to be with you."

"Not yet."

"Where are you?"

She did not answer. Her smile awoke him and for a few moments her image lingered, white and shining, framed between the tree trunks. He reached out his hands and she disappeared. Again he slept and when he awoke the setting sun shone red in the thickets, while above the crowns of the pines, the sky flamed. Jacob remembered that he had not put on phylacteries since he had fled but this was his first day of mourning and so praying in prayer shawl and phylacteries was forbidden him. He moved into the brush searching for food: the blueberries had withered, but not the blackberries, and he gorged himself. Yet he remained hungry. Evening had fallen but the forest murmurs did not cease. Eerie laughter came from the branches, night birds calling. Another nocturnal bird repeated the same shrill warning over and over again like a prophet. The moon rose and dew fell as if through a heavenly sieve. The moss gave off warm, spicy odors. Jacob's head ached. He stumbled through a tangle of underbrush and trees, knowing he couldn't stay where he was. Here he would starve or fall prey to wolves. But there was no path out. He caught sight of a figure among the trees, ran calling to it, and saw it evaporate. Voices were chattering all around him and he wondered if he were already in the hands of the demons. To protect himself, he recited, "Hear O Israel," and then forced himself to envisage each letter of the word, Jehovah. His foot plunged into mud as he skirted a swamp; pine cones struck him as if thrown by hidden hands. He slid on beds of fallen pine needles. He walked toward the moon. The forest was savage yet he knew that even here Providence tended each fern and grub. He listened and heard the many voices around him, each unique, and, uniting all, the inimitable voice of the forest. Overcome by fatigue, he sat down on a couch of moss near a tree trunk. He felt the approach of death and once more cried out to Wanda.

His strength ebbed from him and the earth he rested on became suddenly near and dear. The grave is a bed, he thought, a most comfortable bed. If men knew this, they would not be so fearful.

VI

Sand dunes stretched out and down like steps and at the bottom Jacob saw the Vistula quiet, deep, half silver, half a greenish black. Walking and dreaming, he had come to the edge of the forest. The landscape was as empty as on the first day of Creation. Jacob walked and the moon walked with him. The pleated sand, here and there as white as chalk, brought to his mind the deserts he had read of in the Pentateuch. The sight of the river made him hasten— he had not tasted water since the day

before. The closer he came to it, the wider the river became. At
the shore, bending down to drink from his cupped hands, he
recalled the story of Gideon in the Book of Judges. He sat down
to rest in the cool breeze and saw shadowy nets trembling on the
surface of the water as if cast by some unseen fisherman. Stars
dropped from the sky into the waves and hovering glowworms
flared. Jacob again wanted to sleep but some power warned him
not to, and, overcoming his weariness, he rose, climbed a pile of
rocks and looked about him. Far off to the right, he saw something which could be a barge, a raft, a mill. He walked along the
shore toward it.

Nearing the object, he discovered that it was a ferryboat,
moored by thick ropes to piles; not far from the boat were a hut
and a dog house. As he approached the landing, a barking dog
ran toward him and a moment later a man came out of the hut.
He was as black as a gipsy, barefoot, half naked, with long, curly
hair, and wore trousers turned up to the knee. Scolding the dog
in a rasping voice, he walked up to Jacob and said:

"The ferry doesn't run at night."

"Where does it go?"

"Where? To the other side."

"Is there a town there?"

"A stone's throw away."

"What's its name?"

The stranger informed Jacob. After a moment's silence, he
asked:

"You a Jew?"

"Yes, a Jew."

"How come you're not carrying bundles?"

"I don't have any."

"If you're a beggar, where's your sack?"

"This stick is all I own."

"So that's it. Some have too much, others too little. In my lifetime, I've seen everything. What happened? Were you robbed?"

"Robbers don't worry me," Jacob said, amazed at his statement.

"You're right. What have we got to lose? More than your trousers they can't take. But I do keep a spear, and you've seen the dog. Around here, they'd even run off with the ferryboat if they could. And how far would they get? Once we were crossing and this peasant woman's goose jumped into the Vistula. Two men had to keep her from going in after it. We got the goose back later. I said to her, 'Can you swim?' 'No,' she said, 'not a stroke.' 'How come you tried to jump overboard, then?' You know what she said: 'Well, it's my goose, isn't it?' Where are you from?"

"Josefov."

"Never heard of it. It must be far away."

"It is."

"Well, people come and people go. The kings don't even sit still. Everyone's come this way; the Swedes, the Muscovite, Chmielnicki. Whoever has a sword wants to live by it. But someone's got to do the work or we'd all chew rags. I'm a nobody, but I have two eyes in my head. Time's one thing I have enough of. I do plenty of thinking. You must hungry."

"I don't have any money."

"You're entitled to a piece of bread. Even jailbirds get bread and water."

The ferryman walked into the hut and returned with a slab of bread and an apple.

"Here, eat."

"Do you have a pitcher in which I can wash my hands?"

"Yes. What do you want to do that for?"

Jacob washed his hands with the water that the ferryman brought him and wiped them on his coat. After saying grace, he bit into the bread.

"I owe you thanks, but first I must thank God."

"You don't owe me a thing, or God either. I have bread so I give it to you. If I didn't have any, I'd go begging. God owns everything but the rich receive it all."

"God is the author of all riches."

"If there is a God. Have you seen Him? I had one passenger, an aristocrat, who said there wasn't."

"What kind of an aristocrat?"

"Crazy! But he talked sense. What does anyone know? In India they worship snakes. The Jews put little black boxes on their heads, and shawls. I know. A lot of them used to use this ferry. But along gallops Chmielnicki; there were so many corpses floating in the Vistula the river stank. That's what their God did for them."

"The evildoers will be punished."

"Where? There was a brute of a count in Parchev who flogged I don't know how many hundreds of peasants to death but he lived to be ninety-eight. His serfs set his castle on fire, and down came the rain and saved it. He died peacefully sipping a glass of wine. I say: the worms get everyone, good and bad."

"Yet, you give me bread."

"So! Don't take it as an insult but I feed hungry animals, too."

VII

The ferryman, whose name was Waclaw, took Jacob into his hut and gave him a pillow stuffed with straw. There was only one bench to sleep on so Jacob lay on the floor. The ferryman talked:

"One thing I've learned in my life: don't get attached to anything. You own a cow or a horse and you're its slave. Marry and you're the slave of your wife, her bastards, and her mother. Look at Pilitzky, all his life scared he'll be robbed, while he's being bled dry. When he married that whore, she only had to look twice at a man and he was sending around his seconds. The worst bitch this side of the Vistula. A hunk of filth. She's had a stallion as her lover, and of course the coachman. Did you know her husband finds her lovers? If that isn't being a slave, what is? When I hear such things, I say to myself, Waclaw, not you. You'll be nobody's slave. I'm not a peasant. I have noble blood. True, I don't know who my father was, but what's the difference? My mother came from a fine house. They wanted to apprentice me to a shoemaker and marry me off to his daughter. A dowry and all the trimmings went with her. So did a mother, grandmother, and sisters. The dust didn't settle under my feet. Here at the ferry I'm as free as a bird. I think what I please. Twice a day the passengers come and I do my job. No one bothers me the rest of the time. I don't even go to church. What does the priest want? To put another rope around my neck."

"No, man cannot be entirely free," Jacob said, after some consideration.

"Why not?"

"Somebody must plow and sow and reap. Children must be raised."

"Well, not by me. Let the others do it."

"A woman bore you and brought you up."

"I didn't ask for it. She wanted to have a man, so she did."

"But if there is a child, it must be fed, clothed, and taught, or it will grow up a wild animal."

"Let them grow as they please."

Waclaw began to snore. Yes, it is true, Jacob meditated, only half asleep himself, man goes in harness, every desire is a strand of the rope that yokes him. Jacob fell asleep, awoke, dozed off again, woke with a start. What should he do? Leave and desert the child? But where would he go? What would he do? Marry again? He had already stepped under the canopy twice, and now his two wives and three children were in the other world. He would be more at home there than here. A cold wind was blowing from the Vistula and he tried to warm himself with the heat from his own body. His brain stayed awake and he could hear himself snoring. He mustn't stay here long; people would soon be coming to the crossing, and the dragoons might be on his trail. But perhaps it was better to be caught and hanged.

Jacob fell into a deep sleep, and when he opened his eyes the sun was shining. Waclaw stood over him.

"You got yourself a little sleep, eh?"

"I was exhausted."

"Go on sleeping. There's nothing better. If someone who doesn't belong here shows up, I'll let you know."

"Why do you do all this?"

"Your head must be worth a couple of grivniks…" And Waclaw winked.

As Waclaw left, closing the door behind him, Jacob heard the sound of approaching wagons and realized there must be a road across the dunes. Soon wagons began to pass, shaking the hut, and through chinks in the walls came smells of horse dung, tar, and sausage. He heard many people talking, though it was still early and the ferry wouldn't leave for hours. There was no water in the hut to wash with before praying. So Jacob recited, "I thank," a prayer one could say without ablutions. Blessed spirit, he murmured, where are you now? Your body must have been buried like carrion. He thought of the child, his and Sarah's, the grandson of Rabbi Eliezer of Zamosc and of Jan Bzik. He could not desert it. Did not the first Jacob rear the grandchildren of

Terah and Laban? His own son must grow up instructed in the Torah. For God, whose purpose requires both life and death, there was no such thing as good birth. In God's mills even chaff becomes flour.

Rising, he walked to the front wall and peered through the cracks. It looked like market day outside—everwhere peasants, carts, oxen, pigs, calves. On the ferryboat near a sack stood a strange little man in a prayer shawl and phylacteries, his face turned away from Jacob toward the east. His white gabardine and embroidered prayer shawl were unlike any seen in Poland, and he was wearing sandals and white stockings. He bowed so low praying that the phylactery on his head almost touched the deck; he seemed to be reciting the eighteen benedictions. When he turned, Jacob saw the stranger's white beard that extended to his waist, and knew that this man had been sent to him. Degraded as he was, heaven no longer trusted in his wisdom to choose freely, but was leading him step by step along the road that he must follow. Jacob could no longer remain in the hut, but had to go and present himself to the stranger.

VIII

The man finished his prayers, replaced his phylacteries in their cases and put on an abaya, the kind of coat worn by messengers from the Holy Land and by Jews from Egypt, Yemen, Persia. Jacob approached the man and greeted him with a Sholom, expecting to receive a reply in Aramaic or Hebrew, but when the stranger spoke, it was in Yiddish.

"A Jew, eh? This place is crawling with gentiles. But I say my prayers wherever I am."

"You must be an emissary from the Holy Land."

"Yes, an emissary. The need in the land of Israel is great. We had a drought this year and on top of that a plague of locusts.

When the Arab's in trouble, what's left for the Jews? Starvation is everywhere. And thirst. Water is bought by the cupful. Well, but the Jews all over the world are merciful. Stretch out a hand to them and they give."

"When do you go back?"

"I'm on my way now, though I still must visit a few communities. Then I board ship at Constance."

"How do the Jews maintain themselves in the Holy Land?"

The emissary paused to think this over.

"Which ones? It depends. The majority are paupers and what you don't give, they don't have. But there are a few rich men. All of us were struck dumb when we heard what was going on here in Poland. The news came about Chmielnicki—may his name be blotted out—and we had a second Tischab'ov. We ran to the sacred graves and the Wailing Wall and prayed. But we were no help. The massacres must have been already decreed. How do we know what's going on in heaven? Since the destruction of the temple, the rigor of the law has prevailed. But there are signs, many signs, that the End of Days is near."

"What signs?"

"It would take too long to tell you. The Book of Daniel makes it clear to those who understand that the Redemption will come in the year 5426. Don't think we do nothing. The cabalists are busy and have uncovered all kinds of portents. Of course, everything is in God's hands but much can be done through the power of the holy names. Pure and sacred men dressed in white sit and pore over these mysteries. Are you a man of the Torah?"

"I have studied."

"Have you ever looked into the Zohar?"

"Occasionally."

"Well, the sacred names govern everything. As the Gemara says, there is an angel for each blade of grass. And if that is so, the Redemption will only come through the holy combinations. Our cabalists fast, study all night, and at dawn visit the graves of saints. The older generation is gone; we have been deprived of our pious Rabbi Isaac Luria as well as Rabbis Chaim Vital and Shlomo Alkabetz. But the tabernacle of peace in Sefad still exists and Yephtah is the Samuel of this generation. But can a man live without bread? Even Rabbi Chanina, the son of Dusso, had to have his share of St. John's bread each week. Jews all over the world must do their part. What is your name?"

"Jacob."

"Give me a little something, Reb Jacob."

And the emissary pulled out a wooden alms box. Jacob blushed.

"You won't believe me but I don't have even half a groschen."

The alms box quickly disappeared.

"How can you travel without money?"

"I am a mourner, I should be sitting shivah."

"So why aren't you?"

"I'm escaping from the gentiles."

"Then, it's you who should be receiving. Does it matter where a Jew suffers? We all have the same Father. Why are you running away?"

Jacob didn't know whether to laugh or cry. Again his story must be told. The secrets he had kept for years were now being divulged to everyone. So seemingly chance occurrences led to a predetermined end. He said to the emissary:

"Come into the hut. My story is long. I must not be seen."

"But what about the ferryman?"

"He is letting me use it."

Before seating himself on the bench, the emissary ascertained that there was no cloth there woven of both wool and linen. He was so short his legs didn't reach the floor and Jacob placed a log for his feet. Then, leaning against the wall, Jacob told everything, denied nothing, from the day the Cossacks took him captive until the night he escaped from the dragoons. The emissary nodded, grimaced, chewed his beard, rubbed his forehead, and occasionally pulled at one of his sidelocks. The deeper Jacob got into his story the more pained the emissary became. He spread his hands, raised his eyebrows, tugged at his beard. His eyes expressed sadness, compassion, astonishment. From time to time, he sighed deeply. When Jacob finished, the emissary covered his face with his hands, which were small and bony, and his lips, hidden behind his beard, murmured and shook as if he were reciting a prayer or an incantation. After a while he lowered his hands. His face seemed altered, grayer, more drawn, with deeper pockets under the eyes.

"The community is right. Your wife was a gentile and so is your son. The child follows its mother. This the law. But behind the law, there is mercy. Without mercy, there would be no law."

"Yes, yes."

"How could you have thought of doing such a thing? Well, it's done now."

"I am ready for my punishment."

"What? It's all because of the massacres and the destruction. Don't ask me what I've seen here. Nevertheless you're a learned man."

"It was not within my power to act differently."

"It seems it was not. Free will exists, but so does foreknowledge. 'All is foreseen but the choice is given.' Each soul must accomplish its task, or it would not have been sent here. The sons of Keturah were also the sons of Abraham."

"What shall I do now?"

"You must save yourself and you must save your child. First of all, he must be circumcised. When he grows up, he may have to be converted—I don't remember the law exactly but meanwhile let him be brought up as a Jew. It is written somewhere that before the Messiah will come, all the pious gentiles will have been converted."

"I don't remember the passage."

"It's somewhere in the Talmud or Midrash—what's the difference? I'll give you two guldens and when you have money, God willing, you'll give it back. Not to me personally, but to another emissary. Does it matter? The money goes to the Holy Land. The fact that you found me here is odd: I was to have preached a sermon and I would have collected a nice sum of money. But suddenly I was seized by a desire to travel. That's the way Heaven manages things."

For a while both men were silent. Then the emissary said:

"If she has already been buried, you are obliged to pray today. Take my prayer shawl and phylacteries. I'll wait and then we'll have breakfast."

TWELVE

I

The emissary tried to persuade Jacob that it would be dangerous to return to Pilitz immediately. A man's life is too important, he said, and anyway the infant was too small and weak to
be moved. Besides, the day after tomorrow was Succoth, and
a holiday is a holiday. He suggested that Jacob go to the city
with him and stay there until after Simchath Torah. But Jacob
was unyielding. He longed to see the child, and he wanted to
visit Sarah's grave. Money was hidden in his room; perhaps no
one had as yet stolen it; he could not suddenly start begging.
In his years of slavery and wandering, Jacob had grown used
to overcoming obstacles. Distances no longer frightened him,
nor dark forests, beasts, robbers; even his terror of devils and
hobgoblins had vanished. The strength he had gathered had to
be used. His escape from the dragoons meant that the king was
not as powerful as he had imagined. What would happen to
the might of the wicked if the just were not so craven? Stories
he had heard of how the Jews had behaved during the massacres shamed him. Nobody had dared lift a hand against the
butchers while they slaughtered entire communities. Though
for generations Jewish blacksmiths had forged swords, it had
never occurred to the Jews to meet their attackers with weapons. The Jews of Josefov, when Jacob had spoken of this, had

shrugged their shoulders. The sword is for Esau, not for Jacob. Nevertheless, must a man agree to his own destruction? Wanda had often asked Jacob: Why did the Jews permit it? The ancient Jews of the Bible stories had been heroic. Jacob never really knew how to answer her.

Breakfasting with the emissary on bread, cheese, and plums, Jacob hesitated, then took the two guldens, promising to return them as soon as he could. The emissary who had to stay a few more weeks in Poland told Jacob his route. Passengers, as well as horses, cows, oxen and sheep were still coming aboard the ferry. Amid the hubbub of the peasants, the neighing, bellowing, baying of the animals, the emissary advised Jacob on his future conduct. The Messiah was coming, so why stay in Poland? It was a great act of piety to settle in the Holy Land. When the Redeemer came, the Jews in the land of Israel would be the first to greet him. Moreover, a Jew could breathe more freely in the country of the Turks, where the Torah was respected. Many rich Jews lived in Istanbul, Smyrna, Damascus, and Cairo. Of course there were sometimes hostile edicts and people were falsely accused, but such catastrophes as those that happened in Poland—never. Further, since he, Jacob, had broken the ecclesiastical laws of the Christians, and the Jews too had good reason to censure his conduct, why not bring his child to the Holy Land and settle in a place where scholars were supported? He could always learn a trade or go into business if he wished. God willing by next summer the child would not be too frail to make the journey. The emissary's words were laden with half-spoken promises. He hinted that the Messiah already existed, and that where he was and when he would reveal himself was known to the most esoteric of the cabalists. He said to Jacob:

"My lips are sealed. A word to the wise is sufficient."

The emissary was about to say more, but suddenly the ferry began to move and Jacob jumped ashore. The emissary called out:

"Comfort and aid are coming. We'll live to see it—in our own lifetimes."

II

At dusk Jacob started for Pilitz and reached it by late evening. All the shutters were closed. Pilitz slept. A three-quarter moon shone in the sky. The Succoth booths, covered with green branches, had already been set up, though a few were yet unfinished. Walking abreast of his shadow, Jacob carried an oak stick and in his breast pocket a knife Waclaw had lent him. Jacob now heeded the advice of the Book of Aboth: "If one comes upon thee, to kill thee, rise first and kill him." Passing the market place quickly, he came to the house in which Sarah had died. There was no light, a sign that the corpse had already been removed. Standing momentarily at the door, overcome by terror, he sensed the presence of the corpse, not the body, nor even the soul, but something shapeless and horrible. He pushed in the door. The moonlit room resembled a ruin, the bare floor littered with straw and rags; the body must have been cleansed on the spot. Everything had been removed, all the clothing and linen, even the pots from the oven. There was something uncanny, hostile in the fetid air. The room had a wintry dankness though it was still late summer. What's wrong with me? Why should I fear her? Jacob said to himself in reproach. Wasn't she more a part of me than my own body? But he left the door open; his heart pounded, and he breathed heavily. He searched through the straw mattress but realized immediately that the money he had hidden there was gone. Thieves! And Yom Kippur had hardly passed. The men of the burial society might even have stolen it. Despite his anxiety,

Jacob was overcome with anger. They had devastated his house. The robbed had become robbers. It was a world of grabbers; whoever could, stole, and now they were going to sit in the tabernacle and invite the Holy Guests to join them. Jacob's few books were missing too. "Naked came I out of my mother's womb, and naked shall I return thither."

After kissing the mezuzah, Jacob left. Be a witness, he said. He strode toward the cemetery. Even at a distance, the new grave was visible, a fresh mound of earth far removed from the others. When he reached the mound, Jacob saw a marker, and on it the words: "Here lies Sarah, the daughter of the Patriarch Abraham." Jacob's eyes grew moist. Here lay Wanda, Sarah, the woman he loved. Although he tried to recite Kaddish, he choked on the words. Darkness enveloped him. Had the moon been extinguished? Throwing himself to the earth, he pressed his face against the grave: I am here, Sarah.

He listened as if expecting her voice to issue from the grave. A ghoulish idea came to him: to exhume her body, or at least to thrust his hand into the earth and touch her. He wanted to kiss her once more. It's forbidden, it's crazy, a sacrilege, he warned himself. Even though it was a sin, he prayed for his own death: I have wandered too long in this world. Everyone I love is there. Lying prostrate, waiting for death, he had forgotten the child. For a while his strength seemed to ebb. His legs became numb and wooden, his brain like stone. He slept as though dead, then awoke. His prayer had not been answered. Rising, he began to mumble Kaddish. The marker had fallen to one side; he straightened it.

Brushing the earth from his face, Jacob stepped back a few paces. He looked for a large rock, wanting like the Patriarch Jacob to lay a stone on the grave of his beloved wife, but there were none. Jacob returned to Pilitz. Passing the study house where a single candle burned, he opened the door. An old man sat at a stand, looking into a book. Jacob recognized Reb Tobias, of whose eight children only one daughter, the wife of Naphtali the leather merchant, remained. In the glimmering light Reb Tobias' face with its matted and dirty beard seemed dark as earth. His gabardine was bloated like the garment of a pregnant woman; since he was ruptured, every few weeks his intestines had to be pushed back in place by a woman, the only person in Pilitz who knew how, and the fact that he had to allow a woman to touch his private parts caused him more grief than the physical pain. Now at midnight he sat studying the Torah. He's not a thief, God forbid, Jacob defended him, but a victim of other people's sins. The thieves are a minority.

Jacob stood watching but the old man did not stir. Deaf and half-blind, he held the book so close his eyelids almost touched the letters and at the same time hummed with a kind of moaning singsong. Because of such men as this, God had preserved the Jews. Suddenly, as Jacob stood there, he knew exactly what he must become: an acetic who eats no meat, drinks no wine, does not sleep in a bed. He must atone for his sins. In winter he would immerse himself in cold baths, in summer lie on thorns and thistles; the sun would burn him, the flies and mosquitoes bite him. For the rest of his life and until his last breath, he must repent and ask forgiveness of God and of Sarah's sacred soul. Perhaps then he would not have to linger too long in this most imperfect of worlds.

But what if in that other world Zelda Leah claimed him? She was there with her children. But would she want him after what he had done following her death? They had never belonged together spiritually, had never truly mated; most likely she had ascended to realms of purity that he, a man of earthly passions, could never enter. And as for the children, their holy souls were undoubtedly at the very Throne of Glory.

III

Jacob knew where the young woman lived to whom he had given his child, but in the night, with all the shutters closed, her house was indistinguishable from the others. It seemed to Jacob that during even his brief absence changes had occurred in Pilitz. Lurking outside, he listened for a baby's cry. But he could not remain here forever, so, after hesitating, he decided to try one house. He raised the latch to knock, the door opened, and by the light of the moon he saw two beds and two cradles. A man grunted, a woman woke, and a child began to cry. The man asked harshly: "Who's there, huh?"

"I'm sorry. It's me, Jacob, the baby's father."

In the uneasy silence even the child stopped crying.

"Woe is me," the woman groaned.

"Did they let you out of prison?" the man asked.

"I escaped. I've come for my baby."

Once more there was silence. Then the woman sdd: "Woe is me! Where will you take an infant like this one in the middle of the night? He's too small to be moved. The least wind and, God forbid…"

"I have no choice. The soldiers are after me."

"Make a light. Make a light," the woman told her husband. "They'll arrest us. I've heard the count wants the baby. Woe, Woe. What messes people get into."

"I won't give up the child without the consent of the community," the husband said firmly. "They gave it to me, let them take it back. I don't have to suffer for other people's bastards."

"I'll pay you for your trouble."

"It's not a question of money."

The woman, after covering herself with a shawl, stood at the oven and blew into the embers. Then she lit a wick and set it in a shard of oil. Its dim light illumined the unplastered walls, the smoke-stained ceiling, the two benches – one for dairy dishes, one for meat – on which stood pots, bowls, and in a wooden trough covered with rags a loaf of dough. Diapers, swaddling clothes, and straw whisks littered the room. Garbage floated in a pan of slops. A chamber pot stood next to one bed. In one cradle lay the child who had been crying. In the other, beneath a dirty quilt lay Jacob's son: tiny, red, bald, with a large head and pale eyelids. The baby's face looked old and grief-worn. A smile reminiscent of death touched its tiny lips and unformed forehead. Jacob stared. Only now did he realize that he had a son. The woman stood on the other side of the cradle.

"Where will you take such a little baby?"

"It's murder," her husband said, from his bed where he was propped up. His fringed garment was stained; pillow feathers stuck to his skull cap, and his beard and sidelocks were stippled with wisps of down. In his black eyes there was the look of a man trapped by domesticity. Jacob knew they were right, but he realized that if he did not take the baby now he would never see it again. Recalling the dream and Sarah's words, he girded himself stubbornly.

"I'll take care of him. The night is warm."

"It's not so warm. At dawn it gets cold."

"I don't want Pilitzky to get my son."

No one spoke; this was an unanswerable argument. Jacob took out a gulden.

"This is for what you have done. I'd pay more, but they stole everything, even the dishes."

"I know. I know everything. The burial society really outdid itself. They thought that you, God forbid, would never return."

"They all grabbed except us," the husband said. "They stripped the house."

"They took my money out of the straw mattress. And right after Yom Kippur!"

"Don't fast and don't steal, my mother, peace be with her, always said," the woman commented. "She'll intercede for us in Paradise. Other people's property is sacred, she always maintained."

"That's the reason we live as we do," her husband said. "Where will you take the baby? Well, I'd better not ask."

The woman began to move about the room. She found a basket, padded it with rags and diapers, laid the baby inside and covered it with a quilt. The infant whimpered once. The woman looked at Jacob:

"He has to be nursed every few hours."

"I'll get somebody."

"When? How? Oh Mother."

And the woman began to cry.

Suddenly she said:

"Wait. I'll draw some milk from my breast, Where's the bottle?"

Her husband left his bed. Below the torn shirt, his legs were thin, crooked, hairy. He found the bottle for his wife. The noise in the room had waked the animals. The cat stretched, chickens clucked, worms crawled, a mouse poked its head out of a hole in the floor. The woman turned to the wall and squeezed milk from her breast. After a while she gave Jacob the bottle, its neck stoppered with a bit of cloth, and showed him how to pour single drops into the baby's mouth so that it would not choke. Jacob knew he was risking the child's life as well as his own; carrying the infant, he would be unable to defend himself if attacked. But he could not leave his own child, and Sarah's, among strangers and enemies. If he was destined to live, he would live. Jacob thanked the couple repeatedly, speaking of a debt which only the

Almighty could pay. Then he walked out into the night, moving in the direction of the forest, the Vistula, and the ferry. He lifted his gaze to the stars: "Father, what do you want?"

A passage from Psalms came to his lips: "O spare me, that I may recover strength, before I go hence, and be no more."

IV

The moon had set and it was dark in the forest. Slowly Jacob felt his way along a path, pausing occasionally to listen to the child's breathing or to ascertain by a kiss whether it was warm enough. He had endured many tribulations in his life, but never a more anxious night than this one. Praying so hard his lips swelled, he put himself completely into the hands of Providence, knowing he was acting improperly in relying on miracles. But thrusting his burden on God was now his only recourse. He had nothing left but his faith.

Jacob's footsteps aroused the sleeping forest. Twigs snapped under his feet; birds rose from the thickets; animals scurried for cover. He kept one hand raised over the basket to ward off branches. Every conceivable disaster occurred to him. Bears and wild boars inhabited the forest. Several times he thought he heard a wolf howling and reached for the stick thrust through his belt. Let there be day, let the sun rise, he commanded imploringly, realizing that his ambiguous words meant also: Let the Redemption come, and there be an end to this dark exile. It was safer to keep quiet, but instead he recited aloud passages of the Psalms, the Prophets, the Book of Prayer, and cried out to God: I have reached the end of the road. The waters are swirling around me. I lack the strength to endure these afflictions. Suddenly he had a desire to sing and he chanted a Yom Kippur melody which turned midway into one of the mountain songs. Each note reminded him of Sarah. As he sang, he wept.

All at once, a strange light flooded the forest, and for a second Jacob thought Heaven had heard him. All the birds began to scream and sing at once: the trunks of the pine trees seemed aflame. Far off in a clearing between the trees he saw a conflagration. A moment later, he realized it was the sun. Jacob gazed at the child, sat down, and offered it the cloth moistened with milk. At first it seemed to rebel at not receiving the breast, but finally it started to suck. For the first time in weeks, Jacob was joyful. No, not everything was lost; he still had his son. Let him, Jacob, reach the Vistula, he would cross it on the ferry, and find somebody to nurse his son!

At that instant, the name he must give the boy came to Jacob: Benjamin. Like the first Benjamin, this child was a Ben-oni, a child born of sorrow.

Before long he sighted the dunes that bordered the Vistula and knew he had not gone astray. Coming out of the forest, he looked around for the ferry, and walked in the direction where he was sure the crossing lay. The Vistula flowed, red mingling with black; a large bird skimming the surface dipped so low at times that its wings ruffled the waters. The river's calmness, purity, and radiance refuted the darkness of the night. Set against this luminosity even death seemed only a bad dream. Neither the sky, nor the river, nor the dunes were dead. Everything was alive, the earth, the sun, each stone. Not death, but suffering was the real enigma. What place did it have in God's Creation? Jacob stopped again to look at the baby. Did it already suffer? Yes, there were signs of suffering. But such sorrow did not come from anything it had yet endured. Its wide brow seemed furrowed in thought, and its lips moved as if it were saying something. He is only partly here, Jacob thought, no, not yet here; he is still meditating on his past before birth.

Jacob remembered the words his namesake had spoken on his deathbed: "And as for me, when I came from Padan, Rachel died by me in the land of Canaan in the way, when yet there was a little way to come into Ephrath; and I buried her there..."

His name was Jacob also; he too had lost a beloved wife, the daughter of an idolater, among strangers; Sarah too was buried by the way and had left him a son. Like the Biblical Jacob, he was crossing the river, bearing only a staff, pursued by another Esau. Everything remained the same: the ancient love, the ancient grief. Perhaps four thousand years would again pass; somewhere, at another river, another Jacob would walk mourning another Rachel. Or who knew, perhaps it was always the same Jacob and the same Rachel. Well, but the Redemption has to come. All of this can't last forever.

Jacob lifted his gaze: Lead, God, lead. It is thy world.

PART THREE

THE RETURN

THIRTEEN

I

Almost twenty years had passed and Pilitz, grown into a city, belonged now to the son of one of Pilitzky's creditors, who had taken possession after a protracted lawsuit. Both the lord of Pilitz and his wife Theresa were dead, he having finally carried out his threat to hang himself. The widow had immediately begun an affair with an impoverished young noble and had been so infatuated that she gave him the lot of what she had. One day he disappeared. Theresa became melancholic, locked herself in an attic room in the castle, grew sick and emaciated, and never reappeared. All of her cousins and relatives deserted her. When the new owner moved to dispossess the widow, the bailiff found her dead surrounded by her cats. The peasants commented that although Theresa had been dead for days, her cats, ravenous from lack of food, had not touched the body – evidence that animals are grateful to their benefactor.

The castle had been rebuilt, but the young noble was seldom there, spending most of his time in Warsaw or abroad. The bailiff stole, and Gershon's youngest son-in-law, as dishonest as Gershon himself, now leased the manor fields. The peasants starved; most of the Jews were also poor; yet the city grew. Gentile craftsmen now competed with the Jewish artisans, and the priests sent delegates to the king to revoke the ancient Jewish privileges. But when one trade was taken from a Jew, he found another. Jews sapped the trees for turpentine, sent lumber down the Vistula to Danzig, brewed vodka and beer, made mead from honey, wove cloth, tanned hides, and even traded in minerals. And although the Muscovites sharpened their swords and the Cossacks attacked at every opportunity, nevertheless between invasions they bought Polish goods. Jewish merchants extended credit, conducted business with Russians, Prussians, Bohemians, even with the distant Italians. There were Jewish banks in Danzig, Leipzig, Cracow, Warsaw, Prague, Padua, Venice. The Jewish banker did not waste money on luxuries, kept his capital in a bag tucked into his fringed garment, and sat in the study house praying. But when he gave someone a letter of credit, the recipient could present it in Paris or in Amsterdam and get money.

At the time of Sabbatai Zevi, the false Messiah who later put on the fez and became a Mohammedan, Pilitz was torn by dissension. The community excommunicated his followers, but they retaliated by publicly cursing the rabbi and the town elders. Men not only damned but even attacked each other physically. Some of the members of the sect ripped the roofs from their houses, packed their belongings in barrels and trunks, and prepared to fly to the land of Israel. Some indulged in cabala, tried to tap wine from walls, to create pigeons by the arcane powers of the Book of Creation. Others ceased to follow the Torah, believing the law would be annulled with the coming of the Messiah. Still others ferreted out hints in the Bible that to be utterly evil was the way to redemption, and they indulged in every variety of abomination. There was a teacher in Pilitz whose imagination was so strong that while praying in prayer shawl and phylacteries he could fancy himself copulating and have an ejaculation. The cursed sect considered this so great an achievement that they made him their leader.

After a while, most of the Jews recognized their error, realized Satan had seduced them, and lost faith in the false Messiah. But some still conspired and kept up their pernicious idolatry. They met at fairs in distant cities and made themselves known to each other through various signs. They wrote the initials S-Z on the books, tools and other merchandise sold in their stores, and they exhibited talismans invented by Sabbatai Zevi. They were united not merely by the illusion that Sabbatai Zevi would return and rebuild Jerusalem, but by commerce. They bought and sold from each other, formed combines, worked for each other's profit, and intrigued against their enemies. When one was accused of swindling, the others testified to his honesty and threw the blame on someone else. They soon became wealthy and powerful. At their meetings, they ridiculed the righteous-pointing out how easy it was to deceive them.

The city grew and so did the cemetery, until the graves spread to the spot where Sarah lay. Her grave became an issue. Some of the elders said her bones should be exhumed and buried elsewhere, since according to the law she was not Jewish and it was a sacrilege to let her remain among the corpses of the pious. The opposition maintained that digging up her bones was not only wrong but might have evil consequences. Besides, the marker had rotted away, the mound flattened, and no one was sure where the body lay. The wisest thing was to leave well enough alone. And the cemetery kept on growing. As usual in new cities where there is no book of chronicles and no old men to hand down the traditional stories, Sarah was soon forgotten and even Jacob was seldom remembered. Many of their contemporaries had died; new citizens had moved in; and Pilitz now had a stone synagogue, a study house, a poor-house, an inn – even a community outhouse for those who were ashamed to use the gutter. In a little hut across from the cemetery lived the gravedigger, Reb Eber.

One day in the month of Ob, a tall, white-bearded man, in a white gabardine and white hat, sandals on his bare feet, a bag on his shoulder, appeared at the cemetery. In his right hand he held a stick. He did not look like a Polish Jew. His waist was circled with a broad sash like those worn by emissaries from the Holy Land. Moving among the graves, he poked, searched, bent down to read the headstones. Observing him from a window, Eber wondered what he was doing in the cemetery. Was he looking for someone? The settlement was not old; there were no saints' graves here. Eber went to find out.

"Who are you looking for? I'm in charge here."

"So? There used to be a convert's grave here. Sarah, the daughter of the Patriarch Abraham. They buried her at a distance, but I see the cemetery has grown."

"A convert, here? Has she a stone?"

"No, a marker."

"When did she die?"

"Some twenty years ago."

"I've only been here six. What was she to you?"

"My wife."

"Who are you? What's your name?"

"Jacob. I lived here once, a little after the massacres."

"Was conversion allowed in Poland?"

"She had a Jewish soul."

"I don't know. The place is overgrown with weeds. They added a piece of ground years ago. The whole city fasted."

II

Jacob continued to search, poking with his stick, and sniffing at the ground; then he stretched out on the wild grass, whispering to the earth. The sun was setting when Jacob walked through the city, looked around, stopped, gaped. It was a different Pilitz with different people. Seeing the study house, he entered. A single anniversary candle flickered in the menorah, and above the tables were shelves of books. Jacob took one out, looked inside, kissed it, and put it back. Then he took out another and seated himself. He had come from the Land of Israel to disinter Sarah's bones and take them back. Their son, Benjamin Eliezer, was now a lecturer in a yeshiva in Jerusalem. Jacob had never told him of his mother's origins. There are truths which must remain hidden. Why divide his spirit? Benjamin Eliezer had grown up a prodigy and at thirteen had already dipped into the cabala. This was in the time of Sabbatai Zevi and both father and son were misled by the false Messiah. The emissary Jacob had met on the ferryboat had been one of his legates and in old age had put on the fez.

Jacob had been through so much in those twenty years. The voyage to Jerusalem had taken many weeks and the vessel he had been traveling on had been attacked by pirates. He had seen half of his fellow passengers murdered before his eyes. The baby had suffered from dysentery and would have died if Sarah had not come to Jacob in a dream and given him a remedy. He too had become critically ill. Scarcely had he recovered when a Turk accused him of stealing and the captain had wanted to hang Jacob. A storm had come up and the ship lay on its side for three days. When Jacob arrived at Jerusalem, he found the city suffering a famine. Moreover, there was scarcely any water to drink. Every few years the city was swept by pestilence. Jacob was present when Sabbatai Zevi had been driven out of Jerusalem; he knew Nathan of Gaza and Samuel Primu. During the days of his error, he had worn the talismans of the accursed sect and had eaten on Tischab'ov and the seventeenth day of Tammuz. He had almost put on the fez like all the others. God alone knew how many miracles had happened to him. All that he had seen and endured could not have been told in seven days and seven nights. It is impossible to convey the torment he had undergone when he realized that he was sinking into the lowest abyss! Even his present trip to Poland had been beset by many pitfalls, proving again that no moment is without its misfortune. Every day he experienced another miracle. But that Benjamin should have become an instructor in a yeshiva at twenty and the son-in-law of a rabbi was an unalloyed gift from Heaven. Heaven had decreed that Jacob should not perish a heretic. It had been willed that Sarah and he were to leave issue.

But the disappearance of Sarah's grave was a blow to Jacob, and it seemed that the trip had been made in vain. Jacob wanted to bury Sarah's bones on the Mount of Olives and to prepare a grave for himself close by. He hoped that since he had not been able to be with her alive, at least his body should rest near her in death.

Well, but everything God did was for the good. The older Jacob grew, the clearer this truth became to him. An eye was watching, a hand guiding, each sin had its significance. Not even Sabbatai Zevi had come in vain. False birth pains sometimes precede the true. Jacob, journeying through the Turkish countries from the Holy Land to Poland, had come to know things he had not understood before. Each generation had its lost tribes. Some portion always longs to return to Egypt. There are always frightened spies, Samsons, Abimelechs, Jethros, Ruths. The leaves drop from the tree, but the branches remain; the trunk still has its roots. Israel's lost children live in every land. Each community has within it those who stay apart. Men blossom and wither like plants. Heaven writes the story and only there is the truth known. In the end each man is responsible only for himself.

When Jacob had still been close to the sect of Sabbatai Zevi, they had tried to persuade him to marry. Women of wealth and fine family were available. He had never been free of carnal desire, but a power stronger than passion had said no. Later too, when he had repented, the rabbi and the cabalists had argued that according to the law and the cabala, he should find a new mate. But even when his lips said yes, an inner voice shouted no. It often seemed to him that Sarah was still with him. She spoke to him, he answered. She accompanied him to the ruins and the holy graves, warned him against all kinds of dangers, and advised him how to bring up Benjamin. If he put a pot on the stove and forgot it, she called him when the food was about to burn...

How could he tell such things? He would be considered insane or possessed by devils, but every heart has secrets it does not tell.

Jacob nodded over the book open before him. How wonderful there were study houses and books everywhere! Jacob had never forgotten the years on the mountain when he had to dig Torah from his memory. His love for books had grown continually. Sometimes when they tried to marry him off he wanted to answer, the Torah is my wife. No day passed without his going over a few chapters of the Bible, and he had read the Midrash many times. His love for the Torah had not ceased even when he belonged to the Sabbatai Zevi sect. A chapter of the Psalms was like manna which tasted exactly as each man wished it to. Jacob refreshed himself with the moral truths of Proverbs; he satisfied his hunger with sections of the Mishna. Everything he studied he explained to Sarah in Yiddish, sometimes in Polish, as if she were sitting beside him. On the voyage he had drawn her attention to the waves, the islands, the flying fish, the constellations. Look, Sarah, God's wonders! It was perilous for a Jew to walk alone on the roads in the Holy Land, but he had wandered with her among the Arabs, through deserts where caravans of camels passed. Sarah watched that no evil befell him. Arabs with wild eyes and knives at their waists gave him figs, dates, St. John's bread, and provided him with shelter for the night. Many times he came upon venomous snakes—which turned away from him. "Thou shalt tread upon the lion: the adder and the dragon shalt thou trample under feet."

But why had he been sent on this long journey if he could not find Sarah's bones and bring them to the Holy Land? His son had tried to dissuade him from the trip. The cabalists had pleaded with him, saying that every Jew was needed in the Holy Land. The pangs accompanying the birth of the Messiah were almost over, and signs indicated that the battle of Gog and Magog was imminent. Satan was drawing up a list of heavy accusations. The Lord of Edom girt his loins for the bitter struggle. Soon would come that battle when the evil hosts would attempt to overturn the scale of mercy. Then would Asmodeus, Lilith, each demon, every hobgoblin, bark, hiss, spit, foam; led by the primeval snake, packs of dogs, adders, hawks, and hyenas would march to Batsrah where the final conflict would take place. Not a single pious Jew, prayer, benediction, or act of piety, could be spared with the Redemption hanging in the balance. Jacob was needed here, not in some distant country. Sarah, too, argued against his going: Why bring my bones when soon the underground caverns will be filled with skeletons rolling to the Land of Israel? But for the first time in twenty years, Jacob demurred. An irresistible power within him forced him to make the trip.

Jacob's losses had been great, but he still had the holy books to cling to. Resigned long since to the loss of both the joys of this world and of heaven, he served God without hope, prepared each moment for the fires of Gehenna.

III

The men who came to the study house for the evening prayer greeted the stranger and asked where he came from.

"From the Land of Israel," he answered. "But once I lived here in Pilitz."

"What is your name?"

"Jacob. In those days I was known as Jacob the teacher, or as Jacob, Dumb Sarah's husband."

There was an outcry. Though most of the men present had not known Jacob, a few of the older inhabitants remembered him well. The man whose wife had nursed Jacob's baby clutched his head, and ran to tell his wife the news. She came into the study house among the men and began to cry and scream as if she were praying for someone who had fallen ill.

"Dear man, a day hasn't passed without my thinking of you. How's the baby?"

"He lectures in a yeshiva in Jerusalem and is the father of three children."

"That I should have lived to see this! There is a God."

Once more she began to wail.

The cantor had difficulty keeping the people silent until after the Minchah prayer, and immediately upon the completion of the eighteen benedictions the tumult resumed. Though few had known Jacob and his mute wife, many had heard of them. Even in the villages outside of Pilitz, the story was told of how Jacob had escaped from the dragoons and come in the middle of the night to claim his son. This story had been particularly popular when the Messianists were dominant in Pilitz. That sect had believed in physical action, had contended that Israel should either seize Esau's sword or intermarry with his seed and that of Ishmael until all the descendants of Abraham had become one nation. They cited Jacob and Sarah as precursor of the Redemption. The new lord of Pilitz had even regarded the sect of Sabbatai Zevi with favor. At that time the mound over Sarah's grave was still visible, the marker still there, and women and girls had gone to the grave and recited prayers.

But when it was heard that Sabbatai Zevi had accepted the Koran, the warden of the burial society in Pilitz ordered his men to level the ground over Sarah's grave. Not long after, the new plot of ground was added to the cemetery and soon no one remembered where Sarah lay. Now, hearing that Jacob had returned from the Land of Israel, the secret followers of Sabbatai Zevi approached him, bid him welcome, and one of them invited him to stay at his house. But, refusing to be anyone's guest, Jacob replied he would sleep in the poorhouse. At the mention of Sabbatai Zevi's name, Jacob spat and cried out loudly, "Let his name and memory be blotted out."

Many questions were put to Jacob about what had happened to him. He spoke of the land of Israel, of the Jews living there, of the yeshivas, the holy graves, the ruins. He explained how the true cabalists were attempting to bring about the End of Days. He described the Wailing Wall, the Double Cave, Rachel's grave, and exhibited a few Turkish coins. A young man asked him if on his sea voyage he had seen any of those creatures, half man, half fish, who sing so sweetly that a man must stop up his ears or he will expire with delight. Jacob said that he himself had not seen any. Long after the evening prayer was over, the men continued to talk and converse. Why had Jacob come? someone asked. When he replied that it was to disinter Sarah's bones and transport them to the Holy Land, there was a long silence. Then the warden of the burial society remarked:

"Might as well look for a needle in a haystack."

"It seems that it was not fated," Jacob said.

The people began to turn their backs on him. Everyone had heard of the bones of saints of important people being carried to the Land of Israel—but that a man should return after twenty years to hunt for the bones of some female who had been given a donkey's burial? That was peculiar. Some murmured that the guest must be out of his mind; others suspected him of belonging to the excommunicated sect; still others concluded that he was a liar and had not come from the Land of Israel. The followers of Sabbatai Zevi walked over to him, but everything they said, he disputed. Finally all the older men left, and without Jacob. Soon the woman who had nursed Jacob's child entered, bringing kasha and beef broth for him, but he told her he never ate flesh: neither meat nor fish nor anything else from a living creature, not even cheese or eggs. The woman asked:

"What do you live on? Burning coals?"

"Bread and olives."

"We have no olives."

"Also I take radish, onion, or garlic with my bread."

"How do you keep your strength that way?"

"God gives strength."

"Well, eat the bread."

Jacob washed his hands at the water barrel and sat down to eat the dry bread. A few boys whose turn it was to study at this time of the night began to ridicule the stranger. "Why are you so scared of flesh?"

"We are flesh ourselves."

"What do you take on the Sabbath?"

"The same as on weekdays."

"You're not allowed to torment yourself on the Sabbath."

"Nor must one torment others."

"What do you put into the Sabbath pudding?"

"Olive oil."

"If everybody lived as you do, what would the ritual slaughterer live on?"

"One can survive without slaughter."

One boy tried to convince Jacob that he was breaking the law, while the others pinched themselves, giggled, whispered.

He knew they were ridiculing him, but Jacob answered seriously, clearly. Jacob, who had his own ways of thinking and acting, who interpreted the Torah in his own manner, was accustomed to suspicion and mockery. Even as a child he had been a misfit. Despite his brief association with the followers of Sabbatai Zevi (and even there he had been on the outer fringe), he had always remained aloof. Even his own son, Benjamin Eliezer, had at times reproached him for his strange conduct. In the Holy Land, the community had wanted to support him out of funds given to aid scholars, but he had refused to accept charity, and had done all kinds of hard labor, such as digging ditches, cleaning outhouses, carrying heavy loads usually transported by donkeys. He was offered steady work, but refused to stay long in one place. One day he would go to Safad, another to Shechem; sometimes he journeyed to Jaffa, other times he wandered through the desert on the way to the Dead Sea. When he was sleepy, he would lie down in the sand, placing a stone under his head. There was even a rumor that Jacob was not a born Jew but a convert. Years passed, yet some of those who knew him never discovered that he was a learned man and considered him an ignoramus.

He had always been the same Jacob, in Zamosc, in Josefov, in the hamlet on the mountain, in Pilitz, in Jerusalem. His thoughts seemed clear to him, but others found them confused. At times, Jacob accused himself of stubbornness and disobedience since the Torah itself said that one should accept the majority and follow the leaders of each generation. But even so, Jacob could not be other than he was. Besides he could not forget the years he had spent in Jan Bzik's barn on the mountain, surrounded by animals and savage shepherds. The years with Sarah had left their mark upon him. He had great patience with the weak but he resisted the strong. For long periods he could remain silent, but when he spoke it was always the truth. He had made long journeys to repay half a piastre. He dared defy armed Arabs or Turks. He took the most difficult tasks upon himself, carried the paralyzed, cleansed the lice-infected sick. Men avoided him, but pious women considered him a saint, one of the thirty-six righteous men who are the pillars of the world.

Now Jacob sat in the study house, reproaching himself for having come. Of the money he had saved for the trip, there was not enough left for the return journey. He had placed himself in a situation where he would have to ask others for help, and, God forbid, he might become sick in Poland, or on the ship where those who die are buried at sea. I am mad, he said to himself. My mother, peace be with her, when she called me a rattlebrain, was right. As soon as he had finished the passages he had set himself, he walked to the poorhouse. The boys had told him he could sleep in the study house, but this he considered sacrilege. His rule was to prefer the difficult to the easy. Sometimes Jacob was amazed at the burdens he required his body and his soul to carry.

IV

Opening the door of the poorhouse, Jacob entered. In the darkness, he heard sighing and groaning, snoring, and the uneasy coughing of those he had disturbed. A man's voice asked:

"Who's there?"

"A guest. A stranger."

"In the middle of the night?"

"It's not midnight yet."

"The candle is out already."

"I will do without it."

"Can you see in the dark?"

"I'll lie down on the floor."

"There's a bundle of straw somewhere. Wait, I'll get it for you."

"Don't bother."

"Once I'm awakened, I can't close my eyes all night."

Jacob stood there while his eyes grew accustomed to the darkness and his nose to the stench. Even though it was summer, all the windows were tightly shut. The moon wasn't shining, but the sky outside was filled with stars. Jacob could discern the sleeping forms of men and women. He was familiar with all of the smells, the moaning; it was the same everywhere, in the Holy Land, in the countries of the Arabs and the Turks, in Poland. In whatever town Jacob found himself, he always went to the poorhouse to help the old and the sick, to wash them, rub them with turpentine, bring them fresh straw. Now, bringing a pile of straw and spreading it on the floor, someone was helping him. Jacob had read Shema before coming, so that the holy words need not be defiled by this unclean place; now he only needed to say the last prayer before sleep. He lay down, carefully stretching out his legs to avoid touching anyone. A woman complained:

"All night they drag themselves around, and now they come and wake up sick people. May their legs drop off!"

"Don't curse, woman, don't curse. You'll have time enough to sleep."

"In the grave maybe."

"Who are you? Where are you from?" the man who had brought Jacob the straw asked. He lay on a bench nearby.

"I came from the Holy Land."

"You aren't that Reb Jacob who was in the study house today?" the man said, astonished.

"Yes, I am."

"Didn't anyone offer you a bed? You lived here once. I remember when you first came. You were the teacher. My own son learned the alphabet from you. We were talking about you earlier."

"It couldn't be the same Jacob," a woman said.

"Yes, the same."

"No wonder they call Pilitz Sodom," the man said. "But even in Sodom there was a Lot, and he took in strangers."

"What's your name?" Jacob asked the man.

"Mine? Leibush Mayer."

"Reb Leibush Mayer, one should look for the good in people, not the bad. How do you know no one invited me? The truth is, several men did. But it's not my habit to be anyone's guest. What's the matter with the poorhouse?"

"My enemies should rot in poorhouses," said the woman who had cursed Jacob.

"He knows what he's doing," Leibush Mayer defended Jacob. "How many of you here come from Pilitz? The devil knows where you're from. You land in Pilitz and eat up the town. But I came the very first day. There were only three houses here, then. It was right after the massacres. Gershon, may his soul burn in hell, had already grabbed Pilitzky's fields. In those days we didn't even have a quorum. I came with Menasha, my little boy. I'd lost my wife and the other two children. Menasha's gone too, now. I was a carpenter, and there was plenty of work to do. We had one tutor—he left before you came," he said, turning to Jacob. "Another teacher was supposed to come from the other side of the Vistula. Then you showed up. I remember it as if it were yesterday. What do these beggars know about that. You taught my Menasha and he learned a lot. In a few months he could read. Well, and so you took over the fields from Gershon. What didn't happen, then! We've talked about you; we've talked. Just last week I told these paupers here your whole story. Then you show up! But why did you come back from the Holy Land?"

Jacob was silent for a moment.

"To visit my wife's grave."

"Did you find it? The burial society people blotted it out. Don't think, Reb Jacob, there weren't people on your side." The man's tone changed. "I remember that meeting at the rabbi's the night after Yom Kippur. I went. True, I was only a carpenter, but I was invited. Wasn't I a householder? Didn't I know the small letters? I stood at the door and listened. I wanted to cry out, 'Don't be so harsh. He's punished enough.' But Gershon, his bones should turn in his grave, shook his fist at me. And who gave the verdict? The rabbi, Gershon's son-in-law. We know who was the real rabbi. It was Gershon too who denounced you to the priest. I'll testify to that before God Himself. Gershon almost turned to steam when he heard you'd taken the baby. He almost ruined the man for letting you have it. Did the child live?"

"He has three children of his own now."

"Where is he?"

"In Jerusalem."

"How did you get there with such a small baby?"

"It's a long story."

"They wanted me to be a member of the burial society, but I wasn't going to lick Gershon's boots. They didn't even cleanse your wife's body properly, just threw her into a ditch in her clothes. I was there. I saw it. The beadle was about to recite Kaddish, but Gershon said no. They stole everything you had. The corpse was still lying on the floor, and they were stripping the room. They even took the broom. And they turned the place upside down looking for money."

"I forgave them a long time ago."

"All right, you forgave. But has God? In Heaven everything's written down—from the biggest sin to the smallest. Gershon took to his bed before the year was out. His belly was always big but it swelled up and he looked like a barrel. There wasn't a feather bed large enough to cover him and the town rang with his hiccups. Your wife, Sarah, may she dwell in Paradise, was not at peace in her grave. Maybe I shouldn't tell you, but she came to women in dreams and complained: I am naked and without shrouds. She was also seen walking in the room where she died. Even in summer that room stayed icy. Everyone knew why she walked. The house was finally bought by a gentile."

"It's gone now," Jacob said.

"It burned down. Suddenly one night it blazed up like straw. The women swore they saw her image in the flames."

"Whose?"

"Your wife's."

V

Jacob awoke before dawn. Something heavy lay on his heart; his stomach was swollen; his limbs were weak. Am I getting sick? What's happening to me? he asked himself. His tongue was coated; his head lolled. Never before had he been so ill. He found he didn't have the strength to sit up. He lay amazed, watching the sun through the window, a red ball rising in the east. Dawn was like dusk; the birds twittered feebly. Were the window panes so dusty? Were his eyes misted? Somehow he raised himself and looked around. Men and women lay all about him on straw pallets amid garbage and rags: the old, the sick, the paralyzed, some with distorted faces. They muttered, snored, grunted, whined through their noses. Jacob sank back again, closing his eyes.

He was not asleep, yet he saw Sarah standing near him dressed in luminous drapes and surrounded by light. The joy of the sunrise emanated from her. Smiling at him like a mother, like a wife, with a love greater than he had ever known, she said:

"Mazeltov, Jacob. We have been separated long enough."

Jacob opened his eyes. He knew the truth: his time had come. Well, is this what I came for, to die? Here, and not in the Holy Land? This seemed to him a harsh decree: his son and grandchildren were there; Benjamin Eliezer would not know of his death, would not know he should say Kaddish. But Jacob warned himself not to question the Lord of the Universe. If this was Heaven's decree, so be it. "All that God does is for the good." Jacob glanced at his sack in which he carried his prayer shawl, his phylacteries, and a few books, a Pentateuch, a volume of the Mishnah, a prayer book. How can I recite holy words in this filthy place? he asked himself. He wanted to pray, but his lips would not move. Finally, he began to murmur a chapter of the Psalms, omitting to pronounce the names of God. "None of them can by any means redeem his brother, nor give to God a ransom for him ... That he should still live forever, and not see corruption."

Jacob dozed off, woke, fell asleep, and woke once more. Even as he closed his eyes, his dreams rushed in on him. Phantoms walked, ran, screamed, behaved in indescribable ways. And when he opened his eyes, they remained for a time etched against the glare of the daylight, speaking a tongue that Jacob understood without hearing. He lay there seeming to sleep. A man with a gray disheveled beard and a wrinkled earthy face put his feet down from his bench and nudged Jacob.

"Reb Jacob, it's morning."

Jacob stirred.

"You don't want to be late with your Shema."

"I have no water to wash my hands."

"Wash your hands in the barrel. They don't bring you pitchers around here."

"I'm afraid I'm not well," Jacob said.

"What? You do look a little yellow."

The man stretched out his hand, touched Jacob's forehead, and frowned.

"I'll go for the healer."

"No, don't trouble."

"Caring for the sick is a sacred obligation."

The man put on his gabardine and his shoes and left. Soon the women and the children began to wake; they yawned, coughed, sneezed. One old crone sat up cursing. Everyone deloused himself. Despite his stuffed nose, Jacob was aware of the stench. Worms crawled on the floor and walls. Rabbis had many times denounced the lodging of men and women in the same room in the poorhouse but the practice persisted, the justification being that Satan had no power over the sick and the old. Modesty did not exist here. One woman bared breasts which hung down like empty sacks. Jacob averted his eyes. His wish had always been to die in the shadow of the holy ruins, near the graves of saints, surrounded by cabalists and ascetics, and to be buried on the Mount of Olives. He had imagined himself bringing Sarah's bones to the Mount and had intended to raise one stone for both of them. He had always pictured his son Benjamin Eliezer standing at his grave reciting Kaddish. Yet it was fortunate that he had had the foresight to carry with him a small bag of earth from the Holy Land. He lay silent while half-naked children crawled over him. A woman rebuked him.

"As if it wasn't crowded enough. The devil had to drag in another."

It was some time before Jacob realized that she was referring to him and he wanted to apologize but he lacked both the words and the strength with which to talk. Jacob listened to what was going on within him. How had it all happened so quickly? He had gone to sleep a strong man and had awakened moribund. His stomach had stopped digesting, his intestines were frozen; his teeth felt loose in his gums. Usually in the morning he had to urinate, but today there was no need even for that. He watched from under his eyelids the women and children eating, and the sight seemed foreign to him. But finally he summoned up enough strength to rise. He washed his hands at the barrel, and walked outside on unsteady legs to cleanse himself of urine before prayers. Standing at the wall, he forced out single drops. The heat was already oppressive. The sun blazed. Next to the poorhouse, in garbage and excrement, grew grass and wildflowers—white blooms, yellow blooms, feathery seed puffs, hairlike green fringes. Butterflies fluttered, and blue-gold flies buzzed on a heap of goat turds as if holding a meeting. A dog limped down the street sniffing the ground. For a moment the wind brought the clean scent of the fields, but then shifting bore only the smell of the outhouses. Feathers whirled in the air as in slaughter houses. Roosters crowed; chickens clucked; geese honked. On a patch of grass and weeds a crow picked at the guts from a chicken. Jacob stood openmouthed. This was the world he must soon leave. He returned to the poorhouse and tried to lift his sack. He could not stay there; the room, as the woman had pointed out, was too crowded. It was one thing to go among the poor to aid them, and another to infringe on the space that they needed. Only yesterday the sack had felt light; now he could barely raise it. At last, having pulled it over his shoulder, he said to everyone:

"Goodbye. Forgive me."

"The poor man is sick. Don't let him leave," screamed the same woman who had reproached him for being there.

"Where will you go, Reb Jacob?" voices called to him.

"To the study house."

"Oh, it's terrible. He can hardly walk," another woman screamed.

"Get him some water."

"Thank you. There's no need. Don't be offended."

Jacob kissed the mezuzah and walked to the study house, which was just across the street, taking small steps and stopping frequently to rest. He heard the voices of the men praying and the boys studying. Lingering in the antechamber, Jacob quickly thought over his life and tried to make an accounting, but his brain was as sluggish as his guts were. Nothing but exhaustion remained. Nevertheless, he marshaled his strength, and before saying the words which are customarily spoken before entering a holy place, he dipped his fingers into the copper font. He remembered having read in a book of ethics that even the man who dies in bed is a martyr. The very act of dying is a sacrificial offering.

VI

Jacob became faint during his prayers and fell sprawling in his prayer shawl and phylacteries. There was consternation in the study house. He was lifted to his feet and a man who had no children took him home and gave him a room; the man's wife assisted Jacob.

Chanina the healer was sent for, and all kinds of remedies were applied – bleeding, leeches, herbs—but to no avail. Jacob grew weaker from hour to hour. His voice became so low one could barely hear him. The next morning he asked for his prayer shawl and phylacteries but lacked the strength to put on the shawl or bind the thongs to his arms. The men of Pilitz came to visit him and the rabbi came also. Jacob asked the rabbi to recite the confession. "And for the sin," Jacob said, as it is said on Yom Kippur; with hands that now lacked the strength to close he fruitlessly attempted to beat his breast. He remembered that he had been strong all his life; now he was as weak as he had once been powerful. He couldn't even turn on his other side. Merely to open his mouth and swallow a spoonful of warm water was too difficult.

Jacob wanted only to doze. He lay there with his eyelids closed, absorbed in an activity unknown to the healthy. He did not think but something in him approached the higher truths. From nowhere, images came to him: his father, peace be with him, his mother, peace be with her, his sisters, Zelda Leah, the children, Sarah. Even Jan Bzik visited him, no longer a peasant, but a saint from Paradise. They were debating something among themselves but without hostility, and Jacob too was being consulted. Both sides were in their own way right, and even though Jacob was not sure what the question was or what it meant, he was amazed. If only men could apprehend these things while they were still strong, he said to himself, they would serve the Lord differently. No one would lack confidence. No one would become sad. But how could these truths be conveyed to the vigorous? No, it was impossible. Already there was an impenetrable wall between Jacob and those who came to visit him. They wished him a speedy recovery, murmured the customary words of comfort and hope, gave him all kinds of advice, but though he heard them their words seemed empty, unrelated to anything he cared for. He did not want to recover; he no longer needed his body, and his devotion to it had passed.

Already, several times, he, Jacob had found himself outside his body looking down on it as if it were discarded clothing. The body lay, wrapped in linen, huddled in bed, sick, yellow, crumpled. You have already served your time—Jacob said to it—you are torn and stained with sins and must be cleansed. In one night the healthy Jacob had torn free from the moribund; he had traveled over fields, mountains, seas to the house of Benjamin Eliezer in Jerusalem. He had entered the room where his son sat studying by the light of an oil lamp, had spoken to him, given him a sign, but Benjamin Eliezer, engrossed in his book, had not responded. Before long some power had whisked Jacob back to Pilitz and he had again become imprisoned in his body and its suffering.

Jacob's death agony had begun. He breathed hoarsely, his chest heaved, single words of Yiddish and Polish bubbled from his throat. Those present thought he was dead, but when a member of the burial society laid a feather to his nostrils, it still moved. His body in its own way resisted the sentence of death. It tried to hold on, to function again, to digest, eliminate, belch, sweat, but its efforts were like the twitching of a slaughtered animal. The heart fluttered like a half-torn wing; the blood moved sluggishly; the eyes did not see the burning candle. The flame of life was guttering, and those on the other side, who waited for Jacob like relatives waiting on the shore for the ship to anchor, called to him and stretched out their hands. Jacob saw Sarah near Zelda Leah, and even though his thoughts were no longer earthly, he wondered. Well, but up there things happened differently...

Jacob's body died, but he was already so busy greeting those who had come to meet him that he did not look back. His dark cabin with its rags and refuse was left behind on the ship. The voyagers would clean it out, those who must still continue to journey on the stormy seas. He, Jacob, had arrived.

The men of the burial society lifted the corpse, opened the window, and recited the justification of God's decree. They placed Jacob with his feet toward the door and set two candles at his head. Pious men gathered to recite the Psalms. The news that Jacob had died spread swiftly through the district. Even though he had lived in obscurity for twenty years in the land of Israel, how he had conducted himself was not unknown, and he was thought of as a righteous man. The original cemetery plot was long since fully occupied, so Jacob was given ground in the new part. The body was cleansed and taken to the study house where the rabbi spoke the eulogy. The whole town attended Jacob's funeral. When the gravedigger broke ground for Jacob's grave, his spade struck bones. He began to dig more carefully, and soon a body was seen that had not yet completely decomposed, perhaps because the earth there was so sandy and dry. From the skeleton and from pieces of clothing, the burial society women saw that it was a female. Strands of blond hair still entwined the skull, and it soon became clear that this was the grave of Sarah, who had been buried unshrouded in her own dress. The community had buried Sarah outside but the dead had gathered to take her in. The cemetery itself had ordained it; Sarah was a Jewish daughter and a sanctified corpse.

Pilitz was in an uproar. Women cried; the pious fasted. Many came, even young girls and children, for a look at the body that had lain twenty years in the earth and was still recognizable. The cemetery was as crowded as in the month of Elul when everyone visits the graves. All saw the hand of Providence in this event. It was like one of the ancient miracles, a sign that there is an Eye which sees and a scale wherein even the acts of the stranger are weighed. The elders called a meeting and decided to bury Jacob near Sarah.

Thus judgment was rendered. Jacob, enveloped in a prayer shawl, with shards on his eyes, and a stem of myrtle between his fingers, was buried near Sarah. And the community undertook to erect a common tombstone as recompense to Sarah for the injustice done her by Gershon and his men. After the thirty days of mourning, the engraver began to chisel their stone. At the crest were two doves facing each other, their beaks joined in a kiss. But only the outlines were formed in keeping with the Mosaic interdiction against images. Deeply incised were the names of the deceased: Jacob the son of Eliezer; Sarah the daughter of the

Patriarch Abraham. Jacob was honored with the words, "Our teacher, the saint"; and inscribed near Sarah's name was the line from Proverbs, "Who can find a virtuous woman?"

The epitaph was completed by a passage from the Bible encircling their names: "Lovely and pleasant in their lives, and in their death they were not divided."

A GOD'S MISTAKE

www.ingramcontent.com/pod-product-compliance
Lightning Source LLC
Chambersburg PA
CBHW020409110726
47899CB00006B/1914

A GOD'S MISTAKE

CHRONICLES OF AN URBAN DRUID™ BOOK 11

AUBURN TEMPEST

MICHAEL ANDERLE

DISRUPTIVE IMAGINATION

LMBPN Publishing
PMB 196, 2540 South Maryland Pkwy
Las Vegas, NV 89109

Version 1.00, October 2021
eBook ISBN: 978-1-68500-415-6
Print ISBN: 978-1-68500-416-3

THE A GOD'S MISTAKE TEAM

Thanks to our JIT Team:

Larry Omans
Deb Mader
James Caplan
Rachel Beckford
Paul Westman
John Ashmore
Kelly O'Donnell
Diane L. Smith
Micky Cocker
Dorothy Lloyd
Dave Hicks
Jeff Goode

Editor
SkyHunter Editing Team

CHAPTER ONE

I lean over the scrying mirror on the kitchen table, my druid stones in one hand and a pink Dumbo blankie in the other. The pressure is on. I have to do this. The people I love are depending on me.

"Focus, Fi," Sloan says beside me. "Scrying is an ancient art. Relax yer vision and let the images take form of their own accord."

"You can do this, Fi," Aiden says, his voice strained with the exhaustion of the early-morning hour. "I believe in you, baby girl. Where is it?"

The screaming of the twins upstairs is making it hard to concentrate. I try to block out their upset.

Aiden's right. I *can* do this.

I'm Fiona-freaking-Cumhaill.

I roll my neck and let my vision blur. Scrying is an esoteric practice that allows truths to reveal themselves on an altered plane.

I'm a Celtic shaman.

Esoteric planes are my jam.

Come on truths…reveal yourselves.

I shift my fingers, rolling my druid stones to keep the fae energy active and flowing. Staring at the dark mirror, I draw a steadying breath and squint, tilting my head to make out the image taking form in front of me.

"Well, that makes no sense."

"What?" Aiden says. "What do you see? Anything, Fi. Give me anything to go on."

"I see Daisy curled up in her little bed next door."

"Daisy?" Sloan repeats. "Why would Daisy have Ireland's favorite pacifier?"

"I don't know. I'm telling you what I see."

"Good enough for me." Aiden beelines it toward the back door in his boxers. He doesn't pause before he's gone and Sloan and I are chasing after him.

When I exit the back door of my childhood home, I hustle across the new deck extension joining the back of this house to the back of the house Sloan bought me last December.

I giggle at my brother. "Indecent exposure, Officer Cumhaill. Put some clothes on."

He's in the door of our place and jogging down the basement steps by the time we get to the back door. "Add breaking and entering to the charges."

"I didn't break anything," he shoots back at me.

"Don't scare her." I say it loud enough he'll hear me but hopefully not so loud that I'll wake up the four people sleeping upstairs. "She's a skunk. Scaring a skunk is a bad idea."

He stops in his tracks, and we catch up with him outside Sloan's apothecary room. "Good point. Do you mind doing the honors, Fi?"

I take the lead, smiling. My oldest brother is as brave as they come. He chases down bank robbers in his day job and battles dark wizards and vampires as part of my druid Team Trouble.

But he's scared of our fluffy little skunk.

"I still think I got my wires crossed. Why would Daisy have Ireland's sou-sou?"

"No idea but we've looked everywhere else. No stone left unturned."

"Okeedoodle."

The companions' wall in the man cave downstairs has a habitat space for our family wildlife companions. The big stone cave at the back is where Bruin is sawing logs, curled up in a heaping ball of mythical, brown grizzly bear.

Manx switches between sleeping on the long, flat branch with his four paws hanging loose or the padded platform mounted near the ceiling, where he is now.

Doc Marten has a hammock hanging between two branches and has his face tucked under his tail.

Our wee Daisy girl is sound asleep in her den, which, if truth be told, is a felt cat cave. Whatevs. She lurves it, and that's all that matters.

I kneel on the hardwood and peek into the den.

Oh. My. Heart.

She's snuggled up in a ball, sucking on the soother, with her little paws curled against her mouth to keep it in place. What a sweet thing.

"It's a shame to wake her. Look how cute she is." I'm about to brush her mind with my druid powers when Doc lifts his head and yawns.

"What's wrong?"

"Nothing, buddy. Go back to sleep. We were looking for Ireland's sou-sou, and Daisy has it."

"She needs it." Doc lifts his head. "She hasn't slept in days so I got it for her. I heard Kinu say it works like magic to put the baby to sleep."

"It does, but now Ireland's not sleeping, and Carragh is crying because Ireland won't stop crying."

He sits up and blinks at me, his black button eyes lost in the darkness. "I'm sorry about the babies but please don't wake Daisy up. She's been so sad and tired that she won't even play with us."

Well, that's upsetting.

I look back at Aiden. "What do you want me to do?"

He shakes his head. "It doesn't make sense to wake up one tired girl and make her cry to stop another tired girl from crying."

"Tell me which pacifier it is," Sloan says. "I'll pop to the twenty-four-hour pharmacy and buy her a new one. Hell, I'll buy her fifty."

Aiden shakes his head. "Not that simple. They were part of Gran's baby gift. She bought them in Ireland. I've never seen the same ones here. Kinu thinks it's the shape of the suckle thingy. She loves it."

That eliminates Sloan from the late-night rescue. He could portal to the Emerald Isle, but that distance would drain his reserves, and he wouldn't be able to come back for two or three days.

"That leaves Nikon or Dionysus," I say.

Aiden frowns. "Do we really intend on dragging them into a newborn pacifier crisis?"

"Sure we do. If they aren't busy or sleeping, they won't care." I smile at Sloan. "Would you mind popping up to our room to grab my phone, hotness?"

Sloan is gone in a blink and back almost as quickly with my phone in his hand. "Try Dionysus first. He stays up later."

"What time is... Oh, dear."

Aiden frowns. "Forget it. We'll deal. We don't need to bother the Greeks over a simple soother disaster. People have sleepless nights with newborns all the time."

I ignore my brother and take Sloan's advice, texting a quick message to Dionysus.

Tarzan, if you're up, can I ask a favor? No biggie. No emergency. Just need a ride to the treehouse and back.

I've barely hit "Send" when my skin tingles and Dionysus is standing next to me.

The Greek god of wine and ecstasy is a tall, lanky, athletic guy with long brunette curls and a penchant for being naked. Hellenistic and hedonistic is his motto, and he wears it well.

When he wears anything at all.

Tonight, thankfully, he's got his male bits covered and is wearing his cheetah print loincloth. My fault. I started down the Tarzan path. "Jane, I'm always happy to oblige. You know that. What do you need in Ireland?"

"Gran bought the twins a certain type of pacifier—"

"The only one our little Ireland will accept," Aiden interjects.

I nod. "—but sweet Daisy confiscated it and we can't bear to take it back."

Dionysus bends to look into the felt den, and his loincloth rides up. Sloan and Aiden both get an eyeful of the god's ass and quickly avert their gazes. "Aw, that raises the cuteness factor of the world by like a bazillion."

"Right?"

He straightens and brings his hands up to his face. "The way her little paws are all wrapped around it, and she's suckling. It's adorbs."

"True story." I lean in to have another look myself. I would take a picture, but the flash would come on and scare her. Then nothing would be so cute and we'd all reek for the next three days. "So, you see our dilemma."

"Instead of going to the treehouse, why don't I do this." He snaps his fingers and Aiden is holding a pink bunny basket filled with the beloved pacifier. "Is that the one you need?"

Aiden grins. "Hells yes, it is."

"Then they're my gift to you and the wee ones."

Aiden meets Dionysus chest-to-chest and pats his back. "You rock, Greek. Thank you."

"That's what family is for, isn't it?" When Aiden backs off, Dionysus looks at me and his smile dims. "Isn't it, Jane?"

"Oh, yeah, of course. Coming through in the clutch even at three in the morning."

He nods, pleased with himself. "Good. That's what I thought."

Aiden thanks us again and takes his leave.

Dionysus is emitting a soft glow, clearly jazzed by the win. "Now that the crisis is over, we're free to do something fun."

I bark a laugh and look down at Sloan's t-shirt I threw on when Aiden came knocking on our bedroom door half an hour ago. "Dude. It's three in the morning. Sleep is the only thing I want to be doing."

"Yeah, of course. Right. I forgot mortals need sleep." He looks around like he has something on his mind but then pushes it away. "I guess I should go."

I reach out and squeeze his wrist, my instincts telling me something isn't right. Considering Dionysus only recently moved to Toronto and is adjusting to a new life in a new city, I sympathize that he might be lonely and out of sorts. "How about we pull out the couch and have a sleepover? I'll find one of the must-see movies from the list I made you, and we'll have a glass of wine. But if I fall asleep, you gotta forgive me because it's late and I'm really tired."

He grins so wide his dimples have dimples.

Nailed it.

I look back at Sloan. "Care to join us?"

He leans in and kisses me. "I'll pass if ye don't mind. I have a meeting in Montreal in the mornin' with Garnet and need to get some sleep."

"'Kay. Night. Sleep tight."

When Sloan *poofs* out, I point at the pullout couch and smile.

"I guess it's you and me. Help me with the cushions, and we'll see what movie sounds good to you."

The brass bell rings over the door as I drag my butt into Myra's Mystical Emporium for an eleven o'clock start to my ten o'clock shift. I don't like being late—because I miss too many shifts due to my crazy life—but getting here on time this morning was an absolute no-go.

The only bright spot is, the rogue book that likes to divebomb customers doesn't attack me when I enter.

You gotta take the small wins.

Myra looks up from pricing a set of chakra lanterns and startles. "Wow, you look like something the lions hacked up on the back lawn."

Considering she lives with Garnet's Moon Called pride, I don't even want to imagine what that looks like. I think it's safe to assume it's not a compliment.

"Thanks?" I set the cardboard drink tray on the counter and pull free my strawberry milkshake. "Ireland couldn't sleep, there was a three a.m. druid quest to locate her missing pacifier, and somehow I ended up on the pullout with Dionysus watching the *Pitch Perfect* trilogy until the sun came up. Dayam, that man can sing. I mean, he can really belt it out."

"He's a god. I'm sure there's not much he can't do."

I laugh. "Maybe, but people deserve to hear his voice. It's amazing."

She laughs and grabs the summer slushie I brought her. "So what's up with the god of wine that he ended up singing with you until daybreak?"

"No idea, but I'm worried about him. Despite him being all smiles and craziness, my instincts tell me he's struggling."

"New city. New life."

I suck hard on the straw with minimal success. This shake is super thick. "Why would a man who has the world at his fingertips move into a bachelor pad in Toronto and forgo his native lands, his temple, and his beloved worshippers?"

Myra pulls her straw from her mouth and swallows. "I'd hazard a guess he's evolving somehow, and you help him feel closer to whatever he seeks to become."

I chuckle. "I doubt that. I'm a disaster waiting to happen most days."

"That's not how those around you feel. You have a natural magnetism about you, duck. You emit a powerful draw and the rest of us are the iron filings it pulls toward you."

I roll my eyes. "That's ridiculous."

"Says you."

"Hmph." I take another long pull on my straw and suck in more strawberry bliss. "Dionysus is the freaking god of good times. When I asked Dora about what to get him for his housewarming, she thought he was looking for the connection of family and true friendship. I believe that's part of it, but there's more. My instincts say I'm missing something. I don't know how to help him."

"Maybe that connection of family and friendship is enough for now. There are times when all any of us needs is someone to be on our side, to listen when we need to talk, and to hug us when it gets to be too much."

I know she's right, but I worry.

Dionysus is a skilled warrior and a god of the Greek Pantheon. He's sassy and insouciant, but when you get to know him, he's still a little boy who was given away by his father and who was never accepted by his peers on Olympus.

"Why does he melt my heart so much?"

Myra sets her slushie down and reclaims her pricing gun. "Because you're a mama bear at heart. It doesn't matter if it's orphaned children who need a home or ancient immortals stuck on the fringe. You're a gatherer and a protector."

She's not wrong.

"I'm also a terrible employee who's late for work once again and who needs to get my butt in gear. My boss is very understanding, but one of these days, she's going to fire my ass."

Myra laughs and shakes her head, her electric blue hair swishing against her shoulders. "It'll never happen. You gave me Garnet, Imari, and my own life back. You're a fixture here, duck."

"I'm thankful for that. After finding out about the longevity of living while bound to a dragon, I admit, I freaked out. I can't bear the thought of outliving my family and Sloan, but it's comforting to know I'll have you and Garnet and the Greeks and maybe Emmet for centuries to come."

Myra's brow arches, disappearing under her hair. "Emmet? I didn't know he has immortality?"

I pick up the next box in the shipment and lift it onto the counter to unpack. "I don't know that he does, but he fell into a river of raw fae prana. That might mean immortality, right?"

It's not common knowledge, but that's what happened to Nikon Tsambikos Senior, Nikon's grandfather.

That's how his family gained immortality.

Myra offers me a compassionate smile. "Only time will tell. We have plenty of that ahead of us."

I reclaim my plastic cup and raise it to cheers her slushie. "To lifelong friends—however long that life lasts."

After my shift at the bookstore, I hop into my SUV and crawl through the downtown congestion toward the Acropolis. As the crow flies, it's five minutes away. In midday traffic, it takes twenty. I park in one of the six primo spots Nikon reserved closest to the building and turn off the engine. The posted signs say "Designated for SITFO"—the Special Investigations Task Force of Ontario—and even though it's silly, I feel special having a saved spot.

Having six spots reserved is overkill since more often than not, most of us are with someone possessing portal abilities and we don't arrive with our cars. Driving is old school. Still, the spots are for me, Kevin, Maxwell, Andromeda, and my Da and brothers if they're here working out or checking in.

When the engine cuts off, I pull the door latch and drop out of my truck. Scanning the lot, I check if anyone is around. I can usually count on sidelong glances from the business types working on one of the bottom six floors.

To them, this is an ordinary building where ordinary humans are working the grind. So, when the twenty-something kids get the best spots and enter the building in ripped jeans and concert t-shirts, they're understandably curious.

Who are these people who rank the closest parking spots, you ask?

Nunya business.

A couple of times, men in suits have even rushed to ride the elevator with me to chat me up and find out. That's always fun...

What floor, Miss?

Ten, please.

Oh, you're part of SITFO.

Yep.

That's a task force or something?

Yep.

You have four floors?

Yep.

That's usually when the elevator car bumps to a stop, and they frown. *What kind of task force is it, anyway?*

The top-secret kind. Which is when I make the international sign of locking my lips and throwing away the key. Hilarious.

I push through the turnstile glass doors, wave a friendly hello at the guard at the security station, and head toward the elevator. Sadly, no one is around to chase me into the elevator today, so I'm on my own as I rise to the seventh floor to surprise Sloan with a visit.

Seventh floor—STOA.

The Shrine of Toronto's Objects and Antiquities.

The brakes wheeze as the elevator car bumps to a stop and the gears roll and rumble to open the double doors.

"Oh—" I jump as a long-legged woman in black couture moves to step into the elevator. My shield tingles and I study the dark-haired vixen. "Sorry. Excuse me."

When she backs up a step, I vacate the elevator, and we change places.

"Think about my offer, darling," she purrs, bathing Sloan in a flirtatious smile.

When the elevator doors bump shut, I look at him and blink.

He holds up his finger and shakes his head. "Not in a million years, *a ghra*."

"I didn't say a thing. Did I? Nope. Not a thing."

He grunts, turning me and pressing a hand at the small of my back to usher me into his happy place.

As much as he misses his work with Granda taking care of the Shrine of the Druid Order, he's put together quite a shrine of his own here over the past five months.

"Hey, Manx. I'm glad you're here to keep him out of trouble."

Sloan's lynx animal companion trots over for me to scratch his ears. "Yer coddin' me, right? The boy never gets into any trouble. That laurel rests squarely on yer head, Red."

I grin. With my magnet for mayhem, I do keep things interesting. Still… "The seductress with the ebony hair is trouble. I felt it the moment our eyes met."

Sloan grunts. "That may be true, but she holds no interest for me. She's exactly the opposite of what I love about you."

"Beautiful, sophisticated, and alluring?"

He scoffs. "Don't be daft. Entitled, dangerous, and manipulative."

"Oh, well, I guess that's all right then."

He rests his hands on my hips and bends to kiss my nose. After almost a year of looking into these mint green eyes, you'd think I'd be immune. Nope. Not even a little. "*A ghra*, I'm too far gone to look at another. I'm pathetically, hopelessly, blissfully in love. Besides, ye possess ten times the allure Duchess d'Aboville does."

"Uh-huh. Keep plying me with compliments, and I'll start to think you're hiding something."

"Yer ridiculous."

"Agreed. So, what offer did the dastardly duchess make that she wants you to consider?"

He frowns and waves it off. "Nothing worth considerin', I'll tell ye that."

I cross my arms over my Niall Horan concert t-shirt. "I'll need a bit more to go on so I don't hyperventilate and freak out."

He points at the antique table in the corner, and we both sit. "Ye know how Garnet and I went to Montreal this mornin' to meet with a man about relics?"

"Yes. You mentioned a Monsieur Blaise."

He nods. "That's right. The men in the Blaise family have been the purveyors to empowered families back to before the French settlers arrived in Port Royal in 1604. He's the man to know when dealing with relics in the empowered world in Montreal, and Garnet wanted us to meet."

"Of course he did because Garnet is a wise man who knows you'll rock the shrine keeper gig."

He lowers his chin. "Perhaps that's part of it, but there's more."

"With Garnet, there always is. What did he rope you into? You don't have to do anything you don't want to. Your shrine runs independently of the Guild of Governors. You run your own show."

Sloan squeezes my hand where it sits on the small table and smiles. "Yer sweet to come to my defense but it's fine. His interest isn't about me or my shrine specifically. It seems there's a private event being hosted here in Toronto next week and Monsieur Blaise has concerns about the safety of his antiquities."

"The safety of his antiquities? What kind of event is he hosting? Is it *Antiques Roadshow*? Oh, say it is. Do the fae have their version?"

"No. It's not *Antiques Roadshow*."

"Poop. You got my hopes up."

"My apologies."

I shrug. "No biggie. If not *Antiques Roadshow*, what then?"

"When I tell ye, try to keep it together and focus."

I chuckle. "Intriguing. Okay, yeah, I'll try, but now you've got me all wound up and curious."

"It's the Fae Unseelie Relics Ball. It's—"

"Hold on." I stall out as my mental hamster double-checks what I think I heard. "FUR Ball? It's called the FUR Ball?"

Sloan rolls his eyes. "Aye, it is."

"You're not shitting me?"

"I'm not."

I bend backward, laughing up at the ceiling. "Best. Name. Evah. Hilarious. Is it a Moon Called event? No, wait, you said the anagram was for Fae *Unseelie* Relics. As in dark and evil fae? As in Prince Keldane and his psychotic relatives?"

"I don't know how big the Unseelie presence is on this side of the faery glass, but yes, I suppose it would include Prince Keldane and his psychotic relatives."

My blood runs cold at the mention of Keldane, and I press a hand to my chest. I never mention it to Sloan, but there are times when I wake in a cold sweat, and I can feel the bite of Keldane's scimitar as it scores my flesh.

"I didn't know you would be dealing in dark relics."

"I'm not, and I won't be. Monsieur Blaise called Garnet because he had some trouble over the weekend and now he fears that trouble might follow him to Toronto for the event."

"The FUR Ball."

"Yes, Fi. Try to focus, luv."

"Okay, what kind of trouble?"

"Someone murdered one of the men donating several items for auctioning off during the ball and stole the relics."

I straighten. "Murdered how? Like normal two shots, head and heart or something more Unseelie gruesome?"

Sloan's brow pinches, and he leans in looking concerned. "How is it that ye think getting shot in the head and heart is normal?"

"Well...okay, maybe normal was the wrong word. What I was asking was if we thought it was a mundane human type of murder and robbery or if it was more."

"Monsieur Blaise believes it's more. He said it's not the first time something like this has happened recently. He's noticed a shift over the past year that worries him."

"What kind of a shift?"

"The Culling kind." Sloan frowns. "Although he isn't aware of why it might be happening, he said several people his family has dealt with for centuries have been murdered in their homes, and valuable family heirlooms have gone missing."

"What kind of heirlooms...or do I need to ask?"

"Likely not. Several of the families have lost very powerful relics from personal collections—relics that he believes are magically charged."

"Seeing that he deals with Unseelie fae, I'm assuming the alignment of these relics leans toward chaotic and evil."

Sloan leans back in his chair and winces. "Got it in one, *a ghra*. The pieces he described seem to have ties to violence. The sapphire cocktail ring a woman wore when she was declared a witch and mobbed in the street. A Victorian insect brooch worn by a mage found with his throat slit. A gold bar brooch worn to clasp the cloak of a vampire the night he was burned and left for dead."

"This sounds like stuff Mr. Simchas would be into."

"Is that the weaselly man ye believe sold ye to the hobgoblins?"

"That's him. You should've seen how excited he got when I explained to him what murderabilia is. I should have clued in then he was the Mayor of Creepsville."

I draw a deep breath and exhale. "So what does any of this have to do with the duchess and her propositioning you?"

He arches a brow. "I'm getting to that."

"Fine, get to it faster. Manx and I are hungry, aren't we, buddy?"

Sloan chuckles. "Manx is always hungry."

"Exactly, so let's wrap this up so we can eat."

"Where was I?"

Poor man. I do fluster him some days.

"Empowered people got murdered, and someone stole their jewelry. You're about to tell me how that connects with your duchess and her sleazy offer."

"Not my duchess and it wasn't sleazy."

"So you say."

"I do. Right. So, Monsieur Blaise wanted assurances that if the items to be displayed come to Toronto that he has somewhere safe to store them until it's time to set up the exhibits."

"That's where you and STOA come in."

"Correct."

"So, he vouches for you within his empowered circles, and you secure the evil pieces until the FUR Ball. Am I getting this?"

"Perfectly."

"All right, so you impressed the socks off him, and you came home and…"

"When I returned from Montreal, the Duchess d'Aboville was waiting downstairs. It seems she's one of the FUR Ball donors and tried to come up to see my facility but was unable to access this floor."

I grin. "Too bad, so sad."

Between Dora's warding and Dionysus giving us his godly protection, floors seven through eleven are tightly locked down. I doubt anyone but an extremely powerful person could get up here without an invitation.

"Do you think she was testing our defenses?"

Sloan nods. "Very likely."

"Did you think that's all it was?"

"Likely not."

"So, what does she want?"

He chuckles. "Honestly, I have no idea."

"What! I thought we were getting to the point of the duchess part of your story."

He shrugs and stands. "What I know and what I suspect are two different things. She says she has a collection of valuable pieces that will be included in the exhibit next week and invited me to join her for a luncheon tomorrow in her hotel room to discuss it further."

I snort. "Fat chance. There will be no hotel room meetings with that female. I don't care if she has the Queen's jewels. That's a hard pass."

"That's what I told her. I said she could bring her collection here and I would cater a meal."

"What did she say to that?"

"She said that when dealing with nobility, it's best to learn my place."

"Rude. Well, then, good riddance."

Sloan runs his fingers over his jaw and sighs. "I don't disagree, but somehow, I don't think we've seen the last of Duchess d'Aboville."

CHAPTER TWO

I don't like the idea of a sexy cougar in designer clothes prowling around Sloan and inviting him to her hotel room. Still, I know without a shadow of a doubt there's nothing to worry about. In some stroke of insane fae serendipity, that cultured, male model, genius of a man is crazy about me.

There's no explaining it.

I try not to question it.

"So what kind of tingle was it?" Andromeda asks me an hour later when Sloan, Manx, and I *poof* up to the tenth floor to the Team Trouble Batcave.

"Just a warning tingle. There's no decoder ring to understanding what my shield is telling me when something like that happens, but on a scale between one and ten, I'd say she set off a three… maybe a four."

"So, not as urgent as, 'There's a vampire about to bite into your throat and drain you,' but not as benign as, 'A crazy rocking chair ghost lady is staring at you from next door.'"

"Pretty much."

Andy laughs and unzips her leather attaché case. "Things in your sphere have to be qualified on a unique curve."

"True story."

When she's finished sliding her file folders into her bag, she zips things up and fits a lid onto a banker's box full of files. "I have to run. I'm due at the courthouse at City Hall in thirty minutes, and it seems my brother has forgotten."

"Nikon? That's not like him. Did you text him?"

"I did."

I step over to the war table and call up the map of Toronto and the locator ID for Nikon's Team Trouble pendant. "That's weird. He's not registering anywhere in the city."

Sloan steps over to have a look and frowns at me. "Are ye usin' our law enforcement equipment to track yer friend fer a ride to work?"

"Um...maybe."

He rolls his eyes. "Yer ridiculous. I'm happy to take ye to the courthouse, Andromeda."

"Since when?" I make a face. "You can only go where you've been. When were you at City Hall?"

"When ye took me skatin' at Nathan Phillips Square last winter. That's right outside the front doors, isn't it?"

I laugh. "It is. Good geography, hotness. I didn't think of that."

"*And* I took Kevin over a couple of weeks ago to get his and Calum's marriage license before the office closed, remember?"

"Right, I forgot about that. Huh, you get around, Mackenzie."

Sloan scrubs Manx's ears and pats his head. "Keep an eye on her, sham. She's running on three hours sleep, and it's startin' to shine through the cracks."

He's not wrong.

I fight the yawn pushing at me and close the search on Nikon. "Yeah, you deliver Andy and her stuff to the courthouse, and I'll wait here."

Andromeda pulls her long, blonde hair back into a twist and pins it up. Her hair is straight and well-trained, so it accepts its new position without argument.

The smooth updo transforms her from an elegant, Mediterranean supermodel to a tough-as-nails litigator—who might also moonlight as a supermodel.

It's a Greek immortal thing.

Nikon is the same.

Although, Nikon is aging beautifully now that Hecate lifted her curse. The boy from Rhodes has matured in appearance from his teens into a hunky twenty-something hottie.

He wears it well.

Andy grips the handles of her bag and holds her hand out. "Thank you both. I promise I'll return him without a scratch."

"Thanks. The only woman allowed to scratch him up is me, amirite?" I hold out my fingers and curl them into claws.

Andy laughs, and Sloan picks up her box and gives me a look. "No more all-nighters for you."

When the two of them *poof* out, I head over to Garnet's office. He was on the phone when we arrived and seems to be packing up now too. "Heading home, boss?"

He nods. "I am. I've been working a lot and neglecting my girls. It's an oasis date tonight. I'm picking up takeout, and we're having a picnic in the grotto. Then Contessa McSparkles is going to entertain us with her new dance routine."

"Fun. Hug Imari from Auntie Fi."

"Will do."

"So, is there anything you want me working on? Is anything going sideways right now?"

He lifts his tailored suit jacket off the hanger hooked on his wall and shrugs into it. "No. For once, Toronto is all quiet. Did Sloan tell you about the masquerade ball next Wednesday night?"

"The FUR Ball? Sure did."

"Team Trouble will attend. Clear your schedules. Starting Monday, I want the lot of you on deck to assist Blaise's events team."

"Will do. Night. Have a good one."

"You too, Fi."

Garnet flashes out, and I look around the empty office. "And then there was one."

"And then there were two," Nikon says behind me.

I jump and laugh at myself. One thing about having friends who portal, people pop in and out a lot. "Hey, good looking. Where have you been? I tried to find you a minute ago, and you didn't show up on the Toronto grid map."

He frowns at the war table. "Let me guess. Andy was worried I'd make her late?"

"Uh...no. She thought you might've gotten caught up with something."

"You're a terrible liar, Red. Your pale complexion and freckles give you away. It's adorable, but yeah, you suck at it."

"All right. Andy was a little panicky about not getting there on time. No harm done. Sloan *poofed* her over to the courthouse. No fault. No foul." As I'm explaining, Sloan returns. "Now, he's back."

Nikon holds out a fist to bump with Sloan and nods. "Thanks for taking her, Irish. I don't know why she gets so worked up. I forgot her one time in 1786, and she's never let me live it down."

I giggle. "I guess, with immortal lives you face long memories."

"Apparently."

"Well, you're here now, and we'll vouch that you made it with plenty of time to spare."

Nikon winks. "Thanks, Red."

"So, what kept ye?" Sloan asks.

"Papu needed to see me about vineyard troubles. He senses someone magical in his winery, and he wanted me to come to check it out."

"Did you find anything?" I ask.

"I didn't, but he's been the master of that property for millennia and has a freaky sixth sense about things. His sensitivity to magical power is the strongest of all of ours, and he's sure someone's been through his production house. He tasked me to find out who and why."

"But if ye didn't find anything in the winery, what more can ye do?" Sloan asks.

"I'll be damned if I know, but hey, grandparents are in a special category all their own."

"Absolutely." There's nothing I wouldn't do for Gran and Granda. "So, how'd you leave it?"

"I said I'd look into it."

"Look into it how?" I ask.

He shrugs, holding up a couple of bottles. "I figure I'll ask the Guild lab techs if they'll take on a personal project and test these for me. Then I'll check with other vineyards and see if I can find anything there. Maybe it's a rival vintner or someone sneaking in to see how Papu has managed for so long. No idea."

I grin. "Check with the other vineyards? You mean travel across Europe tasting wine and investigating at all the vineyards?"

He arches a brow at me and chuckles. "I don't suppose all of them, no, but that's where I'll start."

"Well, then, I suppose you'll need a backup team to come with you...just in case you find something."

Nikon chuckles. "I don't know that I should give it that much credence."

"Hells yeah, you should. This is Papu we're talking about. He saved both our lives. We need to treat this very seriously. Sloan and I will sort through our schedules and be ready to snap out tonight. No. Even better, we'll have Dart take us through the portal circle, and he can visit his siblings while we tour around Europe."

Sloan scowls at me. "Och, yer gonna have to give me more notice than that, Fi. I'm still hoping to salvage a meeting with the duchess tomorrow, and Dora set aside time in the afternoon to help me with an herbology problem. And yer on Jackson duty to take him to football practice Saturday morning."

I sigh. "Okay, maybe we can't go if you leave tonight. How about Saturday afternoon? That gives us all day tomorrow to get organized and make a plan."

Nikon laughs. "Why make a plan? You've grabbed the reins and seem to have everything figured out."

"Almost everything." I hold up my finger and grab the Dionysus pendant around my neck. Focusing on my movie marathon buddy, I close my eyes to see if he wants to pop in and chat.

When he doesn't appear, I frown at the pendant. "Huh, maybe he's busy."

Sloan shrugs. "He *is* a god of the Greek Pantheon. I'm sure he has a great many responsibilities pulling at him. There's a possibility he's not even in this time."

"Yeah, you're probably right." Still, I think he'll love the idea of a European wine tour. Pulling out my phone, I text him a teaser.

What have you got going on this weekend? Wanna road trip on a European wine tour with us on Saturday and Sunday?

I hit "Send" and grin up at the two of them. "I bet he'll come. After all, if someone's messing with wine, it's his dominion to protect, and he's the expert of all experts."

Thursday night at Shenanigans is always a good time. That's the night when most of the regulars come to avoid the weekend whiskey warriors, which is what Liam and I call the nineteen to twenty-five crowd that comes out to get their buzz on.

There's nothing wrong with that, but Shenanigans is so much more.

Sloan *poofs* me, Calum, Kev, and Dillan into the private stairwell that leads to the loft apartment above the bar. Emmet and Ciara are already here somewhere. They had dinner with Da and Shannon upstairs and said they'd meet us afterward in the pub.

The five of us find the pair at the back wall with two tables pulled together.

"What's the craic?" I ask as we claim our seats.

Ciara sweeps a hand to highlight an empty table. "Not much craic yet, I'm afraid. I think yer bestie is suckin' exhaust on the bar."

Right, there are no drinks in front of them.

As much as I pride myself as an Irish girl who can handle my whiskey, when seated next to Ciara, I'm Irish-lite at best.

Sloan catches me watching Liam and squeezes my wrist. "Maybe ye should help him out fer a bit, aye? It looks like he could use it."

It does.

We try not to get more than one or two customers deep on the bar, but he has a solid crowd of three-deep crushed up against the unlucky stool sitters.

"You don't mind?"

He shakes his head. "My guess is with the two of ye workin' together ye'll have that crowd cleared out in twenty minutes."

Probably more like thirty, but whatevs.

Popping up onto my toes, I kiss his cheek. "Save me a dance. Oh, and keep an eye out for Suede. She said she might join us tonight."

Sloan nods. "We'll be sure to keep her company until ye return. Have fun."

"Always."

It's true. I shuffle off from the table, swaying my hips to Celtic rhythms and kissing a few cheeks of customers who've known me my whole life. There's something to be said for having a special place where you always feel like you're home.

Shenanigans is that for me.

"Hey, there. What's the holdup with service? Are you guys short-handed?"

Liam rolls his eyes, grabbing two frosted mugs from the chill fridge. "Oh, maybe a little. Jordie's car died in an intersection halfway here. He called CAA, and they towed it for him, but he'll be late. Kady has the flu and threw up half the night. The new kid I hired to bus tables decided the job doesn't live up to his potential, so he no-showed."

"Awesome. Do you want help?"

Liam laughs and pulls a draught. "Is that a rhetorical question? Have I ever turned down your help behind the bar?"

I round the end of the bar and grab an apron. "Why would you? I'm fabulous."

"That you are."

While Liam finishes the order he's filling, I grab a bar towel and catch up on a bit of cleaning and restocking before diving in.

"All right, who's next? What can I get you?"

The two of us dance our dance without pause, and by the end of it, things are back under control, and everyone seems happy.

"Have I told you lately that I love you?"

I wipe up a puddle of melted ice off the counter and pull a four-by-four out of the fridge to restock the cherries, lemons, and limes. "Oooh, sing that to me, in your best Rod Stewart voice, and prove it to me."

Liam straightens, pulls out his phone, and the music takes an abrupt detour to serenade me. "This is my best Rod Steward voice."

I laugh. "It's amazing. Sounds just like him."

The two of us sing behind the bar, catching our breath and getting ready for the younger crowd to arrive at eleven. When I was nineteen, we went to the bar and started drinking around eight-thirty or nine. Now it's not cool to go to the bar until at least eleven or after.

What the hell's with that?

If it was a choice between going out for a drink at midnight or heading upstairs to bed, the only right answer is bed.

King Henry for the win.

By the time the ode to Fi is over, Jordie has arrived and is rushing to put his stuff away in the staff room. Liam flips the music back to the regularly scheduled playlist, and I untie my apron. "Are you good if I go drink with the fam jam?"

"Yeah. Of course. Thanks Fi." He presses his fist against his heart. "I love you, little sister."

I make a face. "Ew, don't do that. You know that weirds me out."

He laughs, pulling the next order slip from the printer. "I know. That's why I said it."

"Just for that, I'm taking my pay in a pitcher for the table."

"Take two. You're worth it." He grabs the rum off the back rack and pulls the lid off the blender. "Hey, has your dad mentioned anything about moving or where he and Mom might end up?"

"What do you mean moving? Like moving out from upstairs?"

"Yeah, I get the feeling that being newlyweds in their fifties and living over the bar isn't their end goal dream of dreams."

I chuckle, but no, I hadn't thought about it. "I guess it's loud when he's off shift and trying to sleep."

He nods. "They haven't said anything to me, but I overheard them talking about how you guys are all grown up, and I could take the bar if they decided to exit stage left."

I hate that idea.

"We haven't even gotten used to Da not living at the house. I'm not ready for them to move out of the pub too. Where would they go? Would it be a place in the neighborhood or are they thinking about something else? What about policing...and SITFO...and this place?"

My voice is getting pitchy, and I stop the panic before Dart senses it and ends up crashing through the wall of the pub to see what's wrong. "I vote no."

Liam barks a laugh. "No one asked us to weigh in. I'm sure that when the subject does come up, we won't get a vote."

"Just because they're adults and decided to get married, that doesn't mean they can knock us all for a loop." I set the two pitchers of draught onto the bar and frown. "Seriously. Did you get a sense that it was idle conversation or planning?"

He shrugs. "It sounded like planning to me. Your dad was asking questions about me taking over the bar and what she'd do if she didn't have to run this place."

"But..." I want to say that Shannon *has* to run this place because she *is* Shenanigans, but that's crazy. "Is it selfish to not want anything to change?"

He shakes his head. "I think it's perfectly normal with all the changes in the past year. But yeah, I thought I'd mention it and see if you'd heard anything or at least give you a heads up if you hadn't."

"Thanks. That would've blindsided me. We still miss Da from him moving out when he married your mom."

Liam nods and takes the next order slip from the printer. "I'm with you."

"Sorry I'm late, boss." Jordie rushes in to take my place.

"Shit happens, Jord," Liam says. "I'm surprised that beater of yours hasn't stranded you before now."

Jordie launches into a defense for his old hunk-a-junk, and I take my pitchers to go.

"There she is." Sloan smiles up at me as I arrive at the table. "How'd that go, *a ghra*? Ye always seem to enjoy bein' behind the bar."

I set down the two pitchers and squeeze past Dillan to sit beside him on the bench. "I do love the bar, but honestly, it's always the most fun when it's Liam and me, and we're crazy busy. We have a rhythm, and that's what makes it even more fun."

I pour a round and sip my first pint of the night. "Is Suede not here yet? I thought she would be."

Emmet nods and hooks his thumb over his shoulder. "She's here. She and Ciara took a girl trip."

"A girl trip" is Emmet's term for women traveling in packs to visit the ladies' room. I take another swallow and jump back up. "Oh, great timing. I've got to pee."

Sloan laughs, and when Emmet opens his mouth to say something, my guy shuts him down. "Let them be, Em. There are mysteries in this world men were never meant to understand."

I'm still chuckling about my closet philosopher as I push the door and find Ciara and Suede washing up at the sinks. "Hello, girls."

"Fi! There you are." Suede rips off a length of paper towel and hugs me once her hands are dry. "I waved to you at the bar, but you were hyper-focused."

I ease back and head into one of the stalls. "Yeah, I get that way. I love it when it's busy like it is tonight. It makes working the bar tons of fun."

"I'm headin' back to the table," Ciara says. "Em texted me our food arrived."

"Okay, no problem. We're right behind you." I finish in the stall, flush, and come out to wash my hands. "Don't let your food get cold on my account."

Ciara leaves, and I open the faucet and check out my elven friend in the mirror's reflection.

Suede Silverbirch doesn't talk about her family, but I've gathered she's the daughter of a powerful elven leader. The fact that she's a Guild Governor means her family must be either royal or politically connected.

Unlike the mages, wizards, and some of the magic-wielding races of empowered citizens, elves and ash nymphs and some other races are considered less powerful because they're simply magical folks, not magically powerful.

Not that it matters.

From the moment I met her during the riverboat luncheon last summer, she's never been anything but my friend. She was my first friend in that room of Guild goofballs—then Zxata and Nikon.

Man, that luncheon set me up for some great people in my life.

"Sorry to horn in on your family night," she says behind me.

I pump the soap and scrub my fingers. "You could never horn in, girlfriend. If you say you need to talk to me, I'm always available to listen."

She purses her lips and tugs on her long, silver hair. "Maybe I shouldn't say anything. I mean…it's probably nothing. Then I'm embarrassing all three of us."

Okay, now my skin is starting to tingle.

"You should definitely tell me. If it's nothing, there's no harm done. If it's something, there'll be two of us to put our heads together and figure it out."

She tilts her head back and forth as if considering that. "Okay, you're right."

She ducks to check for feet, ensuring we have the room to ourselves. When she straightens, she smooths her hair and wets her lips. "You know how sometimes my elf girlfriends and I enjoy some of the more hedonistic pleasures of having the god of ecstasy living in our midst?"

I lean closer to the mirror and check that I'm presentable. "Dionysus mentioned that in passing."

She leans her hip against the vanity and frowns. "It's probably nothing. I mean...it happens to every man, right? That's what they say. I'm not even sure he's having a problem. It's just—"

I lift a finger to stop her. "You're saying Dionysus had a moment when he wasn't ready to sex it up?"

"I am. I mean...I think so. You know him. He never stops moving, but when everyone in a room is naked, you tend to be able to gauge how things are going."

I don't want to envision that too closely. "Do gods even get dysfunction?"

"I have no idea."

"Neither do I." I pull out my pendant and look at his likeness. "How do I bring that up in normal conversation to check in?"

"Please, gods, don't tell him I told you. It's just...when you mentioned earlier that he seemed desperate for some company and you were worried about him, I thought maybe you should know."

"Absolutely." I toss my paper towel and am ready to leave. "It's not the easiest subject to bring up with a friend, but if during one of your free love soirees, Dionysus failed to perform at his usual level of sexual mastery that's a huge deal."

She shrugs. "There were enough of us there that I don't think any of the others caught on, but it wasn't my first time playing the Greek god grind. When I thought back to other times when he played the host card and excused himself instead of joining, I wondered if it's happened before."

Well, that would certainly explain why the god of fabulous might set himself up in a bachelor pad funhouse and hide in a VR room.

"Poor Dionysus. His sexy schmexy self-image is so ingrained in his identity, if things aren't working for him, he must be freaking out."

"That's the only reason I'm bringing it up."

I wave away her concern and shake my head. "You did the

right thing. Sloan and I are planning a weekend away in wine country with Nikon. I'll convince him to come with us. Maybe I can figure out what's wrong and see if I can help."

Suede exhales. "I hope so. Him losing his mojo would be a blow to all womenkind."

I laugh. "I'll take your word for it."

CHAPTER THREE

The next morning, I lay in bed for a long time after my eyes first open. Staring at the carved ceiling of King Henry, my mind is a centrifuge of worry and wonder.

I check my phone and Dionysus neither called nor texted. Do gods have dry spells? Is Suede imagining things? Would Da and Shannon move away? Who is the Duchess d'Aboville and what is she after? What's upsetting Daisy that she's not sleeping?

After stewing for too long, I figure there's only one of those issues I can do anything about right now, and I can't do it from upstairs.

Sweeping the fabric drape out of the way, I roll out of King Henry and pull on a pair of yoga pants. I've grown fond of wearing one of Sloan's t-shirts to bed. It's as dressed and presentable as I'll be until I shower at Badass Bootcamp after I spend an hour or two in the gym.

Heading into the washroom, I pee, brush my teeth and gather my hair in a handful and pull it from my eyes. Unlike Andromeda's golden silk that sits smoothly and looks sleek, my chaotic kinks and curls are unruly and stubborn. They twist out of the elastic like I'm a star in an 80s Guns N' Roses video.

Whatevs.

With that taken care of, I grab a fresh change of clothes, toss them into my gym bag with my toiletry kit, and head downstairs. As usual, I'm the last to rise so everyone is already milling around downstairs.

Taking a quick look around, I check for Daisy, and when I don't see her, I sit with Calum and Kevin at the table. "Oooh, what are we looking at?"

"Pinterest pages of beach weddings." Kevin grins. "June twenty-first is coming fast."

"Two things to celebrate on the Summer Solstice."

Kevin nods. "I thought it was a nice tip of the hat to Calum's new Robin Hood side."

Calum grunts. "Call me Robin Hood as many times as you want. I'm still not wearing tights to my wedding."

Emmet snorts. "You'd look great in green tights and swash-buckler boots, dude. Add a little leather and a hood…you should totally go with that."

"Right?" Kevin says. "At the very least for the Solstice afterparty."

"Dream on, boys."

Kevin winks at me. "A boy's gotta try."

I touch the screen of his laptop and enlarge a picture of an arbor in the sand. The loving couple has their linen pants rolled up their shins, and the water is lapping at their feet and ankles. "This is nice."

"Yeah, I liked that one too. Calum's not keen on having sand stuck to our feet for the rest of the night."

I scowl at my brother. "You're having a beach wedding. There will be sand."

Calum shrugs. "Call me crazy."

"Crazy," Kevin and I both say.

I round the island and pour myself a glass of juice. "How are plans for the wedding coming, anyway?"

Kevin shrugs. "Good, I think. I'm not sure. We've never planned a wedding before."

Emmet waves that away. "If at the end of the day the two of you are married and you spent the day the way you want to, it's a win."

I fill my glass and lean over the island. "Yeah, you don't need big or fancy or flashy if that's not your thing. You guys do whatever feels right, and it'll be perfect."

Kevin nods. "Yep. Good advice."

Calum takes his dishes over to the sink and pours himself another half a cup of coffee.

I check that our conversation is our own. "There's something I want to mention." I tell them what Doc told us about Daisy being super sad and not wanting to play with them.

Calum looks stricken. "Why isn't she sleeping?"

"I don't know, but Doc swiped Ireland's pacifier so she could try that. When I found her, she was out cold and sawing logs, but that doesn't explain why she'd be upset in the first place."

"She hasn't mentioned anything," Kevin says.

I shrug. "I don't know what it's about. Maybe she's worried about the wedding or missing her forest friends or the medication for her seizures is making her feel funny, I don't know."

"Whatever it is, we'll figure it out," Kevin says.

Calum checks his watch and worry darkens his expression. "Wait for me to get home tonight, and we'll talk to her together, 'kay?"

The two of them start chatting privately, so I meet Emmet's gaze.

"What's so funny?"

He's been reading a news story on his phone and chuckling like a little kid. "There's been a downturn in the markets. It seems Viagra, Cialis, Levitra, and Stendra have all taken a hit over the past few weeks. Customers are complaining about the efficacy of their pills, and the pharmaceutical companies can't figure out why."

"That's a downer," Kevin says.

"Soft markets can happen to anyone...or so I've heard," Calum says.

"The stockholders are hoping for a strong upturn," Emmet says, "but so far, nothing's rising."

"That's deflating."

I laugh and let them have their fun. "Is Sloan around?"

"In the apothecary. He's having trouble with one of his plants," Kevin says.

"It's gone limp," Emmet adds.

"Oh no, it's catching," Calum says. "Is everything okay behind closed doors, sista?"

I roll my eyes. Right, he mentioned Dora is going to work with him later on a herbology problem. "Everything's fine behind closed doors. Sometimes a limp plant is only a limp plant."

I leave the three of them laughing and head toward the back of the house and the basement steps.

Dillan and Aiden come in from the back door, both in their blues. I delay my trip to go downstairs to find Sloan and turn back toward the kitchen. "We're all here. Do you guys have a sec? There's something we need to talk about."

Dillan frowns. "Wasn't me."

"Yeah, it was. I saw him do it," Emmet calls.

I shake my head. "It's nothing bad."

Dillan nods. "Oh, good, then it was me."

"Oh, now he's taking the credit. His pants are totes on fire. It was totally me."

I roll my eyes and lean against the breakfast bar. "Last night, Liam told me Da and Shannon are talking about moving. He overheard him ask her about walking away from Shenanigans and leaving it with Liam."

"*What?*" they all shout in unison.

"They can't do that," Emmet says. "Shannon is the Shen in Shenanigans."

Dillan scowls. "That almost made sense but nope. It's a fail."

"The point is, they can't move," Emmet snaps.

"Move where?" Calum asks. "Still downtown? Midtown? Uptown? Farther?"

"Uptown?" Dillan's scowl deepens. "Who wants to live Uptown. Scarborough? North York? Why the hell would they want to live there?"

"No one said they do." I pull the lid off the Tupperware container with the blueberry muffins Emmet and Ciara baked yesterday afternoon, grab one, and peel back the paper. "I said they mentioned moving. He had no idea where or when. You're projecting."

"Well then, no," Emmet says matter-of-factly. "It's bad enough Da moved out of the house. Now they're going to move out of the pub? I vote no."

"My reaction exactly, Em, but I'm not sure we're getting a vote."

Emmet frowns at me. "Majority rules. There are more of us than them."

"Do we have the right to vote no?" Aiden asks.

Dillan sighs. "When Mam and Mark died, Da and Shannon dedicated themselves and everything they did to us. Now, maybe they want their turn."

I fold the muffin paper in on itself and take a bite. "Look at you being all mature and understanding. Where's this coming from?"

D shrugs. "Maybe I'm evolving."

I snort. "All right, what's her name?"

His scowl of indignation is too funny. "What? Why can I only be evolving if there's a woman involved?"

"Call it my druid instinct. You mentioned an unbelievable hookup at Dionysus' housewarming, then nothing. You want a plus-one for the wedding and *Rocky Horror,* and when you're not at work or here, you're suspiciously silent about where you've been spending your time. Single Dillan is all swagger and sass. This is Dillan in a relationship."

"Look at you, Nancy Drew. Think you have your older brother all figured out, do you?"

"Yep. So, what's her name and why aren't we getting the scoop on her?"

"Because there's no girl."

"She better not be married," Emmet says. "We'll kick your ass to hell and back if you're the cheating piece of ass on the side."

"She's *not* married, you eejit."

Emmet's grin is wildly triumphant. "So there *is* a girl. See what I did there? Now who's the eejit, eejit?"

Dillan launches, and Emmet takes off a split second before Dillan's fist flies through the air where his face had been. The chase is on, and the two of them race up the stairs two at a time like a herd of elephants.

"No horsing around on the stairs!" The words are still ringing in the air when I turn to Kevin. "Did I just channel my father?"

Aiden chuckles. "You sure did. If you'd said it with an accent and threw in a 'feckin' eejits' it would've been perfect."

I laugh. "They say one day we become our parents."

Kevin snorts. "Shoot me now. Honestly, Fi, if I ever start making felt clothing for our flower pots or think it's cool to wear black knee socks with shorts, take Calum's gun and shoot me."

Calum waves that off. "Hey, don't knock Ivan and Isabelle. Your parents are amazing."

He grins. "Yeah, fine. They are."

A loud *thunk* over our heads makes me duck, but thankfully, nobody comes crashing through the ceiling.

Sloan *poofs* into the kitchen looking alarmed. "What the hell was that?"

"Emmet and Dillan horsing around." I point upstairs to where grunts and *thuds* fill the air.

"I thought the ceiling had given way," he says.

"We were a floor closer. Imagine how much louder that *clunk* was for us."

Sloan scowls up at the ceiling and the pendant light fixture swaying from the assault. "Should we step in and break it up?"

"They're fine. It's best to go on with our day."

Sloan eyes my bag. "If yer finished with yer muffin, do ye want me to take ye to the eighth floor to work out?"

"Yes, please." I walk to the bottom of the stairs and yell up. "Going to work out. Do you want to come, Em?"

"No, he's good," Dillan shouts, panting. There's another loud *clunk,* and I wince. "Emmet can't come to the phone right now. He's too busy getting his pansy ass kicked by his better."

"I'll go." Bruin lumbers up the back hall. "Goddess knows ye can't be trusted out in the world all alone."

"Too true, Bear," Sloan says. "Too true."

Sloan *poofs* me to the eighth floor of the Acropolis, and I turn on the lights and set my bag down. "How long until you have to meet the duchess? Is that what you're wearing?"

He looks down at the slacks, button-down shirt with a tie, sport coat, and frowns. "What's wrong with what I'm wearing? You said I looked good."

"Too good, hotness. Too good for her, anyway."

His worry drains away, and he gathers me into his arms for a hug. "I enjoy the way ye look at me when I dress well. The fact that she gets to see it should make ye happy because there's not one thing she can say or do that will make me waver. I'm a goner."

I grin. "Good, because I can't be the only one out on that limb."

"I assure ye, yer not. Now, shall I leave ye to yer workout?"

I draw a deep breath and check my phone. Still no reply from Dionysus. "Actually, would you mind popping me up to Dionysus' bachelor pad first? I'm getting worried. He really should've responded to me by now, and I have a bad feeling."

"Ye shouldn't worry, *a ghra*. There are a dozen reasons why he might not have responded to yer text."

I shake my head. "Suede told me something private last night that has me worried. Would you mind humoring me?"

"Of course, luv." Sloan takes my hand, and in the blink of a moment, we *poof* to the open concept loft apartment Dionysus magicked himself as the eleventh floor of the building.

The moment we take form, my breath solidifies in my chest. The place is trashed: the blow-up panda has its throat slit open, the bumper cars are in pieces, and the furniture can now be stacked and used as kindling.

"Oh, shit." I grip Sloan's arm when he moves to investigate. "Hotness, as much as you're going to hate this, I'd like you to go back to STOA and let me handle this."

"Are ye daft? Someone invaded the home of a Greek god and destroyed the place. There's no way on this earth I'm leavin' ye alone here."

"First off, I wouldn't be alone. I have Bruin. And second, no one attacked. If I'm right, Dionysus did this."

Sloan's gaze tightens, and he scans the space. "Why would he do that?"

I sigh. "It's not my story to tell. Trust me. If I'm right, there's no danger to me. He's going through a rough time right now, and I think I'll be able to reach him better without you here."

"Fi, ye know I believe in yer abilities and yer instincts but—"

"Thank you." I cut him off before he can say any more and

reach up on my tiptoes to kiss his cheek. "I'll text you once I assess the situation."

He frowns at the devastation. "Go ahead and text me if ye like but ye won't need to because I'll be standin' right beside ye. I told ye I'm not leavin' and I'm a man of my word."

I scowl at him, but his scowl is much more severe.

He's locked horns and is now wearing a look of Irish determination I recognize all too well from facing off against Da and Granda.

There's no changing his mind on this.

Uhh... Men.

"Fine. You search the VR room and the triclinium. I'll check the bedroom."

"Fine." Sloan stomps off toward the arcade area of the loft, his long, brisk strides carrying him into the distance. Yeah, even annoyed at him, I spend a few extra seconds checking out his ass and the graceful stride of the powerful warrior he holds in reserve.

Enough of that though, I'm annoyed at him.

I frown at the mess, the rubber soles of my sneakers *crunching* glass with every step I take, making my way toward Dionysus' bedroom.

As I near the door, the pressure in my chest is nearly unbearable. My heart is pounding, my mouth is dry, and there are so many terrifying images clicking through my mental View-Master I can't think.

He's immortal.

I've never been more thankful for that simple truth than right now. "Tarzan? You okay?"

Nothing.

I grip the door handle and wait a beat. If Sloan's right, my shield will weigh in.

Again, nothing.

I push the door open and suck in a breath.

CHAPTER FOUR

"Nononono, dude, what have you done? Sloan, in here!"

Rushing to his bedside, I drop to the floor and try to figure out where to begin. He's naked, unconscious, and hooked up to a homemade intravenous feed. There's a rainbow of scattered pills on the bed and floor and half a dozen empty liquor bottles lying discarded like fallen soldiers around his bare legs.

"Let me in there, luv." Sloan rushes forward to fill the space as I make room. The first thing he does is pull out the IV lines feeding into both of Dionysus' arms. As he flings them away, scarlet liquid whips through the air and across my chest.

I catch the scent and scrunch the cotton in my fingers to bring it up to smell. "Wine? He's doing wine intravenously?"

"That's insane."

No argument. "Twenty bucks says he wakes up and has a perfectly reasonable explanation for doing this."

Sloan grunts and the surge of his magical signature raises the hair on my arms. "Dionysus, can ye hear me, sham?"

He doesn't answer.

While Sloan's healing energy roars to the fore, his hands slide over the perfection of Dionysus' physique.

I swallow and press shaking fingers against his throat. A strong and steady pulse comes back at me, and I exhale, my eyes stinging with tears. "You're so lucky you're alive, you big dope. You know the rule. No one dies on me."

My emotions build in cresting waves, and I push back the tears. I'll cry later—there's no question about that—but for right now, I need to stay in the moment in case Sloan needs me.

Searching the chaos of the scene, I grab a purple barrel from the toy pile on his dresser and dump out the two dozen plastic monkeys.

Then, making like a kid on Easter morning, I start crawling around the floor, gathering all the colorful ovals scattered everywhere.

Dayam. I've never seen so many pills.

"Help me get him off the floor, *a ghra.*" Sloan hooks a hold under Dionysus' arms and lifts him toward the mattress. I pull the sheets back, sending a barrage of pills soaring through the air, and help lift his legs onto the bed.

Sloan goes back to working on him with his powers.

I figure it's safe to pull the sheet over his hips and give us all a break from the beautiful but very nakey Dionysus.

Once I do that, I climb onto the bed and lie down beside him. "Hey Greek god, it's me, Fiona. Open your eyes and tell me you're okay."

He doesn't.

His head is lolled toward me, though, so I gently grip the sides of his face and pull open his eyelids.

Yowzers, his pupils are silver, swirling, and freaky weird. "I don't know what this means, but I'm assuming it's not good."

Sloan looks over and blinks. "Och, I can't see how that's good, no."

I pick up a pink, a blue, and a pale green pill between us and sigh. "Man, when you set your mind to something, you really commit."

"He's coming out of it," Sloan says. "Can ye get him a glass of water and a good-sized vomit bin? The next bit won't be pretty."

"On it." I roll off the bed and opt for the puke bucket first. I rush out to the living room and search until I come up with a Pirates of the Caribbean garbage pail in the powder room. "Come on, Jack Sparrow. I have a feeling you're going to be very useful."

Sloan is in the zone when I get back, so I do busy work and stay out of his way. I climb back onto the bed, gather the pillows to the headboard, and discover a medieval-looking gold goblet under the comforter.

By the weight of the thing, it's pure gold.

It's lying on its side, and it soon becomes clear that's where Dionysus kept the pills before they tumbled free.

My hamster takes a detour from my current state of panic to noodle on that. A pure gold goblet, bejeweled and likely five or six hundred years old, used as the party snack bowl.

That's quite a departure from the red Solo cups we use at our place for a night of drunken debauchery.

"He's coming around," Sloan says.

I snap back to the problem at hand and grab Captain Jack, readying for what's to come.

Sloan is right, as usual.

Once the first weak groans of consciousness sound, Dionysus grimaces and starts to lurch.

Sloan helps him get over the bucket, and I follow his trajectory to ensure I've positioned Captain Jack to receive.

As Dionysus heaves forward and spews, I fight the tightening of my gag reflex. Thankfully, I only have a small blueberry muffin in my tummy, so nothing much to slosh around.

I try not to hear the velocity of the splashing.

I try...and fail.

Then comes the smell. I've been drunk on wine and whiskey enough times to tie that scent to some very dire moments of me praying to the porcelain god.

"Fi, ye look green, luv. Do ye need to take a walk and breathe?"

I meet Sloan's concerned gaze, burp, and swallow the burn of bile. "No. I'm good. I'm here."

Dionysus mutters something in tongues, and my focus returns to him.

"Hey, Tarzan, welcome back."

He doubles over again, and another funnel of fluid ejects from within. "What is happening to me? I feel like a mountain goat rammed me in the head and a musk ox defecated in my mouth."

"You paint a colorful picture. It didn't help my queasy stomach much, but it was entertaining."

Dionysus comes further out of his stupor. Groaning, he shakes his head and closes his eyes. "Go. I don't want you here right now."

"Tough titties, Tarzan." I hand Sloan the puke bucket when he gestures for it. "We're here, and we're not leaving. You may not know a lot about family yet, but by trying to kill yourself, you've initiated level one emergency protocols."

He flops on the bed and groans.

After lying there for a while, his face screws up, and he opens his eyes. "Kill myself? I'm a god. I wasn't trying to kill myself."

"Well, you took a boatload of pills, and you were taking wine intravenously. In my world that's a major cry for help."

He presses a hand over his eyes and groans. "Wine always used to make me feel good. Humans take pills to feel good. I wanted to feel good, and nothing was working."

Just like that, I feel a thousand times better.

As I predicted, in his mind infusing his body with wine was a perfectly reasonable means to an end.

Death wasn't the end he was aiming for.

Relief washes away the panic, and my body starts to come down from crisis mode. In the aftermath of the past ten minutes, there's no holding back the tears. "You scared the bejeebers out of me, dude. I thought you were trying to die."

Dionysus looks stricken, but whether it's from my assumption or my state of leaking emotions, I can't say.

Lying on my side facing him as I am, I clutch his hand in mine. "Don't do that again. If you have something weighing on you, tell me you're hurting. I will always make time for you. Family figures things out together."

His fingers tighten, his hold fierce. "Not all families, Jane. The one I'm from exploits weakness and teaches you never to expose vulnerability."

"Then your old family is wrong. It's a good thing you have a new family now."

Dionysus blinks quickly, but there's no hiding that he too is glassing up.

Movement over Dionysus' shoulder brings the return of Sloan through the doorway. He's washed out the bucket and sets it on the bed by our feet.

"Thank you, Irish," Dionysus says.

"Of course."

I meet Sloan's worried gaze and offer what I hope is a reassuring smile. "Go to your meeting, hotness. We'll be fine. I'll text you later."

"Are ye sure? I don't mind stayin'. I can call the duchess and put her off."

"No. You go. I'm going to teach Dionysus the cathartic benefits of an Oprah ugly cry, and you don't want to be here for that."

"All right. Take care of each other and text me or I'll worry."

When Sloan *poofs* out, I swipe my cheeks and squeeze Dionysus' hand. When I was seventeen, Emmet and I volunteered at the youth hotline center at our high school, answering phones. As different as this situation is, sometimes Dionysus could pass for an angsty teen.

I fall back on the counseling training we got.

"I love you, Dionysus. My life is better because you're in it. I understand things aren't going well for you, but I'm here and I'll always be here for you."

He closes his eyes, and we leave it at that, his eyes leaking from between pinched lids. When his breathing slows, and his body relaxes, I take his cue for a nap and close my eyes too.

Everything feels better after a little snooze.

When I wake up a while later, we're still clasping hands, and he's watching me sleep. "Hey there, Tarzan. You feeling better?"

"No. I think my brain is going to explode...and my tongue tastes like a feral animal died in my mouth...and throwing up is very unpleasant. No wonder humans despise it. Been there, tried that, thanks but no thanks."

"That was the first time you ever puked?"

He makes a face. "Yes, and it's disgusting."

"No argument."

"What's with the throbbing behind my eyes?"

"Have you never had a hangover before?"

"No. Is that what this is?"

"Do you feel like death, pounding head, sick stomach, muscle aches, fatigue, sensitivity to light?"

"All of the above."

"Then yes, this is a hangover. Have you never had one of those either? I've seen you party. How could you never have the morning after the night before?"

"I'm the god of wine and feasts. What good would I be if I was hungover all the time?"

"Good point." I think about that for a bit and frown. "So what does it mean that you have one now?"

His expression is somber. "I honestly don't know."

The fear glittering in wide eyes cleaves my heart in two. I

45

squeeze his hand and offer him as much support and confidence as I can. "We'll figure this out. Do you still have the ingredients for Gran's hangover recipe?"

He thinks for a moment and swipes his hand toward the kitchen. "Yes. You'll find everything you need."

"Perfect. Close your eyes, and I'll make up a batch of cure-all and be back in twenty minutes to make you feel better."

He squeezes my hand and winces. "You make me feel better just by being here, Jane."

"Aw, sweetie. Rest now. I've got you."

Dionysus sleeps for an hour, and I don't have the heart to wake him. I text Sloan and update him, then start sifting through the rubble to see what's salvageable. Odds are Dionysus can sweep his hand through the air or snap his fingers and fix it in a flash but cleaning up gives me something to do while I worry.

When a groan sounds from the bedroom, I pour him a mug of Gran's pick-me-up and cut it with coffee. When I get back to the bedroom, he's scowling and flips the sheets to cover his lap. "Oh, you're still here."

"Yes, cranky pants man, I am. I told you I've got you and I take my declarations of support very seriously."

"I feel like bog swill."

I hold out the mug. "That's the way humans feel every time we overdo it with alcohol."

"Yet you do it again? That's masochistic."

I let him sip from his cup for a bit, then get things rolling. "Let's talk about what's upsetting you and see if we can figure it out together."

He takes another long sip and swallows. "Nothing's bothering me, Red. You know me. Life of the party. I'm too shallow to have depth."

"I know better."

He rolls to the side of the bed and frowns at the mess of his room and the apartment beyond. "I'm sorry you saw this. I'll strike it from your memory, and everything will be fixed and back the way it was."

I sit up and raise a finger. "No. Friends don't strike the memory of friends. What happens between us is real, no matter how crazy, messy, or ugly it is. Promise me."

He sets the almost empty mug on the head of the gargoyle beside his bed and rolls out from under the sheets. The move provides me with a glorious view of his chiseled backside.

I drop my gaze. "And put some clothes on. Friends don't flaunt their junk in front of friends. Obviously, there are times when nakedness is unavoidable, but we try to keep that to a minimum."

"No kissing. No sex. No nakedness. There are a lot of rules to being friends with you, Red." The next moment, Dionysus is dressed and holding out his hand to help me off the edge of the bed. "I'm hungry. Are you hungry?"

"I could eat."

"Wanna go out for pizza?"

I laugh. "Are you up for pizza? Gran's concoction is good, but it's not instant."

"Yes, I feel better."

I look down at myself. "I'm wearing sweats and Sloan's t-shirt —which I slept in—and haven't showered. How about we order in?"

I accept his outstretched hand, and the surge of power makes the hair on my arms stand on end. A moment later I'm looking around at beautiful old buildings and cobbled streets, and I'm wearing my favorite ripped jeans and the top Kinu and Aiden gave me for my birthday a few weeks ago.

"Oh, man. What did you do?"

CHAPTER FIVE

Dionysus looks around, then at me, confused. "I thought we were going out for pizza."

I chuckle. "So, naturally we came to Italy."

"Naturally." Dionysus steps in beside me so another couple can pass us on the sidewalk. Then he reclaims my hand, and we follow them down the skinny street. "Thank you for being my friend, Jane. I'm told I'm a nightmare and people tire of me, but I'm trying to do better."

I squeeze his hand and hug his arm. "You're not a nightmare. Whoever told you that was an idiot and given a chance, I'll tell him so."

"You better not. Zeus doesn't like humans much, and he likes dissension even less."

Zeus? His *father* told him he's a nightmare?

I hug his arm and rest my cheek against his shoulder. "He's wrong. He doesn't know how to love someone as special as you."

"Gods don't know how to love at all. At least not the gods in the Greek Pantheon."

I admit, after meeting Hecate, I might've believed that, but not now. Dionysus may not understand how to love yet, but he's full of endless potential.

"You must've loved someone over all the years."

"I was thankful for the mountain nymphs who raised me. They didn't love me, but they were good to me. They were afraid of Zeus, and the dangers that hiding me posed them because Hera wanted me dead. I was angry for a very long time, but then I found when I stopped caring about people, it stopped hurting so much."

The restaurant he brings us to is exactly what I'd expect an authentic Italian restaurant to look like. It has an outdoor patio with black iron tables and linen cloths and a grapevine trellis overhead to block the sun.

When we take a seat, a woman in an apron comes over to greet us. Dionysus speaks to her in lovely, flowing Italian, and when he finishes, he smiles at me. "Do you mind if I order for us?"

"That's fine. I'm not fussy. No wine though. I think you should take a break from the vino for a bit."

"Agreed."

While Dionysus orders, I watch the people passing. Unlike in Toronto, the folks here don't seem to feel the pressure to get where they're going. They're strolling arm-in-arm and pointing up at stone archways and stained glass windows and a church at the opposite end of the square.

I watch an old couple with an equally slow and aged Scotty dog by the fountain a little farther along.

"This is amazing."

"Is it?"

"Yes. Don't you think so?"

Dionysus looks out at the scenery, and his face tightens as if he's struggling to work through a puzzle. "I suppose I used to think so. Somewhere along the line, everything seems to blur together in one long, never-ending fog of existence."

"I'm sorry life left you so alone, but that's over. You're part of Clan Cumhaill now. We live and love and celebrate our family. When things go wrong, and someone in our family is hurting, we're there for that person. You're not alone. We'll figure this out together."

"Thank you, Jane, but I told you, there's nothing to figure out. I'm good."

A young girl brings a pitcher of water, two glasses, side plates, and a caddy with cloth napkins, cutlery, and shaker bottles with herbs and ground peppers.

When we're alone once again, I reach across the table and take his pinky and link it with mine. "You and I are going to talk about what led up to you thinking a wine infusion was a good idea."

"Nothing led up to it. I wanted to feel good."

"I believe that, but before you freak out, I want you to know there's nothing you can't talk to me about. I won't judge you, pity you, or repeat anything said to anyone, not even Sloan. This is a pinky swear, and in the Cumhaill family, there's no breaking an oath of a pinky swear."

His gaze is narrow as he studies me. "Why do we need an oath? What's this about?"

"I want to talk about what's happening with you."

He pales a little and scans the crowd around us. "You're exceedingly more interesting. What have you always wanted, Jane? Do you need a favor? I'll do anything you need. Just ask."

I smile. "That's kind of you, thanks, but what I need is for you to trust me with your pain. Tell me what's happening so we can work on it together."

When he opens his mouth to deny it, I hold up my free hand. "Let me start by saying I already know or have a good idea about what's upsetting you."

His brow pinches and his lips purse.

Our server arrives with two wide, wooden paddles with our pizzas cut in squares down their length. One has sauce, circular discs of white cheese, and spinach. The other one has mushrooms, very thinly sliced Prosciutto, and basil.

"Grazie." I nod. She says something in response, and I smile and look at Dionysus. "Grazie is all I've got."

He speaks with her briefly, and she backs away with a smile on her face. As his focus shifts back to me, his pleasant demeanor vanishes. "There's nothing wrong. Believe it or not, wine infusion isn't my first bad idea or my most reckless. I'm a nightmare, remember?"

"That's not true, and you need to change that tape playing in your head." I draw a deep breath and exhale, ready to come at it again. "Look, I get it. You're the man when it comes to all things sex-tacular. Hitting a glitch in your field of expertise has thrown everything you know into chaos. You're angry and confused and probably very scared about what this means going forward."

A hard mask clicks into place, and my shield tingles to life. "Stop talking, Fi. We're friends, but you don't know me, and you don't know what you're talking about."

I squeeze his pinky with mine. "You can't lie in a pinky swear. I *do* know you, and I know what's wrong. Yes, it's awkward, but it doesn't have to be weird. It happens. You need a friend, and I *am* your friend. Now, let's figure out what's going wrong. There can be a dozen reasons things aren't working the way they should."

He tenses to stand, and I study the side of him I've never known. Gone is the playful god of good times.

This is Dionysus the immortal demigod.

The warrior.

This is the other side of the coin I'm so accustomed to, or in the Greek's case, the other side of the drachma.

I change tack immediately. "Please sit."

The moment of hesitation hangs heavy between us and I recognize this as one of those pivotal moments where relationships change.

Either he'll retreat to the life of selfish oblivion he's known and avoid all the feels, or he'll recognize we have something special and won't want to throw that away.

"Please, stay. I wish you could trust me enough to be honest with me, but I won't push. It's a shame, though, because I'm a great listener and genuinely in your corner.

"If that's not where you are, then stay because there's too much pizza for me to eat on my own. And also because I don't have my purse and I'll be damned if I dine and dash on my first trip to Italy."

His gaze remains locked with mine, his pupils swirling with the silver glow of magic I saw earlier when he was unconscious.

The glare is hard and cold.

It has no effect on me.

I've been glared at by the best, and it doesn't even faze me. When he doesn't stomp off, I take that as my answer. I wait for a moment to see if he wants to serve and when he doesn't, I take the liberty. "Would you like one slice of each to start?"

"That's fine."

I serve him up two slices and do the same for myself. After shaking out my napkin, I set it over my lap and pull out my phone. I swipe up Sloan's contact and send him a quick text.

Went out for pizza. All is well. Love you.

With that taken care of, I look around to see how people do things here. When in Rome, do as the Romans do, amirite?

"Are we in Rome?"

"No. Taormina, Sicily."

I watch the others eat their pizza. Perfect, knife and fork it is. I pick up my cutlery and dig in.

The first slice I try has goat cheese, spinach, and thinly shaved meat. When I take my first bite, I realize how hungry I am. The richness of the flavor is amazing. The blend of sauce and herbs and cheese is both light and delicious.

"Thank you for bringing me here, by the way. I've never been to Italy. It's on my list of places I've always wanted to see. I'm happy to share this first with you."

That seems to thaw him out a bit, and he picks up his utensils. "I'm happy to do anything that puts a smile on your face. I love you too, by the way. Thank you for saying Zeus is an idiot…and for crying when you thought I was dying."

I swallow and smile. "You're welcome."

The two of us eat in silence for a few minutes. I enjoy the pizza. I study the Old World architecture of the buildings and absorb as much of the sensory details as possible. This might only be a quick trip to Italy, but I want to remember everything.

"Are you truly not going to push me into talking about it?"

I pause with my fork halfway to my mouth. "Truly not. I said what I needed to say. You know I'm here for you, and I think it would help you to lean on me. You're a grown man. If you don't trust me enough—"

"I trust you, Jane. If there's anyone in this endless existence that I trust, it's you. It's just…"

"It's incredibly personal and rattles everything you thought you knew about yourself."

He frowns. "Apparently, we don't need to talk about it anyway. You already know everything."

I set my cutlery down and pick up my crust. From what I see around me, it's culturally acceptable to pick up pizza crust and eat it with my hands. "So, are we talking about it or no?"

He rolls his eyes. "I suppose we are, but can we keep it vague or metaphorical?"

"All right. So, the first time it happened?"

"A week after you invited me to your house for the first time to introduce me to your family and friends."

"I know it doesn't happen every time because…well, I've been paying attention over the past months."

"It didn't start as all the time, but now…" he looks down at his lap and shrugs. "I don't know what to do."

I sip my water and set the glass back on the table. "It's a stressful time. You uprooted your life by moving here. All new friends. New dynamics to learn. Stress can be a huge contributing factor."

He shakes his head, his brunette curls catching the early evening breeze. "I don't stress—except about this—but not before this, so that can't be the cause."

"Maybe it's the wine? People use alcohol to enhance their moods, but in reality, it's a depressant and can affect mental and physical health."

"The wine?" The look of horror he shoots me is hilarious. "Now you're just cruel."

"I know you're having a hard time, but—"

"Not hard. We wouldn't be having this conversation if I was having a hard time. I *wish* I was hard."

I giggle, his attempt to lighten the mood easing the tension in his handsome face.

The younger server walks by in time to catch that and blinks at us. Thankfully, Dionysus doesn't seem to notice, or he'd be back to being embarrassed and defensive.

It's awesome that he's joking about it.

When he smirks, I smile too. "This is a momentary setback. It happens to all men at one point or another."

"Has it happened to Irish?"

I take a bite of my pizza crust and chew longer than I need to while I scramble for the right answer. "No, but there have been ideas or positions or timing issues. Things don't always work out perfectly, but it's important not to sweat it. Anxiety compounds problems like these."

"For humans," he whispers, leaning forward. "It's not the same for me. This is my realm of expertise… my Zeus-given dominion. If anyone finds out that I'm having a missile crisis, I'll be the laughingstock of the Pantheon. I'll no longer be capable of holding the claim on my throne, and I'll lose what little respect I've managed to claw together in an endless life of disapproval."

The raw fear in his voice breaks my heart. "Let's step back from the ledge and make a plan. The first thing we do is lay off the orgies and the alcohol for a bit. You've been living hard for—"

I catch his scowl and back it up.

"Sorry, there's that word again. You've been living loose and easy for millennia, and it's put a lot of pressure on you to perform."

He arches a brow at me. "I never felt any pressure until now. *Not* living hard is what's causing the panic."

"So, maybe you need a break. You can expand your interests, catch up on things you've let fall behind. Have you ever wanted to learn to surf?"

"To taunt sharks and have stinging jellyfish tendrils wrap around my junk? No. Never have."

"What about skateboarding?"

"I'm not seventeen, and I'm not wearing my shorts belted across my thighs. If my ass is on display, it's out for the world to see without road rash."

"Snowboarding?"

He frowns at me. "What's with you and the fixation of putting me on a stiff board? You suggested the same thing three times only with different settings."

I think about that and laugh. "Okay, not snowboarding. My point is, it can't hurt to get away and recharge. Nikon, Sloan, and I are planning a wine-tasting weekend as a favor for his papu. He thinks someone magical trespassed into his winery and he wants to know why."

Dionysus grows very serious. "Nikon Senior makes some of the finest wine I've ever consumed. He's on my list of seven. Nikky promised me an amphora every season for helping you way back when we first met, and I've enjoyed it ever since. It's one of my favorites."

"I remember. He gave you another one for your house-warming party, didn't he?"

He nods. "He did."

"So, we're going to check things out and make sure no one is tampering with his vintages. It's in your wheelhouse, it'll distract you from your troubles, and you might enjoy joining in and having fun with us."

Dionysus dabs his mouth with a cloth napkin and frowns. "Wine is not only *in* my wheelhouse; it *is* my wheelhouse."

"That's why I thought you'd get a kick out of joining the fun. Except then you pulled that craziness with the IV lines, and now I'm wondering if you should stay as far away from wine as possible."

He sucks in a breath. "You wound me. Wine is my friend, my lover, my confidante."

I chuckle. "Not this weekend, it's not. This weekend you're going to tour Europe with friends and sample wine with discrimination and moderation."

"Moderation isn't in my vocabulary."

"Trust me. I've noticed."

CHAPTER SIX

Just before six, Sloan *poofs* into the back hall, unlaces his dress shoes, and sets them neatly in the closet on the rack. I greet him with a hug and kiss his cheek. "I'm glad you're home. Today was a day, wasn't it?"

We hug for a minute, and he eases back to study me, and knowing him, check that all is well in my world once again. "How was your lunch with Dionysus?"

I lead him back to the kitchen and continue setting the table. Kevin and I have almost everything ready for dinner and are expecting Calum home any time. I take the fresh bread to the table and set it next to the little pitcher of olive oil and herbs for dipping.

"Lunch was good. Did you know Italians consider it rude to ask for a to go bag? They prefer you eat things hot and fresh and not take your leftovers home."

Sloan's brow arches. "Italy? You said you went out for pizza."

"We did. We went farther than normal."

Something in Sloan's expression tells me he's not happy about that. He doesn't hide it well and strides off toward the powder room to wash up for dinner.

I consider letting it go, but then I think better of it and follow. Leaning on the frame of the open door, I watch him as he suds up, rinses, and dries. "Why don't you like it that we snapped to Italy for pizza?"

"Do you think that was appropriate after what we walked in on? For goddess' sake, Fi, he tried to…" He makes eyes at me, and I shake my head.

"He didn't. It was an ill-thought-out plan to feel better."

"Why would he need to feel better? He's the god of feeling good. Everything he does every minute of the day is one big feel-good moment."

"Yeah, well, not everything is as it seems. He's going through something right now."

"You're not going to tell me what that is?"

I shake my head. "Not if I can help it. I promised him I'd respect his privacy and he needs someone he knows he can trust right now."

"Right. Of course."

I frown at the vigorousness of his scrubbing. At this rate, he won't have any skin left on his hands to wash. "You don't think anything is going on between Dionysus and me, do you?"

Sloan rinses and dries off and folds the hand towel over the black iron rail. Straightening, he extends his hand, and when we make contact, he *poofs* us up to our bedroom. Loosening his tie, he heads into the walk-in to change for dinner. "Not in the way ye mean, no. I trust yer judgment and yer affections."

"Good. But you said, *not in the way I meant*, which implies it bothers you in a different way. Care to share?"

He hangs his tie, unbuttons his dress shirt, and shucks it off his shoulders to hang up. "You'll think it's silly."

"Not if it's upsetting you, I won't."

He frees one of his Polo shirts off its hanger and pulls it over his head and down the glorious ridges of his abs. "One of the things I've been lookin' forward to is us gettin' away and me showin' ye all the wonders of the world I grew up in. I know ye've never been to other parts of Europe than Ireland and want to go, and I like the idea of bein' the one to share it with ye."

"Aw...and just like that, you steal another piece of my heart."

He flashes me a half-smile and rolls his eyes. "Be serious."

"I *am* serious. You wanting to do that for me is lovely and thoughtful. I look forward to it."

"Yes, but now it'll be Nikon and Dionysus who are showin' ye around Europe, and I'll be taggin' along as yer boyfriend."

"Sorry. I didn't mean to volunteer us for this without checking with you first. That was insensitive."

"It's fine. Don't get me wrong. I hold no animosity against them and think it'll be a good time. It's just—"

His words sink in, and I hold up a hand to stop him from finishing his sentence. "Wait. What do you mean you'll be tagging along as my boyfriend? Is that how you see yourself?"

He turns and unbuttons his slacks, stepping out of them and holding them up to clip and hang. "I shouldn't have said anything."

"Yes, you should have." My voice is an octave higher than usual. "You are a shit-ton more than that. Is that the way you feel?"

"There are moments, yes, when yer takin' care of everything and everyone, and I look around and wonder why I'm there."

"You're there because that's where you belong—right beside me as life comes at us."

"Yer right. As ye said earlier, today was a day." He grabs a pair of jeans from the drawer of his organizer and his leather belt.

Before he can step into his pants, I step up to him. "Sloan Mackenzie, you are by far the smartest person I know. You're brave and steadfast and an accomplished fighter. You know more about druid life than anyone except Merlin and maybe Granda— certainly twenty times more than me. You are my rock. More than my lover, you're my mentor and friend and the druid I want to be when I grow up."

He drops the jeans and belt, wrapping one arm around my waist and the other behind my neck. Pulling me close, he presses his soft lips against mine.

My mind fritzes out for a moment and doesn't come back online until he breaks the kiss. "Thanks, *a ghra*. I think I needed to hear that more than I realized."

"Then that's on me. I'm sorry."

"There's no reason for you to be sorry. It's just...sometimes ye have so many people around ye, consumin' yer time and attention. I want to be sure the two of us don't miss out on those special moments ye'll remember forever. In my mind, I pictured us traveling as a way to share new experiences."

I run my hands along his ribs and down to the waistband of his boxers. "I look forward to it, but we can enjoy new experiences right here at home too."

He chuckles, the smooth timbre of his amusement a deep rumble in the enclosed space. "Dinner is nearly on the table, and we've christened every room in the house, including this closet if I remember correctly."

I grin, stretching the elastic of his waistband and sliding it down his hips. "We have fifteen minutes until dinner, and we had sex in this closet. What I have in mind is all about you."

"Ye don't have to—"

"I want to. As you said, there are a lot of people demanding my attention. We don't want to miss out on those special moments."

Twenty minutes later, the two of us descend the stairs with smiles on our faces—Sloan's from being at the receiving end of one of those special moments and me from the smug knowledge that I turned his world upside down and cheered him up.

Yay me!

Calum looks beat as he locks up his Glock and smiles at us coming down. "Hey, guys. Good day?"

"It had its moments," I say, always happy to see the return of one of my brothers from his shift. "Lots to talk about at dinner."

"Give me five to change, and I'll be down."

While Calum heads upstairs, Emmet and Doc Marten come down, talking in pine marten animal language. It used to freak me out to hear Em talking wildlife chitter-chatter, but now it's just weird—awesome, but weird.

When they make it to the main floor, Emmet sets him on the floor and greets Ciara, who's coming up from downstairs.

Emmet's new betrothed spends a lot of time in the basement. I hate to think that she's avoiding me, but there's a real possibility she's given me a wide berth since their handfasting at the Beltane celebration.

"Och, it smells divine up here." She sets her iPad on the little desk area built into the kitchen cabinets. "What can I do to help?"

"I think we're all set," Kev says. "Come sit. Calum will be down in a second to join us."

The five of us sit, and by the time we've poured the wine and settle, Calum returns looking much more comfortable in his jeans and a t-shirt. "All right. Let the games begin."

The six of us being home to have dinner doesn't work out often because of Em and Calum working shifts, and Kevin works odd hours at the gallery. When it does, we try to take advantage of the chance to connect and catch up.

"So, who's first?" Kev indicates that the topic of the day's events is now open.

"I'd like to hear about Sloan's meeting with the mysterious Duchess d'Aboville." I hold my plate forward so Kevin can dish me a slab of lasagna. "Did you learn any more about who she is and what she wants? What did your ring tell you? How good were her treasures? Anything interesting there?"

"Irish." Emmet sets his napkin on his lap. "What the hell are you doing checking out another woman's treasures?"

Calum chuckles. "The only answer to that question is, 'No, the woman had nothing I found remotely interesting. Your treasures are much more impressive.'"

I laugh and wave to allow Sloan to answer.

My guy tilts his head this way and that. "Her relics were interesting. She had some empowered objects, and the jewelry seemed genuine. The Unseelie don't seem to have the same requirements for provenance, so there's not much to be done in the way of verification before the exhibition next week. Then again, I'm supposed to protect them, not verify their authenticity."

The confused gazes around the table remind me that with all the Dionysus drama, I didn't tell them about our job next week. "Sorry, from the beginning, then. There's an Unseelie masquerade ball event next Thursday night, and Team Trouble has a contract to provide security. As of Monday, you'll all be reassigned and off your regular duty roster for the week."

"Noice." Emmet grins.

"What's this about relics and protecting them?" Calum asks.

Sloan straightens. "Well, the event is called the FUR Ball and—"

Cue the choking hysteria.

"Bullshit." Calum looks from him to me and back again. "You're totally making that up, Irish."

He frowns. "Why would I? It stands for—"

"No, don't tell us." Emmet laughs and holds up his hand. "Let us guess. Telling us will end the joy of this moment much too soon."

"Don't be stupid. Yer as childish as yer sister."

"Rude." I stick my tongue out at him. "Okay, boys, give it your best shot."

The table grows quiet as everyone chews, then Calum gives it a try. "Fornicators Use Rubbers."

"Forty Uber Racers."

"Fluffy Urban Rabbits."

"Flying Under Radar."

"Feisty Underwear Reveal."

"Fae Unicorn Riders."

My attention ping-pongs between them as I wait for them to wear themselves out...until I remember they'll never wear themselves out. "No, no, no, and no on all counts. Keep thinking. Go on, hotness. What did you find out about your dark fae stalker?"

He pegs me with a look. "She's far from my stalker. I do know she's empowered and holds an almost covetous passion for antiquities, and yes, when I activated my ring, I did find something interesting."

"Which is?" I take a piece of bread out of the basket and pass it on.

"When my ring removed her glamor, she appeared to me with the shadow of a black cat wrapping itself around her."

Interesting.

Emmet reaches for another piece of bread. "Was it like a melanistic jaguar kind of black cat or a witch's familiar kind?"

He shrugs. "Hard to say. It was a shadow, so it was hard to gauge its size. All I know is that she's something other."

Calum pours a little of the dipping oil onto his side plate and passes me the pitcher. "When you say covetous of antiquities, do you mean in a high-end collector way or an unlawful liberation way?"

Sloan frowns. "It's uncharitable to say, but I'm thinking the latter. Merlin warned us that bringing Laytah into our lives might draw dark energy. Morgana's perversion of her original craftsmanship has left her as a beacon of dark intent."

"Well, if there have already been robberies in Montreal and the duchess is casing the shrine, ye should be ready for an unwanted visitor," Ciara says. "Ye said she's empowered and yer unsure what she is or what her powers are. That leaves ye unprepared."

Sloan swallows a sip of wine and sighs. "I was thinking that myself."

Calum grins. "Em? Remember the drug bust last month where the 55 Division raided that warehouse?"

Emmet's eyes widen and sparkle with mischief. "I like the way you think, bro. Yeah, that's a great idea."

"What's a great idea?" Sloan asks.

Calum finishes chewing and grins. "There was this big bust last month after a CI got killed. The cops who raided the warehouse expected the drug dealers and the guns, but they nearly lost their shit when they ran into the extra security in the money room."

"Why? What did they have in place?"

"A cougar."

"Nice." I laugh, imagining the shock on those cops' faces. "A normal cougar, yeah? This was all mundane and nothing to do with the empowered world?"

"Right. A normal, ferocious cougar locked in the dealer's money room. So, even if someone got in to rob them, they didn't get out."

"That's awesome. How did I miss this story?"

Calum scoops himself seconds and passes me the bread. "It happened while you were busy with the vampire stuff. The gist is Bruin could sleep in the shrine for a few nights and see if our black cat is a cat burglar."

"Oh, and me too." Manx lifts his head from where he's curled up on his bed. "If Bruin gets stakeout duty, I want to go too."

Sloan shrugs. "It's fine by me as long as ye stay out of the locked vault and keep to the main room."

Doc scurries into the kitchen and stands up on his back legs. "Daisy and me, too?"

Emmet and Calum look at one another and check in with Sloan.

"All right, sham," Sloan says. "It looks like it's a companions stakeout mission. After dinner, we'll gather up yer things and I'll portal ye over to get set up."

Doc sits up, twitching his whiskers. "We'll do you proud, Irish. Trust is the glue of life and the essential material for a flourishing relationship. We won't let you down."

Oh, our little philosopher.

Sloan nods. "I appreciate yer conviction, Doc. I'm sure ye'll be a force to keep the thieves at bay."

When he scurries off, the rest of us try not to snicker. I change the subject to keep from laughing. Leaning in, I whisper to Kevin and Calum. "Don't forget about talking to Daisy."

Calum frowns. "We won't. If the animals are having a sleepover, we'll have to talk to her before she goes."

"What's the whispering about?" Em asks, keeping his voice low.

"Doc told Fi that Daisy is sad about something," Kev whispers. "She's not sleeping and not playing with them like usual."

Emmet empties the last of his wine. "Jitters about the wedding?"

Kev and Calum shrug. "No idea yet. I guess we'll find out."

I spend an hour in the grove with Dart while Sloan and Emmet pack an overnight care package for the companion animals, and Calum and Kevin speak with Daisy.

"All of them are going?" Dart asks.

I can tell by his tone he's sad to be left out and I feel bad for him. "Sorry, buddy. You're too big to be in the shrine, but the good news is, tomorrow Sloan and I are heading to Europe, and we thought you might like to spend the weekend with your mother and siblings. If you're up to trying the portal rings, we thought you could take us through after Jackson's soccer game."

He nods but doesn't seem as excited as I thought he would be.

"What's up? Don't you want to see your family? You don't have to. You can stay here if you prefer."

"It's not that. I simply would rather visit Saxa and the dragons in Iceland. Utiss and Bryvanay have so much to teach me, and it seems frivolous to sit around the dragon lair with my siblings when I can be learning more about who I am and my abilities."

I pat the rough scale on his cheek. "Don't forget to be an adolescent and have fun too. I don't want you fast-tracking your development if it means sacrificing the craziness of youth."

His head tilts to the side, and he snorts. "That is an utterly human way to look at things."

I chuckle. "My bad. You do you, buddy."

"Is Merlin planning to visit Empress Cazzienth this weekend? Perhaps he wouldn't mind if I go too."

"I don't know, but I'll text him and ask. If not, maybe visit Scarlett and your siblings this weekend, and I'll arrange for you to get to Iceland the next time Merlin goes if that's okay with him."

Dart bends his head forward so I can rub his horn. "Thank you. That is a fine idea."

CHAPTER SEVEN

"Fi, wake up, luv." Sloan gives me a gentle shake and rolls out of bed. Deep night shadows the bedroom even with King Henry's curtains thrown open and the light of the moon glowing through the windows. My heart jolts awake before my eyes have time to adjust.

"What's happening? What's wrong?"

There's a strange *beep* going off in the bathroom, and it takes a bit for the REM sleep fog to lift.

"The Bad News Bears are calling for help at…" I blink at the blurry red blob on the bedside clock, "six minutes after four?"

"Aye, it seems so. Now hurry, put these on." He tosses a pair of sweats at me as he jogs past to stop the alarm. While I pull them on, he grabs his keys from the bowl by the window and rushes back with his hand outstretched.

The moment our hands clasp, he *poofs* us to the seventh floor reception doors. Like the other floors of the Acropolis, no one can portal directly into the main core of the building. We always arrive in the foyer by the elevators and have to pass through the security protocols to gain access.

A crash follows a loud *thump* inside.

"Well, that doesn't sound good."

Sloan presses his hand on the scanner and unlocks things with his key. We rush into STOA in time to have a brown furry blur race over our feet, hissing. Doc is lit up. Manx growls, wildly running as he swipes his claws through empty air. "I smell her over here. Bruin, can ye catch her?"

She's fast, he says in his spirit form, blowing past. *Really fast.*

Sloan activates his ring and searches the shrine room. The space is big and wide open other than shelving units and display pedestals that hold his antiquities.

"There's a presence in here," I say, my shield flaring with a warning. "Our security flusters her."

"How can ye tell, *a ghra?*"

"I don't know. I just can." I drop the glamor on my eyes and wave my fae freak flag, searching with the odd aura vision that comes with this mode of sight. "Got her. Yeah, good call on the black cat guess, Mackenzie. She's booking it on all fours about the size of a spaniel. Her ruff is up, her tail twitching and propelling her out of reach from our security team."

"What's her aura like?"

"Foul and dangerous."

"Of course, it is. Well, I can't see her even with my ring, so it's up to you and Bruin."

I watch the tainted form of the wannabe cat burglar racing around, evading Bruin. My mind grasps for an offensive that applies. I've got nothing. "How do I fight something in spirit form?"

"Yer the Celtic shaman, not me."

"Oh, good point." Except when Samuel, Quon Shen, Ahren, and I fought the spirits escaping from the Neitherlands, we had a containment area. Well, beggars and choosers and all that. "I'll try."

Striping off my clothes, I close my eyes and focus on my animal form. I've become more accustomed to my Sabertooth panther, and the magic of my transition takes hold without effort.

The first few times I transformed, I thought it was scary and disorienting. Not now.

Now I understand this form much better, and after the days of training I did with the other shamans, I'm relatively confident of my abilities.

The moment my view on the world shifts lower, I scan the shrine. The spirit cat is racing just out of Bruin's reach, both in a translucent shadow self of their physical form.

In this form, I can see them.

She's toying with you, Bruin.

Aye, I noticed that, thanks.

My bad. With a roar to get her attention, I lunge and join the chase. "No stolen treasures for you, Duchess. Too bad, so sad."

I swipe through the air, narrowly missing the cat's back leg.

She hisses, and I smile.

Taking my frustrations out on her is more cathartic than I thought it would be. Invite my guy to your hotel room, will you? Ha, take this.

I lunge, snapping empty air. The speed of Bruin's pass in the opposite direction ruffles my fur. I land, twisting to gain purchase with my mighty paws on a polished stone floor. Even before I stop moving, I fight to change direction to take another swipe at her.

This time, Bruin chases her straight at me.

I track her approach and catch her intention as she telegraphs her intended escape path. With a sprawling lunge, I manage to bat her out of the air.

The cat is knocked spinning and dematerializes even further into a dark mist. Without so much as a goodbye, the mist zooms toward the point where the two glass doors meet the floor.

She siphons through the tiny crack and is gone.

Doc Marten races after the last of her and *clonks* against the door's metal frame. He sits back on his haunches and shakes his little head.

Adrenaline pumping, I shift back, pull my t-shirt back on and step into my yoga pants. "One duchess run outta town with her tail between her legs."

"Yer sure?"

"Oh, yeah. She was no match for the fab five, and she knew it." Bruin takes form and looks up at us, his big body vibrating with laughter. "That was fun."

I head over to check on Doc.

Emmet's pine marten is staring off in a daze like he still sees stars. "Dude, are you okay? You didn't suffer any brain damage or anything, did you?"

"How will we be able to tell?" Manx chuckles. "The way he waxes philosophical, maybe his noodle is already bent or bendy."

I reach down and pick up Doc, holding him in the air to look into his eyes. "You okay?"

"Satisfactory, thank you. Although, a headache seems imminent."

I lay him in the cradle of my arm and brush a hand over his fur. "You boys did a great job."

"Daisy missed it," Manx says. "She'll be sad."

I shake my head. "I don't think she will. The boys kept her home to talk about what's bothering her. I bet she's getting the royal princess treatment."

"Do you think she'll be happy again?" Doc asks.

"I'm not sure, buddy. All I know is that Calum and Kevin love her and want her to be happy, so they'll do whatever they can to ensure our Daisy girl is feeling much better going forward."

"Good."

Sloan is assessing the room and stands up a downed pillar display. "I'm glad I moved all the objects into the vault. Even if they didn't get stolen, they would've gotten damaged in the kerfuffle."

I bend and look at the tiny crack at the joining of the two doors. "The important thing is we know how she got in."

"And she knows we're ready for her," Manx says.

Sloan scrubs Manx's ears and plays with the long, black tufts of fur coming off their tips. "I doubt she'll be back tonight. If yer ready, boys, there are still a few hours of sleep to be had. Shall we?"

Doc jumps out of my arms and joins Manx and Bruin on the floor. "Our shift isn't over. There is still plenty of night left."

"Yer sure?" Sloan says. "Ye don't need to stay."

"We'll stay." Manx checks in with the other two and shakes out his fur. "Even if she doesn't come back, we'll finish out our shift and protect yer treasures."

I study the three of them and gauge their conviction. "Okee-dokee. I'll reset the alarm to call if you need us. We'll see you in the morning."

Bruin nods. "Plug that hole in the door."

I nod. "And we'll plug that hole in the door."

The next morning, Sloan is stepping out of the shower when I wake up. Deciding not to miss the show, I hustle my butt out of King Henry and hurry into the bathroom. Yeah, baby. Soooo worth it. He catches me ogling, but I don't even care. It's my right. "Did you sleep late? You're usually long gone by now."

He finishes toweling off and wraps his hips with a mile of terry. "Och, no. I was up at the crack and brought home the conquering heroes. I made them the breakfast of kings, and now they've gone down to the den for some much-earned rest."

I chuckle and squeeze toothpaste onto my brush. "So much happens while I'm still sleeping."

"Not an issue, luv. Yer an eight-hour girl and I prefer six. To each their own."

Yikes…only getting six hours of sleep is exhausting even to think about. "I was thinking—"

"Och, that's never good."

I chuckle and point at him with my toothbrush. "Hey, not all my ideas end in disaster."

"Yer right. Only most of them. Go on. What were ye thinkin'?"

I run my brush under the faucet and meet Sloan's gaze in the mirror. "While I get ready and gather Jackson for his practice, you should pop into the Batcave and fill Garnet in on what happened last night. If we're supplying backup security for the FUR Ball, it would be good to figure out who the Duchess d'Aboville is and what she's capable of. Maybe he can assign someone to keep an eye on STOA while we're gone too."

He grins. "A grand idea. I'm meeting him in twenty minutes to do just that."

"Oh, well, great minds think alike."

He chuckles. "And fools seldom differ."

Forty-five minutes later, I stroll across the back deck to the other house and knock and walk. "Hello, the house. Does anybody in here know where I can find a monkey in cleats?"

"We're up here," Kinu calls from above. "He'll be ready in two, Fi. Just putting on sunscreen."

"No rush."

I toe off my sandals and walk barefoot toward the front of the house. Meggie is sitting on the couch with a bowl of dry cereal, and the twins are sleeping in the bassinet set inside the entrance to the family room. "Hello, babies."

I lean in and give each of my newborn nieces a kiss.

Ireland's hair is growing in the same russet copper as Aiden's and mine. Carragh's is chestnut brown like Kinu's. All four kids have the light beige complexion of Kinu's Japanese heritage and are a beautiful blend of two attractive people.

"Auntie Fi loves you, babies." I plop onto the couch next to Meggie and kiss her chubby cheek. "Auntie Fi loves you too."

Meg blinks up at me. "Nuggle?"

"I would love a snuggle, baby girl." I set her cereal onto the coffee table and slide her off the cushion and onto my lap. According to the development charts, Meggie's behind on her words, but we've all seen the way she absorbs the world.

She has a sharp mind working beneath the silence.

Snuggle is one of her new words, and she knows we all melt and pick her up for hugs when she asks. Mam's theory in child-rearing was that you could spoil kids with things, but never with too much love.

We seem to be living proof of that.

Dillan comes in, and he's all hips and swagger wearing yesterday's clothes and looking like he's ready to conquer the world. "Morning, sista mine."

"Oh, you've got it bad." I cover Meg's ears. "That got laid parade is becoming a regular thing."

He waggles his eyebrows. "Life is good."

"So, when do we meet her?"

He shrugs. "Soon. With Calum's wedding in the next couple of weeks, I'm running out of time."

"Running out of time? You make it sound like you don't want us to meet her."

He offers me an apologetic smile. "Things are going well—like, incredibly well. Once she meets all of you, the dynamic will change. I like having her all to myself. It's been perfect."

I've never seen Dillan's eyes glitter with such contentment before. It looks great on him.

"Perfect only lasts so long. Then it becomes real. Real is good too. It takes a bit more work, but it's good."

Dillan chuckles. "Aren't you the *younger* sister?"

"I am, but girls rule, and boys drool, right Meggie?"

Meg giggles and Dillan feigns shock. "Rude. Just for that, Uncle Dillan will have to get you both and make you pay."

When he lifts his hands in tickle claws, Meg squeals and wriggles into my chest. I cage her in my arms as Dillan attacks us, tickling and making her crazy.

"I'll protect you, baby," I shout, laughing as my brother tickles me too.

"I'll trade you Megs for Jackson," Kinu calls from the upstairs hall.

Dillan straightens, lifts Meg off my lap, and throws her up in the air to a fit of giggles. "Mommy wants you. Say bye-bye to Auntie Fi, Meggers."

"Buh-bye." Meggie waves.

"Bye-bye, baby. Have a great day."

As the two of them head up the stairs, Jackson comes down holding the railing, his shiny yellow and black polyester soccer uniform shimmering in the light. "Auntie Fi, look. I'm a bumblebee."

"You sure are."

"His bag is by the door. He's all set. Thanks, Fi."

"Not a problem. We'll be back."

Jackson runs ahead of me and grabs his bag, unzipping it to show me. "This is my pack-pack for soccer. Those are my oranges, and my shoes and my shin armor and my water bottle."

"Shin armor, eh?"

"Uh-huh. Daddy says I need to play like a warrior and warriors need armor. Right?"

Sloan steps in and hears that and chuckles. "A football warrior?"

Jackson laughs and rolls his eyes. "No, Uncle Sloan, I play soccer not football. Yous silly."

I finish buckling my sandals back on, grab the booster seat

from beside the door, and we're out and headed for my SUV. "Come on, Mr. Bumble. Time for the three of us to buzz off."

Jackson roars with laughter, and I smile at Sloan. "I kill it in the five-year-old demographic."

After soccer practice, Sloan, Jackson, and I stop at the corner store. I run in and buy a container of mint chocolate chip ice cream. Jackson wanted a cone from McDonald's, but there's no way a five-year-old is getting soft-serve ice cream in the back seat of my truck.

A brick of ice cream to take home is even better. He'll get more than one bowl, and he can share with his mommy and Megs.

"Thanks again, Fi," Kinu says, meeting us at the door. "How was it?"

"I winned!" Jackson pumps his fist in the air, running inside and slipping on the floor with his cleats.

"Won your practice, did you?" Kinu laughs. "He gets that from his father."

I hand over the pack-pack and the ice cream. Once Sloan sets the car seat down, we wave our goodbyes and head home to change our clothes and get ready for our wine weekend away.

"Hotness, can you text Dionysus and Nikon to check on the travel plans? Tell them we're good to go when they are."

"Aye, I can do that."

I grab the away bag I packed for the weekend, check that I haven't forgotten anything, and head downstairs. "All set. Now all we need is—"

"Let the party commence." Dionysus appears in the kitchen, his arms out to the side in a dramatic flourish, and takes a theatrical bow. "How do I look?"

My vision almost fritzes out from his burgundy cotton pants, the matching smoking jacket, and the paisley silk ascot that accents the outfit and matches his pocket square.

"Do I look like a human, upper-class dandy?"

"You sure do."

Sloan jogs down the stairs behind me and stops in his tracks. His eyes bug out, and the man who is a quick thinker in all situations seems thoroughly thrown.

"What?" Dionysus asks. "Too much?"

I wave away his self-consciousness. "Not if you want to look like a dandy."

"I do."

Sloan collects himself and joins us. "If that's yer goal, ye nailed it."

"Excellent." Dionysus straightens. "So, is this bicycle leaving the station or what?"

Nikon flashes in and—"What in the holy horrors of hell are you wearing?"

I giggle. "Dionysus is dressing for the occasion. He's going as an upper-class dandy."

Nikon's eyes couldn't get any wider. "I didn't pack my monocle or my pipe, but other than that, I think we're ready. Are you guys taking Dart through the rings?"

I shake my head. "No, he and Merlin left last night. Merlin plans to visit Cazzienth and the Iceland dragons for a week and was fine with Dart tagging along."

"A week? I bet he was excited."

"Very. I think he has a sweet spot for Saxa and is missing her."

"Ah, young dragon love." Dionysus smiles off into the distance.

"You say that as if you have experience with such matters, Tarzan."

He flashes me a sexy smile. "As my dear friend Eros would say, 'You know it's true love when it's the greatest hello and the hardest goodbye.'"

Nikon squints at him and looks at me. "What the fuck did I miss?"

I wave away the crazy look. "I think this is Dionysus unplugged. It's been almost forty-eight hours since he had a drink. We're trying something new."

Nikon frowns. "Sober Dionysus is weird…even weirder than drunk Dionysus."

I slide an arm around Dionysus' back and pet the front of his crushed velvet smoking jacket. "Sober Dionysus is lovely, and it's a pleasure to meet him finally."

"So, are we ready to go?" Sloan asks.

I jog to the top of the basement stairs and lean over the rail. "Bruin, we're all set, buddy."

"On my way." I wait the few seconds it takes for him to say goodbye to the others and shift into his spirit form. He swirls around me when he reaches the main floor, then the gentle pressure of his presence pushes against my sternum, and we're ready to roll.

I join the others and put my right hand forward in front of them. "All aboard who's coming aboard."

CHAPTER EIGHT

Nikon snaps the four of us to the Tsambikos family vineyard on the Isle of Rhodes in Greece. It's changed very little since the first time I came here in the days of chariots, togas, and temples. The three biggest differences would be indoor plumbing, the trucks in the gravel drive, and of course, the absence of Nikon's grandmother, Helene.

I study the impressive three-story home poised at the edge of a cliff looking out over three tropical seas. The last of the sun's auburn rays gleam off the white marble terraces. The floors are tiered and supported by a span of symmetrically spaced columns and archways that reflect the architecture of the original façade.

In the distance, the dramatic crash of waves breaking brings me right back to the week I spent looking out over the mixing waters of the three seas, wondering if I'd ever get home to Sloan and my family.

"It's as magical as I remember." I face the cliff's edge.

"It is at that, *a ghra*. This is the southern tip of the island, isn't it, Greek?"

Nikon nods and points to the left. "That's the Mediterranean Sea, the Sea of Crete is in front of us, and that's the Aegean."

It's perfection.

"At last, you come." The gruff welcome comes from the crest of the hill leading down toward the grape fields and the winery beyond. "And you brought the better half, I see."

Nikon Senior winks as he joins us and offers me a glimpse of the softer version of the man. Aside from the two of them sharing a name, Papu is the opposite of Nikon in almost every feature.

Where Nikon is tall, lean, and blond, his grandfather is five-foot-ten, densely muscled, and has dark brown hair and eyes. "You look well, young lady. I take it your men are taking good care of you?"

Nikon chuckles. "She can take care of herself well enough, and you know it."

"Still, it's a man's job to pamper the females in his life and make sure they never forget they are cherished."

Nikon snorts. "You realize she's all but married, don't you, old man?"

I laugh and wave his cynicism away. "If Papu wants to fawn and fuss, who am I to argue? He's right. Ladies love to be cherished."

Sloan chuckles. "Yet every time I try to buy ye something nice or do something extravagant, ye get all wound up and tell me not to."

"I can't argue there. I guess I'm not most women. I'd much prefer a bag of Skittles and a kiss than a diamond necklace."

"That's why yer such a treasure, *a ghra*—"

Dionysus steps around me, presents me with a bag of Skittles, and bends to kiss my cheek. "I told you, Red. Anything you ever want, you need only ask."

"You are too cute. Thanks." I tear the top of the bag, grab a handful and pass them around. With the sweet tang of fake fruit exploding in my mouth, I address Nikon Senior. "Nikon said you felt the presence of an empowered trespasser. Can you show us where? Maybe we can figure out what's going on."

Papu gestures back the way he came, and we follow him toward the slope toward the winery. It's a fairly steep decline in elevation, and it strikes me that it's a good thing the fae prana gifted Nikon's grandfather with the strength and vitality of youth. Otherwise, climbing this hill every day for the past two millennia would've been impossible.

Except, when we get to the crest of the slope, I realize there's no need to climb.

There's a golf cart parked off the path.

"Huh, this is new since the last time we were here."

Papu climbs in and turns the key, starting things up. "Many modernizations have been put into place since your days of battling wills and wits with Hecate."

I suppose so.

Nikon climbs onto the leather bench beside his grandfather, Sloan and I take the back seat, and Dionysus steps onto a metal running board at the back and reaches up to hold onto the frame of the fiberglass roof.

The breeze that tugs at my hair as we pick up speed is warm and fresh with the salty mist of the seas below. Solar lights line our path and cast small pools of warm light to guide our way.

It's beautiful.

As much as I love the city, part of me connects to the nature of this place and loves it just as much.

"You're looking old, kid."

Nikon grins at his grandfather, the smile on his face relaxed and easy. "I finally made it through puberty."

"Congratulations."

We all know how much it means to Nikon not to have to look at his seventeen-year-old self in the mirror every day. Now that Hecate's curse has lifted, he should age until he looks thirty-four like the other members of his immortal family.

It's a source of true joy for Nikon.

It's the work of only a few minutes to drive us down the slope to where the winery runs. It seems this is where Papu made the most changes. The last time I was here, there was a brick building where the grapes were cleaned, crushed, and made into wine.

Now there are two massive production buildings.

Papu parks the golf cart, and we all slide out. I laugh at Dionysus' windblown scare-do and reach to smooth out his crazy curls.

Papu turns off the golf cart and leaves the keys in the ignition. "What about your great, furry beast, Red? Have you brought him along?"

I pat my chest twice and nod. "He's here. Do you want to say hello?"

"I would like that. If I remember correctly, he has a good sniffer and might be of some use in tracking down whoever it is who's been tampering with my wine."

Dionysus sucks in a breath. "Tampering with wine is a capital offense. I vow to not only find the fiend but to make him suffer for it. I'm thinking beheading or possibly evisceration."

Yikes. Dionysus takes slights to the wine industry very seriously.

I release Bruin, and he materializes next to me.

Nikon Senior glances down and an appreciative twinkle lights his eyes. "Hello, Bruinior. It's nice to see you again, old friend."

It sounds funny to hear him call Bruin an 'old friend' when we only met in February. For him though, it's been more than four months—it's been centuries.

Sloan gestures toward the winery buildings. "Tell us how ye first realized someone violated yer facility."

"Come inside, and I'll show you."

The moment the five of us enter the Tsambikos winery, my senses tingle. It's not as severe as having my shield kick in with a warning, but it's not *nothing* either.

I scan the space, trying to get a sense of my surroundings. A stack of large white bins sits at the entry point of a sorting conveyor belt that runs the length of one wall while twenty stainless steel fermenting tanks run along the opposite wall. The space in between is fairly open with two forklifts ready to use.

A metal staircase leads up to the back of the tanks, but other than that, not much more.

Papu is right. There's definitely an empowered influence in the area. I flash back to standing in Merlin's cave and how the rat in the corner ended up being a spy for Morgana's son. We can't take anything for granted.

Bruin, take a look around. There's something or someone here that shouldn't be.

Bruin's massive head swings to meet my gaze. *In what way, Red? What am I looking for?*

I'm not sure, but there's an energy here that doesn't belong—no, it's more like a magical signature. See what you can find, and I'll do the same.

"What aren't you saying?" Nikon squints at me. "I know that cranial conversation look. Who are you talking to?"

"Bruin." I hold up my finger and close my eyes. "*Detect Magic.*"

Opening myself up to track the odd pulse of power, I feel unusually apprehensive and queasy. What normally affects me like a burst of energy is hitting me the exact opposite way. The moment I actively start searching, I want to stop, fold up my tent, and go home.

"What's wrong, *a ghra?* Ye look like ye swallowed sour milk."

"That's what it feels like too. Papu's right. There's something or someone here."

Sloan stiffens and frowns as he scans the surroundings. "Gentlemen, why don't ye step toward the door and give us a moment to look around."

The two of us step deeper into the space, and I hold out my

palms. Sloan grips my shoulder and sends me a rush of healing energy. Thankfully, the squirrels in my stomach settle down and stop digging for nuts. "Much better. Thanks, hotness."

"My pleasure. Now, what do you sense?"

Bruin materializes next to me and shakes his broad shoulders out. "I don't sense or smell anyone here. If there is, their magic shields them beyond my senses."

"Thanks, Bear. That's both comforting and not comforting at the same time."

I focus on my spell and let it draw me forward. Passing the first stainless steel tank, I move on to the next.

My spell is drawing me forward, but the urge to stop and retreat remains strong.

It's like an adult game of hot and cold.

With my hands still up, I fight through nausea and the urge to leave and push forward.

The tanks have a foot or two between them and are sleek and cylindrical. "Is there more to these tanks? Like nozzles or feed lines or something like a keg at a pub?"

Papu steps away from the exit and waves me back toward him. He gestures at the metal steps leading up to a catwalk running behind the tanks.

The hollow *clang, clang, clang* of our progress rings out as we climb the stairs and expand my search to the back of the tanks.

The fittings and valves are all neatly designed and attached to the tanks in an orderly fashion. Tracing a finger along the pipes, I follow the snaking twists and turns, searching for anything that sets my magical alarm bells ringing. "What happens to the wine from here?"

"These are the fermenting tanks where the sugar from the grapes turns into alcohol. Depending on the type of wine we're making, we add yeast or carbon dioxide until the process is complete."

"Then what happens?"

"Then we separate the wine from the sediment and press and rack to filter for clarity."

"Whatever it is, it's not here. Where does the wine production process take us next?"

"After fermentation and filtration, the wine is sealed into oak barrels and stacked to age in the next building."

"Perfect. Let's check there next."

Nikon's grandfather leads the way down the steps and out of the building.

I expect the fresh air to relieve the intensity of the nausea, but it doesn't.

If anything, it's building even stronger.

We tromp across the asphalt lot between buildings and approach the second part of the facility.

"Bruin, have a quick look around and see if anything here raises your hackles."

Will do. The sudden rush of wind that blows past me signifies that my bear is off on his next mission.

Papu leads us into the next building, and I stop in the door-way, taking it all in. The warehouse holds a stacked racking system that has hundreds of oak barrels sitting eight rows high for the length of the entire building. It's quite beautiful...not to mention impressive.

Dionysus whistles through his teeth. "This is how I envision the afterlife in the Elysium Fields. Look at all that beautiful wine."

I can see how this would be his heaven.

"It's amazing, Papu," I say.

"It's my life's work."

It's easy to see that. "Okay, so the fermented wine comes from the other building into here to be stored in the oak barrels for what? Months? Years?"

"That's right. The flavor is enhanced by the amount of time

it's aged, so yes, for Tsambikos quality, eighteen to thirty months minimum."

"Then I'm guessing you bottle it over there?"

He turns to the other wall, and we follow. "Yes, this is where the bottling takes place."

Distracted as I am by the immensity of the production, I'm unprepared when the queasy unease in my stomach violently revolts.

I frantically search for—"I'm going to be sick."

Dionysus snaps his fingers and thrusts the Captain Jack puke bucket under my face, and I double over and retch.

Nothing like yakking up half a bag of Skittles in front of your friends and an elder.

Awesomesauce.

I lower myself onto my knees, prop my palms on the cool, concrete floor, and lock my elbows so I'm aiming into the bucket for any further up-chucks.

"Are ye all right, luv?" Sloan whispers next to me.

"Fine. It's not me. It's a repulsion spell. We're close. Whatever is here doesn't want to be found, and it knows I'm looking."

With my head still hanging over the bucket, I hold out my hand. "Dionysus, may I have a bottle of cold water, please?"

"Sparkling or spring?"

"Spring, thanks."

I close my fingers around the bottle, twist the top, swish, spit, and take a few long swallows. When my mouth tastes less like vomited candy, I press the bottle against my forehead. "Okay. Sorry about that, folks. That snuck up on me."

Pushing up to my feet, I hand Sloan the water and pick up the bucket. "Do you have a washroom handy?"

"I'll take it, luv."

I wave off the help. "Not a chance. I clean up my messes when I'm able. You clean up enough of them already when I'm not."

Dionysus snaps his fingers, and the bucket is gone. "You two cleaned up my mess. My turn."

Both generations of Nikons look a little boggled.

There's no helping it.

"All right." I reclaim my water and take another swig. "Show me the bottling process."

Papu points at an intricate conveyor system where the bottles are loaded and filled, corked, lidded, sealed, and labeled. It runs from one end of the building to the other and has hundreds of moving parts.

After two steps, I take Sloan's hand. "Can we please try to avoid another round of heave-ho?"

"Of course, apologies, luv. My fault."

It wasn't, but I don't feel well enough to draw this out any longer than we already have.

As we walk the assembly line, I hold up the palm of my free hand and release the glamor on my fae sight. Nothing comes back to me, which is strange...unless what I'm sensing isn't fae magic.

Reclaiming my blue-eyed appearance, I follow my instincts and continue my search. "All the wines, no matter red or white and no matter how long it aged, go through this part of the process?"

"That's right."

I continue my search and change the game from hot and cold to barf or relief. Whenever nausea abates, I turn back and push toward the feeling of barfing.

My process takes me to the filling stations and specifically to the main feed line above where the smaller conduits branch off to fill eight bottles at a time.

I draw my finger down the main pipe and point at a coupling between two pieces of the line. The metal looks almost the same as everything else, but at the same time, it's different...more polished. "What's this? It's not the same metal. Is it supposed to be here?"

Papu leans in and frowns at a small extension ring of pipe between two clamps. "Absolutely not."

"Bingo. We have a winner," Nikon says.

I take a few long strides in the other direction to keep from doubling over again and sigh when things start to settle. "If you don't mind, I'll wait outside."

CHAPTER NINE

Once I release my spell and get some fresh air, my head clears, and my stomach settles. Sloan stays with Nikon and his grandfather to figure out how to remove the magical pipe extension while Dionysus and I sit in the golf cart and recover.

Well, *I'm* recovering. He's as jazzed as ever.

"Excellent work, Red. You're more my hero than ever. You saved the wine from whatever ill intent some fiend planned and Tsambikos wine is safe once more."

I chuckle, holding up my knuckles for a bump. "Glad to help right your world, my friend. I know Nikon's vintages are one of your favorites."

"This is true. So, when I say thank you, it's with the deepest and most genuine affection."

"I'm glad it helped. Now we need to figure out what that spelled pipe extension was doing to the wine and if it's an isolated attack or if someone compromised the other top vintners as well."

Dionysus' expression grows serious. "What kind of evil are we dealing with that someone would target great wine? It's vile—unconscionable even."

"As the god of wine, I'd say anyone from the magical world who targets wine must know they're stepping on your toes. That makes me think this is personal."

His gaze narrows. "Do you think someone's throwing down a gauntlet? Am I being challenged?"

"I don't know. I was thinking out loud."

Dionysus stiffens and his burgundy upper-class dandy outfit shifts to black leather pants and a battle vest covered in weapons. "If it's war they want. It's war they'll get. Coming after me is one thing but tainting the purity of wine is unforgivable. It is *on*."

I chuckle. "I don't know that it's a declaration of war. So far it's one magical spell cast by someone we don't know to do something we don't know. I don't think it's time to sharpen your weapons."

Dionysus barks a laugh. "You jest, puny human. My weapons never need sharpening."

I arch a brow. "Puny human?"

"Too much?"

"Maybe a little."

CHAPTER TEN

Over the next hour, with the help of Nikon Senior and Dionysus, we sit at Papu's kitchen table and compile a list of the top-quality wine producers. We need to ascertain if the magical tampering is a one-off event or something more widespread. While I realize that there are many impressive wine regions located on other continents, three of the top four are Italy, France, and Spain, so we start there.

Thankfully, the expertise of Papu and Dionysus makes the task quick and efficient.

Then, to incorporate my theory that this might be personal, we have Dionysus list all his personal favorites and any he drinks regularly.

Once we're satisfied that our list is complete, Nikon—who played the part of our secretary—shares it to the group chat and I scroll through it.

"Holy schmoly, there's a lot of ground to cover."

Papu nods. "I'll call those I know and tell them to expect you. While I won't be able to explain about the magic, the fact that anyone touched their pipes should be enough to have them help you remove it."

Nikon chuckles. "Yes, no one wants his pipe touched without permission."

Dionysus grins. "Speak for yourself, Nikky. I pride myself on being an interactive touch station."

I giggle and speak to Papu's point. "That will be a great help, thank you, Papu. Now that we know what we're looking for, we shouldn't be underfoot for long."

"Assuming the placement of the spelled pipe extension remains the same," Nikon says.

Sloan sets down his third sample of wine and swallows, frowning. "I've been thinkin' about that. I believe the placement is key. If the magical perpetrator simply wanted to affect a vintage or a batch, he—"

"Or she," I interject.

"—or she," he amends, "could've placed it anywhere along the process, on the fermentin' tank, on the nozzle of the press, or somewhere along the filtration process."

"But it was in the bottling feed," Papu says. "I see your point. In any of those other places, the spell wouldn't have touched every vintage. The process is slightly different between reds and white and different again depending on the result we're aiming for."

"So, by putting it in the bottling feed, all wine produced here would pass through it," I add.

Sloan nods. "That's right. Maximum coverage with minimum effort."

I don't like the sound of that. "What are you getting off the wine? Can you feel anything?"

"No. Not a thing." He looks at Nikon. "Did the lab technicians find anythin' in the samples ye gave them to test, Greek?"

"Yes and no. They found a definite trace of magic, but it didn't seem to activate or attach itself to any purpose. They were stumped."

"Do you think it's like one of those terrorist plots like you see on the cop crime shows where the bad guy poisons the water to take down society or mutate them into a mindless army?"

Sloan frowns. "Ye truly need to stop watchin' those programs, luv. Ye have a hard time separatin' fact from fantasy."

I laugh. "Because hello, fantasy is real, magic is real, so who's to say it couldn't happen?"

"Point to you, Jane." Dionysus sniffs at the wine and frowns. "Maybe if I have a few sips I can help."

"No. You've done really well today on the sober train. Let's see how tomorrow plays out before you go back to the bottle. Who knows, maybe giving you some distance will heighten your sensitivity, and you'll be able to pick up something you couldn't before."

I collect the glass out of his hand, and my skin tingles with magic. "Is that you doing that?"

"Doing what?"

I frown and hand the glass to Sloan. "Hold this and let me take it from you like I just did with Dionysus."

Sloan does as I ask and I collect the glass from him without any tingles.

"Nikon. Now you."

It's a testament to either my oddities or their patience that they don't pause to question me. Nikon picks up the glass, and I take it from him. Again, no niggling surge of magic tingling over my skin.

"Dionysus, let's do that again." I set the glass on the table and let him reclaim it. He lifts it to his nose and sniffs it, as before, and I take it before he can sip it.

My skin tingles with a second wave of magic, and I frown. "I think we figured out why the wine carries a magical signature but didn't respond to anything the lab techs tried."

"I'm almost afraid to ask," Nikon says.

"Yep. It's targeting our god of grapes."

Dionysus stiffens. "Rude. So this *is* a declaration of war. All right, gird your loins, people. I'm taking off the gloves."

As it turns out, gloves aren't the only thing Dionysus takes off. Pacing the villa in a toga, bronze greaves, and arm bracers, he reverts to his warrior self of old. Battle-ready and anticipating a foe to fight, he stalks the perimeter of the triclinium, swinging a flaming short sword through the air as he rants.

"To what end?" he snaps. "I dedicate my life to pleasing people. I celebrate life. I am the poster boy for champagne and orgasms. Who would target me? Do you think it's one of my miserable Pantheon?"

"Maybe. Hecate might still be pissed you helped Calum and I win her trials."

He frowns. "This seems too subtle for Hecate. That bitch likes to be in your face so you know who's screwing you over."

Sloan frowns. "Speaking of screwing people—and excuse the crassness of that segue—have ye considered it might be the result of yer dedication to pleasing people that prompted this attack? Maybe our wine fiend is a disgruntled lover or a husband of an indiscretion?"

Dionysus frowns. "How would that be my fault? I don't pursue lovers. They come to me. Is it my burden to determine if they're making a wise decision?"

I laugh. "I don't know if you'd realize it if it were or weren't. Wise decisions don't seem to be on your radar."

"Agreed, so, how is it my fault if a wife or husband ends up smiling in my sheets?"

Sloan chuffs. "Families are torn apart from such things. Parents forever walkin' on eggshells. Children left wonderin' if and when that strain will pull their world apart."

"Are we talking about me or you, Irish?"

"Ye must realize there's more to life than drunken revelry."

"Says you."

"Feckin' hell, man, decisions have consequences. Ye can't play the victim when yers have finally come around to bite ye in the arse."

I launch off the couch as Dionysus turns. The energy in the room just flipped my holy hell meter into the red. "Passions are high, and this topic obviously has personal implications. Let's slow the crazy train. We'll know more tomorrow once we visit the other wineries. Let's call it a successful night and get some sleep—"

"Sleep?" Dionysus turns, his gaze swirling silver. "There is no sleeping when someone is bearing down on you. Whoever this is, they've struck a blow. They've poisoned not only my passion but also my purpose. Who is the god of wine who cannot drink wine? He's the god of nothing."

I rush over to him, stomping out the sparks of flame he's raining around the room. The sword-swinging is getting dangerous. With the fury raging, we need to diffuse this or risk burning down Papu's house.

"Okay, outside." I point at the open glass wall and step out to the back patio. "Give us a moment, boys. We need some air."

Dionysus follows me without comment, and I point for him to walk with me.

"We'll figure this out," I say, giving him space while he parries and thrusts into the darkness of night. "The important thing is we know what's coming at you now. The magical alteration of the wine and the fact that someone directed it at you is likely the source of your other issue as well."

"I thought of that, too. As much as I hate to say it, thank Zeus for that. You warned me that too much wine could give me wangxiety and limber my timber, but I didn't believe you. Now, I'm hopeful you're right."

I step closer, pointing for us to take the path toward the

orchard. "Someone with a grudge knew the best way to hit you where it hurt was to taint your wine and steal your manly mojo. Knowing this is a big step to righting the wrong. How are things beneath the toga? Any improvement there?"

"Not yet, but for the first time in weeks, I'm not going to panic. This is it, Fi. I know it is."

I feel the same way. "Can you extinguish your sword so we can talk without me worrying about setting the world on fire?"

The sword ceased flaming immediately.

"Sorry. I'm not good with betrayal."

I bump his shoulder and smile up at him. "I think your response has been quite understandable. Whoever did this hit below the belt, quite literally. Now we need to figure out who and why."

"Sloan is upset with me. He doesn't get me."

I hug his arm and rest my cheek against his shoulder. "Sloan was raised in an oppressive and unhappy home much like you were. It left him with rigid views on what's acceptable and unacceptable. He doesn't always understand the gray areas of life, but I'm working with him on that."

"Funny. Similar childhood, yet he's rigid with rules, and I can't stand to be constrained by any."

"He doesn't judge though, so don't think that. He just gets frustrated sometimes and needs a moment to process a change in perception."

"I would never knowingly cause strife in a marriage or break up a family."

"I know you wouldn't, but maybe, in the past, you never cared enough to consider the consequences either."

He shrugs and squeezes my hand where it wraps around his arm. "In the past, I never understood commitment or family. It was only after watching you and Calum fight for Nikky that I realized there are people in this world who will risk everything for someone else—and not even someone they were bound to."

"Nikon is part of our family, as you are. Being bound to someone isn't about blood or marriage. In my experience, the most significant bonds between people are those we choose."

"I still don't understand why you chose me."

I stop under the screen of trees in the orchard and look at him. With the light of the moon breaking through the thin veil of fruit trees, shadows dance across his face and in his eyes—which, thankfully, have stopped swirling silver.

Dionysus hasn't aged over the centuries—he's as youthful and beautiful as any son of Zeus would be—but in this light, he *does* seem older somehow.

"I chose you because you chose me first. When Nikon approached you for help, there was no reason for you to step out of your lane and go against Hecate on our behalf."

"Except going against Hecate. I think you miss the appeal there."

I reach up and palm a lemon hanging over my head. It's not ripe yet, but the entire place smells lovely. "Pissing off Hecate was your first impulse, yes, but then you chose to get involved. You shed your life of superficial indulgences, and you stood for something."

His eyebrow arches and disappears under his hair. "You give me too much credit."

"No. I don't." I face him and take both his hands in mine. "You're an intelligent, capable man, yet in some ways, you were living half a life. That's neither good nor bad. You chose what you knew and what you're good at—celebration, revelry, and instant gratification."

"All the good things."

"Some of the good things," I correct. "You didn't have a frame of reference for love, and that's what you gravitated toward when you chose us. I think you saw something more than what you had, and you wanted to learn more about it."

"I admit, the way you and Calum worked together and

supported one another through Hecate's trials astounded me. None of my siblings would ever lift a finger to help me or keep me safe."

"Yet you worked with us and helped us win. That's what caring about others does—it builds bonds."

"I never thought about it like that."

I pull him into motion. "You're the strongest of all immortal demigods, right?"

"Right."

"Living as the god of wine and ecstasy brought out your Zeus-appointed god-self, right?"

"I suppose."

"With us, you're exploring your human side. You never knew your mother, and she never got the chance to nurture you, so there's a gap of understanding. I think being part of Clan Cumhaill is teaching you about trust, loyalty, love, and finding peace in the knowledge that there are people in this world that will set everything aside to have your back when you're in trouble."

I stop under the lemon tree where I summoned him that night I was waxing philosophical under the moonlight. "I've got you, no matter what comes at you. *We've* got you. When people see you, they might see the sexy and suave god, but I see the boy raised by mountain nymphs that never loved him. I see a kind, funny, and steadfast kid who hides deep inside you because he's too afraid no one could ever love him."

Dionysus swipes his cheeks and exhales in a rough breath. "Wow. You don't hold back, do you, Jane?"

"Not with people I love, no. Sorry, but I want you to know I see you, and I get you."

He leans forward and pulls me into a tight hug.

Magical current courses through my body and I hold on tighter, savoring the contact. His power is in flux, and I have no doubt it's because his emotions are so raw.

He's the one who pulls back, breaking away slowly as he studies me. "Sorry," he whispers. "I think I've needed to hear that for a very long time."

"No apology needed. We're family and friends. If you need a hug, I'm right here."

He straightens. "I like being in the friend zone. It protects this connection. Too much of a good thing might be too much for you and ruin us."

I laugh, giving his stomach a light smack. "I think I can manage a hug without getting all panty-damp and trying to seduce you."

He bumps my shoulder the way I'd done earlier and starts back toward the house. "Come on, puny human. You need sleep. As you said, we have a lot of ground to cover tomorrow."

CHAPTER ELEVEN

The day passes like any other in this crazy life of mine. My boyfriend looks up the address for each of the top wineries, and my immortal Greek friend magically teleports us there so we can remove the spelled sections of pipe tainting Europe's wine to make my Greek god friend impotent.

That's perfectly normal, amirite?

I sigh as the day winds to a close, wanting to flop onto the nearest couch and not get up for two days.

"One last address, *a ghra*." Sloan passes his phone to Nikon to use the Google Earth view to pinpoint where to snap us. "If ye would, Greek."

Nikon flashes him a strange smile and offers the phone back. Once everyone is ready, we all link up and snap out.

It takes me a moment to figure out that something is weird about this destination. I scan the sandy beach and the beautiful turquoise waters and shake my head.

"What's here? Not a winery."

Sloan winks. "No, that last one ended our list. This stop is all about yer first trip to the south of France. I rented this private compound fer tonight so we can regroup and hopefully recharge a little at the same time. Tomorrow begins our duties with Monsieur Blaise and the FUR Ball."

Dionysus and I chuckle. "FUR Ball."

"You're both coming as part of Team Trouble, right?" I ask the Greeks.

"Hells yes," Dionysus says. "Can you even ask that with a straight face? Me miss a masquerade ball? Not likely."

"Well, it's a black and white ball, so break out your finest togas."

Nikon grimaces. "Greeks wore himations. Romans wore togas. You wound us, Red."

"Sorry. I've never heard of a himation."

Dionysus waves that away. "The point is we'll be there with bells on."

"Not literal bells though, right?" Sloan asks.

Dionysus waggles his brows. "What, and ruin the surprise?"

I laugh and take another look at the beach and the tropical waters. As my body relaxes, I wrap my arms around Sloan's waist and lay my cheek against his chest. "Amazing. How did you know I was about to lose it?"

"I pay attention, luv. Ye've had enough fer today, so pull off yer shoes, roll up yer pantlegs, and soak in a bit of the ambiance of France. Boys, yer in the pool house. Come and go as ye please but fer the next few hours, I'd like Fiona to myself if ye don't mind."

Nikon waggles his brows at me, and Dionysus kisses my cheek. "Don't do anything I wouldn't do."

"Which is what, exactly?"

He laughs. "Exactly. See what I did there?"

I laugh. "Try to stay out of trouble, boys."

"Here, take these." Sloan hands them the bag of tainted pipe fittings we removed today.

"Nikon, you take them and keep them away from Dionysus.

The spell might affect him specifically, like the wine, so I don't want him handling them—just in case," I add.

"Even though we're taggin' out fer a few hours," Sloan continues. "If ye happen to figure out somethin' time-sensitive, feel free to interrupt."

"Interrupt?" A grin spreads across Nikon's face. "Is that an invitation to join you?"

I laugh. "Nice try, Tsambikos. Off with you."

The two of them stride off toward the sprawling beach house behind us, and I take a moment to wind down. Closing my eyes, I tip my face to the late afternoon sun and breathe in the fresh sea air.

Sloan steps behind me and rests his chin on my head. "I apologize fer chasin' them away, but I needed one of those moments we talked about. We've been bouncin' across Italy, France, and Spain, and ye've yet to see anythin' but vineyards."

I cover his arms where they wrap around my waist. "Not that the vineyards and wineries weren't lovely—because they were— but you're right, this is much better. Where are we?"

"Sainte-Maxime."

"What water am I looking at?"

"The Gulf of St. Tropez."

"It's beautiful. Thank you."

"I'd give ye the world if ye let me."

I turn in his arms and smile at the rattan chairs beneath the oversized canvas umbrella a few yards closer to the stairs leading up to the seaside house. "Are those our chairs to use?"

"If ye'd like to sit out here and watch the gulls swoop sailboats, yes. They're ours to use."

I tug him behind me, my shoes sinking in the smooth, beige sand as I run. It doesn't take me long before I have my shoes and socks off and I'm shimmying my pants down my thighs.

"What's happenin' here?" Sloan chuckles.

"I don't have a bathing suit, but as luck would have it, my bra matches my undies today, so I'm going with it. When in France, do what the French do."

"And that's swim in their underwear?"

"In this instance, I'm going with yes." I toss my pants on one of the chairs and cross my arms to pull up the hem of my t-shirt and free my hair. "Come on, hotness. The goddess wouldn't have given you that body if she didn't want you to flaunt it once in a while."

I flash him a smile and run toward the surf, giggling and filled with renewed energy. I realize I'm running too fast, too late as my feet catch in the water and I trip forward.

My faceplant is epic.

The surface of St. Tropez smacks my face and stings like a bugger. I don't care. As long as only Sloan saw that, I'm good.

Maybe he didn't see.

There's a chance he was busy stripping down.

Twisting in the water, I surface and tip my head back to keep my hair out of my face. After wiping my hands over my eyes and forehead, I blink away the water and turn back to the shore.

Sloan is standing on the edge of the beach laughing, and Nikon and Dionysus are standing in the backyard of our rental property, looking over the railing.

They're holding up large signs and laughing their Greek asses off. Nikon gives me a four-point-five and Dionysus gives me a ten. Either he doesn't understand the scoring system, or he thought it was perfect that I faceplanted.

I wave to the fans and shoo them away.

Sloan has stripped down to his boxers and is seizing the day. Good for him. I stand, my toes curling in the sand beneath my feet, and wave him in. "Join me, Mackenzie. The water's fine."

Sloan and I swim with the fish, explore our rental, have a shower, enjoy some downtime together, and take a nap. It's pretty much a perfect afternoon, or at least I think so until the sizzling scent of seafood on the grill filters into my world. Then it's even more perfect.

"Oh, that smells good," I say, joining the Greeks busying themselves on the pool deck. Dionysus is fussing with the outdoor table setting, and I have to admit it looks like the setup at a five-star restaurant. "What's for dinner?"

Nikon is in charge of the searing and is basting our dinner as it sizzles over the open flame. "Surf and turf, baby. Steak and sea bass with a mango salad. Good timing, by the way. We're all set."

My stomach growls, and I grab a plate and pass one to Sloan. "Thank you both for putting this together."

"It's the least we can do." Nikon grabs the tongs and sets a sea bass fillet on my plate. Then he moves over to where the steaks are resting on a side pan. He cuts me off a wad of meat, and I take it over to the table.

Dionysus pulls out my chair for me, and I nod. "Thank you, kind sir."

"My pleasure." He tucks me in, and I settle, spreading my napkin over my lap while the three of them grab theirs and join me.

Sloan pours the wine, and when Dionysus takes his, I reach for his hand and focus. Holding his wrist, I ensure there are no magical tingles. "Nothing. You're good."

"Excellent." He holds up his glass. "A toast to the love of family, new adventures, and the pleasure of untainted wine."

We all *clink* our glasses to that.

The glass is delicate, and I sip the wine. It's white and dry, and I'm not sure I'm a fan. "What is this?"

"It's a Sauvignon Blanc. It pairs well with white fish. The earthiness of the pour enhances the flavors of these fish and plays well on the palate."

All righty then.

"I'll give it the benefit of the doubt. I'm more of a red, fruity, and robust girl as a rule."

Dionysus waves, and a second set of wine glasses appear with red wine. "Ask, and ye shall receive, Jane. Grilled fish works very well with lightly oaky red wines as well. The charcoal smokiness toys with the light vanilla of the oak. For that, we have a Pinot Noir."

I smile. "Wow. I know you drink a lot of wine, but it never occurred to me you were also highly educated in the intricacies of wine pairing. Well done, you continue to surprise me, Tarzan."

He beams, taking that as the compliment I meant it to be.

"So, how was your timeout?" Nikon asks as we settle in for a delicious meal.

"Lovely, thank you." I groan as I take my first bites of steak. The flavor is rich and juicy. It's tender and practically melts in my mouth as I chew. "Nikon, seriously? You can cook like this, and you let me make your burgers? I'm horrified."

Nikon takes a bite and winks. "Don't be horrified. I like your charburgers and how you try to mask overcooking them with layers of barbeque sauce."

I sample the sea bass, and I close my eyes and savor the flavor. I can't even be annoyed at his comment because when you grill like this everything else must taste like hockey pucks. "New rule. If you're at our house, you help me on the grill. I'm now your apprentice."

Nikon drops his chin. "I have much wisdom to impart, grasshopper. Prepare to be amazed."

I chuckle and check in with Sloan. He's staring off at the water below, obviously not listening to the conversation at the table. "You okay, hotness?"

He blinks out of his reverie. "Of course, luv. My apologies, I was thinking about the winery tampering and how we might be able to find the culprit."

Dionysus sits straighter and grins. "What did you come up with?"

"Earlier, Fi told Nikon to keep the pipe fittings away from you in case they could still cause harm."

"Do you think they will?" I sip my wine.

"No. The idea that their spell energy still charges them has me wondering if we can somehow track the magical signature back to its source. Maybe then we could figure out who cast the spell in the first place and what their gripe is against Dionysus."

Dionysus leans back, savoring his wine like a long-lost friend. "You don't think it was fae, correct?"

Sloan and I both shake our heads. "No. The spell isn't showing up with my fae sight or Sloan's bone ring. I think it's safe to say it's other."

Dionysus rolls his eyes. "How much do you want to bet it's someone from Olympus? Why can't we all just get along?"

"If they don't get you, it's their loss." I spear the last of my steak. "We'll figure out who and we'll take care of it. If they thought they could take a cheap shot and we wouldn't find out and fight back, they were grossly mistaken."

Dionysus raises his glass. "Here's to exposing the fiend trying to destroy me and making him pay."

I raise my wine glass and sip—

It happens so fast.

There's no time to react.

An ebony-haired man flashes in behind Dionysus.

My shield blazes to life.

He grips Dionysus' shoulder and flashes out.

The three of us are on our feet and pivoting, searching the landscape for some clue of what happened.

"Who was that?" I snap, my heart racing.

Sloan frowns. "Someone with the power to highjack a god. We might've met the fiend who targeted Dionysus, and he's not happy we interceded."

"It's worse than that." Nikon looks grim. "That wasn't only some fiend seeking revenge on Dionysus for an indiscretion—that was Loki."

"Loki? What do you mean? Like, Thor's brother? The trickster prince of Asgard?"

"That's who I mean. If he's pissed at Dionysus, our boy is in more trouble than we thought."

I try to wrap my head around that. "Are you sure? That man looked nothing like Tom Hiddleston, he wasn't wearing green leather, and he didn't have those gold horns he always wears."

Nikon swings his gaze to Sloan. "Is she serious? What am I missing?"

Sloan offers him a sympathetic smile. "Fi tends to invest herself in television and movie characters and confuses them with reality."

I flop back into my chair and finish my wine. "No, I don't. I understand the difference. I just don't get how that man was Loki. Anyway, forget it. How do we find him? I don't suppose either of you knows how to portal to Asgard, do you?"

Nikon reclaims his wine as well. "Sadly, that would be a no. Still, I might know a way. I'm sorry to cut our stay here short, but we'll need to go."

I gather the dishes and stack plates, handing them to Sloan. He *poofs* them inside and is back a moment later for another armful. Nikon snaps out and is back with his bag as well as Dionysus'.

Once the dishwasher is running, I rush to the bedroom to pack ours. It's the fastest rental property checkout in history.

Ten minutes later, the three of us meet back up at the patio door, and Sloan and I nod at Nikon.

Hang on, Tarzan. We're coming.

Nikon snaps us back to his home in Toronto, and I set our bag next to the two he drops on the marble floor of the foyer. "Andromeda?" he calls, his voice echoing off the hard surfaces of white marble in the grand entryway. "Politimi? Are either of you home?"

I have my phone out and am about to text Andy when she strides across the balcony on the floor above. "I'm here. What's wrong?"

"We have an emergency," I say.

"Scale of one to ten?" She rounds the newel post at the top of the stairs and jogs down to join us.

"Eleven."

"Oh, dear. What's happened?"

"Loki took Dionysus." The words tumble off my tongue but my poor hamster trips in his mental wheel. "It seems the Prince of Asgard had a plan to take Dionysus down by poisoning him through the finer wines of the world. We foiled that by figuring it out, so he took him."

Nikon reaches for his sister and squeezes her arm. "Do you or Politimi still keep in contact with Hel?"

Andromeda shrugs. "I haven't spoken to her in centuries. I don't think Timi has either."

"But neither of you are on bad terms or anything?"

"No. Nothing like that. We simply run in different circles and lead different lives."

Nikon lets out a long sigh. "Do you have any way to get in contact with her? Do you know where she is?"

"She doesn't have a phone plan if that's what you're asking. She's the Queen of Helheim. I assume she's overseeing her realm."

I'm trying to keep up, but I admit, I'm not up on Norse mythology. "Who is Hel to Loki and how can she help us find Dionysus?"

Andy gestures at the parlor set just off the entrance, and we go in and sit down. "Hel is Loki's daughter and the only one in that dysfunctional family who likely has an idea of where Loki is. She has two siblings, the world serpent also known as Jörmungandr, and Fenrir the Wolf. They have no relationship with each other and roam in separate places in the world."

"But she keeps up with their father?"

"As much as any of them do, I suppose. Or at least she did. As I said, it's been centuries."

"But assuming nothing has changed?"

"Loki and Hel always shared a bond. He felt responsible for Odin throwing her down into Helheim but true to her character, Hel dusted herself off and made the place her own."

"Helheim is the equivalent to our hell? Am I right?"

"Sort of. It sparked the etymology of using the word *hell* as a dark purgatory world within Christian beliefs. It's much less about demons and tortured souls for eternity and more a feast and celebration of the lives and warriors who end up there."

She pulls a thick, leatherbound text from the bookcase against the wall and brings it to the sofa to sit next to me. "The Norse believe that those who die bravely in battle go to Valhalla and those who die of old age, disease, or anything not on the battlefield go to Helheim."

I turn to Nikon. "You think his goddess daughter will know where her trickster father is?"

"She'll have a better idea than anyone else I can think of, but the pantheons don't recognize her as a goddess."

"Depending on Hel to find Dionysus isn't ideal," Andy says to her brother.

"No, it's not, but there's no way we're approaching anyone from the god side of things. Odin, Thor, Frigg, Hod...that's suicide."

"Entering Helheim is better?" she asks.

I have faith in Nikon's judgment, though. If he thinks this is our best play, I'm game to try. "Okay, how do we get to her? Please don't tell me we have to die."

Andromeda shakes her head. "No. Nothing as dramatic as that —well, at least to get there."

"That doesn't fill me with confidence."

Andromeda turns a page and shows me a lithograph image of a gruesome wall of skulls, bones, and snakes. "The Helheim Glacier is located on the eastern side of the Greenland ice sheet. The Corpse-gates are within the Gnipa cave."

"We can go to this cave and contact her?"

"In theory—if it all works out—it could be that simple, yes."

"And if it doesn't all work out?"

She flips the page and leans deeper into the cushion of the sofa. "The Corpse-gates are guarded by a hellhound, Garmr, who howls to signal new arrivals. That draws the dragon Nidhogg to suck the blood out of all the dead so it's easier for Hel to transition them into her army of the dead."

I roll my eyes. "Seriously? A dragon's going to try to suck our blood and enlist us into her undead army?"

Andromeda sends me an apologetic look. "I did say it isn't ideal."

I huff. "That's an understatement."

CHAPTER TWELVE

The four of us go over the logistics of the Hel plan and getting to Helheim. When we think we have it nailed down, I text Merlin to let him in on the plan. If there are blood-sucking dragons involved, I'd like backup from our dragon master and his family of scaled beasts.

While we await his thoughts on the dragon part of entering Gnipa cave, Nikon snaps us home to get winter coats and boots.

Even though we've only been gone for the weekend, it's good to be home.

Our house seems remarkably quiet.

"Hello, the house," I shout as we drop our bag in the hall and move to the front of the house. "Olly olly oxen—freaking hell, Emmet!"

I spin away from the living room but not before my retina burns out with images of my brother and his betrothed carnally corrupting our leather sofa.

"What the hell, Fi?" he snaps.

"Why are you yelling at *me*? You're the ones naked in the living room."

"You're the ones away for the weekend in Europe. Kevin and

Calum went to Kev's parents. Sloan said you had a place in France. We were supposed to have the house to ourselves."

"I'll go get our warm clothes," Sloan says, his back to the living room. "Nikon? Would ye care to join me?"

Nikon grins. "No, I'm good. I want to see if Fi's head actually explodes or if it just seems like it will."

I make a face at him. "Har-har, Greek. How would you like it if you came home and Andromeda or Politimi was naked in your living room getting lewd on your leather?"

He busts up laughing. "It happens once a month at least. On my sofas, kitchen counter, defiling my pool table, the bar in the den, the hot tub, the seat of my motorcycle. Honestly, after a few centuries, beds become boring. We try to keep out of each other's way."

"Thanks, Greek," Emmet says behind me. "Besides, we're not naked. I have my vest and utility belt on."

I vaguely remember that but refuse to turn back. "So, you're playing dress up?"

"Sexy cop stripper, actually," Ciara says. "Sorry, Fi. We honestly did think we had the run of the place."

I sigh. "Fine. Let's pretend this never happened. We're off to Greenland to find Loki and free Dionysus. There will be hellhounds and dragons, and that's only to access his daughter. If you want to join the fight, you'll need to put away your nakey bits or risk frostbite."

"Yeah?" Emmet says. "We can come?"

"Yes. In fact, your help is key to the plan, Em."

"Cool. Okay, close your eyes if you don't want a show because I'm streaking upstairs to get dressed."

I do as prompted and follow the sounds of him climbing the stairs and walking to his room on the floor above. "What about you, Ciara?"

"Och, my clothes are back in place. Yer brother caught me doin' work on my laptop here on the couch. The sexy stripper thing was all him. He has a spontaneous streak to him, which ye know already, and is a bit of a nutter."

I draw a deep breath and stretch my neck from side to side. "I may have noticed that, yeah."

The amusement on Nikon's face is hugely annoying.

"Shut up, Greek."

"So, this is Greenland." I raise my gloved hand to fend off the glare of sunlight reflecting off ice and snow as far as I can see. The magnificence of the Helheim Glacier is daunting. We're standing on the crest of the ice sheet, and the only interruption in the textured white ground is the ink blue water dotted with icebergs below. "Man, there's nothing like feeling small and insignificant in the vastness of nature, is there?"

"It's humbling," Sloan says.

It is.

"Dayam." Emmet studies the sheer drop of the glacier wall down to the frozen waters below. "It's like we've gone north of the Wall in *Game of Thrones*. Everyone beware of wildlings."

"You know nothin', Jon Snow," Ciara says.

I hold my fist up for a bump. "Well played, Ciara. Point to you, girlfriend."

Emmet chuckles. "No, seriously. How big is this Helheim Glacier anyway, Irish?"

"A hundred and twenty-four miles long, four miles wide and over three hundred and twenty-five feet high."

"Wowzers. That's impressive."

"It's not nearly as cold as I thought it would be," Ciara says.

Emmet nods. "No, this is what a Toronto early spring feels like. Crisp but not violently cold."

"Och, then I'm less worried about my first winter as a Canadian."

I fight the urge to laugh. Winter is still going to be a rude awakening for her.

Nikon holds out a finger to point at the long lake below. "Ice and snow used to cover this whole area, but with iceberg calving and glacier retreat, the topography has changed a lot since the days of old."

"Does that make it easier or harder to find the entrance to the cave?" I ask.

"Easier, I suppose. It does, however, change the landscape from what Andromeda told us to look for."

True story.

I don't see any of the land markers Andromeda mentioned.

The five of us are assessing how to handle that when a long, gut-wrenching howl echoes from a distance.

"Is that our hellhound?" I turn to pinpoint where exactly the sound is coming from.

"I believe it is." Sloan takes my hand. "Nikon, can ye get us up closer to that rise of mountains?"

"Sure can. Hang on, everyone. Let's do this."

The five of us clasp hands, and Nikon snaps us toward the direction of where we heard the baleful cry of the hellhound a moment ago. "Does anyone see the mouth to a cave?"

"Is it a rock cave or an ice cave?" Emmet asks.

"Rock, I think." Nikon doesn't sound sure.

"Wait a moment," Sloan grows still. "We need a privacy veil. No one move."

The five of us stay where we are as Sloan casts a spell enclosing us in a bubble of secrecy. His words are still hanging in the air when an olive green dragon flies overhead and lands eighty feet to our right.

"Good call, Mackenzie," I whisper.

It was. Andromeda mentioned the dragon would come to suck the blood out of the new arrivals, so, yeah, that shows us right where the entrance is.

There's a moment of silence when the dragon lands, followed by a ball-shriveling scream. When the scream dies, the dragon turns and stares off in the distance.

On schedule, Merlin in his dragon form swoops into view, followed by Cazzienth, Saxa, Dart, Bryvanay, and Utiss. They rise and fall, soaring to heights and cartwheeling through the air in playful maneuvers.

The Helheim guard dragon, Nidhogg, takes off and follows as we hoped he would. "Okay, Em, you're up. Do you think you'll be able to communicate with Garmr?"

"I'm catching his awareness, but it's not strong enough to form a bond or have a conversation from here. I'll have to get closer."

"What if Em's gift doesn't work the same way on Hel's creatures as it does on the goddess'?" Ciara asks.

I thought of that but didn't want to bring it up. So far, Emmet's never met a wildlife creature he hasn't been able to win over. Hopefully, that trend continues with mythical Norse beasts. "All he needs to do is to keep Garmr from howling out our arrival and drawing the dragon back."

"And keep the blood-sucking to a minimum." Emmet gives us a goofy grin.

"Yes, please. That."

Ciara makes a face at him. "Can we not joke about that, please?"

Emmet shrugs. "Keepin' it real, baby. If you're having second thoughts, you can wait here, and we can play *Titanic* when I get back."

As if inspired by Emmet's teasing, the ground beneath our feet lets out a loud *crack* and our footing jiggles.

I hold out my hands and my heart rate triples. "What's happening? Are we under attack?"

The druids tense and brace our stances.

Nikon looks at us like we're nuts. "It's the natural recession of the glacier. This entire area is adjusting to air currents and global warming and natural water currents."

"Thankfully, it was only a little tremor," I say.

Nikon chuckles. "That little tremor is all that's needed to cause shearing on the ice wall—yeah, check it out. It's starting."

I follow his pointed finger and watch as massive chunks of ice break off the wall and crumble into the icy fjord below.

The *crunch* and *crack* of ice are like a slow-motion video in real-time, and sure enough, the first erosion seems to set off shearing other chunks all along the length of the wall.

The ground rumbles, and I'm awestruck by the magnitude of it all.

"Come on, guys. I want to be gone before it cracks and sucks us under. The big one's coming," Nikon says.

"Seriously?" I swing my head around, and he bursts out laughing. "You suck, Greek."

Nikon's chest bounces as he gestures for us to get moving over the snowy terrain. "Sorry, Red. Sometimes you're just too trusting to pass up."

It's a sore point with Emmet that Calum, Dillan, Aiden, Da, and I were gifted offensive abilities from the warrior statues in Fionn's fortress while he ended up with the nakey man. His buffering ability, heightened connection for healing, and communication with wildlife and fae creatures are all awesome, but they're defensive powers.

He doesn't get to shine as he would like, but there are times, like now, when his strengths are what we need.

"So, all I need to do is make friends with the hellhound and keep it from baying and calling the blood-sucking dragon of the dead?"

"In a nutshell, yeah." I choose my footing to scale a particularly jagged patch of frozen ground.

The terrain between us and the mouth of the rock cave gaping dark against the brilliance of snow and ice is treacherous.

"We're sure Emmet's gift will work the same with mythical hell creatures as it does with woodland animals?" Ciara asks again, her voice tight.

"There's no way to be sure," Sloan says, "except for trial by fire. We'll have to see how things go."

I don't like the idea of trial by fire when Emmet's involved—not one bit—but I also can't think of a way around it.

I'm still twisted up about that when my brother's head cocks to the side and his gaze pivots to focus on the cave mouth.

"What is it, Em? What do you sense?"

"He knows we're here and that we don't belong. Stay still. I'll try to explain."

"Explain quickly," Nikon says, "because if he calls for the dragon, things will go to shit fast."

We pause, frozen in our tracks, and give Emmet the reins on this part of the plan.

The worry marring Ciara's face is genuine and profound. It warms me to her a little more. I really do want my brother to be deliriously happy. If Ciara's his heart's other half, I'll get over my initial dislike of her.

Eventually.

I draw a deep breath and study the surroundings. It doesn't take long. Jagged, crunchy snow drops off to our right to frozen water with jagged, crunchy snow, and off in the distance is the rise of mountains crested in jagged, crunchy snow.

I see the pattern.

Should it be taking this long? I throw the question at Nikon, unsure if his communication channels are open and he'll pick it up.

How long should it take? Is there a FAQ sheet on subduing mythical beasts somewhere we missed?

Hilarious. You're a laugh and a half today, Greek.

Sorry. I'm worried about Dionysus. I hate not knowing what's happening to him.

Ditto.

We wait in silence a few more minutes, my breath escaping in white puffs of condensation.

What's our exit plan if we need to retreat?

Studying my brother as I am, I catch when his quizzical look changes to alarm. His head spins around, his eyes wild and wide.

Instantly, my shield flares, and my muscles tense with the imminence of danger approaching.

The hellhound steps out of the darkness of the cave mouth. Growling long and low, he stalks forward, his ebony fur standing up at the hackles in wiry patches. The noise Garmr makes vibrates deep in my chest, and even though I don't have Emmet's gift of communication, the message comes across loud and clear.

Leave. You don't belong here.

Emmet breathes deep and slow, holding his palms open at his side as he edges closer. "It's okay, boy. No one's here to cause trouble. We only need a moment with your mistress."

The beast's aggressive stance as it prowls forward makes my pulse race. "Em, maybe we need to rethink. It doesn't look like he's falling for your charms."

"It's fine. I've got this. None of you move. I need his focus on me."

That's the part of this I hate.

I'm accustomed to being the target of violence—not my family. I don't like to be in the safe zone while one of them is in the crosshairs.

The hellhound pierces us with a cold, yellow gaze as Emmet inches forward.

The beast is larger than any species of canine I've ever seen, including Moon Called wolves. His legs are thick with muscle, his shoulders rounded with tension, and his wiry fur hangs low and matted from his belly.

With each step closer, the *scratch, scratch* of his claws slicing through the frozen ground raises the hair on the nape of my neck.

Emmet shakes out his fingers as he continues toward the approaching beast. He's now closer to the hellhound than he is to us and the vulnerability of that makes me want to vomit.

"Please be careful, Em," I whisper, my voice catching in my throat.

The hellhound snarls at me, light glinting off the long, ivory canines exposed in its gaping maw.

Emmet doesn't respond, but I know he heard me.

He's hyper-focused.

The colossal hound pauses his approach, tilting his head as if considering something Emmet is suggesting. For a moment, I think it might be as easy as all Emmet's encounters with communication.

Not this time.

A feral growl vibrates through my body as the hound shakes its head and launches forward. Head down, he charges and catches Emmet in the gut. With a powerful flip of his head, my brother is tossed into the air like he weighs no more than a straw scarecrow.

A deranged roar echoes in the air as Emmet crashes to the icy ground. Brittle *snaps* crack off, and I can't decipher if it's bones or ice crunching.

"Emmet!" Ciara rushes forward, hands raised.

"*Stop!*" Emmet shouts. "Seriously...I've got this."

What's happening? Bruin asks. *Do ye need me?*

We might. I press a hand against my racing heart and focus on settling down. *Emmet's trying to tame a hellhound. If it goes badly, you need to take the beast on while we evacuate him to Wallace's clinic.*

Understood.

The massive beast positions himself above Emmet and throws us a warning.

"Screw you, doggy. You don't get to claim my brother as your chew toy." I give the group a sidelong gaze and read their readiness to attack.

"Emmet," Sloan says, his tone smooth as whiskey, "what's the word, sham?"

"Stay." Emmet coughs, and scarlet spittle speckles the pristine white of the snow. "Hold your position. He's confused."

Confused or not, he broke something in my brother.

I eye up the massive predator straddled over Emmet and a chill races the length of my spine. Em is six feet tall, but the hound dwarfs him and envelops him in the beast's black coat. "Sloan, when I release Bruin, you *poof* Emmet to the clinic."

"No," Emmet snaps. "Seriously, Fi. I'm working on something here. Shut up and let me do my thing."

I purse my lips and bite back my objection.

I hate staying on the bench when people are in danger. It doesn't help that my shield is singeing my back.

The hellhound seems to sense my rising impatience and locks me with a glare.

Screw you, pooch. If you have a battle you want to wage, do your worst.

"Fuck, Fi," Emmet snaps. "You're making this more difficult than it needs to be. Stop challenging him."

Sloan and Nikon edge toward each other and block me out. When the screen closes me off, I feel even more helpless than I did a moment ago.

Man, this sucks.

I stand there, unable to see what's happening, listening to the scuffle and *crunch* of movement scraping against the frozen ground. After what seems like an eternity, the boys shift to the side, and I find Emmet standing next to the hellhound, looking smug.

He has one hand wrapped across his chest and the other stroking the head of Garmr, the hellhound guard of the Corpse-gates.

"Great job, Em." I keep my gaze on the ground and adamantly try not to incite his canine companion. "You rock my socks, brother."

The beast seems even more massive with Emmet standing beside him. True, Em's not able to stand upright at the moment, but even so, the dog's boxy noggin reaches his chin.

"Okay, guys," Emmet says, his voice calm and level. "Bring it in, slow and steady."

Nikon exhales, scrubbing his fingers through the shabby-chic blond spikes of his hair. "That was intense, Emmet. Well done."

Emmet lifts his chin in acknowledgment and smiles. "The interface is super cool. He never meant to hurt me. He's stubborn and fought the connection. S'all good now though. Promise."

"Except that yer hurt?" Ciara says, hesitant to reach for him.

"A couple of broken ribs, babe, but I'm still breathing so nothing tore into my lungs or heart."

Awesomesauce.

That little ray of sunshine does nothing to ease my nerves. "Sloan, could you *poof* him to your father for a tune-up, please? Greenland isn't far from Ireland, is it?"

Sloan chuckles. "Not as far as Toronto, no."

Emmet waves off the suggestion. "I'm good. I've been working on my healing and think I can take care of myself. Just let me sit here with Garmr, and I'll be fine."

I shift my gaze from him to Sloan. "You and Ciara stay with Em. Help him heal if he needs it and take him to your father if things get worse. Nikon and I will go find Hel."

Emmet bends to the side, gripping his chest as he coughs. A fresh wash of blood stains the snow at his feet.

I point at the Jackson Pollock on the snow. "Heal yourself fast, or they're taking you in. I believe in your abilities, but I'm not taking chances with your life."

Emmet wipes his mouth with the sleeve of his jacket and gives me a weak nod. "Understood. Love you too, by the way."

CHAPTER THIRTEEN

The Corpse-gates of Helheim aren't so much gates, but an ominous, textured wall blocking our way to what lies beyond. Rising from the icy floor of the Gnipa cave, it stretches upward and connects to the jagged ceiling. Within that wall stands an elaborate archway covered in Norse symbols and rune carvings.

The wall's surface isn't like anything I've ever seen—though, to be fair—in the dim light of the cave entrance, I can't tell what material it is. It shows weathering in spots and bits of the detailing have fallen to the cave floor.

I pick up a piece of the fallen design and screech, throwing it back down. "Finger. Finger. Finger…" I wipe my gloves against my pant leg while jumping around in my freak out. "So gross. So, so gross."

"Not only fingers." Nikon leans close and scrunches up his face. "If I'm not mistaken, we also have some tongues and peens here."

I cast another glance at the wall. The size. The sheer scope of the artwork. How many body parts did it take to decoupage this horror show? "That's seriously disgusting. Like, truly disturbing."

"No offense, Red, but it *is* the Corpse-gate. It's in the name."

"Okay, well, when you say it like that, it seems obvious." I wave that away. "Never mind. The point is, don't touch anything."

I lift my hand, thankful I have gloves on.

"Not unless you want to go insane and spend your ever after here with me," a woman says, walking through the archway engulfed in a burst of gold.

"Contact with things here makes it hard to fight off the dread that burrows into the soul of living things. And, by the looks of things, you are still living."

She sounds a little disappointed by that.

She doesn't open the door. She simply walks through it as if it isn't there. My mind barely has the chance to wonder about that because I'm too dazzled by the wolf head hanging over her shoulder.

Dressed in ancient warrior garb, she looks like she's ready to take on a hostile army. A flutter in my gut has me hoping that's not us. She wears a green tunic beneath a brown leather and chain mail vest and across her shoulders is slung a wolf pelt.

She's tall and broad like a shieldmaiden of her heritage, but that's not the most startling thing about her.

Nope. Not even close.

Don't stare. Nikon's voice rings strong in my head, and I try to soften my gaze.

Hel reminds me of DC's Two-Face. With a line running straight down her spine, half of her body is that of an eerily pale goth woman with blonde hair shaved close to her scalp and braided by her ear, and the other half of her is blue-skinned with navy blue hair.

"Lady Hel." Nikon bows as he speaks. "I am Nikon Tsambikos, brother of Andromeda and Politimi Tsambikos."

Thankfully, Nikon's introduction distracts her enough that I have a moment to regroup.

"Nikon. I remember your sisters speaking of you. I take it

they are well?"

"Well enough, yes."

The air falls still and quiet. It's embedded in my nature to jump into awkward silences and get the convo rolling, but Nikon warned me specifically about this. With people of Hel's level of rule, they get to ask the questions and open the door to conversation, not the other way around.

"What brings you to my gates, Nikon?"

"Your father, actually."

Her expression tightens. "I don't get involved in Loki's dealings, and he returns the favor. I'm sorry you've wasted a trip. Give my regards to your sisters."

When she turns to leave, I step forward. "He's kidnapped our dear friend."

She holds up her hand, and a rush of nausea and foreboding hits me like eels in my belly and bowels. "As I said, I don't get involved in—"

"I'm not sure what Dionysus did to piss off your father—honestly with him, I'm almost afraid to guess—but he's been poisoning and torturing him."

"Dionysus?"

I don't know what our beloved god of wine means to Hel, but something changes with the mention of his name. Hel spins back to me and her gaze narrows. "Your friend, you say?"

The impact of her full attention presses on my lungs and makes my belly eels squirm again. I'm hoping it's only for effect because I don't think there's a washroom handy if something truly foul happens.

"Yes, my friend. We kind of adopted him and made him a part of our family. That's why we're here. It's been hours since Loki took him and we're worried."

Hel lets out a long-suffering sigh. "You are right to be concerned. If my father took Dionysus, it wouldn't be to catch up on old times."

"So they know each other? They have a past?"

"In a fashion, yes."

Garmr's baleful howl echoes from everywhere all at once. I pivot as Sloan jogs into the mouth of the cave and sends us an apologetic shrug. "Not much to be done about it, I'm afraid. There's a new arrival."

He points at a tall, rugged man stepping into the cave, looking a bit lost and a lot dead.

The screech of a dragon in the distance means our time has run out.

"Will you help us?"

Hel escorts Nikon, Sloan, and I back out to the ice and snow and gestures for the dragon, Nidhogg, to pass us and continue toward the Corpse-gates. I have no interest in the blood-sucking or army of the dead part of her process, so I welcome the chance to leave.

"Let me deal with the new soul and call someone to man the gates. Then, I shall track Loki and see what damage he's done now."

It's upsetting that Dionysus is the damage in that statement but what's more upsetting is her use of the singular. "You mean 'we' will track Loki down, don't you? This is a team effort."

She looks me over and scans our group. It's easy to tell she finds us less than impressive, but regardless, that's her short-sightedness and not my problem. "I shall take care of things, and Dionysus can find you once I find him."

I shake my head. "No offense meant, but that doesn't work for us. Dionysus is more than our friend—he's family. We might not look like an intimidating offensive, but I promise you we've taken on people as powerful as Loki and come out on top."

Hel frowns. "No. You don't look like an offensive threat."

"That's fine. Being underestimated doesn't bother us. If you're not comfortable with us coming, tell us where he is, and we'll go ourselves. Either way, we're not standing down while Dionysus is in trouble."

Her gaze narrows. "Are we talking about the same Dionysus? Greek demigod. Insufferably self-involved. Incapable of evolving past the wants and needs of a lust-filled child?"

The cutting edge in her tone sets off warning bells, and the big picture comes into focus.

Maybe Loki's reason for punishing Dionysus isn't about what happened between the two of them, but something that happened between Dionysus and Hel.

Fathers can be protective. I know that firsthand.

"He may have been that way when you knew him, but he has evolved. He's a valued member of our family and has saved my life more than once. Yes, he's self-involved, but he is also sweet and generous and incomparably eager to embrace life."

She frowns. "It's difficult for me to reconcile the man you describe with the man I once knew."

I shrug. "He's a work in progress, but we love him."

Another rush of squirmy eels hits me, and there's no mistaking the anger and jealousy storming in Hel's coal-black eyes. "You love him? That is a mistake."

I hold my hand out and pull Sloan against my side. "I am in love with Sloan." I hold up my hand and his so she can see our matching bands. "Dionysus is family, and we don't leave family in the lurch. Whatever is going on, we're with you."

Emmet rises from the rock he was sitting on and strokes the scruffy ears of the hellhound. The connection between the two seems to take Hel by surprise.

"Very well," she says, "You may join me, but I won't be held responsible for your safety. My father is unpredictable at best and treacherous at worst. He might kill you on a whim, and there will be little I can do to help you then. You are not Norse, are you?"

I shake my head. "No, Celtic druids."

She nods. "I have no dominion over your death."

A brutal gust of wind picks up and smacks us all with a wall of cold. I cringe and turn to block my face. A moment later, Dart and the other dragons land around us.

Hel's eyes widen, and Merlin transforms into his human self. "Lady Hel, it's been a great many centuries. It's a pleasure to see you again."

She drops her chin and takes in the brood of dragons. "Merlin. What brings you here?"

He tilts his head toward me as Dart postures beside me, and I reach to rub the horn on his nose. "They're with us. Again...part of our extended family."

"This family of yours is rather unconventional."

I pat Dart's cheek and smile. "Maybe, but it works. We love and protect our own, and Dionysus is one of us."

"Would he want you to endanger yourselves on his behalf?"

"That's not his call. We accept responsibility for our safety and won't stop until we have him home."

She takes us all in and draws a deep breath. "All right, but don't say I didn't warn you."

Thankfully, she heads inside to take care of her gate duties. With any luck, we're one step closer to getting out of the cold and finding Dionysus.

Hel may be the daughter of a demigod, but she doesn't have the gift of portal transportation. Since there's no way to Google locations and Sloan's never been to the location Hel describes, we discuss the option of riding the dragons.

Merlin doesn't like the risk of exposing the existence of the dragons to Loki and whoever might be involved with him at the other end. Dart protests, but in the end, Merlin vetoes the discussion and sends my boy back to Iceland with Cazzienth and the others.

They'll be called as backup only if we need them.

To counteract the "no signal" problem, Nikon snaps the seven of us to Gran's and Granda's as a pitstop.

"Och, look who's here. What's the craic, kids?" Gran straightens from working in the garden and brushes the dirt from her hands. "What an unexpected pleasure."

The five of us take our turns hugging Gran. Then she smiles at Merlin and a confused-looking Hel.

"Who might this be, children?"

"Gran, this is Lady Hel. Dionysus is in a bit of trouble, and she's helping us find him."

Gran's smile dims. "Trouble? Well then, our thanks fer yer help and don't let me distract ye. What do ye need to get our boy home?"

"Just your Internet and a quick refresh in the treehouse," Emmet says, hiking his thumb over his shoulder. "Give me two minutes, and I'll be good to go."

"I'll come with ye," Ciara says. "I need the jacks, and there's a box of sweets in the cupboard. Ye'll need sugar after a healin' like that."

"A healin'?" Gran says, her gaze following them as they climb the ladder to our home away from home. "What's happened?"

"Nothing worth worrying about, Gran," I say, reaching to squeeze her hand. "Emmet's coming into his own more every day. He'll be fine."

Hel frowns, holding her hand up toward the treehouse. "I feel Dionysus' power here. Why?"

"Because he and I built the treehouse together fer when he and the kids come to stay," Gran says. "It was a labor of love."

Hel's mouth quirks up at the side in an uneven smile. "Dionysus built a treehouse?"

"It was a gift for us," I say.

"He truly is part of your family?"

"He is."

Something in her expression shifts. "That's why my father chose now to target him after all these years. He finally learned to love someone other than himself."

Emmet and Ciara return, and I kiss Gran's cheek and check in with Nikon. "Are we good to go?"

Nikon puts away his phone and extends his hand.

Gran kisses Emmet and Sloan and steps back. "Find him, kids. Find him and bring him home."

"Will do, Gran," Emmet says. "We'll keep you posted. Love you."

The palace Hel brings us to is like nothing I've ever seen before. It's massive and beautiful and so incredibly impressive I can't even begin to imagine who might live here. Or how many people it might hold.

Dozens? Hundreds?

"What do you think the mortgage on this place goes for?" Emmet scans the façade. "I mean. I think it's out of my budget on a cop's salary, but maybe I could pick up some pay duty."

I laugh. "Dream on, dude. You'd have to be a president of a country to be able to afford a place like this."

Sloan grins. "There are a great many stunning palaces in Austria. What always impresses me is that as awed as we are, imagine how much more unfathomable a building like this would've seemed to the common folks of the 1500s."

"That's cray-cray." I stare at the place lit up against the darkness of night. "I have to admit, hotness, your love of big old buildings is growing on me."

Sloan grins. "Then my evil plan is working."

Merlin scratches his head and scrubs a hand through the

stubble on his chin. "How paranoid is he about being found? Will he have spells cast and wardings up?"

Hel shakes her head. "Not usually. Loki is cocky but also enjoys the surprise of a twist of fate. If someone were to find him here, it would only make the trouble he's causing more fun. He'll have guards, though."

Guards we can deal with. "So, where do you think Loki is and what makes you think he's here?"

"Oh, he's here." Hel frowns at the grand residence. "But with over fourteen hundred rooms, the trick will be to find him."

"What about my pendant?" I pull my silver likeness of him out from under my shirt. "Can we use it for scrying Dionysus? It has his energy and is supposed to connect with him to notify him when I need him."

Hel cuts me with a scathing glare, and I take a step back. Okay, I gotta remember to bite my tongue about Dionysus and me being close.

This girl had it bad at one time—and still does—and is scary as hell—or Hel, I suppose.

Holy schmoly, is that where the saying comes from?

Scary as Hel?

Hilarious.

"Fi? Yo, earth to sista." Emmet waves in front of my face and blinks. "Where'd you go there?"

"Sorry. Brain tidal wave. I got pulled out by the undertow. What did I miss?"

"Merlin asked you to take the pendant off so he can empower it as a pendulum."

"Oh, of course. Sorry." I pull the pendant over my head and free it from underneath the length of my hair. "Do your thing—and thanks for coming."

Merlin nods. "Dionysus is a friend, and after getting to know him at your birthday party, a dear one at that. I want to help bring him home. Now, let's see where this pendant takes us."

CHAPTER FOURTEEN

Merlin's locator spell on my pendant works like a charm—because um, yeah, it *is* a charm. The moment he empowers my Dionysus pendant, it swings forward in the air and points our way.

We walk outside the palace for as long as possible, then take the cobbled path to a side entrance. From what I gather, much of the palace is open to the public for tours, and the rest remains private.

The area we need to get to is on the private side of things, and —of course—the door is locked.

Under normal circumstances, I wouldn't condone breaking and entering, but this is a unique circumstance.

Sloan passes a hand over the lock plate and turns the knob. "Ladies first." Sloan sweeps his hand through the air to usher us forward.

"Thanks, hotness." I wink as I follow Hel inside.

The rest of them fall in line behind us, and I hold out the pendant to see where we're supposed to go next. "Up the stairs," I whisper, keeping to the shadows of the elegant corridors.

We climb the stairs as a group, silent as *Silent Stalk* can make us. Second floor...third floor... When we get to the top of the stairs on the fourth floor, I hang a left and point at a set of ornate double doors.

Hel tries the doors and, once again, they're locked.

Merlin does the honors this time.

The moment we open the door, a six-man team jumps to their feet and—

"Game on!" Emmet shouts, diving behind a leather club chair.

A bolt of magic zings past my head and crashes into the mirror behind me. It shatters, sending jagged shards through the air and raining down on the floor.

I dive behind Emmet's chair, shove my pendant in my pocket, and call my armor forward. "Not even a hello; who are you. Rude."

"I guess they don't like uninvited guests."

"Guess not." I release Bruin and call Birga to my palm. "Have at it, Bruin. We're going after Dionysus."

Pushing back up onto my feet, I peek around the back of the chair, orient myself, and book it through the outer room.

Merlin, Emmet, and Ciara fall back to help secure these goons while Sloan and I follow in Hel's wake.

Yep. She's just as scary pissed off and culling her way through a crowd.

Between the three of us, we have two with guns to fight. Our group has cut the others off.

"Deal with them," Hel says. "I'll find my father."

Sloan and I comply and clear Hel's path as she storms into the next room. I cast a curious glance inside but now is not the time for being a rubbernecker.

There are men to battle.

Spinning Birga in my hands, I take comfort from the whistle of her spear tip cutting the air. There's nothing like battling with a weapon that feels as natural in your hands as an extension of your reach.

I rush the one closest to me, deciding at the last moment to abandon the sharp and pointy end of Birga for the blunt end of her staff.

Cracking his wrist with a hard strike shatters the bones, and his gun falls to the floor. As he doubles forward, gripping his wrist, I follow up with a braced elbow to the side of his head.

He drops like a rock.

Straightening, I find that Sloan has disarmed his guy too. By the blood streaming down his face, I'd bet he also broke his nose.

"You good?" I check him out.

"Fine. Let's go."

Sloan grabs the guns of the two and tosses them out the open window. I check the battle in progress behind us and am pleased to see that everything is under control.

Flipping my attention to what's in front of us, I stop inside an ancient parlor. Fifteen-foot ceilings...gold-gilded everything... and a very "not Tom Hiddleston" Loki arguing with Hel.

"—don't care," Hel shouts. "He and I were centuries ago. You had no right to dredge it up."

"I have every right!" Loki shouts, his fists glowing blue. "That man disgraced you. Humiliated you. Humiliated me."

Hel laughs. "How does me falling in love with a Greek god ill-suited to love me back humiliate you? This has nothing to do with you."

"Of course it does. You are my child. I told you then he would pay one day and now that day has come."

While the two of them are screaming at one another, it doesn't slip my attention Dionysus isn't in the room.

"Where is he?" Emmet races in to join us.

"Maybe back there?" I point at a door behind the desk where Loki is standing. "Bruin? Can you check?"

Bruin pushes off in a lumbering run and dematerializes as he goes.

Loki seems to register the invasion of our group and raises a hand. My feet are instantly rooted to the ground, my arms locked in place. Bruin rematerializes and lets out a thundering roar.

"What happened?"

"He bounced me back from the door and made me take a physical form."

I don't know what Loki can do.

Sadly, I don't know anything beyond what happens in the Marvel movies, and like Sloan keeps pointing out, that's not real life. We should've gone over things with Hel before this, and maybe we wouldn't be playing the part of trees rooted to the middle of the room.

Thankfully, Hel doesn't seem affected by Loki's magic and strides around the desk to confront him. "Stop this, now. If you think you're doing this for my benefit, you're wrong. You don't need to punish Dionysus on my behalf. I never asked for that, and I don't want that."

"You don't mean that."

"I do. I told you that centuries ago, and I meant it then too. Why dredge all this up now?"

Loki frowns. "Because centuries ago there was no point in punishing him. He cared about no one. He didn't value anyone above himself."

Hel chuffs. "So you buy into what they've been saying too? You honestly believe the god of personal gratification has learned to care about others?"

Loki shrugs. "I've waited and watched, biding my time until I was sure he'd suffer from the loss as I tear his life down. He has friends, people he genuinely cares about, and I will destroy those bonds as well as his reputation."

"You're bent on destroying a man because he broke it off with your daughter?" I say, regretting the burst of poor choice even as the words are falling from my tongue. "That seems a little dramatic, doesn't it?"

Loki turns a heated glare on me, and my shield burns hot. "Stay out of this, freckles. You're the reason we're all here."

"Me? What did I do?"

"He loves you. Don't try to deny it."

"So what? He's a good guy. We love him too."

Loki turns back to Hel and grins. "You see? Now he has something to lose."

Hel raises her hand and points at him. "Enough. Let him go, right now. I stay out of your way, and you need to stay out of mine. My past with Dionysus is my business, not yours. Go torture some other poor fool. I'm sure there's someone out there somewhere that deserves your brand of punishment."

"Yes. Dionysus is one of them."

Hel groans and pushes past her father, going for the door behind him.

Before she gets there, Loki drops his hands and scowls. "You're making a mistake, daughter."

"It's my mistake to make. Go. Leave him to us."

When Loki disappears, it takes a moment for the spell to release and for my feet to come off the floor.

"Everyone all right?" I ask, doing a slow turn to check on the fam jam.

Emmet shakes out his legs and checks on Ciara. "Yep. Is he gone? Did we get Dionysus back?"

Hel is already through the door behind the desk and rushing toward a battered and bloody Dionysus.

"Dude." I shake off the last of the lead-footed sensation and launch into action. Dionysus is bound to a chair, the shackles around his hands and feet made of animated razor wire. The barbs are writhing around his wrists, slicing into his flesh. "These bindings are unbelievable. Merlin, can you get them to shut off?"

Merlin moves in to help Hel. "Hello, my friend. How's the party been? We came as soon as we could."

Dionysus tilts his head up, his eyes swollen shut and purple, his lips split and swollen too. "A little wilder than I like."

Merlin releases first one wrist shackle, then the next. They fall to the floor, but they're still wriggling as if searching for something to slice open.

Charming.

I kick the sadistic shackles across the floor and take his hand in mine. "Glad to have you back, buddy. How about we get you home?"

"Home?" Hel pegs me with a scowl. "You're a human. You aren't welcome on Olympus."

I chuckle. "I don't suppose I would be. I meant the home he's made for himself. Come, we'll show you."

Hel shakes her head. "No. The only reason I got involved was because of Loki. You asked me to help get Dionysus back. I held up my end of the arrangement, but I won't let you draw me into anything beyond that."

Dionysus mumbles something, but his mouth is so swollen it's incoherent.

She takes a step back and frowns at the purple pulp that is Dionysus' face. "I have nothing to say to you." Then she points at Nikon. "Return me to Helheim."

"Of course, Lady Hel." He bows his head. As he moves in on her, he meets my gaze. "I'll drop Merlin back with the dragons and meet you all at the loft?"

I check with Sloan. "Can you *poof* four of us? How much energy did you use up in the battle?"

"Hardly any. I'm fine."

Patting my chest, I encourage Bruin to bond with me. Once he's on board, I grip Dionysus' arm and reach out to Emmet. "Yep. See you there, Greek. Safe home."

Sloan *poofs* us straight into the bedroom in the loft, and we get Dionysus settled on his bed. The place is still a disaster zone, but I straighten up around him and close his door to let him get some rest.

"Why isn't he healing?" Emmet asks. "He's an immortal demigod. He shouldn't stay banged up like that."

I glance over my shoulder and lead them away. "Loki poisoned the wines he knew Dionysus drinks, and it's affected him on several fronts, one of those being a stunting of his god powers."

"Is that what the destruction remodel is all about?" Ciara asks.

The smash and trash of the loft ooze anger and desperation. The majority of that was because of losing his other abilities, but they don't need to know that.

"That's what it's about, yes."

"So, now that the poisoning has stopped, how long will it take for him to recover his powers and heal back to full strength?" Emmet asks.

"No idea. As far as I know, he's never suffered anything like this before."

"And hopefully never will again," Sloan says. "It's late. I'll take the two of ye home. Fi and I will stay the night here."

"Are you sure?" Emmet checks in with Ciara. "We can stay and help clean up."

I wave that away. "Odds are by morning, he'll wake up and snap his fingers to restore everything to its proper state. There's no sense in us killing ourselves tonight."

"We don't mind stayin'," Ciara says.

I raise my hand. "No, really, it's fine—"

Nikon snaps in and looks around at the ransacking. "This was one hell of a party."

"He was working on his rock star reputation for hotel trashing."

"Nailed it."

I chuckle and reach up to hug my brother. "Thanks for your help today. You were great. And a super high-five on healing yourself. I'm proud of you."

Emmet musses my hair and eases back. "Thanks, Fi. It's nice to be able to contribute."

I wave that away. "You always contribute, Em. Don't ever think you don't."

Sloan steps forward and holds out his hand. "Greek, are ye able to stay with her for five minutes until I get back? I'll grab our overnight bag and some takeout."

"Happy to. We'll be here when you get back."

Sloan *poofs* out, and Nikon and I head over to the living room seating area. After we set two leather couches onto their legs, we plop down opposite one another and take a load off.

"Well, that was exciting," he says.

I grunt. "I wish the four of us were back at the beach eating surf and turf."

Nikon closes his eyes, his mouth curling in a soft smile. "It was a fun couple of days, Red. Thanks again for horning in on my promise to Papu and making it a wine weekend."

I reach across the space with my extended fist. "Mischief managed."

He chuckles and meets my knuckles with a bump. "Mischief managed."

The morning comes sooner than I'm ready for, and it takes a moment for me to figure out what the buzzing is. "Hotness, your phone." I blink at the empty couch across from me and roll off the cushions to the floor. Crawling the short distance between me and the coffee table, I grab his phone and answer it. "Hello. Sloan's phone."

"Oh…would Mr. Mackenzie be available?"

"One moment, I'll see if I can find him." I mute the call and shout, "Hotness? Are you here?"

My voice carries through the open concept of Dionysus' loft, and nothing comes back to me.

Unmuting the call, I swallow and try to clear the groggy out of my voice. "I'm sorry, he doesn't seem to be around. Could I give him a message?"

"And you are?" The question is polite, but his voice is icy.

"His girlfriend, Fiona. We had a friend with an emergency last night and aren't at home at the moment…but you don't care about that. My point is, I'm not sure where he popped off to. It was a long night."

"If you could tell him to contact Monsieur Blaise."

"Oh, of course, Monsieur. The moment I see him."

We say our goodbyes, and I set Sloan's phone back where I found it. It's weird that it's here if he's not.

Who leaves their phone at home anymore?

Crazy.

A sound by the rock wall has me slipping on my sneakers and heading over to investigate. It takes me a bit to track it down, but after a moment, I find Sloan nestled in a beanbag chair in front of Dionysus' large screen TV playing Halo.

"What's happening here?" This is the least likely thing I expected to find Sloan doing alone in a room.

"Yer brothers are in fer a rude awakening the next time we have a drinkin' night. I won't be the one wakin' up naked."

I laugh. "I see. Logging some extra hours of game time, are you?"

"I am, and I'd appreciate ye not lettin' on. I have a little manly pride to win back."

I watch him for a moment and haven't got the heart to tell him he'll need a lot more practice time if he expects to one-up my brothers.

"Monsieur Blaise called you a moment ago. He'd like you to call him back."

That seems to draw him back to being the no-nonsense man I know and love. "Och, is it nine-thirty already?"

I flip my wrist and read the time off my Fitbit. "Yep. Did you have a call set?"

"I did. I do." He sets the controller down and rolls to extricate himself from the shifting sack of chair. "I need to call him right back if ye don't mind."

"Have at it. I'll head in and check on the patient."

Sloan leads the way across the living room. "I checked on him at seven. The swelling on his eye is down considerably but not enough to suggest his powers have come back online."

Poop. "All right. I'll see what he wants for breakfast. Any preferences?"

He wakes his phone screen and shakes his head. "I'm happy with whatever is on the menu."

Good to know.

"Knock-knock," I say, rapping my knuckle on the frame of his bedroom door. "Are you decent?"

"Am I ever?"

I chuckle and let myself into the room. "You're decent enough."

Dionysus is lying on the bed, feet crossed, dressed, and looking better than yesterday but not as good as the day before that.

"Loki's poison hasn't made it out of your system yet, eh? Your healing is still offline?"

"Seems so."

"Well, this is a learning opportunity. You can suffer through healing like the rest of us. Did Sloan take the sting out of things?"

He shakes his head. "He offered to alleviate the damage, but I told him I would wait for things to take their natural course."

"Sloan's healing is natural. He's a druid."

"I'm fine. I'll take my punishment like a man."

I draw a deep breath and exhale. "That's a little masochistic, but whatevs. You do you."

I crawl onto the bed and flop on the opposite pillow. "What do you want for breakfast? Are you well enough to snap to our place so we can cook you up something? Do you want to hit Cora's or Sunset Grill or one of the other diners you like?"

"No. I've had enough babysitting. You two go, and I'll take care of myself."

I frown. "Are you cranky because you're hurt or because Loki said or did something that upset you?"

"I'm not cranky. I'm the god of fun and frivolity. I'm everyone's favorite lush. I simply would like to be left to my own devices."

I sit up and sigh. "All right. I can take a hint. Feel better, and we'll check in with you later."

"If you must."

I roll off the bed as Sloan pops his head into the room. "Breakfast will have to wait. Garnet called. He has news on the duchess."

"Perfect, this morning keeps getting better and better." I step past Sloan and collect our overnight bag from where it's lying open by the couches. "Let's see what his highness the lion king found out."

Sloan frowns. "Is everything all right?"

"Peachy keen, jelly bean. Now, let's go find out about your femme fatale."

CHAPTER FIFTEEN

The Batcave is buzzing when we arrive. Andromeda and Maxwell are working on something in his office, Da is looking something up in one of the databases, and Garnet is flipping through screens on the conference table computer, scrolling images and news articles on the photo array on the monitor wall.

"Good, you're here," Garnet says without preamble. "So, Maxwell and I spent the weekend looking into your Duchess d'Aboville and I must say, it's been an intriguing search."

"Yeah? I got a black widow vibe from her. She marries rich men and sucks them dry, amirite?"

"Not even close," Garnet says. "We're almost positive she's a mandagot."

"A what? Sorry."

"A mandagot. It's a mythical creature mentioned all through stories in southern France. It's basically a person who also has a spirit in animal form."

"Like Bruin?"

"Similar, but more like an evil spirit."

"Like a ghost?"

"More like a demon animal."

I give Sloan a sidelong glance. "You should reconsider running away with her. I know the two of you share a passion for fashion, but her having a demon animal can't be good."

Sloan gives me a droll stare. "Is she a black cat by choice or by nature? Can she take other forms?"

"I'm not sure about that," Garnet says. "From what we discovered, mandagots most often tend to be a cat, dog, cow, fox, or rat."

I sigh. "Does this help us? We kinda already figured the spirit cat in the shrine was her."

"That wasn't the part of our discovery I thought you'd be excited about. Here, check this out." Garnet picks up the remote that controls the monitor wall and brings up a dozen police reports.

Da comes over and starts hitting the high points of what we're looking at. "From what we've pieced together, yer duchess is a literal cat burglar and has been for over a century."

"Dayam, she looks good for a biddy."

Garnet arches a brow. "Biddy? Really?"

It strikes me then that shifters have long lifespans and Myra is a hundred and ninety-five years old. "Sorry. My bad. You guys, of course, aren't biddies or geezers."

"No. We're not."

"Okay, so back to the duchess. How do we know it's her and not other black cat burglars?"

Da *clicks* to change the screens. "Mostly because she's quite active in the society pages and seems to enjoy havin' her picture taken."

He *clicks* through pictures of the Duchess d'Aboville decked out as a stiff Victorian, a spunky flapper, and a Hollywood starlet standing next to a crooner at one of those old-fashioned microphones.

"Wow, she excels at changing with the times. I don't know if I could pull off a flapper dress."

"Of course ye could," Sloan says, "but that's not the point. The question is, how does this woman's popularity in the upper crust peg her as a multi-generational thief?"

Da flips back to the police reports and highlights the dates. "Because in each case, one of these robberies coincides with a social event where she's involved as either the host or the major benefactor."

"Let me guess," I say, catching on, "she's got some bougie event coming up."

Da nods. "Got it on one, *mo chroi*. She's in town for Blaise's big Unseelie fundraiser Thursday night."

I stare up at the woman's painted-on smile and everything in me wants to throat-punch her. "Well then, it looks like we've got a busy week of relic protecting ahead of us. At least now, we know who we're up against."

Sloan and I *poof* home. After we shower and are ready to begin again, I head downstairs to start breakfast while he takes a moment to *poof* over to STOA and ensure all is well.

"Fi, tell us the truth." Dillan scowls at Emmet and Ciara sitting at the table. "Loki? Seriously?"

"Yeah, seriously. Dionysus and his daughter Hel got involved at some point, and he didn't appreciate how it ended. He told her he waited until Dionysus could understand the loss of love and has been targeting and torturing him for months."

"Did he, by chance, hit him where it would hurt most?" Emmet asks. "Like maybe disrupting the funk in his spunk?"

"Not my story to tell, but it's safe to say that women of the world will celebrate us putting a stop to the personal pain he's been suffering."

Calum holds up his phone. "Which explains the sudden recovery of all the peen pill companies. Suddenly the men of

North America are getting their mojo back, and the pills are working again."

Ciara laughs. "Ye think that was Loki's doing?"

Dillan nods. "Inadvertently, yeah. Knowing Dionysus, I wouldn't be surprised if the little blue pill and the other sextacy tablets are part of his dominion. Poison the god, poison the well, so to speak."

That makes so much sense.

In a bizarre and convoluted way.

Emmet snags the last strip of bacon from the plate in the center of the table and takes a bite. "If the customers are happy again and the stocks are rising he must be doing better, right?"

I pull out the pancake mix, the milk, and my favorite mixing bowl. "He wasn't himself this morning. I'm not sure what Loki did to him, but he's not over it."

"Give him time, *a ghra*," Sloan says, coming down to join us. "He's been poisoned and beaten and embarrassed and likely a dozen other things he's emotionally ill-equipped to handle. He'll come around."

I measure out the pancake mix and dump it into the bowl. "I hope so. He's been doing so well."

"Speaking of doing well." Calum gets up from the table and reaches into the cupboard to grab Daisy's seizure medication. "Our wee girl is back to her sweet and happy self and sleeping like a baby."

"Excellent. What was upsetting her?"

Kevin looks to see if she's around. "Garnet and Kinu have had a couple of preliminary discussions about setting up a Children's Aid-type organization for empowered folks, and Calum and I were asking about adoption or fostering. It's still very much in the theory stages, but expanding our family would mean us moving out as well as another child vying for our attention."

Calum leans his forearms on the island and lowers his voice. "Between the idea of leaving Doc, Manx, and Bruin, and worrying about us loving a child, she was more than a little upset."

"Aw…the poor thing."

"What about the house next door?" Sloan asks.

My head cranks around on a pivot and I laugh. "You can't keep buying every house on our street, hotness. You've got funds but they aren't inexhaustible."

He shakes his head. "I wasn't suggesting I buy it, but we know the owner is renting it out. Maybe we contact him and discuss a long-term lease."

Calum chuckles. "I love the way you think, Irish, but the rent on a whole house would be more than we can manage on the combined income of a cop and an artist."

He grins. "Fostering comes with a monthly stipend for expenses. That would help, and if perhaps yer workin' with Kinu and Garnet on bein' a safehouse fer emergency placements, ye might be able to squeeze even more out of the Guild."

The room falls still, and we all blink like little owls.

"Hotness, that's a fantastic idea. The Guild is loaded. I bet I could sway Garnet without too much trouble." I collect two golden pancakes from the griddle and lay them out on a plate for him next to the cut fruit. "It's certainly worth looking into."

Calum looks at Kev and shrugs. "Yeah, I suppose it couldn't hurt. We aren't ready to make any changes yet. Hell, we're a week and a half away from the wedding. We already have a lot on our plates."

Sloan heaps both of our plates with berries and I grab the icing sugar and syrup. "But it's a great idea and if not next door, maybe the party palace across and down. It'll be empty until the end of the summer, and maybe the owner is getting tired of dealing with frat boys and noise complaints."

"I know Da is," Emmet says.

Calum chuckles. "Yeah, it's almost time for the warden to get his groove on and lay down the law for the newcomers."

I chew my pancakes and pour Sloan and I each a mug of peppermint. "It would also alleviate some of Daisy's anxiety too. If you're next door or across the street, she can come over all the time and be with the others."

Calum nods. "Yeah, it's a decent idea. We'll definitely talk more about it after the wedding."

"And after we take care of the impending robbery at the FUR Ball."

"FUR Ball." Emmet snorts. "Sorry. It's still funny."

Sloan rolls his eyes. "Well, it won't be funny if the duchess manages to make away with chaotically aligned Unseelie relics. The woman is dangerous, and no good can come of it."

Emmet forces himself to straighten up. "Sorry. I forget how seriously you take life, Irish. My bad."

Sloan looks at me as if he doesn't quite know what Emmet is talking about. "We need to secure the artifacts, catch the duchess, and prove to Monsieur Blaise that he can trust us to contain his dark treasures."

I finish my breakfast and wash the syrup off my fingers at the sink. "Maxwell called in the SITFO unit, so you'll all be off rotation this week. We have four days to figure out what happened in Montreal and secure the exhibits until the event on Thursday night."

"All right." Emmet waggles his brows. "First question. Where is the event being held?"

"In the Casa Loma Conservatory."

"Are Xavier and the vampires involved?"

"Nope. Just a normal event rental of the castle facilities. Nothing vampire going on, thankfully. We have enough to worry about anyway."

"Then I guess we better get our butts in gear and get to the Batcave."

"What can I do?" Ciara says.

"Yeah, me too," Kevin says. "We want a job."

I slide my plate into the dishwasher and straighten. "There is something. If you two don't mind being our personal shoppers, we're all going to need formal masquerade wear. Go through our closets and see what will work and what won't. It's a posh, harlequin event with masks."

"Costume party!" Emmet raises his fists.

Dillan groans. "Can't we wear black suits? We all have one of those."

I grab my purse from the chair at the breakfast bar and pull out my wallet. "Take my Guild card and buy whatever you need. The theme is a black and white masquerade ball. Nikon said he's at your disposal for the day in case what you need isn't in Toronto."

Ciara grins at Kevin and the two light up like kids on Christmas morning. "We won't let ye down," Ciara says. "Prepare to be amazed."

Dillan grunts. "I don't want to be amazed, and if you buy me those diamond checkerboard tights and a spangly hat with bells, I won't wear it."

Sloan shakes his head. "No, nothin' like that. This is a sophisticated event, and we'll need to blend in as part of the 'A' crowd."

Ciara and Kevin stand, grab Kev's laptop, and rush off to the dining room.

I put my wallet back into my purse and grin. "All righty then, saddle up. We leave in ten."

Clan Cumhaill arrives en masse at the Batcave ten minutes later. Da and Maxwell are standing at the conference table, looking at a different photo array on the monitor wall than when we left an hour ago.

"Who are we looking at now?" I ask.

Maxwell sweeps a hand toward the wall of images. "Meet the key players attending the FUR Ball."

I bite my lip and studiously avoid looking at Emmet. "Uh-huh."

"With the murder in Montreal, we're not only concerned about safeguarding the relics but also protecting the guests attending the event. Monsieur Blaise made it very clear if another of his guests falls to foul play, there will be a clash of violence from the Unseelie community like we've never seen in our streets."

"Threatening us isn't going to change anything."

"It's not a threat, little girl," a man with a thick French accent says from behind me. "It's a warning to take the consequences of things seriously."

"Monsieur Blaise, I presume?"

He nods. "*Oui.* And though Monsieur Grant assures me this team is well-suited to the task of crowd security, I admit I have reservations."

"Assuming there is an event at all," another Frenchman says, his jowls jiggling as he walks in to join us. "The relics arrive tomorrow, and if you people are not as good as you say, there won't be anything to exhibit by Thursday night."

"I assure ye, sir," Sloan says. "We have that part of the preparations well in hand. Once the relics are in our possession, I will personally guarantee they will arrive at yer event in time fer set up at the ball."

"Guarantees are only worth as much as the blood oath you write them with."

Ew.

Thankfully, Garnet takes that as his cue to usher the squires of evil back into the other room so we can continue with our ops briefing.

"Go ahead, Max." I gesture at the faces on the screens in front of us. "How are we breaking this down?"

After Max finishes going through the A-list attendees and explains which ones are most likely to cause trouble for us, the boys go with Da to the event site to size up the preparations already in place. Sloan and I *poof* back to Dionysus' loft to check on him. He's not in his bedroom, so I go on a hunt.

"Marco…"

Nothing.

"Dude, where are you?"

"Wherever he is," Sloan says, "I don't think it's here, luv."

"Maybe that means he's feeling better, and he went out for some fresh air."

"Possibly."

"Buuut?"

"If he feels well enough to go out, why wouldn't he put his bachelor pad back together? When we were talking during the winery tours, he mentioned several times how eager he was to get home and set his place right again."

I frown at the disaster area we're standing in. "Yeah, that's weird. Honestly, though, there's no telling what Dionysus will do from one moment to the next. He's unpredictable."

"A rapscallion, wasn't it?"

I giggle. "Yeah. That's his favorite."

After confirming that our god of good times is nowhere around, I send him a quick text.

Don't forget about the masquerade ball Thursday night. There will be danger and drinking, and probably life will explode into chaos and cover us with crazy shenanigans shrapnel. I told Ciara to get you a mask. Hope you're feeling better. Call me.

CHAPTER SIXTEEN

First thing Tuesday morning, Sloan, Calum, and I *poof* to the Royal York and work on locating the elusive Duchess d'Aboville.

"Why can't we arrest her?" I ask for the eleventh time.

"Because we have nothing that ties her definitively to any of the past crimes or the attempted robbery of STOA. At most, the only offense we can prove is that she made a play for Sloan's pretty-boy affections."

Sloan rolls his eyes. "Why would ye fan yer sister's delusion? Are ye tryin' to wind her up?"

Calum chuckles. "I don't need to say or not say anything. Fi's a woman and another woman flirted with her man right in front of her. There's no way I'm saying anything Fi hasn't thought of herself."

"I think ye underestimate yer sister."

Calum laughs. "Fi, picture this scenario. You and the duchess are locked in a room together. There are two things on the table between you, a dagger and a plate of brownies. She says she wants to be your friend, but then the lights go out. What do you go for?"

"The brownies."

Sloan nods. "See. Ye thought she'd go for the dagger, didn't ye."

Calum laughs. "Fi, why'd you pick the brownies?"

"Because while she reaches for the dagger, I called Birga and my reach is way longer. I spear her through and keep all the brownies for myself."

Calum chuckles. "Yeah, you do."

Sloan frowns. "All right. You don't get to be left alone with the woman."

"Do I still get the plate of brownies?" I ask.

Calum grins. "I'll make you brownies, baby girl."

"Excellent."

Sloan shakes his head and leads the way to the reception desk to speak with the man on duty.

"Can I help you?" The cutie behind the desk finishes what he's working on before lifting his head to make eye contact. The moment he gets a good look at Sloan, his pupils widen, and he seems to melt a little in his chair.

I cast a casual smile at Calum, who notices the spike in his gaydar too.

"Yes, the Duchess d'Aboville invited me to come to her room for a luncheon, but my assistant neglected to get her room number. Could ye help me with that, Brad?" Sloan reads the guy's nametag.

Brad wets his lips and swallows. "I'm sorry, I can't give out that information. It's against company policy to share information about our guests."

Sloan nods. "Then perhaps ye could call up to her room and connect me usin' the house phone?"

"Yes, that I can do. If you'll give me a moment..." He scrolls his mouse and clicks a few things on his screen before keying in digits on his keyboard. "It's that phone there, sir."

Sloan strides down to the end of the marble desktop and

picks up the phone. Calum and I join him and wait. "It's ringin'. Still ringin'."

We wait a minute more, then Sloan hangs up the phone. "She must not be in her room."

"Any luck?" Brad asks, coming over to check on us.

"I'm afraid not."

"Thanks anyway." I lift my hand to wave it. The three of us retreat, and I sigh. "Well, that was a bust."

"Not entirely," Sloan says. "We've confirmed she's still stayin' here."

"Do you want me to pull my badge?" Calum asks.

Sloan shakes his head. "No. They're no more bound to tell you with a badge than they are without. Unless we have a warrant, they won't tell us anythin'."

Calum smirks. "Are you law-splaining me, Irish? I'm a cop. I know about warrants."

"Apologies. I'm simply thinkin' while my mouth is movin'. No offense meant."

I draw a deep breath and exhale, looking around the lobby. "What now? Can we use a locator spell or truth spell or something?"

Sloan considers that. "Perhaps. Not a locator spell exactly, but I could...hold on."

He strides back over to the desk and waves off the woman, beckoning Brad back to talk to him. "Would ye have a pen and a slip of paper I could borrow, sham? I want to write somethin' down."

I watch from a distance, wondering what he wants to write down. Once he has the pad and pen, he extends a hand in thanks. "Ye've been a great help, Brad."

Sloan holds his hand and smiles while Brad stares star-struck for a little longer than is comfortable. When they part ways, he sighs and goes back to his desk. Sloan stops and jots something down on his way back to us.

"What was that?" I ask.

Calum laughs. "Poor Brad should sit down. I think his ovaries exploded."

Sloan rolls his eyes and hands me the slip of paper.

Room 769.

I read the room number and turn to follow him toward the bank of elevators. "How did you find that out?"

"Ye gave me the idea."

"Yay me. How so?"

"Ye mentioned usin' a truth spell, and that got me thinkin' about him lookin' up the duchess and the information being in his most recent memories."

"And you can wipe and alter memories."

He grins. "Indeed, I can. So, when I shook his hand, I accessed his recent memory and saw the information on the computer screen as he looked it up."

"Booyah, Irish," Calum says. "So much more than a pretty face and a rocking six-pack."

I hit the call button on the elevator and step inside as the doors slide open. "But boy, let's not downplay the power of those things. Yeah, baby."

Sloan hits the seven, and the doors bump shut. "I'm glad ye like what ye see, *a ghra*, but if I have to use it a bit to win over the duchess, remember it's simply a tool in my arsenal. I have no fondness fer the woman."

How could he?

Beyond the fact that she's beautiful and rich like him, and shares his passion for fae antiquities and relics, what's to like?

The doors open, and we check the room sign arrow and take a right.

I draw a deep breath and exhale. "Fine. If you have to flirt, I can restrain myself and not kill her."

"That's very big of you, luv. Thank you."

Calum knocks on the door, and we wait for a moment while

nothing happens. Then, he sets a hand on the keycard reader, and when the light flips green, he opens the door and peeks in.

Hesitating in the doorway, he steps back to the hall and frowns. "I don't think you killing her will be a problem. Someone beat you to it."

Built in the 1840s, the Royal York hotel is an iconic luxury hotel in the heart of the downtown core. It's architecturally interesting, tastefully decorated, and a place locals and tourists alike recognize as a gem of Toronto. Murder in their rooms seems incredibly out of place.

"How did this happen?" I can see the body on the suite floor from the hallway, and it looks gruesome. "How can she be dead?"

Calum comes out from examining the body and shrugs. "I say it has something to do with her throat being slit. Call me crazy, but that's my take on things."

"I meant because we thought she was the bad guy."

Calum pulls the door closed behind him and leans against the wall while I do the same on the opposite side of the hall. "This does kinda blow our theory that she's the burglar and killer from Montreal."

"Unless she had a partner and got double-crossed," I say, thinking about the workaround.

Sloan frowns. "Either way, we're no closer to finding the person responsible for the Montreal murder or the missing antiquities."

"Technically, we don't need to find the missing antiquities. We need to prevent the remaining relics from being stolen."

My phone vibrates in my hand, and I read the incoming message. "Garnet and Anyx are flashing over right now. He says to close the door and wait in the hall for them to arrive."

Sloan is scowling at the door. "I don't like that someone murdered her on our watch."

Calum waves that off. "We found her. We did nothing to cause this."

"How important does a person have to be to be considered assassinated instead of murdered? She's a duchess. Does that count?"

"She *was* a duchess," Calum says.

"Do you think it has something to do with the Culling and the dark side working to gain more dark power?"

Sloan lifts a shoulder. "I don't know what to think, luv. Anything is a possibility, though I expect this is more about the relics and robbery."

Calum scrubs the back of his neck and exhales. "How well-advertised is the Culling? I mean, we'd never heard of it, and that's understandable because we're still shiny new pennies in these circles, but is it common knowledge or little-known info?"

"That's a good question," Sloan says. "We've been operating under the assumption that it's a known fact, but what if it isn't?"

"What if it isn't what?" I ask. "How does it being common knowledge change things?"

"I have two thoughts on that. The first is that if we know who's aware of and invested in the Culling, it might help us narrow down who we're up against."

"But how do we know who knows? You know?"

Calum frowns. "We'll circle back to that. What's your second thought, Irish?"

"The second is that maybe we need to spread the word among those aligned to the good side of things. If it's not public knowledge, maybe we're putting ourselves at a disadvantage by not amassing allies."

"*Ní neart go cur le chéile,*" I say, repeating the words from the Celtic rocking chair lady. "There is strength in unity."

Calum looks at me, and his mouth falls open. "Do you think that's what she meant? Was it a warning to start amassing allies?"

"Maybe. What do you think, hotness?"

Sloan shrugs. "It makes as much sense as any other explanation. I'd still like to know who she was—or is—and find out why she's stalking Fi."

"You and me both." I think about the woman watching over me from the upstairs deck of the rental house next door. "I get the feeling I'm supposed to know her, but I can't figure out how."

Movement down the hall brings our attention to the arrival of Garnet and Anyx. The two of them marching side-by-side would be pee-your-pants intimidating if I didn't know them both well enough to trust they wouldn't morph into their lion forms and end us.

"Any trouble?" Garnet asks as they stop in our little hall huddle.

"Nothing beyond a dead woman in her suite." I point at the door.

Calum passes a hand over the keycard reader again, and the light flashes green. "Other than verifying her state of deadness, nothing was touched or moved."

Garnet nods, and he and Anyx head inside.

"So, back to the idea of letting the good and light people know we're coming up to a battle. Could we assume the dark might be doing the same thing? Maybe that's a way to track who we have to worry about and how big their forces are getting?"

Sloan nods. "A good thought, *a ghra*. If we can somehow find their communication network and tap into what they're saying on their side, we might have a better understanding all around."

Calum nods. "We can put Emmet on that. He's good at computer stuff. Maybe there's a dark fae web or something."

"Garnet will know," I say. "Our lion king has his paw on the pulse of the empowered world. We'll talk to him when he finishes with the body."

My words are still rolling off my tongue when Garnet comes out frowning. "He's done with the body. Or rather, he's done because there isn't a body."

Hubba-wha?

I push off the wall and look into the room. He's right. Where the Duchess d'Aboville was lying dead ten minutes ago, there's nothing but a blood-stained carpet. "Well, crappers. What does that mean?"

Garnet looks at me and shakes his head. "Fuck if I know."

While Sloan and Anyx search the suite for the collection of relics she showed Sloan on Friday, Calum, Garnet, and I flash over to Casa Loma to check on the preparations for the masquerade ball. The evening will begin with the reception drinks, and dinner held in the conservatory. Then guests will move into the ballroom for the remainder of the evening.

"So we thought if there was a dark web for the empowered, we could start searching for who's gathering allies on both sides," I say, filling Garnet in on our new theory. "But we need to know what's out there and how to access it."

"There is a dark web, but there are also FaeBook and Witchipedia."

"Exsqueeze me?" Calum chuckles. "FaeBook? You're serious?"

"Do I look like I have a sense of humor?"

Calum frowns. "Not even a little. All right. If you don't mind forwarding the info on how to access those three platforms, we'll look into things on that side."

I'm still giggling to myself about FaeBook. "Is it mostly the older sector on there? Is there a young and hip crowd somewhere else?"

"Monsieur Blaise," Garnet says, ignoring me and striding away. His hand is outstretched when the two meet, and after they greet one another, Garnet gestures at Calum and me. "I believe you've met Fiona Cumhaill. This is her brother, Officer Calum Cumhaill. They're two of the druids who will be heading up the security on the relics."

Monsieur Blaise lifts his saggy chin and looks down his nose at me. "Her? Isn't she Monsieur Mackenzie's girlfriend?"

"Among other things, yes."

"Well, we needn't bother having a member of the weaker sex as part of our security contingent. I'm certain you gentlemen can handle things better without the drama and hysteria that estrogen brings into things."

I laugh. "Seriously? If you think women are the weaker sex, you've never tried to take back the covers on a cold winter night."

Outwardly, Garnet looks annoyed, but the slight upturn of his mouth tells me a different story. For Garnet, that's pretty much busting a gut. "I don't think our Lady Druid is measurable on any sexist scale you deem accurate. She's an enigma. A warrior with strength and style all her own."

Blaise doesn't seem swayed by Garnet's evaluation, but whatevs.

Haters gotta hate, amirite?

Garnet isn't about to get into a pissing match with a client, and I don't expect him to. People have underestimated and judged me enough in my life that it doesn't faze me.

"The reason we're here," Garnet takes control of the situation again, "is that when Fi, Calum, and Sloan went to question Duchess d'Aboville about a history of murders and robberies she's been in proximity to, they found her dead in her hotel room."

"Dead? *Mon Dieu.* That is terrible news."

Garnet nods. "It's alarming, yes, but we found a few things at the scene that we believe will advance our investigation. We're that much closer to figuring out who's involved in these murders."

"You have my complete confidence, Monsieur Grant. Please keep me up to date on your progress. I shall contact you once the exhibition pieces are ready to be received."

"Of course. We'll speak again soon." Garnet nods and steps back, signaling for us to take our leave.

"Everything okay?" I study the false smile he painted on while speaking to Monsieur Blaise. "What happened there? What did we find at the scene? Did you bluff our client?"

"I wanted to catch his reaction. There are very few species of empowered that can guard their emotions well enough to mislead the heightened senses of the Moon Called. I mislead him to register his reaction."

Calum smiles. "Because as the man in charge of this event, he should be relieved we found evidence at the scene of the murder."

"Exactly, yet his visceral response wasn't relief or even hopefulness."

I check back over my shoulder and ensure no one is listening. "So what was his visceral emotion?"

Garnet waggles his brows at me and smiles. "Fear."

CHAPTER SEVENTEEN

When Sloan catches up with us in the conservatory of Casa Loma, Garnet, Calum, and I have already finished walking the ballroom with Mr. Stark, Blaise's head of event security. The guy is former law enforcement and has a good sense of what needs to happen to prepare for an event like this. Which—I've learned—is a lot.

He seems to have planned a comprehensive defense against any kind of infiltration or attack from outside the event. My question is, what if the danger comes from one or more of the guests?

Or maybe the event's coordinator.

"If one of the attendees or staff is involved, what are the contingencies if the danger is already in play?" Garnet asks my question, and Mr. Stark rolls right into an explanation of the security cameras above and the body cam tie pins all floor security will wear.

"Oooh, these are lovely." I touch the row of silver tie pins where they lay nestled in black foam. They're small and elegant and won't interfere with the masquerade theme at all. "They'll even go well with a lady's dress."

"Where is the feed being monitored?" Calum asks.

"Come, I'll show you."

As he points the way and heads across the dancefloor, I point at Sloan coming in where staff members are setting up the podium. "You guys go ahead. I'll catch Sloan up."

I veer off and meet my guy in the middle of the dance floor. "Care to tango, Mackenzie?"

He chuckles, but other than that, he remains completely professional. "What have I missed?"

"Not much. We met Mr. Stark and got the tour. Oh," I lean in closer and whisper, "Garnet fibbed to Blaise and told him we found something at the hotel room that might lead us to the killer."

"And?"

"He said instead of being relieved, your Frenchman friend reeked of fear."

Sloan arches a brow. "All right. If he's a suspect, you and I need to go over the Blaise family tree and the past events where someone killed people. Maybe the Duchess d'Aboville isn't the only common denominator."

"Good idea." I pull out my phone and send Garnet and Calum a text telling them where we've gone and why. Then I slip my phone into my pocket and take Sloan's hand. "Can we stop at Dionysus' loft first? I want to check in on him."

Sloan nods and escorts me into the shadows and out of view in case any non-magicals are around. The surge of his wayfarer magic makes my skin tingle. Then we *poof* into the middle of Dionysus' living room.

"Tarzan? You here, dude?"

If he is, he's not making any noise.

I make quick work of searching the place, then give up and join back up with Sloan. "Okay, I guess he's still out."

"That's a good thing."

"I hope so."

"Do ye want to stay fer a bit or go?"

"There's no sense staying. He could be anywhere or anytime."

"True enough."

I scan the interior one more time and then pull out my phone.

Big day in the Batcave. Join us if you're up for some murder and intrigue. Text me if you want me to come hang. Heart you big.

I hit "Send" and slide my phone back into my pocket.

"Are ye all right, *a ghra?*"

"I guess so. Something isn't sitting right. I feel like I'm missing something and the shoe is about to drop."

"With yer history, yer not likely to have to wait long. And instead of a shoe, it's likely an anvil."

"You're probably right."

"I'm sure things will become clear soon enough."

I hold out my hand, thankful he's right there with me. "To the Batcave."

We materialize one floor down at the Batcave, and I stride over to the conference table to hug my father. "Hey, Da. How's the craic?"

"Och, it's wicked craic today. Ye know how I love a special assignment I can sink my teeth into."

"I do." I study the files set out on the table's surface and read some of the sticky notes attached to them. "You're tracing the event host for these?"

"Aye, I am. The duchess was the easiest link to make, but with her death, we need to dig deeper. What did you kids come to do?"

"Dig deeper, actually." I pull out a chair to step up and sit on the table. "We came to see if there was a link to Monsieur Blaise and the robberies and homicides of the past events."

"Blaise? What cast the pall of shadow over the man in charge?"

I fill him in on Garnet's play to catch him off-guard. "Maybe he's afraid we'll find out it's him."

"Or maybe he's being coerced and is afraid fer the safety of someone he loves. Or maybe he's afraid the bad publicity will tarnish his reputation. Or maybe it's something different altogether. Don't lead the evidence, *mo chroi*. Let the evidence lead you."

"Yes, Obi-Wan. Teach me the ways of the Force."

Sloan spends the next hour working with Emmet and Ciara on the computer, and I get some one-on-one time with Da.

"This is nice." I hand him a file when I'm finished with it and reaching for another. "We haven't spent much time together now that you moved in with Shannon and I moved in with Sloan."

Da sets the file down and smiles. "Aye. One of the things I love most about bein' a father is spendin' time with my kids. Ye've all grown into such amazing individuals. I couldn't be prouder of the lot of ye. I want ye to know that."

"Thanks, Da." I drum my fingers on a police report from 1934 and frown. "Da? Can I ask you something?"

"Of course, *mo chroi*. What is it?"

"Liam overheard you and Shannon talking about moving. Are you two planning on leaving? Did he maybe misunderstand? He did, right?"

He stops fiddling with files and bathes me in a sad smile. "Ye know I love ye all with all of my heart, aye?"

I draw a deep breath, not liking this lead-up to things. "Yeah, I know."

"Liam didn't misunderstand what he heard. Runnin' the pub takes a lot out of Shannon. She's been a one-woman force for almost twenty years and even before that, Mark could only help when he was off rotation."

"Yeah. I get that."

"But it's not only because of Shannon that I've been considerin' a move. I missed nearly forty years with my parents. Druids tend to live a little longer than most, but there aren't so many years left that I want to waste any. Mam is seventy-two, and Da just turned seventy-six."

"You're thinking about moving to Ireland?" I hear the crack in my voice, but there's no helping it. My emotions are leaking through my usual tough-girl persona.

"Now that we have people like Nikon and Sloan in our lives and the dragon portal at Drombeg, Ireland is as close as midtown, closer even."

I blink at the tears blurring my vision as a piece of my heart crumbles and breaks off. "But what about family dinners and giving us hell for being idiots and being Granda to my kids?"

Da pushes his chair back from the table and pulls me into his lap like he used to do when I was a kid. "I'm not talking about pulling out of yer life, Fi, just about layin' my head down at night a little farther away. I'm well past my eligibility to retire from the force and have been talking to Maxwell about makin' the SITFO a full-time gig. I'll still see ye here when there's work to be done, and I'll still come runnin' every time yer world detonates into a hape of insanity."

I laugh. "Well then, why am I worried? If that's the case, I'll see you all the time."

"Exactly right, my wee girl." He brushes my tears away with his thumb. "I will always be yer da and granda to yer kids. I can't tell ye how much I'm lookin' forward to that."

"It won't be for a while, I know, but couldn't you just wait around putting your life on hold until we're ready to stand on our own?"

We both get a chuckle out of that.

"Yer ready, Fi. Instead of waitin' around, how about I spend time with my bride and my parents? Brendon's death took a lot out of me, *mo chroi*. There's part of me that will never recover. I'm tired, and my heart hurts, and I need some quiet time to heal."

Another round of tears springs free and my breathing hitches. I press against the ache that fills my chest every time I think about losing Brenny. "I get that."

"I know ye do. Ye all do. I need time to sip a coffee in the mornin' and watch the sun come up knowin' I don't have to rush off to the station and be at my best. I want to spend time in the grove of my childhood and replenish my energy. I want to help yer Gran in her garden and help Granda rein in the Elders of the Order. Do ye understand?"

I draw a deep breath and wipe my cheeks. "I do. I guess I thought you'd always be right here with us."

"And I will, *mo chroi*. Fer every moment that matters, I'll be standin' at yer side. Nothin' and no one could ever keep me away."

I lean to the side and rest my head on his shoulder. "I love you, Da. Forever and always."

When he lifts his hand and offers me his pinky, I hook mine with his and close the link. "I love ye more, *mo chroi*. Forever and always."

I'm not sure how long I sit there, soaking in Da's strength before I realize the whole room has gone quiet. Sitting up straight, I look over Da's shoulder, and Emmet is standing there with tears glistening on his cheeks too.

"Do you want to get in on this, Em?" I chuckle at the mess of us.

"Yeah."

I get off Da's lap, and my father stands to meet Emmet chest-to-chest. "I'm going to miss you, oul man."

"I'm not gonna be gone anywhere long enough fer that to happen. Ye'll see."

"So, is it a done deal then?" I ask. "Is it a plan?"

Da looks at me and shrugs. "It's what we want. The only problem was that we didn't know how to bring it up. Now that it's out in the open, I suppose it's got the makings of a plan."

Emmet punches my arm and frowns at me. "Way to go. If you'd kept your mouth shut, we could've trapped them here longer."

I rub my arm and laugh. "Yeah, maybe, but then you wouldn't have gotten the chance to cry in the Batcave."

Emmet scrubs his hands over his cheeks and wipes his hands on his pants. "I don't know what you're talking about. I had an allergic reaction to something in the air—pollen, I expect."

"Your only allergy is to dairy, and I didn't see you getting milk in your eyes."

He shrugs. "So, where are you thinking, Da?"

"Well, if ye don't mind, we talked about movin' into the treehouse Dionysus made ye. It would be close to my parents, and we'd see ye that much more often. If ye don't mind, of course."

I draw another deep breath. "I don't mind. I think that's a great idea. In fact, you can have Emmet's room."

"Hey." Emmet scowls at me. "Rude."

When we get back to business tracking down the relic events of the past, whether or not murder and robbery connected them, we find the same organization has been involved time and again —La Boutique Blaise.

"Most of them, yes," I say, going through the list, "but not all of them. There are six that Blaise doesn't host. Four by Marché Mystérieuses and two by a sole proprietor.

"How much do you want to bet those sole proprietors are customers of Blaise or have a connection somehow?"

"I don't think they were involved," Da says. "In both cases

where a sole proprietor was involved in hosting an event, they were the one killed in and left in the wake of the robbery."

"So, maybe customers then." Sloan pores over the scattered paperwork.

"Or competitors," Calum adds.

Da knocks his knuckles against the table and sighs. "That's conjecture at this point, and we're runnin' out of time to make the connection."

Garnet flashes in with a carrier of burgers, fries, and rings and sets them down on the other end of the table. "The event is fast approaching. What are we up against?"

"That's what we were discussing." Da grabs a burger and takes a seat. "Knowing who is only part of the problem. Knowing how is as much a mystery."

"How so?" Garnet hands me a box of fries before taking one for himself.

"Four of the robberies happened at the actual event when armed men came in guns a-blazin'. Several of them happened after the fact once the crowd cleared and they were takin' things down, and others happened in the day or two leadin' up to the event. There's no clear MO for us to prepare for."

"Well, we're now in the day or two leading up to the event," I say, "so I guess we should be on our toes.

"I don't think it's time to panic yet," Sloan says. "The relics haven't arrived."

"When is that happening?" Garnet asks Sloan.

"I haven't been given a specific time or day. All Blaise told me is to expect a call from him when his brother-in-law, Gerald, flashes to town with the items up for exhibit."

"They're to be secured in the shrine vault?" Garnet asks.

"That's the plan, but I have a bit of a twist in mind to throw off any burglars."

I'm halfway through my burger when a thought strikes me.

"What about the duchess' missing body? What do we know about that?"

Garnet shrugs. "One of three things. Either mandagots respawn at a place of origin, or their corporeal bodies dissolve upon death, or someone flashed in and took the body to keep us from learning more."

"Does anyone feel like we have more questions now than when we started?" Calum asks.

I raise a fry.

Da chuckles. "That's often the way of things in our line of work. The good news is, even though there's much we don't know, there is also much we do."

Maybe, but it doesn't feel like that.

CHAPTER EIGHTEEN

After we finish looking into past events, I help Da pull together the files and clear the conference table. "Can I ask you something else?"

"Of course. What's on yer mind?"

"When a man goes through something traumatic, why does he pull back and shut down instead of taking the help offered to him?"

Da turns to face me and leans his butt against the table. "That's a complicated question. Is everythin' all right with Sloan, *mo chroi?*"

"Oh, perfect. He's magical."

"Then yer brothers? Has somethin' happened?"

"No. Not them either. Loki targeted Dionysus because he had a relationship with his daughter Hel and from what I gather, it didn't end well. Fast forward, and Loki's been poisoning him with tainted wine and causing his masculine energies to suffer. Then, when we figured that out, Loki kidnapped him. I'm not sure what happened in the hours before we found and rescued him, but he's definitely off."

"How long ago did this happen?"

"The poisoning has been months, but we only figured it out on Saturday and got him back from Loki yesterday."

Da reaches forward and chucks my chin. "Och, luv, if it was yesterday, he simply hasn't bounced back. Give him time. He's been a god for eternity. I'm sure he's not accustomed to feelin' like a victim."

"Yeah, maybe that's it." I search within myself to sense whether or not that feels right. It doesn't. "I just feel like something's still off."

"All ye can do is let him know without question that ye care about him and yer there if he needs a friend."

I sip the last of my soda and toss my empty cup to Calum beside the trash can. "I've done that."

"Then ye've done what ye can. To answer yer question, it *is* different fer men—it shouldn't be—but it is. Oftentimes, men are conditioned from a young age to dust themselves off and stay strong. Culturally, we're not supposed to show our emotions freely or cry or let our vulnerabilities show."

"That's stupid."

"Aye, it is, but it's been the way of things since the world first started turnin'."

"But Dionysus and I have shared those moments of vulnerability, and he trusted me with his heart. I don't know why he's not trusting me now."

Da pulls me against his chest and sets his cheek on my forehead. "Sometimes ye remind me so much of yer Mam it hurts. Yer heart is as open and tender as hers, and like her, ye'll find a way to comfort any wound ye come across. It's simply in yer nature."

I chuckle. "Sloan and Emmet are the healers."

"Healers of the body, maybe. Yer most definitely the healer of the soul."

I like the sound of that.

"All right. I think I'll see if I can reach him again before we head home. Thanks, Da."

"Anytime, *mo chroi*. Anytime at—"

"Here we go," Sloan says, reading the screen of his phone. "The relics are on their way now. I'm to meet Blaise and his brother-in-law downstairs at STOA to receive them."

Garnet grabs a napkin and wipes his fingers. "Ready?"

I step back from Da, kiss his cheek, and jog toward Sloan, hand extended. "Ready."

The empowered objects and antiquities for the FUR Ball arrive in a lockable upright chest on wheels. It's brought to us by Blaise, his brother-in-law, Gerald DeMarco, and two burly goons, who, if I'm not mistaken, are shifters of some kind. They give Sloan an inventory list, and we go over it as Gerald points out each of the twenty-six pieces one by one.

Since the moment the case doors swung open, my shield has been tingling, and the butterflies in my stomach have been hell-bent on migrating north.

That's some bad juju.

"I trust everything is in order?" Monsieur Blaise says, smiling at Garnet expectantly.

Garnet checks in with Sloan, and he straightens and closes the doors. Raising his hands, he casts a binding spell securing the contents within and touches the top, sealing the entire case in a layer of stone. "Aye, everything is in order."

Garnet accepts the clipboard with the manifest and contract and signs for the pieces. Then he hands it to Sloan, and he signs as well.

Blaise arches a brow and watches as Sloan rolls the stone-encrypted case into the vault. "That's it? You're simply putting them into a vault? You assured me you had a top-quality security plan."

"Och, and I do. Don't you worry, sir. I've staked my reputation on keeping them safe until delivery and put up a large sum of collateral as insurance. I guarantee yer possessions are in the best possible hands."

Blaise and Gerald don't look so sure, but there's nothing to be done about that. "Then that's that."

Sloan nods. "It is indeed. You can contact Garnet and me at any time for further preparations, but you won't have access to these treasures until Thursday afternoon for event set up."

Blaise looks like he might argue, but then Garnet gestures for them to head back out to the elevator area to take their leave.

When Sloan and I are alone at last, he kisses me, activates the spell on my watch, and steps back. "Safe home, luv. I'll see you in two days."

I step into the vault, place my left hand on the chest of treasures and my right hand on the dragon band encircling my left arm. The moment I focus on transporting to the dragon lair, I zap through the distance and find myself standing in front of my favorite leprechaun. "Hello, Patty. What's the craic?"

"Fi!" He's all smiles as he fights with his recliner to get his feet to the ground. After he sets his controller onto the charging station, he shuffles over to me, lickety-split. "Och, yer a welcome sight. Are ye here fer a visit?"

"I am." I lift my wrist and the two timepieces I have strapped to my arm. One is my Fitbit, which won't be able to keep accurate time here in the lair, and the other is my Niall Horan, One Direction watch, which we spelled to count down so I arrive back in Toronto in time to set up for the FUR Ball. "I'm sticking around guarding this for a few hours if that's all right?"

"All right? It's a grand surprise. Come, let's tuck that over here so the kids don't knock it, and we'll go see who's around to say hello."

"Who's around? Are the kids allowed to be out and about on their own now?"

"A great deal more than they were, aye. There have been a lot of changes around here in the past weeks, Red. A lot of changes. Now, what have ye brought?"

I wheel the case of the relics over to his seating area and sit on the coffee table. "The mission, if you choose to accept it, is to help me un-evil as many of these cursed and evilly aligned treasures as we can in the next…" I lift my watch, "six hours."

His snowy eyebrows arch. "Where did you come across a treasure trove of evil objects, Red?"

I grin. "That's the entertainment part of this visit. I'm going to fill you in and tell you all about it."

Merlin snaps in with the Perry twins, and I wave them over. "Are we late? Sloan just texted us."

"Nope. I just got here myself. Thanks for helping."

Merlin nods. "Well, as the only people with clearance for the dragon lair, we're happy to be included."

"Anything we can do to join the Fi fun is a yes from us," one of the twins says.

"Not to mention helping to rid the world of cursed and tainted objects," the other says.

"Awesome. Thanks, guys." I don't dwell on that too long because once again I've forgotten their names.

Damn it!

What is it about these two that keeps me in the dark?

It's insane.

Moving on from that, I place my hand on the case and release the energy that created the stone tomb. Then, I remove the binding spell and move to the lock.

Open Sesame doesn't work.

Neither does. *Gain Access.*

"Huh."

"What, huh?" Patty asks.

"Merlin, will you take a shot at this lock? It's fighting me. I think it's spelled to resist opening."

Merlin steps in close and I shift back and out of his way. He tries a few things and is just as stumped. "Huh."

"Right? What do you think?"

He tilts his head. "It's spelled to resist magic. What about lock-picking? Patty, have you got any fine tools that might work?"

"I do. It might take me a bit to locate them. They're in my treasure room somewhere."

"Oh, boy." I've seen the state of Patty's treasure and laugh. "Excellent. In the meantime, I'll check in with Dart and the other kids."

The first time I toured the old dragon lair—the one that Granda now uses as the shrine for the Order—I couldn't get over how big it was. That hollowed-out area buried deep in the Cliffs of Moher was home to one dragon.

This lair is home to over twenty.

It's beyond massive and has a warren of tunnels that allow the Westerns and the wyrms to access the surface. The wyverns have a lagoon grotto that leads down and out to the water beyond, much like Merlin's cave beneath Tintagel Castle.

I feel my boy long before I see him.

Since our bonding took hold and our union began, Dart holds a presence within. It's not the same kind of presence as when Bruin is physically within me. With Dart, it's more like a sense of belonging and strength that grows the closer we are together.

"Fi, Merlin mentioned a mission against evil. Is everything all right?"

"So far, so good. We're going to work on making it even better. How are things with you? How's your stay with the Iceland dragons going? Are you having fun?"

He chuckles. "You're thinking of me as an adolescent again. Our union has unlocked centuries of knowledge, and with the help of Utiss and Cazzienth, I've gained a great many new skills."

It's odd to hear Dart talk like that. He sounds so grown up. After scrubbing my hands over his center horn, I bend and kiss him. "It doesn't matter how big and wise you get. You'll always be my blue boy."

He lowers his head and stretches out his wings. "And you'll always be my Mother of Dragons. Now, follow me to the flight cavern. I'm anxious to show you what I can do."

"I've only got a few minutes before Merlin and Patty will need me."

"Then I will return you straight away."

"Deal."

It doesn't matter what's going wrong in the world, riding a dragon can fix it...at least for a time. Now that Dart and I are bound, and our union is strengthening, I'm much more comfortable riding him.

When we arrive at the edge of a stone plateau, Dart supersizes and I swing up onto his elbow and jog over to my saddle on his first spike. With a two-handed grip and my feet planted, I brace myself for the raw power of his launch to take off.

I've found there are two kinds of liftoff.

One when he runs and launches up, and I brace against the forward thrust, and the other when he runs off a ledge and the world drops away, and my stomach flips like a sudden drop on a rollercoaster.

S'all good.

There's no bad way to ride my dragon. As we get warmed up, I make small adjustments with my footing and grip, and soon we're cutting the crisp air of the cavern like a missile in flight.

Glancing back, I notice he's still wearing all three saddles from when we were sucked back to Tintagel, so I practice releasing my hold and navigating his back while in motion.

I don't have the grace and confidence of Merlin, but I'm getting better.

Fi, can you hear me?

Even with the wind whistling in my ears, I hear him as clearly as if we were standing next to one another in my living room. *Loud and clear, buddy.*

Perfect. When you feel the tingle of my magic take hold, accept it and become one with my efforts or you'll cause a ripple in the illusion.

Illusion? Cool. *How do I accept it?*

It's instinctive. Let it wash over you and become one with my intention to hide us from sight.

I jog back to the saddle wrapped around his first spike and take my stance. *Does it matter if I move?*

Not if you're within the glamor's proximity. If you dive off or get thrown into the air, it'll drop you from the glamor, and you'll suddenly pop into view for anyone who's watching.

Hilarious. *Okay, I'll try not to let any moves throw me off.*

An excellent idea.

Dart banks right and we soar toward two other Westerns, both green. Being the terrible mother that I am, I don't recognize who they are. I'll call them Green Guy and—Oh, I think that one's Chezzo.

The two of them are amazing to watch.

My skin tingles with the signature of Dart's magic, and I snap back to paying attention. I welcome the intent of his glamor and allow it to wash over me as he asked.

I'm not sure what to expect, but a faint iridescent film slicks over us and wraps us together like magical cellophane.

I move my arm to test its parameters, and it flexes and moves with me.

Cooleroo.

"Great job, buddy. You're doing it!" I'm so relieved. If Dart can glamor his presence, it makes him living in the city so much less alarming.

Sure, he might soar across the sky to save me from a vampire attack, but he can conceal himself and save Garnet and his team three days of following up and wiping all traces of magical exposure.

Oops.

Not that it matters. No one regrets him breaking the rules to save me from Xavier. We handled the exposure, and the next time the unthinkable happens, maybe it won't have to be.

"You rock my socks, buddy."

We reach the far end of the cavern and make a wide arc back toward the plateau. I blink up at the iridescent shimmer of his glamor, and my chest swells with pride.

I love you huge, Dartamont Cumhaill.

I sense the surge in pride as we near the plateau and he lifts his head to prepare to land. *Ditto. And as much as I love to fly with you, I believe my time is up.*

Dart escorts me back to the main cavern, and we find Merlin, Patty, and the Perry twins still working on the lock and looking frustrated. Well, crappers. Sloan and I talked a lot about what I should do if the relics fight me or the dark energy is too strong, but we never considered not being able to open the freaking case.

"Seriously? We're still stumped?"

Merlin frowns at me. "Lock picks did nothing. I've tried druid magic. Patty's tried too. We've cast spells and enchantments. Nothing's working."

"If we knew the source of the spell," Patty says. "Maybe we could do somethin' but fer now, we're runnin' out of ideas."

I bend down and look into the keyhole. It seems to be an old standard lock...only it's unpickable.

"Can we warp the metal of the case or expand the metal of the lock or pop it out of place or something?"

"What are you thinking, Fi?" Merlin asks.

I scratch the back of my neck and shake my head. "It's a bizarre idea. Kinda gross, actually."

Patty pushes his spectacles up his nose with his stumpy finger. "We're all friends here, Red, and yer plan is dead in the water if we don't get this case open."

Merlin shrugs. "We've tried everything else. What have you got?"

"One of you to piss in the lock, and I'm going to *Freeze Water*."

The twins look gobsmacked.

Yeah, they aren't used to me yet.

"Are ye serious, then?" Patty asks.

"Yep. One of you whip it out. Who's got good aim and needs to go?"

The four of them look at each other, but no one volunteers.

"Yeah, you're probably right. It was a dumb idea."

Patty grunts and steps up to the case, reaching for his fly. "I wouldn't do this fer anyone else, Fi. But yer ideas often work, and we've tried everythin' else. Tell me when enough is enough."

I chuckle. "How do I know? Do you think I've done this before?"

"Only the goddess knows. Just say when."

I try my best not to think too deeply about what's happening and keep my sight focused on the lock.

As the stream of liquid comes into view, it reminds me of the water gun game at a fair where the first squirt is off-center, then you adjust to hit your mark and make the monkey climb up the rope and ring the bell.

I also try not to think about the fact that Patty's pee smells like clover flowers. Cute but not something you need to know about your friend.

"*Freeze Fluid*," I say, focusing on the metal lock.

Nothing.

I wait a few more seconds and try again. "*Freeze Fluid*."

The lock frosts over.

"Okay, Patty. Hold your fire."

Merlin moves in to look and holds his finger against the frosty lock. *"Freeze Fluid."*

The snap of metal precedes the metal tumbler popping out of place and rolling on the stone floor.

"Huzzah!" I say, holding up my arm. "Patty pee for the win. Well done, sir."

Patty chuckles and tucks things away. "I do love yer kind of crazy, Red. Ye never let things get boring."

"You're welcome. Now. Let's not lose that lock. We'll have to put it back and mend it when we finish."

Merlin grins. "Go ahead and pick it up then. Your plan. You get the honor of picking up the pee lock."

I clutch my fist and give it a little pump. "Yay me!"

It takes the five of us almost five hours to dissipate the negative energy of Monsieur Blaise's artifacts and replace their signature with fake negative energy that will dissipate over the next few years. Our thought is that by that time, Blaise might sell the pieces and the alteration won't be tied back to us.

Even if it does, it won't be for a couple of years.

The important part is that these items won't be useful for any dark fae during the Culling.

Yay team!

"How do you think we did overall?" one of the Perry twins asks.

I'm checking the pictures I took of each tray and making sure all the trays are in the proper slots and looking exactly as they did before. "I think we rocked it."

Merlin grins. "I agree. Other than that one dagger with the sapphire hilt, we've rendered them pretty much harmless."

"Anyone using that dagger with evil intent will suffer the same injury back on them." I grin. "Nikon taught me that one."

"With forty-five minutes to spare," Patty says, checking my watch for the countdown. "Just enough time fer ye to help me clear the next task on Animal Crossing before ye need to go."

"Absolutely." I close the doors on the storage case, and after Merlin re-engages the lock and mends it, I bind it closed and seal it with stone. "I'll put on the record, and you can set us up."

"*Little Less Conversation?*"

"You bet. It's my fave. Long live the King."

Merlin chuckles as I jog to the gramophone. "On that note, we'll leave you two to your fun. Dart will take Darcy, Davin, and I topside, and we'll drop them home on our way back to Iceland."

"Thank you all so much." I plunk into my recliner and accept my controller. "I appreciate your help."

"Our pleasure," the Perry twins say in unison.

Darcy and Davin.

Darcy and Davin.

I've got to remember that for the next time.

When we're by ourselves, I smile at Patty. "Your help was invaluable. You're a marvel with treasures, and tonight you proved you're willing to go above and beyond for the success of a mission."

He pinches his fingers at his brow and tips an imaginary hat. "Always a pleasure, milady. Yer more trouble than most but worth the effort."

I check my watch. "All right. If we've calculated things correctly, we have thirty-eight minutes until it's Thursday after-noon back home."

"Perfect, just enough time to get some bait and try to catch a coelacanth."

I laugh. "Whatever that is."

CHAPTER NINETEEN

When the alarm goes off on my watch, I hug Patty goodbye and focus on transporting myself and the case to the ballroom at Casa Loma. The way my dragon portal band works is the first time I grab it, the magic transports me to the lair. The second time, I can steer myself and land anywhere I focus on. If our plan has gone off without a hitch, Sloan should be waiting with Garnet for my arrival.

"Here goes nothing."

"Good afternoon, Lady Druid."

I meet the smiling faces of Sloan, Garnet, and Monsieur Blaise. "Good day, gentlemen. I hope I haven't kept you waiting."

"Not at all, *a ghra*. Yer perfectly on time." Sloan steps close, kisses my cheek, and presses his hands on the stone encasing the relics. When the layer of gray rock vanishes, he removes the binding and spins it on its wheels to face Monsieur Blaise.

"Monsieur, if you'd like to check your collection, I'll have ye sign off on the contract that everything is as it's supposed to be."

"I still don't understand why your girlfriend is the one delivering my goods. I hired *you* to protect them, Monsieur Mackenzie."

Sloan nods. "I put them in the safest place on this planet. In an underground lair, under the watch of two dozen dragons."

"And one Man o' Green," I add.

"And one Man o' Green," Sloan adds.

I'm not sure if Blaise thinks we're joking or if we've thrown him so far off his game that he doesn't know how to respond. Either way, his gaze narrows on me for a long while before he gives up and decides to check out his collection.

I paste a smile on my face and cross my fingers. If luck be the lady tonight, he won't notice the lock has been tampered with or our fake evilness vibes.

We need to pass his inspection.

Odds are he'll only check the objects themselves for authenticity and verify no one switched them out, right?

I doubt he has a way to check the alignment of cursed and empowered treasures at a glance like this...

Right?

Man, I hope so.

I chew on the inside of my cheek as I wait for this inspection to end. It's nerve-racking, and I have to rub my palms on my pants.

"Monsieur?" Garnet holds up two pieces of paper. "If you're ready, I'll have you sign off on our protection and delivery of goods, and you can begin placing the items into the exhibits."

Monsieur Blaise waves over his brother-in-law and gestures at the case. "You can begin the exhibition setup. Everything is in order."

Garnets smiles and beckons Anyx and Thaos closer. "My men will stay with you and monitor the security of the exhibits while the rest of us go home and change for the big event."

"The reception doors open at six-forty-five," Blaise says. "The bar at seven."

"Looking forward to it."

Sloan meshes his fingers with mine and *poofs* us straight to our bedroom. "How did things go at the dragon lair? I assume you neutralized the relics?"

"They have been. There was one hiccup, but nothing we couldn't handle."

"Oh? What happened?"

I fill him in on the problem with the lock and my pee and freeze solution.

His brow creases. "Why didn't ye get Patty's water pistol and use that?"

I bark a laugh. "Because I didn't think of that."

"So, yer first instinct was to have a man pull out his Johnson and pee?"

"Hey, I have five brothers. They say go with what you know. I'm accustomed to guys peeing wherever and whenever it's needed."

He laughs, leaving me standing in the center of the room as he strides off to our walk-in closet. "Other than that? How was your visit?"

"It was great. Merlin and the Perry twins came to help. Patty was, of course, magical with the treasures as you predicted, and I got a chance to fly with Dart in the cavern of the dragon lair. He learned how to glamor."

"That's wonderful."

"Yeah, he's super jazzed. Then, we finished in time for me to play a little Animal Crossing with Patty and we rocked out to some of our Elvis favorites."

"It does sound like you had a great time."

I toe off my shoes and leave them and my pants in the middle of the floor. Releasing Bruin, I scrub my hand over his broad brow and tickle his ear. "I'm napping for a couple of hours. Feel free to eat, sleep, and be merry."

Bruin slaps his tongue up the side of my face and laughs when I wince. "What time of day is it? The dragon lair has me turned around."

"It's half two," Sloan says, checking his watch. "We're off-duty until six. So, we'll rest until five and head back to be in place for when the doors open."

"Gotcha. Holler if ye need anyone killed."

"Will do, buddy." I beeline it for King Henry. "I've got lair lag. Come lay with me and tell me what's been going on here, hotness."

King Henry welcomes me with such comfy cozy bliss I might not make it through Sloan's account of our hours apart. "Did I miss anything exciting?"

Sloan climbs in beside me and flicks his finger to encourage me to roll onto my side. I do as prompted, and he slides one arm under my neck and the other over my ribs.

Wriggling back, I yawn as he spoons me and snuggles in. "Och, it was an eventful time. It seems yer not the only source of mayhem."

"Do tell. Did our plan to lure a break-in work?"

"Our plans always work."

I laugh harder. "But never in the way we intend."

He brushes my hair behind my ear. "That's true. This one came close, though. I spent my days working with Garnet and Mr. Stark at the event center, and Manx and I spent our nights in the vault camping out with Doc and Daisy."

"Good. I'm glad she got to take part in a stakeout."

"She did, and she enjoyed herself quite a bit."

"Did our burglar take the bait?"

"Not at first, but at three o'clock this morning, we did have an unexpected visitor."

"Who?" I twist to look over my shoulder. "Did we get him?"

"Did we capture the intruder? No, but you could say we tagged him…in a fashion."

"How so?"

"When the door opened, we were all sound asleep. It was dark in the vault, and when the intruder eased inside, he stepped on Daisy's tail and scared her."

"Oh no!"

"Oh, yes."

"And she tagged him."

"Definitely."

"Did you all get skunked?"

"We did, but yer gran sorted us out soon enough."

"Yay, Gran."

"Indeed."

"What did you do with your clothes?"

"Washed in baking soda and hanging on the back fence. Lara said it'll take a few washes and up to three weeks for the smell to be gone."

I close my eyes, chuckling while imagining Daisy taking out a prospective cat burglar with her skunky stink. Girl power!

"So, since we both need a few hours, let's close our eyes and get ready to face the world once more."

My eyes have already shut, and my consciousness is drifting from my body. Yeah…sleep now.

The world will have to take a number.

I'm deep in my dream of warm summer sun and splashing in exotic waters when Sloan pats my shoulder and jiggles me awake. "Sorry, luv. Our respite has ended. It's time to get ready for the ball."

"FUR Ball." I giggle while still half asleep.

"Yes, luv, the FUR Ball. Now, if ye hurry, ye'll have time fer a shower and get something to eat before ye need to get dressed."

"Do you have time to *poof* to the Samosa Hut and get me some butter chicken samosas?"

"Fer you, I'll *make* time. Do ye want rice with it?"

"No. I'll nuke up some veggies, thanks."

"All right. I'm going to have a quick turn in the washroom, and I'll do that."

"Perfect. Thank you. I appreciate it."

Sloan kisses my cheek and winks. "It's my genuine pleasure, *a ghra*. Now, make sure you don't go back to sleep. Ye'll be cranky if ye don't have time to gussy up before such a fancy event."

True story.

It doesn't take me as long to gussy up as most women, and since Ciara and Kevin were in charge of our wardrobe, I only need to shower, slap on some war paint, and pin back my hair.

Easy peasy, lemon squeezy.

Rolling to the opening of King Henry's drapes, I drop my legs to the floor and grab a pair of dressy black undies and the matching bra from the back of my unmentionables drawer.

By the time I pull that together and toss the clothes I'm wearing into the hamper, Sloan's exiting the bathroom. "All yers, luv." His kiss is minty fresh, and I pull him back for another taste. He chuckles and reclaims his freedom. "No time fer seconds right now. If the night goes well, though, I'd like to come back to that impulse when we get home. I missed ye."

"You read my mind, Mackenzie."

It's always odd to spend time in the Wyrm Queen's dragon lair and return to reality after the timeframe has distorted. Gran and Granda said it was from being around great power for long periods.

After spending almost a week with the five dragons in Merlin's cave, time seemed to flow normally.

Either it's the Queen of Wyrms specifically, or it's Patty, or it's a combination of the two of them.

That's a thought for another day.

I make quick work of my shower, shave my legs, and end up sitting in front of the vanity mirror, leaning in close to give myself smokey eyes. There's no sense doing my lips yet because I haven't even begun devouring my butter chicken samosas.

Mmm, even the thought of them makes my stomach growl. Grabbing my bathrobe, I cover up and head downstairs.

"Fi!" Emmet waves from the table. "You're back. How'd it go with the relics?"

"Good. I babysat them at the dragon's den, we diminished their dark power, and we returned them this afternoon as contracted. Blaise had no choice but to sign off on the delivery. If he or someone else planned to take them and hold us responsible, they missed out."

"Noice."

"Did you hear about Daisy's foray into battling robbers?" Calum rises from the computer at the kitchen desk. He has Daisy in his lap and lifts her to snuggle against his chest.

"I did. Sloan said she was instrumental in foiling the would-be robber."

"I stunk him," Daisy says. "I didn't mean to, but I stunk everyone."

I wave that away. "Sloan said you were awesome and Gran had a remedy to un-stink everyone."

Emmet opens the fridge and frowns at the interior. "Are we out of beer? Fi, no more road trips for you. You remind us of these essentials."

I do. "I think there's a backup case in the basement bar. You know what Da always says. It's better to have it and not need it—"

"—than to need it and not have it," he and Calum chime in.

Emmet closes the refrigerator door and strikes off toward the back stairs. "Excellent. I'll get it."

I check the fridge for leftover veggies that might need eating, but there aren't any, so I grab a couple of cans from the pantry. "So, other than the attempted relic heist at STOA, did I miss anything?"

"Nope."

"What about the wedding? How's that coming along?"

Calum grins. "Good. I think Kev's got all the things sorted the way he wants them."

"What about you?"

He laughs. "I told him to tell me where to show up and when. As long as he's there to say his vows, it's my perfect wedding."

"Aww...point to you, bro. So sweet. I can't wait."

Calum shrugs. "Honestly, other than it being nice to celebrate with the family, it won't change much for me. He's been my other half for a decade. We live together. We love each other. Having a wedding license from the city doesn't mean more than that."

"No. It doesn't. Still, it'll be lovely."

"What will be lovely?" Kevin asks as he and Ciara come into the kitchen from the back hall. Their arms are full of garment bags with little tags hanging around the neck of each hanger.

"We were talking about the beach nuptials," I say, reaching up to take my veggies out of the microwave. "Calum says you've got everything pretty much nailed down."

Kevin grins. "Ciara and I finished with the last of the arrangements yesterday. Now we only need to stay on top of things over the next week, and unless something unforeseen happens, we're golden."

Emmet is back with the case of beer from downstairs. "You two make quite the team."

Ciara nods. "Honestly, we had a great time plannin' the celebration."

"We definitely did," Kevin says. "I have the artistic flair for things, and Ciara was already in the wedding planning groove from the handfasting."

"I enjoy event plannin'," Ciara says. "It's fun to take the imagined event and make it a reality."

"And spending other people's money is fun too."

Ciara laughs. "I think I showed great restraint."

"For sure, you did."

It strikes me as I hear the two of them talking that they do enjoy creating together. "Maybe the two of you should plan a few more events together and see if you might like to make a business of it. Ciara's certainly attended and helped with enough Order events to know her way around magical celebrations, and Kev's right. He has a flair for colors and artistic impression."

"That's a cool idea." Emmet hands out a round of beers. "You two should think about it. It could make a great side hustle."

Calum laughs. "You just want an excuse for more parties."

Emmet grins. "Guilty as charged."

Sloan *poofs* in with an aluminum platter and sets it on the trivet on the island counter. "I got twenty-five butter chicken and twenty-five assorted other flavors. The woman says to match the color dot on them to the menu to know what kind they are."

While the gang huddles around to check out the options, I snag five butter chicken samosas and put them on my plate with my veggies. "Thank you, hotness. You're my hero."

Sloan winks. "Then my plan is workin'. Soon ye'll realize ye can't live without me."

He's joking, but his words hit home. There's a strong possibility that one day, I'm going to outlive him.

"I already know I don't want to live without you. If it comes down to it, I may have to take you to the Cistern of the Source and dip you in the river of prana."

"A modern-day Achilles," Nikon says, snapping in with Dionysus. The two of them are both in black-on-black togas with black sandals. "It does our hearts proud to have you waxing philosophical with Greek mythology, doesn't it, Dionysus?"

"Of course."

I pop the last of my first samosa into my mouth and rush over to hug them. "Are you here for a pre-drink beer before the ball?"

"FUR Ball!" Calum and Emmet both shout.

I laugh. "Hilarious."

Sloan rolls his eyes. "Yer all the same."

"True story." I hug Nikon and move to Dionysus. His hug is stiffer than usual, but I suppose after what Loki did he's likely still processing. "I love the black toga. It's stylish and still fits the theme of the event."

Nikon clucks his tongue. "I told you, Red. Greeks wear himations, not togas. That's the Romans."

"Ha! It's all Greek to me."

We all get a laugh out of that. All of us except Dionysus. "Did you see what I did there? It's all Greek to me...Julius Caesar..."

He laughs. "My apologies. I was distracted."

"You okay, Tarzan?"

"Of course. Why wouldn't I be?"

I squeeze his arm. "No reason. Just checking in."

"How about a beer?" Emmet makes his way over.

"Just one." I head back to my abandoned plate on the island. "We need to be in top Team Trouble form for tonight."

"Hello the house," Dillan calls from the back.

"Ha! We start handing out beer and look who shows up uninvited."

"I heard that." Dillan joins us. Oh, and he brought a date. "Uh, everyone...this is Evangeline, the lovely lady I've been spending my time with. Evangeline, this is everyone...well, almost."

He steps to the side so we can meet her, and I admit, I'm taken aback. The woman is lovely—truly radiantly, lovely—I've simply never known Dillan to get involved with anyone who wasn't a vertical replica of a stick, and on the supermodel scale.

Aww, my brother is growing up.

Evangeline is a full-figured blonde with corkscrew curls, a genuine smile, and a power signature that makes the hair on the nape of my neck tingle. When I meet her gaze, I'd swear her piercing teal eyes seem to be backlit to glow. She's wearing a full-length white dress with ruching in the bust, a curve-hugging bodice, and a flowing gossamer skirt.

I rush forward, hand extended. "Evangeline, it's so lovely to meet you. I'm Fiona, and this is my other half, Sloan. Welcome to our home."

Dimples crease her round cheeks as she smiles and shakes my hand. A surge of magic tingles under my skin. Wow. She's got juice...but it's such a lovely sensation it's hard to describe. "Please, call me Eva, and thank you. It's lovely to be here."

"We thought maybe you were made up," Calum says, coming forward. "D kept talking about this amazing woman he met, yet he kept you all to himself."

Dillan chuffs. "Eva, this is my brother Calum, and that's his partner, soon-to-be husband, Kevin."

"Oh, that's the wedding next week," she says.

Kevin beams. "Nine sleeps...but who's counting?"

Emmet's up next. "I'm Emmet, and this is my betrothed, Ciara. It's good to meet you."

Eva greets the two of them and smiles at the boys. "Wow, you all look so much alike."

Dillan nods. "Yeah, me, Brenny, Calum, and Em all got our Mam's black hair and green eyes. Fi and Aiden take after Da with the red hair and blue eyes."

"But even so, your auras are so similar. There's no missing the fact that you're family."

"And extended family," I say, doing the honors of introducing the Greeks. "These two lovely men in himations—definitely not togas—are our very dear friends Nikon Tsambikos and Dionysus."

Nikon shifts the handshake and bows to kiss her knuckles. "It's a pleasure to meet you, angel."

"Back it off, Greek. There's no hedonism happening here. Keep working on my sister."

Nikon chuckles. "Your sister and her boyfriend shut me down every time. I'm starting to get the feeling it's a no for the two of them."

I laugh. "Oh, just starting to get that feeling, eh?"

Nikon gestures at my silk robe and arches a brow. "You can't blame a guy for dreaming. Is this what you're wearing? I thought it was a black and white masquerade. I didn't know it was clothing optional."

I go back to my dinner, fork in a bunch of carrots, and nod. "I haven't been given my outfit yet. I take it that's what the garment bags were for?"

"Yes indeed," Kevin says. "Speaking of, I think it's time you all get dressed and shuffle off to the ball. You have a big night ahead of you. Thieves to fool and murderers to catch."

I grab my last two samosas to go, and Kevin hands me the garment bag with my name hanging off the hanger. "Thanks. I hope you two were kind to me."

Ciara and Kev share a conspiratorial smile. "We've done you proud, Fi. Trust us, you'll look amazing."

CHAPTER TWENTY

"What the actual fuck?" I say, staring at my reflection in the mirror. "I can't wear this in public."

Sloan is standing behind me, studying my bra through the sheer black gauze that is supposed to be my dress. It's a see-through sheath from my shoulders to high on my thighs. "It's..."

"Sleazy?"

"No. It's much too elegant for sleazy. I'd say aggressively enticing?"

"I don't want to be aggressively enticing. I want to be sleek and pretty and blend into the shadows."

"Ye won't blend in wearin' that. I'd wager it's fair to say ye'll be the focus of many wanton glances."

"I don't want wanton. Wanton is unwanted."

He offers me an apologetic smile. "What about somethin' from yer closet? Have ye a little black dress ye could wear? Isn't that a staple in a woman's closet?"

"It is, but my little black dress was from before my druid days. My body shape has changed with all the workouts. Besides, it's too short. If I have to fight in that, I'll be showing the crowd as much as if I'm wearing this." I groan, checking out my abs and midriff. "Had I known this was in store for me, I would've gone shopping myself."

"Maybe it won't matter. Ye'll have a mask coverin' yer face."

"But Garnet will know it's me...and Anyx...and Da. Good grief, I don't want my father seeing me in this dress. If I wanted the men in my life to scan my girl parts, I would prance around naked."

The soft knock on the door brings Ciara peeking in. She's taller than me and slimmer and far more elegant. Her dress is stunning and clings to all her curves like it was custom-fitted. "Fi? From the other side of the wall, it sounds like yer freakin' out. Do ye not like the dress?"

I hold out my arms and shrug. "What dress? I might as well go to this thing in my lingerie."

Ciara blinks and comes in to join us. "Ye *are* in yer lingerie. Where's the dress? That's the slip."

She glances around the room and finds the garment bag. She splits the two parts, frowns at the empty interior, reaches down below the zipper, and pulls out the other half of my outfit. "This is yer dress."

"Oh, thank the goddess." I reach for what she's offering. "I honestly thought it was some kind of haute-couture horror show."

Ciara laughs. "I wouldn't do that to ye, Fi. At least, not anymore. Between Kevin and I workin' on it, I think we found ye the perfect dress."

"At this point, if it covers my hoo-haw and the girls, I'll be happy."

Ciara laughs harder. "Och, maybe I shouldn't have told ye. It would've been a hoot fer ye to come down to the kitchen in yer slip."

I roll my eyes and point at the door. "Thanks for your help. Buh-bye now."

"All right. I'll wait downstairs fer the reveal. Och, and Fi?"

"Yeah?"

"Yer welcome."

Dear Goddess, please forgive the uncharitable thoughts that flitted through my mind as I stood in front of my dressing mirror, wanting to kill Ciara and Kevin. I panicked. I'm calm. I'm beautiful. And I never want to get out of this dress.

I've never been a vain person or particularly impressed with myself. In the right outfit and with the right lighting, I generally figure I clean up pretty well. With Sloan on my arm, there's no chance of getting an overly inflated opinion of myself.

Today is different.

This dress makes me feel beautiful and sexy, and all the things a girl wants to feel when stepping into an elegant conservatory decorated for a classy event that I normally would have no business attending.

"You look amazing, hotness." I cast a sideways glance at my escort.

"I pale in comparison to yer beauty, *a ghra*. I can hardly breathe."

I like the sound of that. While Sloan often says things like that to me, tonight I feel like it's true. "I like these masks. I say we keep them on and play masquerade ball, the home edition, later in King Henry."

"As entertaining as that is, Lady Druid," Garnet's voice says, coming into my ear, "let's not forget we've got the entire team on comms tonight."

I make eyes at Sloan as my cheeks flush hot. "Oops. Sorry, Da."

"It's fine, *mo chroi*." Da is across the room at the champaign fountain, but his voice is as clear as if he were standing right beside me. "Let's pretend that was yer way of testin' the comms."

"Yes, let's."

Sloan and I stroll around the outside of the room. The space is massive, with an easy three hundred people here looking posh in black or white. The only people wearing color are the servers in harlequin costumes with gold, red, and black diamonds, and Monsieur Blaise, who has a deep red suit jacket.

It's so schmancy it's amazing.

Arm-in-arm, we do our tour, then start visiting each of the exhibit pedestals.

"Fi, I need you to adjust Sloan's tie clip," Anyx says into my ear. "Stark says his camera is set too low. All we're seeing are chests and shoulders. Be nonchalant. You're just a woman sprucing up her man."

"Oh, you're crooked, hon." I slide my fingers behind the silk of his tie, unpin it, and move it up a little. Before I release it, I tilt the silver head up. Hopefully, they can get a clear look at faces. "There. Is that better?"

"Better," Anyx says. "And Sloan's right, Fi. You look lovely."

"Thank you—" I'm about to call him Puss, but remember how much he hates it. "—Anyx. Is Zuzanna here tonight?"

"Over your right shoulder sipping champagne by the urn of white roses. You can't miss her. She's radiant."

I smile as I scan the ballroom and find his mate without difficulty. She's wearing a shimmering white dress with her long blonde hair swept up and off her neck. She has a mask on a stick versus the kind Ciara and Kevin got all of us.

They went with the ones that tie at the back of our heads with ribbon in case we need our hands.

Smart choice.

I lift my chin and smile at Zuzanna, and she gives me a subtle lift of her champagne flute.

With my brothers here, the Greeks, and Ciara... We've got this place locked down.

"Some of these relics are really cool." I point into the display case closest to us. "Oooh, and they have their origin stories on their little plaques. Cute."

Sloan chuckles and leans down to read about the ancient trylle hair clip. "I love that ye think they're cute, *a ghra*. Although, I don't think cute is what Monsieur Blaise is going for."

I scan the ballroom for our host and find him speaking with a group of gentlemen. "How come he's wearing a red jacket?"

"I suppose if yer the host ye wear whatever ye like."

"I suppose so."

I'm dying to talk to Sloan about Dillan's date, but the comms make that impossible. I like her. And I love the way she brings my brother to life. He and Eva are by the bar. He's getting her a drink, and I don't know that I've ever seen him so enraptured.

Dillan has always been our grouch. If there's snark to be spread or a cutting remark to be said, he's our man.

It's all a defensive wall.

Once you get to know him, you find he's as sweet and silly as the rest of my brothers. It usually takes the women he dates time to find that out.

It seems Evangeline is the exception.

She seems to have completely disarmed him, and happiness looks good on him.

Sloan follows my gaze and smiles. "It's a good night all around."

"Yes, it is."

"Ladies and gentlemen," Monsieur Blaise says, stepping up to the podium. "I want to thank you all for coming tonight to the sixty-fifth annual Fae Unseelie Relic Banquet and Ball."

The room responds with a round of applause.

"Many of you have been here before, and it's wonderful to see so many familiar faces in the room. Please drop by our table and say hello to Genevieve and me at some point through the evening. For those of you who are new to the event, welcome."

"Eyes on the crowd, folks," Anyx says over our comms. "Several of the past attacks occurred during opening remarks. Fi? Are you sensing anything?"

I scan the crowd, but nothing seems off.

"Nothing so far," I whisper.

"Unseelie Relics first became a passion of mine as a child of nine," Blaise continues. "My *pépère* came to stay with us and gifted me with this insignia pin."

He straightens and turns so everyone can see it. "It signifies belonging to a band of banished Sluagh Sídhe—an unsanctified group of the dead who fly above the earth, stealing mortals and taking great pleasure in being brutal with them. I, of course, was hooked."

"Of course." I make eyes at Sloan, and he makes them back at me. "Who wouldn't be. Kidnapping, torture, and murder —oh my!"

"Easy, Lady Druid," Garnet says across the room. "Heightened hearing is real. Bottle up that saucy goodness for later, please."

I paste on an innocent smile. "Got it."

"Then, when I was seventeen," Blaise says…

Kill me now.

I scan the room and notice Nikon's downturned mouth. Ha. Someone I can talk to without getting into trouble. *What has you frowning, Greek? Getting a draft up your himation?*

He meets my gaze, and his scowl clears. *Breezes are always welcome.*

Then why the face?

It's probably nothing.

What is?

Dionysus is acting like a dick. He was an ass when I went to pick him up, and he was an ass just now when he hit on Zuzanna.

What? He tried to pick up Zuzanna? Anyx will shred him for that.

That's what I told him, and that's when he upped the dickdom.

Do you think it's still a Loki aftertaste?

Maybe, but he better snap out of it, or this party is going to get violent.

Aren't we the ones paid to ensure it doesn't get violent?

We're getting paid?

Aren't we?

No idea. Anyway. You're the best at wrangling him. I suggest you get out your lasso, cowgirl.

Yee-freaking-haw. I tap Sloan's arm and smile. "I'm going to excuse myself for a moment."

"Is everything all right?"

"There seems to be a problem with the wine master. I should go check—"

"Are we to stand around all night and listen to this drivel?" Dionysus strides out of the shadows from the bar with a bottle of wine in his hand. "Life is too short, Frenchman. Get to the fucking point."

"Oh, crap."

"You embrace the dark side. You have a collection of trinkets that get you off. And you want everyone here to pony up donations because your company is floundering since your brother-in-law started attending high-stakes gambling events and paying for call girls."

There's an overall gasp that escapes the attendees as a collective.

I push off the wall and head straight for my guest. "Sorry for the disturbance everyone, the actors for the interactive Greek tragedy are booked for Saturday night. Someone must've got their wires crossed. Carry on."

I make it to Dionysus' elbow at the same time Nikon grabs him from the other side. "Don't touch me!"

The pulse of magic that erupts from him knocks me back, and it's only because Sloan is tight on my six as backup that I don't end up on the marble floor.

"What the fuck, dude?" Emmet says.

He and Calum pick Nikon up off the tiles as Mr. Stark moves in with his security team. "It's time for you to leave, sir."

"But the party is just beginning." He throws up his palm and the doors all slam shut. At the same time, an almost invisible barrier forms around him. Stark's security men try to get to him, but there's no getting through.

He's like Dr. Who standing in an invisible Tardis. "You know what this circus needs?" he asks. "Animals."

He snaps his fingers, and it takes me a moment to figure out what's happening.

The comforting pressure of Bruin's presence is suddenly gone, and my bear materializes in the middle of the gala. Not just him. Zuzanna, Anyx, Garnet, and Thaos have all shifted and are roaring mad.

"Fuckity-fuck," Dillan says, escorting Eva into our group. "What do we do?"

"Get Dionysus out of here," Da says.

"Bring on the clowns!" Dionysus throws up a hand, and the twenty servers in harlequin costumes start racing around the room bopping people, tossing hors d'oeuvres, and pulling off masks.

The lions are now running between tables, and people are screaming and stampeding in every direction.

"Talk him down, Fi." Da points at where Dionysus is standing in his invisible phone booth, eating popcorn and laughing like a petulant child.

"I'll try. I've never seen him like this." I smack the wall of his barrier, my ring *clinking* against the hard surface as if it were glass. "Dionysus, dude, what the literal hell? Cut it out."

"What? You aren't having fun?"

"No. I'm not. This was an important night for Sloan and Garnet, and you screwed them."

"Screwing people is what I'm all about. Didn't you know that?"

He takes another handful of popcorn from his bucket and turns to watch the mayhem unfold.

Bruin growls, tossing his head wildly as he backs into a table and overturns it.

Are you okay, buddy? What's happening?

I can't get him out of my feckin' head. He's drivin' me mad.

Garnet roars, jumping onto a table, his tail twitching like a whip.

"Dionysus, stop this! You're hurting Bruin. Whatever this is about, you're punishing the people who care about you."

"Not my circus. Not my monkeys. Oh, ha! It *is* my circus." He snaps his fingers, and two dozen people turn into monkeys and leap onto the tables. "And now we have monkeys."

Whoop. Whoop. Whoop.

As the alarm goes off, I curse and try to figure out what else is going wrong. It's hard to tell. There's so much to choose from.

"Sloan!" Dillan shouts, grabbing a monkey off his shoulders. "The relics case behind you is open."

I follow my brother's pointing finger and curse.

"Dammit! We're being robbed."

"Of course we are," Sloan mutters under his breath. "Because what better distraction could there be than this clusterfuck?"

There's no arguing his point. As far as distractions go, I think Dionysus just stole Emmet's crown.

"Boys, focus." Da points at the pedestals. "Someone's after the exhibits."

The siren is blaring, adding to the cacophony.

"Seriously, Dionysus." I bang on the barrier. "Your point is made. Stop this before someone gets hurt."

"Why should I care? Do you think you mean something to me? You and your family have been amusement. A joke. Only you don't realize you're the punchline."

My eyes sting. I can't tell if the tears building are more fury or betrayal, but either way, I refuse to let them fall. "You don't mean that."

"The hell I don't." He lifts the bottle to his lips and drinks. From the bottle...

I push back the mayhem of the moment and take a mental beat. None of this feels right. None of this feels like Dionysus. It hasn't felt like him since we rescued him and brought him home...

He has friends, people he genuinely cares about, and I will destroy those bonds as well as his reputation. The words spoken between Hel and her father ring in my mind, and it all clicks into place.

"Loki." I look at him smiling at the chaos, and I'm more sure than ever. "You bastard. What have you done with Dionysus?"

The man in the invisible box stops laughing and looks at me. "Now you've gone and ruined all our fun."

"Where is he?" I seethe, banging the barrier with both hands. "Give him back to us."

"Not until I've had my fun, which should be in...oh, a thousand years or so."

"You can wipe that smug look off your face, asshole. We'll find him. We won't stop until we do."

He shivers and belly laughs. "I'm shaking in my sandals, little girl. You want him? Come and get him."

CHAPTER TWENTY-ONE

The moment Loki is gone, the monkeys turn back into people, the servers stop acting like clowns, and the Moon Called and other shifter species in the crowd return to their two-footed, elegant forms...except for the ones who apparently can't manifest clothing.

They remain naked.

I run my fingers over my hair and rush to check on Bruin. "Are you okay, buddy?"

He shakes his head and lets out a long growl. "Not even a little. When yer safe at home tonight, I have a lot of pent-up energy to burn off."

"Beware the lady bears of the Don Valley."

"Exactly."

"What the fuck was that?" Garnet grips my shoulder and spins me to look at him.

Bruin launches forward and headbutts him back with a roar.

I hold up my hands and get between them. "Enough. I'm fine. Garnet, I know you lost your hold on things there, but manhandling me in front of Bruin when he's just as wound up isn't going to help."

Garnet tips his head back, and a long, threatening rumble vibrates in my chest. "Someone shut those fucking alarms off."

When he looks at me, his eyes aren't the beautiful amethyst they usually are. They're the solid gold of his animal side.

"First off, I'm sorry you all got drawn into this. Second, you should know it wasn't Dionysus. That was Loki. It's a long story, but Loki and Dionysus have bad blood. Loki's been poisoning him.

"We figured it out, so he kidnapped him to torture. We tracked him down and thought we brought Dionysus home. Only it wasn't Dionysus. It was Loki."

"Fucking tricksters," Garnet snaps. "So, where is he now and where's Dionysus?"

"Loki left as soon as I figured it out. I have no idea where Dionysus is."

"Monsieur Garnet, what in the five realms of evil is going on?"

Garnet shakes his head. "I have no idea. It seems you had a party crasher. Loki of Asgard decided to ruin your ball."

"Why would Loki come to this event?" He glares from Garnet to Anyx to me.

I shrug. "I guess it's a trickster thing. He was here for shits and giggles."

Garnet pegs me with a look and sighs. "Thankfully, Fiona figured it out as quickly as she did. As soon as she confronted him, his fun was over."

"Didn't he arrive with you?" Blaise asks, his gaze narrow.

"Did I bring Loki to your party? No, sir. Absolutely not."

Technically, it was Nikon.

"I had no idea Loki was here until just now when I pieced it together."

"They're gone," Sloan says, jogging back, winded. "Four men in masks raided the cases during the commotion and got away with about half the relics."

"*Mon Dieu*, I'm ruined," Monsieur Blaise says, fanning himself.

"So, is it true?" I ask. "Has Gerald plunged you into bankruptcy?"

Blaise sits, drops his head into his hands, and his wife rushes over to comfort him.

While she talks to him in French, I look around for the rest of my family. "Where is everyone?"

Sloan winks. "I had Stark bug several of the more important pieces without telling anyone on his or Blaise's team. He and yer family are trackin' down the thieves."

"Yay, you. Damn, you're smart, Mackenzie."

"Great work, Sloan." Garnet draws a deep breath beside me and exhales. "I apologize for being rough with you, Fi. As much as it's a slap to my ego, Bruin had every right to knock me flying."

Sloan stiffens and glares at Garnet. "Rough with her? What the hell did ye do?"

"Stand down, hotness. He only gripped my shoulder and wasn't in complete control of his lion. The truth is, Loki revved everyone up specifically to cause dissension. He was trying to alienate us from Dionysus."

"So it's been Loki and not Dionysus all along?"

"It has. Which means we never rescued Dionysus and we still need to find him."

Sloan and I take Ciara and Eva home to our place and I text our change of venue on the family channel so the boys won't worry. I also let them know it was Loki and not Dionysus who caused all this, so they don't stay pissed at the wrong demigod.

"You all seem to be taking this in stride," Eva says. "Does that mean you're highly adaptable or this type of bedlam isn't uncommon?"

"Both." I peel off my heels and tilt my head toward the stairs. "Kev, can you get the ladies a drink? We have to change and go after…" I stop and address Sloan. "Do we go after the robbers first or Dionysus?"

Sloan frowns. "We don't know where to start with Dionysus. We'll catch up with yer brothers and see if we can help there. Then, once that mess is taken care of, we'll have Nikon snap us back to Helheim."

I close my eyes, the pressure in my chest uncomfortable. "I should've known it wasn't Dionysus. How did I miss that?"

Sloan disconnects his tie clip and pulls out his comms. I pull my comms out of my ear and set all of it in a dish on the counter. Grabbing the tea cozy, I set it over the dish. "Big Brother is watching and listening, people. We'll come back for these in a bit."

Upstairs, we make quick work of getting changed, and I hang up my pretty dress and laugh at the slip. I really thought Kev and Ciara screwed me over.

I should've known better.

Apparently, my instincts are seriously out of whack.

"I need to find Dionysus." I pull a t-shirt on and top that with my Team Trouble flak vest. "I should've known, and I didn't, and that's on me."

Sloan finishes with his belt and transfers his wallet and phone from his dress pants to his black jeans. "Ye didn't know. None of us did."

"But I should've." Shame and disappointment sting my eyes and I swipe at the tears. "I'm the closest thing he has to family, and I didn't figure it out. Loki has had him for five days doing gods only know what to him, and he probably thinks we're not coming for him."

Sloan squeezes my shoulders and bends to look me in the eyes. "Fi, one of those days we were actively hunting for him, and almost three of them, you were in a time distortion in a dragon lair. I know ye feel like ye let him down, but ye didn't. Dionysus won't think so either."

I exit the walk-in and splash cold water on my face in the ensuite. After patting my face dry, I push down the melt apart and pull up my big girl pants. "Okay, let's get this done. I don't have time to be dicking around with relic thieves when there are more important issues to deal with. Dionysus is my priority."

"That's perfectly understandable. Let's grab our comms, figure out where everyone is, and join the hunt."

Sloan and I catch up to Clan Cumhaill, Mr. Stark, and Anyx in a full parking lot outside a bar in the Bloor West Village. The two of us weren't able to *poof* right into the heart of the area because this entire eight-block strip of businesses and the surrounding neighborhood is wizard territory, and they've heavily warded it against magical infiltration.

Handy if you want to avoid being surprised by an incoming force. Not so handy if you want to escape one quickly and can't portal out.

"What are we looking at?" I ask when we arrive.

Da and my brothers are still looking dapper in their black-tie duds, but that won't stop them from getting the job done.

"We tracked the relics to this location, but that's where the trail went cold." Da holds up several tiny, round tracking discs. They're clear and sticky and about the size of the end of my pinky finger. "We found these on the sidewalk here."

I look up and down the street and sigh.

Bloor West Village might be known as a small village in a big city but it boasts over four hundred bars, restaurants, shops, and services, including a lively nightlife scene. It's a block from High

Park, home to the High Park Zoo, an amphitheater, and a nature center.

Plenty of places to blend into a crowd.

Our bad guys could be anywhere.

"The good news is, if they came here then found the trackers, they likely aren't far. They can't flash out and probably think they can hunker down and hide until the danger cools down and they can make their escape."

"How do we prove them wrong?" Calum asks. "Canvassing the neighborhood won't do us any good. This is solidly dark wizard territory, and no offense Fi, but you've kind of ensured Cumhaills aren't the most popular faces in these circles."

"True story."

"Luckily, this isn't a popularity contest," Da says.

Luckily is right. I'd never win one.

I'm still considering that when Anyx finishes a call. "What's our move?" I ask as he tucks his phone into his inside jacket pocket.

"That was Garnet. He's been interrogating Blaise and his brother-in-law Gerard. He's confident Blaise isn't behind the robbery but said neither of them seems surprised. The men who run the underground gambling ring in Montreal made it clear they would call in Gerard's debts one way or another."

"Would these men of the Montreal syndicate be dark wizards by any chance?" Da asks.

"It seems so."

Da nods. "Thus the connection to the West Village wizards. Dollars to donuts they've got family or associates here who will help them evade our attempts to bring them to justice no matter what we do."

"Where does that leave us?" I ask.

"Unless one of ye have a bloodhound handy, I don't know that there's much to be done."

"Can't you smell them?" I ask Anyx. "Sorry, I don't mean to

imply you're a bloodhound, but don't Moon Called have heightened senses?"

Anyx doesn't seem offended, which I'm glad about because I've insulted people enough to know I can say things that set people on edge.

"I do have heightened senses, and I might be able to track them as a lion," he says. "But it would be hard to either mask or explain a lion trotting down Bloor Street at eight o'clock on a Thursday night. Also, the only things we have with their scent are the tracker discs, and they wore gloves. Even if I did shift, there's not enough for me to go on."

I draw a deep breath and exhale. I don't have time for this. Dionysus is out there. He needs a rescue. We need to end this. But there's no lead to follow and no way to track a non-existent scent...

"Wait a minute." A shot of adrenaline kicks my brain into high gear. "I don't have a bloodhound, but I do have a bear. Bruin can track scents in his spirit form. Maybe he can find our robbers."

Anyx shrugs. "I told you, Fi, there's not enough scent on these chips for anyone to follow. No disrespect to your bear, but not even he is that good."

"That might be true, but maybe he can track down a different scent...maybe one that might still be lingering on someone's clothes or in an apartment around here...maybe something super skunky from a failed attempt at breaching the vault at STOA."

Calum grins. "The guy Daisy skunked."

I nod. "If the guy got skunked last night, even if he disposed of the clothes, they'd stink for two or three more weeks."

"He's a wizard. He might've taken care of it," Sloan says.

"He might have, but we're druids, and even with Gran's super de-skunking spell, your clothes still have a musky taint."

Anyx nods. "That musk is very distinguishable. It's our best shot."

"Well done, *mo chroi*." Da grins. "Let's give it a try."

I speak to Bruin and explain what he's looking for, releasing him to see if he can track a skunk scent that doesn't belong to an urban skunk in the area. "I think you'll smell it at the entrance of a building, or in a dumpster, or a bag of garbage on the side of the street."

On it. Hold tight. This is a lot of area to cover.

"Good luck, buddy." When he's gone, I nod at the group. "He's off to do his thing."

Emmet is all grins. "If we're lucky, the vault intruder will be a clothes whore like Sloan."

"Who are ye callin' a clothes whore?"

Emmet laughs. "You. If our bad guy *is* as attached to his clothing as Sloan, his outfit might be soaking in his hideout and lead us straight to him."

"Yeah, I vote for that."

While we wait for Bruin to return, I give them a more detailed debrief on what went south at the FUR Ball. All I told them before was that it was Loki and not Dionysus. "Although, I still haven't worked out how that happened or when he took his place."

"Ye say, Hel told Loki to piss off, and he flashed out before ye went into the next room to rescue Dionysus?" Da asks.

"Yeah."

"Well then, Dionysus may never have been there to begin with, or if he was, Loki could've swapped him out before ye came through the door."

"Aye, that's what I figured too," Sloan adds.

I guess that would explain it.

I replay that moment in my head and frown. "It had to have been split second timing. We were through that door quick as a lightning strike."

Da squeezes my arm. "I'm sorry, *mo chroi*. I know ye feel like ye failed him, but there was no way to know what happened until after the fact. Ye figured it out as soon as could be expected."

"We'll agree to disagree on that, but what I haven't figured out is now that we know, how do we find him?"

"Back to Hel?" Nikon asks.

I worry my thumb over my Dionysus pendant and try to breathe past the tightness in my lungs. "Maybe. Although, she didn't seem happy about helping us the first time. I doubt she'll be thrilled about a return plea for assistance."

"It's her father who's behind this," Dillan snaps. "It's because of her affair gone bad Loki's doing it."

"I know. Maybe Hel is the answer. If we don't think of anything better, it's certainly an option."

A gentle breeze swirls around me and lifts my hair. I get my mind back on the case at hand and focus. "Is that you, buddy? Did you find anything?"

Was there any doubt?

I chuckle. "Pardon me for questioning your skills. I'll rephrase. Hey, Bruin, tell me the good news. What did you find?"

Much better. Now, come along, and I'll show you.

Bruin leads our group half a block farther down the street into a dark side alley between two apartment buildings. Both are older brick structures with six floors and no architectural characters—just run-of-the-mill brick rectangles sitting side-by-side.

Red, do ye see the fire escape above Nikon's head?

"Yep. I see it." I point at the metal, extendable ladder and the others follow my pointed finger.

Third floor. Three men. Heavily armed.

I relay that to the group.

Do you want me to take point?

"Is Bruin on point?" I ask.

Anyx and Da lock gazes with one another and nod.

"Aye, that's a good idea," Da says. "Fi and Emmet secure the lobby and the elevators. Mr. Stark and Nikon, yer on the back door. Bruin goes in when Anyx flashes Dillan and Calum up to the balcony to infiltrate the window. Sloan, we're on the stairs. Once we get into the stairwell and ye can see up them, ye'll *poof* me to the third floor to cut off any runners. Understand?"

Everyone nods.

"Good. Safe home, everyone."

Normally, I'd be annoyed about being given the lobby. Yes, I'm a bit of an adrenaline junkie. I also suffer from wicked FOMO. Tonight, I'm happy to cover Emmet's butt. He gets pushed to the safe zone more than the others, and I know it bugs him.

Still, there are moments when his skills are exactly the ones we need to get the job done.

I think about that as the two of us enter the building and get situated. The lobby is what you'd expect from a building of this style and age.

From the entrance, there is a wall of small, brushed-metal doors with numbers engraved on them for mail pickup. The interior is painted cream and could use a little sprucing up. The floor is a mottled brown and beige tile. The two elevators are straight ahead.

Da and Sloan walk in with us and push through the door and into the stairwell.

When we're on our own, Emmet walks over and pushes the call button to bring at least one of the elevators to the ground floor. "If it's down here, we cut the odds they'll jump into one to escape."

"Point to you, Em."

He looks at me with his head cocked to one side. "Are you okay, Fi?"

"I will be once I get Dionysus home."

"We'll get him. We won't stop trying until we do."

"I have an idea about how to locate him, and you're the key to making it work...if it works."

He scans the lobby as the front door opens and two university-aged girls come in with ice caps. They both eye him up, but he's oblivious and solely focused on our conversation. "Name it. I'm in."

Of course, he is. That's Emmet. Always game to try anything to help out.

"I'm not even sure if it's a thing, but—"

A huge feedback spike rings in my ear, and I wince and pay attention to what's being shouted on the comms. "—blew a hole through to the next apartment and bolted out the fire escape over there."

"Oh, crap."

Emmet takes off first, and I follow, exiting the double glass doors right on his heels. He banks left and is in a full run, heading into danger without a second thought.

Reality strikes.

Not only isn't he dressed for this kind of an outing...he has no weapon.

As a cop, Da and all my brothers carry Glocks. When we go out to battle, he has the knives Kevin bought us to carry in our vest. Tonight, he has nothing.

Not even the right shoes.

He reaches the corner of the building before me, takes a quick peek, and he's gone.

For the few racing heartbeats that he's out of my sight, my belly squirms.

Da put me with Em to cover him, and I'm not in a position to do that. Dammit.

I round the corner and—"Freaking hell!"

I drop to the ground as a conjured ball of something disgusting narrowly misses my head. It sails past and hits the side of a van parked against the curb.

Thunk.

I wince as the sphere of wriggle and jiggle detonates and hundreds of spiders scramble and spread. The eight-legged horrors cover the side panel of the van and thoroughly gross me out.

Bruin's roar brings me back into the mix, and I curse the sound—yeah, that will draw attention.

By the time I round the dumpster, Bruin has a man pinned on the ground and is bouncing on his front paws, dropping all his considerable weight on the man's chest like a kid bouncing on the bed.

Emmet is standing beside Sloan, chuckling and looking not only amused but healthy and whole.

Sloan, as always, seems to understand my fear and winks at me, extending his hand. "And a good time was had by all."

"Did you get the ones upstairs?" I ask.

"They did. Anyx called Garnet and asked for a vehicle to use for evacuation. Mr. Stark is assessing the relics, which he believes are all accounted for. And we all live happily ever after."

I smile. "The end."

Emmet laughs at the two of us. "You guys are cute."

I smile up at my guy. "I think so."

"You're lucky, Fi. I honestly didn't think you'd find someone who would get you and all your Fi-ness."

Hilarious.

I've thought the same thing about him for years.

I pat Sloan's chest and wave Calum and Da behind the dumpster to cuff our guy so I can get my bouncing bear out of sight. "There's nothing wrong with my Fi-ness. It's simply an acquired taste."

"Like Brussels sprouts," Emmet says.

I make a face. "Thanks a lot. I'm way better than Brussels sprouts, you jerk."

Sloan chuckles. "Och. No need to fuss, *a ghra*. I love Brussels sprouts."

Da gives us all a look and shakes his head. "Could ye maybe gather yer bear and talk about yer vegetable preferences later when yer at home?"

I chuckle and break away from our convo. "Sure, Da. We're on it."

CHAPTER TWENTY-TWO

O nce Garnet's team arrives, and Anyx and Mr. Stark load the three wizards into the truck, Sloan and Nikon portal everyone home. I check the time on the stove and chuckle. "The night is still young."

"If we weren't a man down, I'd say we should put on some music and have a gala event all our own," Dillan says, striding over to join Eva on the sofa.

"I like the way ye think, D," Sloan says. "Unfortunately, we'll have to postpone our elegant house party in favor of finding our missing mate."

Kevin frowns. "What happened? All we know is that the event went wacky, then Fi sent a text saying it's Loki and not Dionysus, so don't be pissed at the wrong demigod."

I stride over to the living room bar and grab the open bottle of Redbreast whiskey and a few tumblers. As I catch everyone up on what went down tonight and what we think it means, I pour a few rounds and we start to shake off a bad night.

"Fi thinks she has an idea," Emmet says on the second round of pours. "You mentioned my abilities being useful. What were you thinking?"

I pull my Dionysus pendant out from under my t-shirt. "Dionysus gave me this to call him if I need him. Merlin powered it as a pendulum for a locator spell and we thought we found him, but what about calling him here? Could Emmet's buffer powers increase my pull of needing him enough to bring him home?"

We all look at Sloan for an answer because he's the most knowledgeable of all of us on druid things. Except, he doesn't look very hopeful. "I can't see that workin', luv. I'm sorry. Yer suggestin' that we could overpower whatever hold Loki has on him. Even with Emmet's buffer ability, he's not stronger than a demigod."

"Then what do we do? He's been a prisoner since Sunday. We have to get him home."

Nikon frowns. "There's still Hel."

"Yeah. Maybe she's our only shot in this."

"May I make a suggestion?" Eva raises her hand to ask. "I know I'm new to the group, and I don't pretend to know your strengths or limitations, but I have a thought."

I open my palms to her and smile. "Please. We always have an open floor for ideas and opinions."

"What are you thinking, angel?" Dillan asks.

She looks around at all the expectant gazes, and her cheeks flush pink. "I think Fi's idea to use Emmet's power-boosting abilities is a good one, but Sloan's right. It's doubtful you'd be able to negate Loki's hold on a prisoner."

"So, where does that leave us?"

"Well, every pantheon has a distinct power signature whether fae or Greek or Norse or celestial or other."

"Right."

"My thinking is that since Dionysus is a demigod himself, holding him prisoner would be causing a large flux of both Greek and Asgardian power in the same location. Dionysus will be trying to escape, and Loki is likely exhausting power to keep him."

I brighten. "I'm with you. Go on."

"So, perhaps if you search for that clustered power output instead of the man himself, you might be able to pinpoint where Dionysus is and go to him."

"How do we focus the spell?" Sloan asks.

"You'd need something from each of them that carries their power. Fiona's pendant was a gift from Dionysus, powered to notify him when you need him. That carries his energy. If you have something of Loki's, you could bind the two power signatures and work on tracking down your location."

I blink and look at Sloan for confirmation.

"In theory, it makes perfect sense. The problem is finding something that carries Loki's magical signature. It's not like he left us with anything of himself."

Something of Loki's...

Right. It's not like he gave me a pendant to call him.

"Maybe that's where Hel comes in." Ciara finishes her drink and sets her glass on the end table beside the loveseat. "She's Loki's daughter. She carries his magical signature."

"Nice one, babe." Emmet kisses her temple.

"Yeah, good thought. Okay, Nikon, can you please try to convince Hel to help us? Emmet, you'll probably have to go too since you're our hellhound whisperer."

"I'll go too," Aiden says. "I don't like the idea of Em facin' that beast alone again."

"While you're gone, the rest of us will work on devising a spell to bind the power signatures and track the spot of output."

Nikon, Aiden, and Emmet break to grab their winter jackets and snap off to Greenland. I run up to collect my laptop, and when I return to the kitchen, I open a video call with Gran and Granda, hoping they can fill in the blanks.

"Sloan is pretty sure he knows how to amplify the spell to act as a locator but isn't sure how to bind two power signatures from two different pantheons."

"How comprehensive is yer apothecary, luv?" Gran flips through her spellbook. "Do ye have the ingredients fer *Effuse* and *Enfetter*?"

"I'm not sure. What would I need?"

Gran holds the page up to the camera and Sloan frowns at the ingredients list.

"No. I've only grown or gathered half of those."

"That's fine. Let's see what else we can find."

While they work on that, Anyx drops Da off, and he joins the meeting of the minds. "What about dactylomancy?" he asks Granda. "The practice is deeply rooted in the Greek pantheon. If we could find an ancient ring or set of rings, maybe Nikon could enhance their power to seek out Dionysus."

Granda scratches his head. "That's not technically what they were for."

"I understand that, but in theory, they might pick up his signature."

"In theory."

"I thought we were using my pendant," I say. "What is dactylomancy? It sounds Jurassic. Does it have anything to do with pterodactyls?"

"No, *mo chroi*. And we *are* usin' yer pendant, but once we find the signature, we need to bind it. The power transfer of yer pendant is supposed to send a message out into the world and let Dionysus know yer callin' him. My hope is the dactylomancy rings will lock onto that signature and allow Nikon to snap to that location."

"Think of it like going fishin', luv," Granda says. "Usin' the magic of divination rings is like attaching a barbed hook to the end of yer call. Instead of simply pingin' him and yer call dissolvin' as a message sent, if Niall is right, yer hook would attach to the energy signature and give ye a destination to reel yerselves toward."

"Okay, I get it. It's like how the divining rod dragged Emmet through the forest to the source of the ley lines when we first started."

Calum laughs. "More importantly, dragged his junk through the poison ivy."

"Hey, Ciara, how's the rash on Em's man bits?" Dillan asks. "All cleared up now?"

Ciara rolls her eyes. "He's right. Yer both eejits."

That just makes them laugh harder.

Ignoring the peanut gallery, I go back to the next problem. "The next question is, where do we find dactylomancy rings?"

Sloan shakes his head. "I don't have any and Blaise didn't have any in his collection. Since they were most popular in the Greek and Roman eras, maybe Andromeda or Nikon know where to find some?"

"Where to find what?" Nikon asks, snapping in with Emmet and Hel in tow.

"Dactylomancy rings," Sloan says. "We have the budding of a plan, but we're not sure where or how to find them."

Nikon chuckles. "That's not an issue. Between Andromeda and Politimi, I think they have like thirty. How many do you want for your plan?"

Da looks first at Granda, then at Sloan. "One fer each of us while we cast the spell would be ideal."

Nikon nods. "I'll text them and borrow a dozen. If we need more, we've got them."

"If they aren't busy, I would love to see your sisters," Hel says. "Would you ask them to join us and say hello?"

Nikon smiles. "I'm sure if they're around, they will. I'll ask and be right back."

When he snaps out, it strikes me that I haven't hugged him lately and truly expressed how amazing I think he is. Nikon is always here to help. He snaps us all over the world on errands, missions, and misadventures. And he never complains or asks for anything in return.

I make a mental note to award Nikon an Oh Henry! bar when all this settles down.

Until then, I've got my eye on the finish line—bringing Dionysus home.

It's hard to fathom the daughter of Loki standing in my living room, but here she is. "Thank you for coming. Can I get you a drink while we wait?"

"Do you have any mead?"

"We do." Sloan straightens from the laptop. "I'll run downstairs and fill a horn. Back in a flash."

Fill a horn? Hubba-wha?

A flash is right. I have no idea where he's going, but it isn't downstairs.

"You don't have mead, do you?"

I shrug and shake my head. "Not that I know of, but hey, he surprises me every day, so maybe he has a secret stash. I have no idea."

Hel's stern scowl softens a little. "He's a good man, and he obviously adores you."

"He is, and yes, he does. There's no explaining it."

"Look at you," Andromeda says, snapping in with Nikon and Politimi. "Hel, you look amazing."

Hel turns to greet Nikon's sisters and her stern disposition softens even more. "As do you both. It has been much too long."

Nikon's sisters are the visual representation of sweet delight and endless night. Andromeda is a lovely blonde with a warmth she spreads over everyone she encounters. Politimi is dark-haired with a pall of Gothic gloom and antisocial annoyance for any who dare look at her.

I leave them to catch up and check in with Nikon. "Did they have some of the rings?"

He holds up a Ziploc bag of ancient relics and shakes it to make them jingle. "Like I told you. They have a bunch."

"They keep them in a sandwich bag?"

"No. That's what I grabbed for transport."

I chuckle and look them over. Simple silver bands lay clustered along the bottom of the plastic bag, their surfaces either worn smooth or carved with basic engravings and runes. "So, these are the mood rings of ancient Greece, are they?"

"That's them."

I smile over at his sisters chatting with Hel, and I'm pleased that not only did Politimi come, but she's smiling. It's a little unnerving.

"What's the look, Red?"

I shrug. "Nothing. I've simply never seen Politimi smile. I don't think she likes me much."

"That's an understatement. She hates you." He catches my reaction to that and laughs. "Don't take it personally. She hates everyone. Although, you didn't help your case by goring me with Birga."

"The memory of that still makes me sick."

Nikon wraps an arm around my shoulders and tilts his head against mine. "I'm fine. I forgave you before I even collapsed. Yet here we are in the chaos of yet another trickster."

"Yeah. I've gotta say, I'm not a fan."

"No. Most people aren't."

"Here ye are," Sloan says, striding in with a large, polished horn in his hand.

Hel steps back and reaches for what he offers. "In an auroch horn too. Your offering is well received, druid."

Sloan stands straighter and is pretty much busting his designer buttons. "Is there anything I can get fer the lovely Tsambikos sisters?"

Andy chuckles. "Whatever's going. Wine? Beer? A Cosmo? Whatever is handy."

"We have margaritas," Ciara says.

"Perfection. I have a feeling if Loki's stirring up trouble, we should all be drinking."

Hel laughs and takes a deep swallow from the rim of her horn. When she eases back from it, she nods at Sloan. "It's very good."

Sloan nods and leaves them to their visit.

When they've gone back to their conversation, I tug on Sloan's shirt. "What is happening? Since when do we have mead and Norse horns?"

Sloan sobers. "I have contacts. The point is Loki's daughter is in our home and helping us with a problem that has no current relevance to her. In the spirit of the whole strength in unity motto of late, I thought it best to make powerful friends whenever possible."

I cast a sideways glance at Nikon and shrug. "It's hard to argue with that."

Nikon chuckles and holds up the rings again. "That's our Irish. Always thinking."

Sloan grumbles at us, but there's no heat in his expression. He knows we're kidding and we adore his intellectual prowess.

"We better get focused before the mead and margaritas start influencing the night," Nikon says.

"Good point. Let's see if Da and Granda have come up with a solution on how to set the hook."

The plan is all worked out, but by the time Da and Granda finish explaining what needs to happen and how it works, I'm utterly lost. Most days, I think I've got a solid handle on all things druid. Then, a moment like this arises, and I realize I'm still only a junior in druid magic next to Granda, Da, Sloan…and of course, Merlin.

Thankfully, I don't need to understand *how* it's supposed to work, only what I'm supposed to do. Which is almost nothing. Yay, me!

Winner!

Sloan and Nikon will be the stars of this show.

We druids will each wear a Greek mood ring and funnel Sloan as much power as we can. Then, he'll cast the spell to throw our metaphorical fishing line into the pond where Loki is holding Dionysus.

Then Nikon will power the transport.

The tricky part is that Nikon won't know where we're going, and that's a key element of his portaling ability.

Granda assures me that with Hel's connection with Loki, our combined intention, and Emmet power-boosting the whole shebang, Nikon won't need to know where we're going. The spell will set the destination. I hope they're right.

Nikon doesn't seem so sure.

I don't want to waste any more time *not* rescuing Dionysus.

Still, ten minutes after the explanation ends, those who need to use the bathroom before the trip have gone, my armor is up, we've drawn our weapons, and everyone in our circle of travelers is wearing the pterodactyl rings.

Da points at me to start the kickoff. "Fi, when Emmet's ready, press yer pendant and call to Dionysus like you normally would. Sloan, off we go."

I hold the pendant between my finger and thumb, and Sloan squeezes my hand. "Don't look so worried, *a ghra*. This will work. Intention is everythin'."

I want to mention that intention isn't everything if we haven't got the spell right, but that sort of defeats the entire thought behind intention is everything, so I stuff a sock in it and think happy-happy successful thoughts.

Sloan and Da start reciting the spell, which is in Irish, and unfamiliar, so I tune it out. I have complete faith that they know what they're doing.

Emmet rubs his thumb up and down the wrist of my pendant-pressing hand. I know he's nervous, but I have faith in him too. He amazes me every day.

After a moment, he squeezes. "Okay, let's do this."

I suck in a deep breath, close my eyes, and press.

CHAPTER TWENTY-THREE

The power surge that sweeps us into the distance is dizzying. I'm not sure if it's Emmet's boost or Da and Sloan's spell added to Nikon's portal snap or what, but the ride is short and ends with a stinging whip across my skin and a whorl of my anxiety flipping in my belly.

"Och, feckin' hell." Ciara winces and probes her bare arm. "That is unpleasant."

I'm about to respond when my surroundings kick in, and I drop my pendant. Gripping Birga's staff, I ready for the incoming assault.

If the Greek rings were our fishhook, we just landed the big one. We're standing in the dark dampness of a medieval dungeon with a maze of crumbling corridors snaking off in every direction.

There are a few sporadically spread torches keeping things from being pitch dark, but even still, a couple of us pull out our phones to give us more to go on.

The muffled sounds of male voices bouncing off stone walls and the agonizing screams of prisoners raise goosebumps on my arms. There's too much echo stimulation to pinpoint which way it's coming from.

"Do we split up?" Emmet asks.

I turn to Dillan. "What's coming up on your radar? Have you got anything?"

Dillan's cloak of knowledge is on, and his hood is up. He frowns as another round of howling hits us and closes his eyes. He grows annoyingly still, and my anxiety dials up a notch. I'm sure it's only a few seconds, but it feels like an eternity.

If that's Dionysus crying out, Loki has tortured him like that for four days and nights.

"This way," Dillan says. "It's a bit confusing, but I think that's because there's more than one option."

"My father has always found rats in a maze to be quite amusing," Hel says. "For what it's worth, I'm truly appalled he's done this to Dionysus. I never wanted him punished for not having feelings for me."

"Fathers will go to great lengths to protect their children," Da says. "I suppose for a man who is morally ambiguous, that opens the door to more options."

I grip Birga tighter.

My arms are trembling, and I'm not sure if it's desperation or fury that's giving me the shakes.

We're coming, Tarzan. Hang on.

We snake our way through the stone tunnels quickly and quietly, eight druids, a Greek immortal, and a Norse demigoddess. With every turn and corridor taken, the male voices get louder and clearer.

So do the moaning cries.

When we're finally close enough that we're approaching Loki's minions, Dillan raises his arm, closes his fist, and stops us at an intersection of tunnels.

His lips move in silent speech and I feel the tingle of his spell settle over us—a privacy spell.

"We've arrived at our destination," he says. "Please take note of your surroundings and take everything with you as you disembark."

Da scans the last hall separating us from the men beyond. "Once we round that corner, I have a feelin' we'll be knee-deep in it. Fi, release Bruin and ask him to get us the lay of the land."

Did you hear that, buddy? Da needs to know what we're walking into.

On it.

"Okay, he's on the clock."

"He better not take them all down." Dillan draws his dual daggers. "I've been itching to cull my way through a hostile crowd."

"For Dionysus' suffering," Calum says. "Let's make them hurt."

Da frowns. "Don't ever let anger make ye forget what we stand fer, boys and girls. Revenge is poison. We're here fer a purpose. We'll rescue Dionysus and end Loki's ideas of justice. We don't kill unless there's no other option. Our strength comes from our connection to nature."

"Tell that to Killer Clawbearer." Emmet scowls.

Da grunts. "Bruin has lived a long time and weighs his own choices. If ye need a conscience, I'm right here. Now, get yer minds off brutal violence and get right and tight, or the three of ye will be benched and sittin' out."

"Fine," Dillan snaps. "But I'm not going to be nice about it."

"Fair enough." Da swings his gaze to me. "What's your shield sayin', *mo chroi?*"

"Nothing so far. S'all good."

Bruin breezes back and materializes among us. "Six men are standing guard at this end of the corridor and four at the other. There are eight cells, each with a captive in one form of torture or another. All with black bags over their faces. All in different states of bloodied and battered."

"So you can't tell where Dionysus is?" I ask.

"No. I can't see, and the stench of blood and excrement is so strong, I can't smell him either."

Da waves that away. "Then we free them all and sort it out when the dust settles. Bruin, take position in the center of the corridor and charge the four at the far end. That will turn the other six away from us and give us a chance to attack from behind."

"Yes, Da."

"Sloan, once ye get around the corner, take Dillan and Ciara and portal to the far end to fight. Aiden, Calum, and I will take the closer group. Nikon, Emmet, and Fi, yer on freein' the prisoners and findin' Dionysus. Hel, if ye wish to get involved, I ask that ye handle yer father if that's possible."

Hel's scowl is deadly. "Oh, I'll handle him, all right."

Da smiles at us all. "Safe home, everyone. Watch yer backs and the back of the person next to ye. Now, off we go."

Two seconds after Bruin disappears and spirits off, there's a wild roar, and the chaos detonates. Sloan swings around the corner to look down the hall and holds his hand out for Dillan and Ciara. They *poof* off almost instantly. At the same time, Da, Aiden, and Calum charge the ones staring at Bruin, and Nikon, Emmet, and I start running along the stone walls, going for the cell doors.

While Emmet and I use our magic to unlock the prison cells, Nikon looks in the peek window and snaps in without effort.

Handy.

The first man I encounter is black and long dead. I don't even bother taking off the bag over his head because who needs that image in their mind.

Emmet has the second cell. I glance in quickly as I'm passing, but it's not Dionysus. Still, he's getting him unshackled and easing him to the stone floor.

I rush to the third cell and press my palm against the locking pad. *"Open Sesame."*

Bruin's right. The stench of bodily fluids is rife in the air. I suppose there's no getting away from that if someone is alive and chained to a wall.

"Dionysus?" I'm halfway across the disgusting space when I realize this can't be Dionysus. He's not tall enough and has too much of a beer belly. He shrinks back as I approach and I realize he has no idea who's coming at him.

It wouldn't be much better if he could see me either. I release Birga and my body armor and approach slowly. "My name is Fiona. I'm going to remove the bag from your head, and we're going to get you out of here."

I do as I say and meet the man's terrified gaze.

"You're going to be okay. My family will make sure of it." I unlock his shackles and barely catch him as he sinks to the ground. "Rest here. We'll come back for you once we've finished with the guards."

I don't know if he's hearing me or not, but he makes no effort to respond. I leave him and return to the hall.

Emmet is coming out of the next room and has to duck as Bruin tosses a guard through the air. I check the status of the battle. Clan Cumhaill has their groove on, and things are well in hand.

"You good, Em?"

My brother glances over his shoulder and gives me a nod. "Yep. Still not him though."

I move to the last door on this side of the hallway while Nikon snaps some poor soul out to the hall and rushes to the last door on the opposite side.

"He has to be here," I say, panic starting to set in. "Please, Earth Mother, please let him be here."

Nikon winks and nods. "Let's do this."

The two of us take the last cells by storm, and I gasp at the battered body hanging by bloody wrists. The poor man has knives and daggers stuck into him, and my heart sinks. If he's human, he's dead.

If he's Dionysus... Holy schmoly, Loki's turned him into a living pincushion.

I raise my palm and throw a ball of faery fire at the bindings hanging him from the ceiling. While that's burning through, I reach up and untie the black bag. The damage done turns my stomach. I'm torn.

I'm half-hoping it's him and half-hoping it's not.

Pulling the bag free, I gasp and cup his beautiful square jaw in my hands, tears welling.

"Got him!" Nikon and I both yell at the same time.

I look back toward the open door, and across to the cell opposite the one I'm in. "What? Are you sure?"

Nikon looks at his prisoner and back at me and mine. "What the fuckity-fuck is happening?"

I look at my Dionysus, and he offers me a soft smile. "I knew you'd come, Jane."

"Of course," I say, my mind spinning. Straightening, I catch Nikon's attention. "Bring him in here."

Nikon snaps his Dionysus into the same cell, next to mine. "They're identical."

Same injuries. Same loose brown curls matted with blood. Same glassy, swirling silver eyes.

"Plot twist," Emmet yells, scowling at the two of them. "Hel, is Loki into cloning?"

"Not that I know of," she shouts from the hall.

I sigh. "But we know Loki likes to play dress up and steal someone else's life."

Hel rounds the corner and lets out a string of curses in a language I don't recognize. "Whatever you think you're doing, Father. Stop. This is beyond screwed up."

Both Dionysus prisoners look up at me like they're confused.

"Why would Loki stay and pretend to be Dionysus?" Emmet asks. "The jig is up."

Hel grins, and it's more than a little creepy. "I'm jamming his powers and blocking his exit. Fool me once; shame on you. There won't be a twice. Screw you too."

Ha! I like her.

"First things first," I say, eyeing up the damage. "Take the blades out and let the healing begin. Porcupine isn't a good look for him."

Calum and Nikon work on the other Dionysus, and Emmet and I start pulling hilts and freeing my guy from the torture he's been suffering.

Once that's done, Hel comes in and looks them both over. "They are visually indistinguishable."

"Maybe, but there's only one Dionysus. No matter how your father looks, he'll never be more than an imperfect replica."

"Thank you, Jane," Nikon's guy says.

My guy frowns and looks at me. "He's lying, Jane. I'm your Dionysus."

I study them as they talk to me and I can't tell. Dammit. What kind of friend am I that I can't tell them apart? "For my birthday, you filled the pinata with—"

"Sex toys," Nikon's guy says.

"Where did we meet for the first time?

"Hecate's temple," my guy says.

Dammit. I have no idea how long Loki's been watching Dionysus or what he might know or not know. How do I prove who's who?

Then it hits me.

"Help them stand." I think my idea through. Yeah, this could work. "Dionysus is the god of sexy schmexy. Each of you is going to kiss me, and I'll know who is the god of ecstasy."

Sloan and my father both frown, but I hold up my finger. "Who's first?"

"Me," Nikon's guy says. He cradles my face with his hands, moves in, and lays one on me. I feel the surge of his energy as he tries to sweep his tongue into my mouth, and I refuse to give him the access he wants.

Straightening, I end the kiss and face my guy. "Your turn, Dionysus number two. Time for a lip lock."

"Ew. You're not going to make me do this, are you? You promised you'd never try to seduce me. What happened to no kissing, no sex, no nakedness?"

I chuckle. "I hate to tell you, but you're naked."

He glances down, and a pair of boxers appear across his hips. "Friends don't flaunt their junk in front of friends, right?"

"Exactly right. Have I found the real you, Tarzan?"

He holds up his pinky, and I lock it with mine. "In the Cumhaill family, there is no breaking an oath of a pinky swear. I am me."

I throw my arms around him and kiss his cheek. "And there is only one you."

My celebration is short-lived because the moment Loki realizes he's beat, his illusion drops, and he's glaring at us. "How dare you involve yourselves in my business, little girl. This is a family matter."

"Exactly right," Da snaps, pushing forward. "Ye targeted one of our own, and our family put a stop to it. If Dionysus did yer daughter wrong, that's up to them to sort out. Ye overstepped, and one look at yer daughter will tell ye she doesn't appreciate it. Now, if ye don't mind—and even if ye do—we'll leave ye to work out yer family issues."

Hel looks us over and shrugs. "I apologize for all of this. Don't worry. This is over. I'll make sure of it."

Da slides an arm under one of Dionysus' shoulders, and I get his other side. Together, we exit the cell and leave Hel and Loki to sort themselves out.

When the dust settles, everyone calls it a night and heads to their respective homes. It's late. It's been an emotional and adrenaline-filled night. And as basic as it sounds, all is well that ends well.

"I'm almost afraid to believe it's over," Dionysus says after he snaps his fingers and his loft is set back to its original state.

"It's only been a few hours. Sloan and I can stay if you want... or just me. I'm happy to crash and keep you company while you heal."

He looks down at himself and shrugs. "One of the perks of being a god. I'm all healed up."

On the outside, maybe, but I know him, and he's hurting. Loki humiliated him, hurt him, and shook the very foundation he set his life's truths on.

This will take time to get over.

"I have an idea." I check my watch and sigh. "It's now Friday morning. We're all bagged and likely taking a three-day weekend. Come crash with us, and we'll have a PJ movie marathon—some *Die Hard, Lord of the Rings, Deadpool*. Then you won't have to be here by yourself. You'll be with people who love you."

His grin tells me that I hit a home run with that one. "There's only one problem, Jane."

"What's that?"

"I don't own PJs."

I pull up my phone and Google adult onesies. "Here, look. You can be a dinosaur, or a shark, or a bear with cute little ears. Here are sports teams and lumberjack plaids, and unicorns and pandas. Whatever you want."

"Can I pick for everyone?"

I chuckle. "I'm sure, under the circumstances, everyone would let you pick."

"Will you sleep on the couch bed with me and snore like you did last time?"

I burst out laughing. "I don't snore."

He and Sloan both burst out laughing.

"Okay, I don't snore unless I'm exhausted."

Sloan nods. "All right. I'll give ye that."

Sliding my phone back into my pocket, I hold out my hand. "What do you say? Weekend sleepover?"

He takes my hand and nods. "Sloan, if I get you a bunny pajama with floppy ears, you'll wear it, right?"

Sloan's mouth falls open, and I giggle. "You bet he will. What happens on a onesie weekend stays at the onesie weekend."

"Excellent. I think I'm a unicorn."

I laugh. "You definitely are."

CHAPTER TWENTY-FOUR

We lounge around like shut-ins for all of Friday and half of Saturday before Nikon gets a text from his sister wondering where he is. I pause the *Santa Clarita Diet* marathon while he takes the call.

"Do you have to get back to reality?" I ask.

He extricates himself from the mountain of pillows on the floor and gets up. He's wearing a giraffe onesie, and when his hood is up, he has little brown ears flopping off the side of his head. "Hel's at my place and wanted to know if she could come over and talk."

I check in with Dionysus to gauge his reaction. He's got Daisy curled up in his lap and looks as content as she does. "Of course. That's fine with me."

I giggle at us. "Are we presentable?"

Dionysus eases the black and white ball of fur onto a stack of blankets and flips back the covers. "Hel has seen me at my best and worst. I don't think me wearing a unicorn onesie will make much of an impression."

I grin at Sloan in the panda jammies Dionysus settled on for him and chuckle. "Then I guess we have company."

Sloan widens his eyes and glances around at the mayhem of an all-out adult slumber party. "Can we at least meet her upstairs where we can see the floor?"

"Deal," Nikon says. "Meet you up there in two."

When he snaps out, I scan the rest of the room. "If you need bio-breaks, food runs, or any other interruptus type events, do that now. You have fifteen minutes."

Calum laughs and hands Kevin the bowl of Doritos. "Now she's even scheduling our free time."

Kev takes the bowl, sets it down, and pulls Calum to his feet. "Come with me, fiancé. I have a surprise I want to show you in the apothecary room."

Emmet snorts. "When a man says he's got a surprise to show you—it's his penis."

"Yes!" Calum laughs. "Just what I was hoping for."

Sloan looks horrified. "Stay away from the plants under the sun lamp on the back wall. Very bad things will result if you touch them with bare skin."

I laugh and look at Em and Ciara snuggled up in the oversized club chair. Picking up a blanket off the floor, I toss it over them. "Looks like you've got the room. Fifteen minutes—and no sexy cop stripper moments."

Emmet laughs. "It'll take us fifteen minutes to get out of these onesies."

I wave over my head. "Whatevs. You do you. I don't want to know how that looks."

Sloan, Dionysus, and I jog up the stairs and find our Nikon giraffe in the living room. Hel turns to look at us, and I'm not sure if she looks more confused or amused. "What have I interrupted?"

I chuckle, swinging side to side so that my dragon tail swishes behind me. "Dionysus had never had a pajama day movie marathon. In honor of his homecoming, he got to pick the PJs."

Her smile is thoughtful. "That's nice of you to succumb to his whims."

I laugh. "It was my idea. No succumbing was necessary. So, do you want to steal him away to chat?"

She looks at Dionysus, and her smile dims. "No. I didn't come to tear you away from fun with your family. I wanted an opportunity to apologize for my father and all the trouble he caused."

Dionysus closes the distance between the two of them and sighs. "It's me who should apologize, Hel. I didn't know…I didn't understand what you felt for me. I thought we were having fun. All I knew throughout my entire existence until now was how to live on the surface of emotions. Your father was right to be angry. I didn't value you or your worth. I was oblivious."

Hel looks at us and shakes her head. "Who would've believed that the first woman Dionysus would fall in love with isn't even a romantic interest?"

Dionysus turns to me and smiles. "Fi and her family have taught me so much about myself, and my relationships, and the things I value. If I were the kind of man to fall for a woman and be overtaken by love, you would be that woman."

"But you're not," she says.

"At least not yet. Maybe in another decade or century or longer, I'll be that guy, but for now, it's all Greek to me." He looks over his shoulder and waggles his brow. "Did you see what I did there?"

I circle my finger and point for him to give Hel his attention.

"Right, sorry. So, here I am, a work in progress. I'm a man learning what love and responsibility and family are all about. I have great teachers, and I'm hopeful when I've learned life's lessons, I'll be a better person."

Hel steps in to kiss his cheek. "You're already a better person. This life looks good on you. If you ever want to branch out your friendships, look me up. I'd like to know this new version of Dionysus."

"I would like that. Thank you for not hating me."

She shrugs. "Can you hate a cloud for raining or lightning for striking? You were always true to who you are. It's wonderful that you found a family to love you because of that and not despite it."

He winks at me and smiles at Sloan. "Yes, it is."

She takes a step back and holds her hand out to Nikon. "I've said what I came to say. If you don't mind, I'd like to go home to my realm. At least there, I understand what's going on around me."

When Nikon snaps out with Hel, I hug Dionysus. "You did good, Tarzan. You should totally go to Greenland in a few months and take her a small gift and mend that fence."

He squeezes me once and eases back. "I didn't even realize I'd broken the fence. How many others did I trample over in the name of a good time?"

"The important thing to remember," Sloan says, "is that yer immortal, so ye have time to reflect and hopefully correct yer mistakes. Makin' amends is another of life's lessons that comes with carin' fer people."

Dionysus breathes deep and exhales. "That might be a very long list of people I need to reconnect with."

I side-hug him and lean my head on his arm. "It's not always easy to love someone exceptional. Especially someone who's on a path of massive life growth."

"Preach." Sloan grins at me.

I laugh at his use of jargon as Nikon returns. "What? Are you pointing at me, Mackenzie?"

"If the analogy fits…"

"But I'm easy to love."

He chuckles. "Yer easy to love, yes, but ours is not the easiest love to manage. Ye mentioned a path of massive life growth. I don't know if ye realize it or not, but yer life is a bit of a train wreck most days."

I open my mouth to argue, but I've got nothing. "Train wrecks can be fun."

Nikon screws up his face. "Not usually, no."

I laugh and head over to the fridge. "Come help me make sandwiches. Everyone's getting hungry again."

I no sooner say it when two platters of sandwiches and wraps appear next to a platter of cheese and veggie nibbles. I arch a brow at Dionysus. "Thank you, but you don't need to do that. We're capable of making meals."

Dionysus picks up one of the platters. Sloan and Nikon follow suit with the others. "But this way, we stick to our allotted break schedule and get back to being lazy faster."

I laugh, leaning over the railing at the top of the basement stairs. "Incoming. Put everything away that's not fit for sibling viewing."

———

When Merlin texts me that he's arrived home and Dart is on his way, I grab the weekend treats for the grove fae and head out to the back yard. The warmth of the summer day is dissipating with the coming of dusk, but the air is still a bit humid. I breathe deep and feel the influx of ambient power that fills my lungs.

It's amazing to have the added trees since the expansion of the backyard grove. Now that Pip and Nilm are expecting, our fae friend numbers will be expanding as well.

I stroll through the trees, delivering the snacks to those who care to receive them. After setting out a bounty of fresh berries for Flopsy and Mopsy, I give the deer a new salt lick. I open the bag of cookies and pull the tray free, setting it on the big rock near the hot spring pool. Then, I unclip the jumbo bag of Chicago mix and set it at the base of Pip's and Nilm's new tree nest.

It still makes Sloan crazy that we're corrupting the nutrition of our fae family, but hey, no one else is complaining. The fae love it.

I don't call up to our brownies to let them know the junk food is here. Emmet says Pip isn't enjoying her pregnancy and Nilm is worried she's not resting enough. I leave them to discover their treats on their own and set out a few handfuls for anyone else who wants them.

I sense more than hear when my blue boy arrives.

"Nest, sweet nest," Dart says behind me.

I turn as the mirage of my back fence wavers and dissolves, and my dragon appears. "Great job on the glamor, buddy. You nailed it."

His toothy grin tells me how proud he is of himself.

He should be. It's well-deserved.

"One step closer to you having more freedom to explore life here in the city."

He lowers his chin and sizes down from his super-sized flight mode. "I can't say I missed the city while I was away, but it's wonderful to get home to you and the grove and my friends. Oh, and I like your costume. Is that a testament to you missing me?"

I chuckle and give him a runway turn of me as a blue dragon. "I absolutely missed you. Dionysus picked the dragon duds, but I thought it was a great choice. A week was a long time to be away from you."

He nods. "I missed you too. Although, it was a wonderful week away. Bryvanay taught me aerial maneuvers and dives, Utiss and I worked on fighting with my tail, and Empress Cazzienth taught me ancestral fireside songs at night."

"Wow. I can't wait to see and hear all those things. What about Saxa? You didn't mention her. Did you have a nice time with her?"

A soft purr vibrates from his chest. "Saxa was as lovely as always. She's kind and patient, and we spent a lot of time flying together."

The affection in his voice is obvious. My boy has got it bad for that yellow dragon. "Saxa is a very special lady dragon. You're fortunate to have her in your life, and she's equally fortunate to have you in hers."

He nods. "While I was with the Iceland dragons, I thought about what you said before about spending time with Scarlett and my brood. You were right. I *should* spend time with them. Maybe I can teach them some of the things I've learned from the Iceland dragons."

"That's an amazing idea. When I was there this week, Patty mentioned most of the Westerns are now able to size up for flight. The Perry twins have been working with Merlin to get them used to saddles, but they can't glamor yet."

"Then we should definitely spend time there. Maybe Utiss and Bryvanay would visit and teach them as they taught me."

I scrub a hand over the rough scales of his cheek. "That's a great idea. I'll be sure to speak to Merlin about it the next time we talk."

Dart yawns, his mouth stretching wide, his long, dagger teeth glistening in the afternoon sun. "I also missed my nest."

"I'm sure you did. We're having a lazy, stay-at-home weekend. Why don't you have a nap and I'll check on you after dark?"

"Perfect." He turns toward the trees but then turns back and licks my cheek. "You know where to find me if the world goes crazy and you need help."

I smile, content to watch him waddle deeper into the trees in the direction of his beloved nest. "I love you too, buddy. Now, snuggle in and get some rest. You never know what tomorrow might bring."

By the time I get back inside, Dillan has arrived with Evangeline, and everyone has moved upstairs to the living room to visit.

Thankfully, they're all still in their onesies so I don't feel like a goof in front of Dillan's new girlfriend.

"Welcome back," I say, joining the conversation. "I worried that after Thursday night we might've scared you off."

Eva's cheeks dimple as she smiles at Dillan. "Oh, no. I don't scare so easily."

I'm not sure what the underlying context is, but it's obviously a private joke between her and my brother.

Dillan winks at her and addresses the room. "I was telling everyone that when Eva and I returned from our walk in the woods just now, Mrs. Graham across the road caught us for a chat."

"Did she make a pass at you in front of your girlfriend?" Emmet laughs. "She's had the hots for him since he built her fence for college money."

Eva chuckles. "Fit men wielding hammers and glistening in the summer sun do have a certain lure to them."

"Bow-chicka-wow-wow," Kevin says.

I laugh. "I love that song. Yes, Eva's right."

"All right." Dillan waves his hands to stop the chit-chat. "Can we focus, please?"

"Sorry, D," Emmet says without an ounce of regret in his voice at all. "What did your cougar girlfriend have to say that is so interesting? If her bedroom window is stuck shut and she wants you to come up and help an oul girl out, I suggest taking a pass."

Dillan flashes Em a middle-finger salute and looks at the rest of us. "Mrs. Graham said that the party palace sold last week, so we have new neighbors coming."

The others in the room share my surprise. "Sold? I didn't know it was up for sale."

"Neither did she. It was a private sale. Someone with deep pockets contacted the owner and told them to name their price."

All heads in the room turn to look at Sloan.

I laugh. "Are you buying up the block again?"

"Not this time—but I would have if I knew the owner was keen to sell. I still think Kevin and Calum havin' a place to start fosterin' fae kids is a great idea."

Calum nods. "Yeah, we've been talking about that quite a bit and agree. Once we're back from our honeymoon, we'll contact the owner of the rental house next door and try for a long-term lease. We're anxious to start a family and Garnet says finding good long-term homes for fae placements is tough."

I grab a carrot off the veggie platter and dunk it into the creamy dip. "Then we should get that established. Between you guys and Kinu and the rest of us, I'm sure we can make it work."

"If ye like," Sloan says. "I can look into it and do the groundwork."

"You don't have to do that, Irish," Kevin says. "You're busy and already do enough for us."

"It would be my pleasure," he says. "I enjoy havin' pet research projects to keep me busy."

I chuckle. "Because we're not busy enough?"

"Och, well, not so busy that I couldn't do it."

"You're just annoyed that someone beat you to the purchase. You were thinking about that place more than you let on, weren't you?"

"No comment."

Emmet laughs and finishes his beer. "So, what did you two decide for the honeymoon, anyway?"

Kevin grins. "We're borrowing Nikon's home in Florence for a few weeks. He says there's a beautiful view of the city with an art studio set up and it's close to galleries and museums and wine tours. He's snapping us there right after the party at Shenanigans."

"Sounds perfect." I meet Nikon's gaze where he's sitting on a stool at the island. *Thank you, Greek.*

My pleasure. I adore them. You know that.

The sincerity in his emotions makes me ache for him. I want

Nikon to find his perfect mate. He's been alone long enough. Now, with the threat of Hecate's jealous retaliation ended, he deserves to be deliriously happy.

"But, before we get to the honeymoon, there has to be a wedding," Kevin says. "I can't believe it's next weekend."

Calum grins. "As far as I'm concerned, it was a done deal a decade ago. The formalities give us an excuse to celebrate."

Emmet laughs. "Clan Cumhaill doesn't need an excuse for that."

"Hells no, we don't," I say, "but it's still going to be fabulous, and thanks to this conversation, I know the perfect gift to get you two."

CHAPTER TWENTY-FIVE

"All set, Fi," Emmet says. I press a finger to the comm bud in my ear and nod at Sloan sitting at the piano. He starts off the rhythmic notes of *Don't Stop Believin'*, and I smile as Calum's favorite song rises to greet family and friends sitting in the neat rows of white chairs set out on the sand.

Journey was the first concert Calum and Kev went to together, and my brother said it was during this song that he first wondered if maybe his feelings for his best friend went beyond friendship.

Obviously, they did.

Dionysus lifts his mic to his lips. "Just a small-town boy..."

Eyes widen as he begins to sing, and Myra's jaw drops. I wasn't kidding when I told her Dionysus' singing voice is incredible. He's amazing, and I dare even the most devout Steve Perry fans to say he doesn't nail it.

And yes, we took a little liberty with the lyrics to make it a male-male love song because yeah, that's why we're here.

From the white tent behind the audience, Meggie leads the wedding procession. Instead of a traditional carpeted aisle because we're on the beach, Da and Aiden set up a temporary wooden boardwalk leading up to the altar.

I wave to Megs and urge her forward. It took a few practices last night, but she understands now. The little monkey peddles her way forward on her tricycle and every few feet, she stops, grabs a handful of flowers out of her bike basket, and tosses them out into her path.

Jackson follows her, pulling a white wagon with Daisy sitting like a princess on the top of a silky pillow. Calum's beloved companion is a beauty this afternoon, all groomed and brushed and surrounded by colorful flower petals in the light of the setting sun.

Having a skunk in the wedding party seems to shock some of the guests on Kevin's side of the aisle, but there's no getting around it. Daisy being part of this celebration is non-negotiable.

The *snick, snick, snick* of the camera shutter at the front of the aisle is all Aiden's doing. He's on his knee taking pictures and signals for his kids to keep it coming all the way forward.

"Great job, Megs," I whisper as she makes it to the front row.

Da gathers her and her tricycle and hands her off to Gran before coming back to help with Jackson and the wagon. He pulls them to the side and parks the wagon in front of him and Shannon.

At the same time, Emmet and Dillan stride up the aisle looking like they're trying not to bust up laughing. I'm not sure what's going on in the tent...and honestly, I doubt I want to know.

The two of them are still snickering when they join Ciara and me up at the front.

Neither of them makes eye contact with anyone, which is probably a good thing.

Merlin arches a brow at me, but I shrug and stick with the program. It strikes me that Dora officiated Emmet's and Ciara's handfasting in all her flamboyant glory and now Merlin is binding Calum and Kevin.

The past months were full of many changes, but there are still things we count on that never change.

Calum's love for Kevin is a constant.

The boys line up at the front with us, and Kevin and Calum face one another and raise their fists for a bump.

"You ready for forever?" Calum asks.

"Yeah, baby. Let's do this."

"To the couple of the night," Da says, holding up a tumbler of whiskey and addressing the private crowd at Shenanigans. "Calum is one of my middle boys. He's been a source of parental pride, a thorn in my side, and an officer I'm pleased to work with."

"That's not what you say at the station," one of the officers says in the back.

"Pipe down, Hoover, or I'll have ye cut off. I've got connections with the bartenders."

Liam and I laugh and wave from behind the bar.

"As I was sayin'," Da says, throwing a look to the back of the room. "Calum has been my son from the moment his Mam and I brought him into this world, but I was fortunate enough to have Kevin as my son not long after. The boys hit it off from the start —skippin' school to fish at the river, breaking the upstairs window and blamin' a freak gust of wind, and gettin' banjaxed as teens and callin' me to pick them up despite it bein' three in the mornin'. Good boys, the both of them."

Calum laughs. "Thankfully, I think your idea of 'good boys' got skewed by Aiden, Brendan, and Liam."

Liam whistles and points at Aiden, nodding. "You're welcome."

"Be that as it may," Da says, laughing. "There was never any doubt the two would get on for a lifetime of friendship. Findin' more together is one of life's blessings. Ivan and Isabelle, as Kevin's parents, I welcome ye both into our family. It's a bit crazy at times, but it works most days. Kevin, ye've always been one of my boys, and I'm pleased it's official."

Kevin raises his glass in reply.

"To the grooms," Da says.

"To the grooms!"

Da waits for the chaos to die down and holds up his finger. "Enjoy the night. Shannon and I are coverin' the bar tab, so drink to yer fill but get home safe. I have a dozen off-duty chaps in blue available to drive people home. Take advantage and arrive alive."

The bar erupts in a roar of applause, and I hug Liam. Then I take the two lemon drop shots I made and head down the bar. "I'm going to check in with the loving couple. Whistle if you need me."

He laughs. "Fi. You're not working tonight. It's Calum and Kevin's wedding."

I wave that away. "But if you need me, you'll whistle. I want the liquor flowing tonight. I'll be right back."

I leave him, round the end of the bar, and find Kevin and Calum saying hello to a couple of friends from his station and their significant others.

When they finish and step away, I hand them the shot glasses and grin. "Happy wedding day, boys. I heart you both hard."

They *clink* the shot glasses and down them in one.

Kevin takes a moment after he swallows to lick the sugar off the rim. "Dayam, Fi. Those go down *waaay* too easily. Delish."

"I know, right."

Reaching into my server's apron, I pull out a letter-sized envelope full to bursting. "For you. Happy wedding day. May you always be as happy as you've always been."

"Thanks, baby girl." Calum leans in to hug me and flips the

envelope over in his hand. "I thought we weren't opening presents until we got home."

"You'll need this present for your honeymoon. Go ahead. Open it."

Sloan comes over to stand with us and smiles when he sees Calum sliding his finger under the flap. "This is a very fat wedding card."

I laugh. "Your wedding card is in the pile for home. This is your real present."

"What is it?" Kevin looks over.

"Last week, you mentioned museums and restaurants and wine tours. I got busy, and Nikon snapped me there to arrange a few special surprises. I may have paved your way for a fabulous holiday without lines."

"Noice." Calum grins. "That's awesome, guys. Thank you."

Sloan shakes his head. "No. This gift is all Fi. The gift from us as a couple is in the pile to unwrap upon yer return."

"Thanks, Fi," Kevin says. "Man, what did you do?"

"You have open-ended reservations at the five finest restaurants—bills already covered, a private guide to take you for a tour of the sites standing by—his name is Alfredo, and two days in Tuscany staying in a private villa in a winery. You also have backstage passes to the Accademia and Uffizi Galleries and time booked with the curators and restoration teams. Kev, whatever you've ever wanted to learn about art is awaiting you."

Kevin's mouth is hanging open, his eyes glassing up as he stares at the brochures and my notes on who to call for what. "Fi, this is too much. It's beyond amazing, but it must've cost you a fortune."

"Nope. Brenny paid. My gift with Sloan is from the two of us, but I wanted you two to have the adventure of a lifetime. I think Brendan would've approved."

"Yeah, he would've." Calum tears up. "Damn it, Fi. You did it again. It's perfect."

I hug them both, thankful for a day as perfect as today and the family and friends we shared it with.

As Da said, it's a bit crazy at times, but it works.

Emmet jumps up on the bench at the family table and *clinks* a knife gently against the side of his glass. "All right, married couple. Let's see a little PDA."

I laugh and step back to get out of their way.

As Calum cups Kevin's jaw and kisses his new husband, my heart swells with all the warm and fuzzies. The Greeks give them a shout-out, the heirs raise their pints, and Gran and Granda couldn't look happier.

I scan the loving faces of Da and Shannon, Aiden and Kinu, Emmet and Ciara, Dillan and Eva, and Sloan, standing at my side like always.

Life is good.

Sloan's right. Our love might not be the easiest to manage, but it's a lock. Cumhaill love is a constant.

Who wants easy anyway?

Thank you for reading – *A God's Mistake*

While the story is fresh in your mind, and as a favor to Michael and me, click HERE and tell other readers what you thought.

A star rating and/or even one sentence can mean so much to readers deciding whether or not to try out a book or new author.

And if you loved it, continue with the Chronicles of an Urban Druid and claim your copy of book twelve:
A Destiny Unlocked

NEXT IN SERIES

The story continues with *A Destiny Unlocked,* available at Amazon and Kindle Unlimited.

Claim your copy today!

AUTHOR NOTES - AUBURN TEMPEST

WRITTEN OCTOBER 19, 2021

Thank you for reading A God's Mistake, I hope you enjoyed it. And thank you even more for enjoying the series enough to stick with it for eleven and soon to be fifteen books.

Yes, that's right... your encouragement in the reviews urged me to contact Michael and suggest another three books in the series. We amended my contract this week. I told Michael the readers think Clan Cumhaill still has stories to tell and he is game to let me run with things as long as you're happy and I'm still enjoying the writing.

I am if you are.

So, off we go toward a fifteen-book series—which is amazing and unexpected and incredibly humbling. Thank you.

When I first emailed Michael and said our writing styles and story philosophies seemed to mesh, I knew we could have fun and tell a great story. He took a chance on signing me up and things took on a life of their own. The stars aligned, the series is doing well, and now the Chronicles of the Urban Druid are coming out in audio and German translations.

I believe Michael is empowered—he makes magic happen.

Last night I finished book 12, A Destiny Unlocked, and after I have a chance to take another pass at it, I'll send it to Michael and his team for a buff and polish and to get it ready for you.

Thanks for all the hours you've entrusted in my stories and all your feedback. Those 'one person found this helpful' comments on the reviews are me, checking in and making sure you're still having fun.

I am if you are.

Blessed be,
Auburn Tempest

AUTHOR NOTES - MICHAEL ANDERLE

WRITTEN OCTOBER 18, 2021

First, thank you for not only reading this story but these author notes in the back as well.

Casino Royal

Ian Fleming has a book titled *Casino Royal*. Two items of note before I tell this story is:

1) I'm not a huge James Bond reader as I don't read much to do with spies, *and*

2) I know very little about the Principality of Monaco.

So, Judith and I find ourselves landing in Nice (sounds like "Neese"), France, and taking a taxi to Cannes.

We were there for business purposes (MIPCom).

The taxi trip doesn't take too long (maybe thirty minutes), but @#%@% was it expensive! While we are in Cannes, we find out that Monaco—and the famous Monaco casino where the James Bond film and story were set—was just a little over an hour via train away from Cannes.

COOL!

Except, we were too jet-lagged on the Sunday before

MIPCom to jump on the train and go see anything except the insides of our eyeballs.

We get through Monday...Tuesday...Wednesday...and it has come to Thursday, and we have to leave the next day to go to Paris for one night and then on to Frankfurt for the Frankfurt book fair.

We need to try to get to Monaco.

I figure we will jump up early and get on the train and try to make it to Monaco.

We do not.

What we do is wake up late because we are STILL jet-lagged. Then, we work on laundry (how sexy is that in a foreign country? Spoiler—not very) and work projects. By the time we can get away to go to Monaco, it's heading towards 3:45 PM.

I decide "Screw it, we will take a taxi to get to Monaco." Except the effort to get a Taxi downstairs is frustrating me (the desk person dialed to get a taxi. We got stuck on hold.) Fine, we head out and start walking about ten minutes down toward the beach and the train station.

The "down to the beach" direction is important because it means we are heading *downhill.*

There are a LOT of up and down hill streets, and my legs have been complaining at me all week about the torture of the exercise (and perhaps the thirty extra pounds) they are having to move about.

We arrive at the train station with about twenty minutes to spare. But, I spy five taxis lined up, and we head over there to chat about a taxi to Monaco. Sensing the impending closing of the opportunity to see the little area, I cut a very poor, very expensive deal, and we get into Taxi #1 and head towards Monaco.

We find ourselves in traffic not three streets away.

As we putter along for twenty minutes instead of at most *five,*

I'm thinking my desire to get to Monaco faster than on a train is an abject failure.

Eventually, we get on the freeway, and our taxi-driver is not a speed demon, but she isn't slow, either (we had examples of both of those later that night and the next morning on a trip to the Nice station.)

We arrive in a bit under an hour in Monaco and pass the train station where we would have arrived at a good twenty-two minutes ahead of when the train was scheduled to arrive.

GO US!

Assuming time is money, I'm eyeing where that damned casino is…only to find out that we are heading for the palace.

You know, the one where the Prince of Monaco resides and you can walk around certain areas?

Way back in the 1500s, they stuck castles and shit up the tallest locations to rain cannonballs down on the unlucky bastards below. Trying to get up a tall hill with thirty or more pounds of armor sucks hard.

But we have a car, right?

Well, you can CLIMB up that sumbitch if *your taxi driver doesn't happen to know how to DRIVE up the side of the @#!@@# hill.*

Ours, of course, did not.

I find myself going ever-so-slowly-up-the-side-of-five-million-steps. I jest, it was probably no more than a couple hundred thousand.

Perhaps a few less than that. Whatever. My legs were screaming at me and didn't have anything positive to suggest about our taxi driver. Especially when we get to the top and there are plenty of vehicles up there…

Including *taxis.*

If I could have screamed in frustration, I might have. Unfortunately, I was sucking in air like a goldfish and couldn't produce a squeak.

We tour a bit of the palace grounds (quite nice) and the chapel where Princess Grace was married (very, very nice). View the gardens a bit and the water (amazing view.)

I find a telephone that says TAXI by the Oceanography building and pick it up. My wife speaks French, so I hand her the phone.

They speak an alien language; we sit there for about eight minutes to wait for the taxi. I don't bitch, I don't squawk, I just sit there knowing my future isn't falling down that huge fucking hill to my death in the waters below next to a few fifty million dollar yachts.

The taxi arrives.

We jump in and finally arrive at the casino...and the name above in (fairly) simple letters is...

CASINO *ROYAL*.

It is at this moment that I realize it is a statement of who owns the casino so much as it is the name. The Prince and his family own the casino (or did in the past and is now part of the government? I'm not quite sure.)

Either way, the momentous learning experience for me is the name of the James Bond book was a statement of where the story had scenes, not a title as much.

Eyes opened, we went inside to play roulette at the Casino *Royal*. Because, if you are in the Casino *Royal*, shouldn't you at least try a lucky number on the roulette wheel?

(*Editor's Note: I won nine francs in that very casino in 1981 at roulette. A little over two dollars. I was very proud of myself.*)

I missed hitting big by just one number.

A bit of my heart and all of my wallet were left in Monaco. But I'll always think about that damned hill and how my taxi driver screwed me. Yes, I feel it is personal. Give me another couple of weeks, and I'm sure I'll be happy again.

Have a great week or weekend, and talk to you in the next book!

Ad Aeternitatem,

Michael Anderle

ABOUT AUBURN TEMPEST

Auburn Tempest is a multi-genre novelist giving life to Urban Fantasy, Paranormal, and Sci-Fi adventures. Under the pen name, JL Madore, she writes in the same genres but in full romance, sexy-steamy novels. Whether Romance or not, she loves to twist Alpha heroes and kick-ass heroines into chaotic, hilarious, fast-paced, magical situations and make them really work for their happy endings.

Auburn Tempest lives in the Greater Toronto Area, Canada with her dear, wonderful hubby of 30 years and a menagerie of family, friends, and animals.

BOOKS BY AUBURN TEMPEST

Auburn Tempest - Urban Fantasy Action/Adventure

Chronicles of an Urban Druid

Book 1 – A Gilded Cage

Book 2 – A Sacred Grove

Book 3 – A Family Oath

Book 4 – A Witch's Revenge

Book 5 – A Broken Vow

Book 6 – A Druid Hexed

Book 7 – An Immortal's Pain

Book 8 – A Shaman's Power

Book 9 – A Fated Bond

Book 10 – A Dragon's Dare

Book 11 – A God's Mistake

Book 12 – A Destiny Unlocked

Misty's Magick and Mayhem Series – Written by Carolina Mac/Contributed to by Auburn Tempest

Book 1 – School for Reluctant Witches

Book 2 – School for Saucy Sorceresses

Book 3 – School for Unwitting Wiccans

Book 4 – Nine St. Gillian Street

Book 5 – The Ghost of Pirate's Alley

Book 6 – Jinxing Jackson Square

Book 7 – Flame

Book 8 – Frost

Book 9 – Nocturne

Book 10 – Luna

Book 11 – Swamp Magic

Exemplar Hall – Co-written with Ruby Night

Prequel – Death of a Magi Knight

Book 1 – Drafted by the Magi

Book 2 – Jesse and the Magi Vault

Book 3 – The Makings of a Magi

If you enjoy my writing and read sexy/steamy romance, my pen name for the books I write in Paranormal and Fantasy Romance is JL Madore. You can find me on Amazon HERE.

CONNECT WITH THE AUTHORS

Connect with Auburn

Amazon, Facebook, Newsletter

Web page – www.jlmadore.com

Email – AuburnTempestWrites@gmail.com

Connect with Michael Anderle and sign up for his email list here:

Website: http://lmbpn.com

Email List: http://lmbpn.com/email/

https://www.facebook.com/LMBPNPublishing

https://twitter.com/MichaelAnderle

https://www.instagram.com/lmbpn_publishing/

https://www.bookbub.com/authors/michael-anderle

OTHER LMBPN PUBLISHING BOOKS